RE...
THE D...

AMY ANDREWS

NAVY OFFICER
TO FAMILY MAN

BY
EMILY FORBES

MILLS
BOON

RESCUED BY
THE DREAMY DOC

BY
AMY ANDREWS

First published in Great Britain 2011
Harlequin Mills & Boon Limited,
Eton House, 18-24 Paradise Road, Richmond, Surrey TW9 1SR

© Amy Andrews 2011

ISBN: 978 0 263 88573 6

Harlequin Mills & Boon policy is to use papers that are natural, renewable and recyclable products and made from wood grown in sustainable forests. The logging and manufacturing process conform to the legal environmental regulations of the country of origin.

Printed and bound in Spain
by Litografia Rosés, S.A., Barcelona

When their gazes swept each other's paths there was the merest moment of pause before they skittered on like two opposing lighthouse signals.

But in that fraction of time it was as if they were the only two people in the restaurant, and Sebastian couldn't remember if a woman had ever had such a startling effect on him.

It was actually kind of exhausting—this level of awareness. The slow but inexorable build of tension tightening every muscle, sizzling along every nerve-ending.

All he wanted was to fast-forward to the end and the kiss that he knew, deep in his bones, was the inevitable conclusion.

It couldn't happen fast enough.

Amy Andrews has always loved writing, and still can't quite believe that she gets to do it for a living. Creating wonderful heroines and gorgeous heroes and telling their stories is an amazing way to pass the day. Sometimes they don't always act as she'd like them to—but then neither do her kids, so she's kind of used to it. Amy lives in the very beautiful Samford Valley, with her husband and aforementioned children, along with six brown chooks and two black dogs. She loves to hear from her readers. Drop her a line at www.amyandrews.com.au

Recent titles by the same author:

VALENTINO'S PREGNANCY BOMBSHELL
ALESSANDRO AND THE CHEERY NANNY
A MOTHER FOR MATILDA

Dedication

*To my amazing editor Lucy, who said yes
when everyone else said no. You gave me wings.*

And to Phillip. Come back to us. We love you.

CHAPTER ONE

SOME days you just weren't meant to get out of bed. For Sebastian Walker today was one of those days. His first day on call as a police negotiator in a new city, a new state, and he'd hit the ground running. He was supposed to be spending the day putting his riverside apartment to rights. But his pager hadn't co-operated.

Thank God it wasn't a full-time gig.

He navigated past the multitude of half-opened boxes that sat strewn all over his floors and seemed to be multiplying in every room. After a year in far-flung foreign hotspots he craved the familiarity of his things but today obviously wasn't going to be the day to get reacquainted.

He swallowed the last of his toast as he knotted his gun-metal grey tie. His pager bleeped again as he shut his front door on the mess.

I'm coming. I'm coming.

'What have we got?' Sebastian asked fifteen minutes later, after approaching the hive of police activity and flashing his credentials to the officer in charge.

'Jumper. With a gun. Her name's Noelene. She won't say anything else. Refuses to talk to us. Says she'll only talk to Callie Duncan.'

Sebastian heard the cluster of groans around him as he strapped on the bulletproof vest he was handed. 'Who's Callie Duncan?'

'A pain-in-the-butt community mental health worker.'

Sebastian nodded. 'Okay. Let's get her in here while I have a little chat with Noelene.'

'Callie, call for you on line one.'

Geraldine Russell, head social worker and director of the Jambalyn Community Centre held out the receiver and placed it in the crook of Callie's shoulder as she watched her colleague juggle a stack of charts in one hand and her pager in the other.

Callie shrugged her shoulder high so the phone fitted snugly against her ear. 'Yo,' she said.

Gerri watched her friend nod a couple of times and then say, 'I'll be there in fifteen.'

Callie dropped her shoulder and Gerri hung up the phone. She raised an elegantly groomed eyebrow. 'Be where in fifteen?'

'Grey St Bridge. They think Noelene Sykes is going to jump. She's asking for me,' she said casually as she dumped the charts on her overflowing desk, knowing Gerri was going to go ballistic.

'Oh, no.' Gerri's impressive bosom shook with the vigorous shake of her head.

Callie grinned. Gerri was a large Aboriginal woman whose statuesque presence carried an undeniable authority. Not many people crossed her and only the exceedingly foolish couldn't see beyond the dramatic tribal-print flowing caftans she wore to the savvy, street-wise operator beneath.

'It's Noelene, Gerri. *Noelene.* As if Noelene's going

to jump off a bridge. There's obviously been some mis-
communication. She's asking for me.'

'No. Not that bridge. Not today.'

Callie smiled at her friend and colleague of ten years,
knowing she was just trying to protect her. 'Yes.'

'I'll go. I'll do it.'

Callie shook her head. 'She wants me.'

'No.'

Callie picked up her keys. 'I'll be fine.'

'Callie Duncan, you walk out of those doors and I'm
firing you.'

Callie grinned over her shoulder. 'Ha! Promises,
promises.' They both knew they were chronically un-
derstaffed and they needed all the good people they
could get.

And Callie Duncan was very, very good at her job.

Callie snorted and placed her hands on her hips, staring down the insistent male whose name she'd already
forgotten in her haste to get to Noelene. She didn't care
if he was a cop or, for that matter, so damn sexy he could
have been in the movies.

He was in her way—that was all that mattered.

'Noelene is not going to shoot me.'

Sebastian returned her blazing amber gaze with a
much-practised calm, pale green one of his own, dropping his head to the side a little and stretching his
neck. He repeated the process on the other side before
straightening.

'You're not going out there until you put it on.'

Callie glared up at him, all brooding, broad immovable male. *Way up.* At six feet in her comfortable flats,
craning her neck wasn't something she did much of but
with this man it was a necessity.

The morning sun shone on his red hair, gilding the golden highlights. He wore it closely cropped at the back and sides but longer on top where it flopped across his forehead. His ginger brows rose above the palest peridot eyes.

He had a fashionable three-day growth of stubble stretched along his strong jaw and long-faded freckles gave his complexion a lived-in look, hinting at summer days on the beach and a penchant for surfing. Spare cheekbones sloped to interesting hollows near his mouth.

And his lips? Oh, man, don't get her started on those suckers.

Frankly he was sexy as hell.

The admission irritated her even more. *She was working, for crying out loud!*

'It's not necessary,' she insisted, desperate to claw back some control of normally sane thought processes. 'I've known her for ten years. She's not dangerous.'

He pushed the offending item towards her. 'Maybe. But it's the only way you're going out on that bridge.'

His voice was deep and even with a slight gravelly quality. Very measured. Very calm. But there was an edge to it that brooked no argument.

Damn cops!

Behind what's-his-name she could see that their little stand-off was drawing quite a crowd. Most of the cops she recognised. You didn't work for a decade in this business without having a close working relationship— sometimes love, sometimes hate—with the police. And she'd worked long and hard to gain their respect.

Sure, she knew they regarded her as a right royal pain in their posteriors. But she also knew there was grudging respect—she was the first one they rang when they had a situation or needed advice—and she was damned if she was going to cede it to this man.

Not without throwing down a gauntlet or two.

It was imperative, particularly that the three very interested, very rookie-looking officers standing behind knew she didn't wilt at the first sign of authority. She needed them to know she wasn't afraid of them and that her client's needs would always come first.

'Fine,' she said through gritted teeth, grasping her loose black T-shirt by the hem and hauling it off over her head. She glared right into his peridot eyes, ignoring the guffaws and wolf whistles, and held out her hand. 'Give me the damn vest.'

Callie gave him his due. While the jaws of the three fresh-faced newbies dropped to the ground, he didn't bat an eyelid. He didn't even lower his gaze for a quick once-over of her lace-clad assets, like every other male in the vicinity. He just passed her the offending item and waited with crossed arms over a chest broadened further by his own Kevlar padding for her to put it on.

'You know you could have just put it on over the top of your shirt, right?' he said after she'd rectified her clothing.

'Not likely,' she snapped. 'Do you think a bulletproof vest engenders trust?' Did the man get his negotiator skills in a cereal packet? 'Can I go now?'

He swept his hand in a flourish before her, indicating she should precede him. The action pulled his half rolled-up sleeves a little higher and she noticed thick reddish-blond hairs gracing strong, freckle-faded forearms.

'I'm right behind you.'

'Imagine my surprise,' she threw over her shoulder, tossing her head.

* * *

Sebastian watched her stalk off and smiled for the first time today, following at a more sedate pace. Callie Duncan was one angry female! It wasn't often in this field that he met someone who didn't seem to know or even care who he was, and he liked it. It was refreshing.

She was refreshing.

He kept his eyes firmly glued to her back, distracted by the vigorous swish of her shoulder-length auburn hair as she strode towards her goal. The sun picked up the honey streaks and for a moment he felt like he was on the set of a shampoo commercial.

Her back was ramrod straight—Kevlar would do that to a person. And her long-legged stride pulled the denim of her jeans across a backside that was…interesting.

In fact, Callie Duncan was just plain interesting all over.

And he liked that too.

And despite her stern glare he could tell she was used to laughing. Her mouth tilted up, as did her incredible amber eyes, and there were soft laughter lines emphasising their appeal.

He put her in her late thirties and was relieved that she wasn't some twenty-something, new grad all peppy and cute with stars in her eyes out to change the world. In fact, nothing about Callie Duncan said peppy and cute.

But, then, neither did she seem jaded, like so many people of her age working in a field where triumphs were small and thanks almost non-existent. Instead, striding towards her goal, she looked strong and fearless. Committed. Confident.

Her Amazonian frame moved with single-minded purpose.

As for what she had inside that lacy black bra…he put that thought firmly to one side.

'Oh, thank God, Callie, it's you.'

'What's going on, Noelene?' Callie grouched as she tripped slightly over one of the barricades the police had used to cordon off the area. No doubt what's-his-name wouldn't approve of it as an opening statement but she knew Noelene well enough to know she could take it.

That didn't mean she wasn't hyper-aware of a certain sexy red-haired negotiator and the rest of what appeared to be the city's police force watching her intently.

'I was just out for a walk…thinking,' the hollow-cheeked mother of four said, the breeze whipping wispy blonde strands of hair across her gaunt, prematurely aging face.

Noelene moved closer to the railing. Callie's gaze followed her movement, aware of the drop behind. She kept her gaze trained firmly on Noelene's anxious eyes as her heart thudded like thunder in her chest.

She would not look down.

She hated heights.

And she certainly wouldn't let any of the city's finest catch a glimpse of the screaming girly inside.

She hated this damn bridge. Any bridge, actually, but this one in particular.

'With a gun?'

Noelene looked down at the gun as if seeing it for the first time. 'What, this?' she asked, waving it in the air.

Callie heard the unlocking of safeties and sensed the closing in of every policeman behind as they drew a little nearer, tensed a little further, poised for action.

'Noelene,' she said, raising her hands in a stop

motion. 'You're making the cops really nervous. Is it even loaded?'

Noelene frowned at her. 'Of course not.'

Just as she'd suspected. 'Can I have the gun?' Callie held out her hand for it.

Noelene looked at the weapon. 'It was Dad's.'

After a quick review of her client's chart, Callie knew it was a year to the day that Noelene's father had passed away. She nodded. 'I know.'

Noelene handed it to her meekly and Callie heard the loud snicker as who knew how many safeties were restored to their off positions and guns were holstered. She passed it back to what's-his-name.

She quirked an eyebrow at him. 'Unloaded. Fancy that,' she muttered. 'Think you can call your boys off now?'

Sebastian smiled at her defiant expression. Her bluster was very, very sexy and it reminded him that it had been a very long time since he'd been with a woman.

Since before the Gulf.

His gaze dropped to her mouth for a second, wanting to kiss that smug look away before returning to her face. 'Oh, I know you know that's not how this works.'

Callie swallowed. The gravel in his voice slid into all her empty places. Her lips felt as if he'd actually stroked his tongue along them and she curtailed the urge to taste them.

How was it possible to be exceedingly irritated and exceedingly turned on at the same time?

Sucking in a steadying breath, she gave him a grudging nod. 'Yeah, yeah, I know.'

'Bring her in,' he murmured.

Callie nodded and turned, walking the few paces back

to Noelene, who was now leaning on the rail, looking down at the river sparkling in the morning sunshine.

'Dad loved this bridge,' she said absently. 'He helped build it, you know? He used to always bring us kids here.'

Callie nodded. 'Do you think we can talk away from here, Noelene? I really don't like heights.'

Noelene nodded, moving slowly towards her. 'I just thought it would be fitting, you know, to mark his anniversary. His service weapon was his most treasured possession. I thought it'd be...right to throw it off the bridge. He was in Korea, you know?'

Callie nodded, holding out her arm and putting it around Noelene's shoulders. 'I know,' she murmured. 'You can tell me about it on the way to the police station.'

Noelene looked at her. 'I was just looking down at the water, minding my own business.' She frowned. 'And this cop car pulled up, telling me not to jump... I had no intention of jumping. But they were yelling and coming towards me and I got scared.'

'I know. Don't worry, we'll get it sorted. I'll be with you.'

'I need to be there to pick the kids up from school.'

'Yep. Don't worry, I'll be with you, expediting the process.'

They reached the barricade. What's-his-name held out his hand for Noelene and helped her through the maze of barricades. Callie was grudgingly impressed by his gentle smile and his unhurried demeanour as he made sure Noelene didn't trip.

Then he turned back to her. 'Thank you,' he murmured, holding out his hand.

Callie's gaze locked with his and she felt a giddy

shift—not something she welcomed, standing on a bridge.

But, damn, the man was sexy. His frank gaze, his lips curled into a slight smile, his height and breadth surrounding her, his voice oozing over her like warm honey.

The background noises faded, their surroundings dimmed, as time and motion coalesced in this one electric moment. If they'd been in a bar she would have taken his hand and led him to the nearest dark corner.

But they weren't. They were on a bridge—a damn bridge, for crying out loud—surrounded by what seemed like a hundred policemen. She ignored the hand. 'All in a days work.'

'Hey, Zack, how's it going?' Callie asked, the phone pressed to one ear as she blindly hooked a hoop earring into her other ear.

'Good thanks, Aunty Cal.'

Callie smiled at her ten-year-old nephew's chirpy greeting. It was good to hear her little man's voice. Since he'd gone back to live with his mother a couple of months ago she hadn't known what to do with herself. Some of the anxiety that had knotted her stomach over the heart-wrenching decision had dissipated, but after eight years in her care, it was hard to let go entirely.

And he would always be her brother's son.

'How'd you do in the cross-country today?'

'I came second! You should have seen me, Aunty Cal.'

Callie's heart strings twanged painfully. She hadn't missed a school event since he'd started pre-school six years ago. But she was trying to step back, give Aleisha a chance to bond with her son.

'Mummy said I ran like the wind.'

Callie gripped the receiver hard. Her brother, Zack's father, had been an athletics champion at school. He'd had such promise.

Until everything had gone wrong.

'I bet you did, my Za Za.' She smiled.

Her nickname for him fell easily from her lips but sat very uneasily in her churning gut. She wanted him here with her again with a startling ferocity. She wanted to put her arms around his skinny shoulders and hug him tight.

Like the polite little boy she raised him to be, he asked, 'How was your day, Aunty Cal? How many people did you help?'

She smiled at how grown-up he sounded. Callie knew that Zack was very proud of the way his aunt helped people like his father—even if he didn't really have an understanding of what that meant.

'Zillions,' she joked, and laughed as Zack's boyish giggle warmed her down the phone line.

He was too young to tell him about her day. About her morning on the very bridge his father had thrown himself off eight years earlier. Zack had never really known his dad and that wasn't the way Callie wanted him to remember Andy anyway.

She hung up a few minutes later just as a horn beeped outside. Callie looked at her watch. Argh! She was running late and two earrings did not make her dressed for dinner!

Sebastian thought he'd actually conjured her up when Callie Duncan appeared in front of him at the restaurant. After all, she'd rarely been out of his head since that morning so seeing her in the flesh again seemed almost natural.

'We meet again,' he murmured, taking in her sexy pin-striped trousers, soft, white, collared blouse with a deep V neck, and very large frown.

'Oh, hi.' Callie's mouth dried as she took in the commanding redhead from the bridge and turned to Gerri. What the hell was he doing there?

Geraldine raised an eyebrow. 'You've met?'

'Er...yes, um... He... That is...' She gestured to the man with that floppy fringe and that voice and that stare and whose name she still couldn't remember. She could hardly call him what's-his-name to his face!

Sebastian quirked a brow and smiled at her verbal groping. 'Sebastian,' he supplied. 'Or Seb. I answer to both.'

Callie nodded, relieved. For a moment. And then realisation slowly dawned. *Sebastian?*

Uh-oh.

Sebastian Walker?

'Sebastian was the negotiator today,' she said automatically as her sluggish brain tried to catch up.

She glanced at him and the intenseness of his gaze stole her breath. It was still there, that thing from this morning. Big and large and growing between them as she took in his casual dress shirt, the rolled-up sleeves, the top two undone buttons.

'At the bridge,' she added completely unnecessarily.

'Huh, what a coincidence,' Gerri said, looking from one to the other. 'Well, as you know, as of next week, he's the new temporary psychologist at Jambalyn.'

He was Donna's maternity leave replacement?

Sebastian Walker? *The* Sebastian Walker. One of the most eminent and renowned young psychologists in the country? Who'd written the modern-day bible on PTSD?

She hadn't quite been able to believe it when Gerri had told them that he'd applied for the one-year relief position in their lowly community mental health centre. It was even harder to believe that he was the man from the bridge.

And she'd flashed him!

Callie sat, frowning, still not quite figuring it out. She felt like a complete airhead. 'So, you're not a cop?'

She'd just assumed this morning...

It would have been much easier if he had been. She could have put him in a neat little box. Police officer. Off-limits. *She did not sleep with cops.* She did not trade hot looks or share silent vibes with them. She did not give them any encouragement at all.

Never.

Cops were off-limits. Her reputation was paramount and cops were, after all, by and large, a great big boys' club. And, as with a lot of boys, bragging often got the better of them. A close friend of hers had found that out the hard way.

Of course, *work colleague* should have sent up a big red flag as well. But frying in the knowing heat of his stare, it came a poor second.

Sebastian shook his head. 'Afraid not.' He grinned. 'I have experience in hostage negotiation. The police, like a lot of organisations, sometimes outsource. I've worked as a civilian negotiator for different police forces from time to time. The Queensland police were eager to have me.'

Of course. Revolutionising psychotherapy for prisoners and being a leading expert in PTSD obviously weren't enough feathers in his cap!

He shrugged. 'The pager rarely goes off.'

'Lucky me,' she murmured, dropping her gaze, desperate to break the incendiary connection she felt every time she looked at him.

This could not be happening! She'd really been looking forward to tonight. To meeting him and to working with him, but with his frank gaze prickling awareness across her skin she wasn't so sure.

It felt dangerous.

And she was no adrenaline junkie.

'Speaking of which,' Christopher Martell, another of Jambalyn's psych nurses, butted in. 'We heard you flashed every cop in Brisbane this morning. I think the news helicopters even got a gawk. You're quite the talk of the town.'

Callie blushed and risked a look at Sebastian. His eyes told her that while he'd been determined to not play her game that morning, his peripheral vision was twenty/twenty.

More than that—they told her he'd liked what he'd seen. That he wanted to see more. That in this restaurant there was a secluded spot in the alley outside and what the hell were they doing here when they could be there, their lips locked, pushing aside clothes, and to hell with inhibitions and social mores?

She dragged her gaze from Sebastian and gave a careless shrug. 'You learn to get bolshie in this job.'

The conversation moved on and Sebastian let it flow around him. His new colleagues were articulate, expressive and dedicated. Chris, Magella, Cynthia and Callie were the nurses. Gerri and Donald were social workers. Ross was the lawyer. Rodney was the receptionist.

They'd obviously been together for a while and could laugh and unwind—debrief—effectively. But more than that, they liked each other, respected each other and he looked forward to working with them and the challenge of community-based mental health.

Even if it was only temporary.

It would certainly be a very welcome change of pace. Exactly what he craved after the chaos, the day-to-day tensions of his last gig. Exactly what he needed before heading back to his private practice and the *real* world.

It was gratifying to see that none of them were too awed by his reputation and he quickly slipped into a groove with them.

Except Callie.

She was distracted.

Distracting.

Her gaze kept wandering in his direction and he was drawn to the way the roundness of her breasts flirted with the soft fabric of her blouse, clinging briefly before shifting, gliding with silky fingers over her bra before settling again.

Even the way she talked and smiled as she indulged in banter with her friends was distracting. She dropped her head to one side as she listened and absently ran the silver pendant at her throat along its chain. And when she laughed? It was full and throaty as if it had come all the way from her toes. Her eyes crinkled and she tossed her head, baring her neck.

Other diners looked around at her laughter and smiled.

When their gazes swept each other's paths there was the merest pause before they skittered on like two opposing lighthouse signals. But in that fraction of time it was as if they were the only two people in the restaurant and Sebastian couldn't remember if a woman had ever had such a startling effect on him.

It was actually kind of exhausting, this level of awareness. The slow but inexorable build of tension tightening every muscle, sizzling along every nerve ending.

All he wanted was to fast-forward to the end and the kiss that he knew, deep in his bones, was the inevitable conclusion.

It couldn't happen fast enough.

CHAPTER TWO

As THE evening drew to a close, Callie was aware of Sebastian becoming quieter, his gaze more intent as a weird kind of charge grew and then arced steadily between them. Like an approaching storm.

Laden. Ominous.

It enthralled and frightened her all at once. She knew she should get up and leave while she could but she felt powerless.

Even when Gerri called for a doggie bag for the massive pizza she hadn't been able to finish and the others took their leave *en masse*, she was helpless.

Sebastian quirked an eyebrow at them. 'Coffee?'

'Kill for one,' Gerri agreed.

'That would be lovely,' Callie murmured.

She should have declined. She knew that. But her fingers itched to push back the unruly lock of hair flopping across his forehead and overrode all her common sense.

No seemed to have been stricken from her vocabulary.

Besides, Gerri was giving her a lift home so she had to stay. Right?

Sebastian beckoned a waitress over and they placed their orders. As she left, Callie became aware of a raised voice behind her and all three of them turned to look at what was happening.

They were sitting in the alfresco area of a restaurant in a trendy new footpath strip in Fortitude Valley. The suburb was up-and-coming, quite hip with the movers and shakers but by and large it was still less than salubrious in places with a lot of cheap boarding-house accommodation. With a large client base here and Jambalyn being located a stone's throw from the restaurant, Callie knew the area well.

A dishevelled man, probably homeless, definitely down on his luck, was asking customers at the tables closest to the street for spare change for food. A young, preppy-looking man in an expensive suit at a table full of suits had taken it on himself to loudly lecture the unfortunate man, who was shuffling his feet, his head downcast, much to the delight of the other suits.

Callie turned away, unable to witness such callous inhumanity. She felt sick. *How could he?* What would a preppy inner-city suit know about the difficulties some people faced and how life could go down the drain so rapidly? How could he judge so cruelly someone he didn't even know?

Her gaze fell to her lap where her hands shook, and she twisted them together to still the tremor. Her heart thumped like a gong in her chest and the meal she'd just eaten felt like a lump of lead in her belly.

Gerri placed a hand over hers. 'Are you okay?'

Callie looked up into Gerri's concerned eyes. She could see a frown knitting Sebastian's brows in her peripheral vision. Callie's gaze darted to Sebastian's and back again. She nodded but the ugly scene had opened the floodgate on memories she'd been trying to keep at bay all day, from the bridge to Zack's little-boy voice, and she felt like she was suffocating.

Sebastian was surprised by the sudden change in the previously animated Callie. She'd gone very pale and there was an unbearable sadness in her expressive amber eyes. The arrogant fool confronting the homeless man had obviously upset her. After her fearless performance on the bridge today he'd half expected her to march over and verbally eviscerate the conceited guy, but she looked like she was about to faint.

'Excuse me,' he murmured.

It was Callie's turn to frown as she and Gerri watched Sebastian's progress towards the altercation.

Sebastian drew level with the table and looked down at the offending man just as he finished suggesting that the obviously itinerant man get a job. 'Have you quite finished?'

Sebastian didn't usually court danger. In fact, he'd had enough of danger this last year. He was certainly no he-man. He didn't pick fights or go around looking for trouble. But some things just couldn't be ignored and this man's attitude was abhorrent. Hopefully after tonight he'd think twice about using someone else's misfortune to make himself look good.

'I…I beg your pardon?' the younger man blustered. He looked around at his friends and the rest of the people in the half-full restaurant, obviously embarrassed to be called on his appalling behaviour.

Good!

'Feel like a big man now in front of your friends, humiliating another human being who was just looking for a bit of decency and compassion?'

The man stood, the scrape of his chair loud in the

suddenly charged atmosphere. 'Who the hell are you?' he demanded.

Sebastian noted the younger man pale when he realised that Sebastian had four inches and several muscles groups on him. He lowered his voice. 'A concerned citizen.'

Callie shivered as the rumble of quiet menace in Sebastian's voice was felt all the way around the restaurant. Her heart hammered and her palms felt sweaty where they gripped the table.

'Look…I'm sorry, mate,' the man said, holding his hands up. 'I didn't mean any harm.'

Sebastian jaw tightened. This guy was nothing but a bully. Picking on someone helpless but backing down at the first sign of superior strength. He needed to apologise. He looked over to the street but the homeless man had obviously seen his opportunity and fled the ugly scene. Sebastian could see him shuffling away, his shoulders slumped.

Callie looked back at her hands as Sebastian suggested the man bring his best manners next time he came out. He was being amazing—calm but firm—and she felt ridiculously like bursting into tears.

Pressure built in her chest and she suddenly felt as if she couldn't breathe. She half stood. 'I…I need some air.'

Gerri inspected her face closely and then gave a brisk nod, handing over the doggy bag. Callie took the offering and slipped out of the restaurant, sagging against its door briefly, grateful for the cool night air on her heated face.

She saw the hunched old man farther down the street and hurried after him, pressing the leftover pizza into his hands when she caught up. He avoided her gaze but Callie could see the tears shining in his eyes as he mumbled his thanks. She smiled at him and backed away, not wanting to humiliate the man any further by trite words or useless platitudes.

Sebastian, who had followed her out of the restaurant, walked towards her slowly as she retraced her steps. Where was his tall, proud Amazon from the bridge, eyes blazing? Was brave Callie the real deal or was the real Callie the woman walking towards him now? Softer, more vulnerable. He'd wanted to kiss the woman on the bridge senseless. This Callie he wanted to wrap up in his arms and shield from the big bad world.

Which one was she?

'You okay?' he asked as she approached.

Callie stopped in front of him, still too emotional to meet Sebastian's eyes. She bit the inside of her cheek. She would not fall apart now. It didn't matter that she seemed to be an unwilling rider on an emotional roller-coaster that was flinging her hither and thither; she would not crack.

The memories. Her brother—years of not knowing where he was or if he was alive or dead. The bridge. Zack.

They would not break her. Not right now.

She cleared her throat. 'Fine.'

Sebastian stopped the snort that rose automatically. Callie was nowhere near fine. Still, he admired her stoicism. Did she spend all of her life putting on a brave face?

He regarded her for a few moments. 'I think our coffees are getting cold,' he murmured.

Callie heard the soft don't-spook-the-horses note in his voice and braced her shoulders. She hated it that he'd seen her like this. She didn't need his pity. 'Can't have that,' she quipped, raising her chin and striding towards the restaurant.

Geraldine rose when they arrived back at the table. She looked from Callie to Sebastian and then back again. 'Everything okay?'

'Fine,' Callie said, uncaring how overly bright it sounded as she sat. Still unable to look at Sebastian, she picked up her spoon and stirred the cappuccino that had arrived during the fracas.

The others followed suit and for a few moments no one said anything as they contemplated their lukewarm coffees. But Callie could feel Sebastian's intense gaze on her and suddenly she wanted nothing more than to wrap herself up in all that intenseness and forget every detail of this horrible day.

Geraldine pursed her lips, about to say something, but her mobile rang, interrupting her. She spoke briefly then ended the call. 'Sorry,' she said standing. 'Tahlia thinks she's in labour.'

Callie looked up from her coffee, her teaspoon clattering against the saucer, everything prior to the call disappearing in an instant. Tahlia was Gerri's daughter and this was the first grandchild. 'Oh, my God, Gerri!'

'I have to go.'

'Of course,' Callie urged. 'Go. Just go.'

Gerri looked at Sebastian. 'Can you see she gets home?'

Sebastian looked at Callie and it was the first time their eyes had met since she'd walked out of the restaurant.

Inevitability smacked him in the face. *There was no way she was going home alone tonight.*

'Of course.'

Gerri nodded. She looked at Callie as if weighing her

up and then looked back at Sebastian. 'Ask her about the bridge,' she said, before hustling out of the restaurant.

Not that Callie noticed her friend's departure, caught up as she was in his stare, her belly tightening, her breasts aching—knowing, now that her safety net had disappeared, there was only one way this night was going to end.

'Are you sure you're okay?' Sebastian murmured.

Callie nodded. 'I'm fine.'

Sebastian didn't believe her for a second. 'Do you need to talk about the bridge?'

Callie regarded him silently for a moment then said, 'No.'

'Really?'

Callie nodded, trying to temper the action and not betray how desperately she did not want to talk about the bloody bridge.

Damn Gerri!

He continued to hold her gaze, seeking answers, and she couldn't bear it. She leaned forward, lifted her hand and gently pushed his floppy fringe back a little. His skin was warm to touch and she heard the quick intake of his breath.

She dropped her hand. 'Sorry. Couldn't resist it.'

Sebastian, his forehead tingling, held her gaze for a little longer then nodded. Whether she knew it or not, she did need to talk. 'My place is ten minutes away. I have...' he looked down and grimaced at his cappuccino '...hot coffee.'

It wasn't a question, it wasn't a command. It was just there, and the way she saw it she could go home by herself and try not to think about the very thing she'd been avoiding all day. That hammered at her skull even now, tearing at her shields. Or she could go home with him.

But she sure as hell didn't want coffee and conversation.

Not tonight.

They didn't speak as Sebastian drove the short distance to his apartment. They didn't speak in the car park. Or the lift. Or as he opened his front door.

Neither did they touch.

He didn't even switch on a light.

Instead, he watched as Callie strode across his lounge room, dodging boxes, towards the moonlight streaming in through his uncurtained French doors.

'Sorry 'bout the mess,' he murmured as he drew level with her, his chest close to her back, his lips near her ear.

Callie frowned, dragging her gaze from the alabaster river below, and looked round, her shoulder brushing his chest. She hadn't even noticed them. 'I didn't notice.'

Sebastian nodded slowly. 'Callie. The bridge?'

She shook her head. 'No.'

He regarded her quietly. 'You know, maybe it'd help if you—'

Callie leaned forward and kissed him, cutting off the words she already knew back to front. It was a fierce kiss. Hard. She didn't open her mouth, neither did he. But she felt it right down to her toes.

'The only therapy I want tonight,' she said, inching slightly back from his mouth, 'involves us being horizontal.' She snaked her arms around his neck and pressed her mouth to his again.

Sebastian felt her words all the way down to his groin. And when her tongue lapped against his lips, seeking entrance to his mouth, he granted it on a strangled groan, burying his fingers in her hair.

It felt good to be kissing a woman again. To get lost in one. To feel curves pressed against him and suck in all that sweet female aroma with each jerky breath. And not just any woman. A sassy but vulnerable one who had blown his mind on a bridge a mere twelve hours ago and was doing her damnedest to blow it again.

But as the kiss grew increasingly wild—desperate— his conscience pricked at him. Even though he couldn't think of a time when he'd been this aroused, he knew this was about more than hot stranger sex for Callie.

The psychologist in him knew there were bigger things driving her.

Her fingers had worked three buttons undone by the time he managed to pull himself out of the sexual fire scorching his common sense. He covered her hands.

'Stop,' he whispered, kissing her eyelids, her cheeks. 'Hold on for a moment.'

He ignored her mewed protest and the fascinating sight of her ravaged mouth. 'Why don't we get that coffee first?'

Callie, still dazed and weak-kneed, would have slumped to the floor had she not been leaning against him. She returned her ministrations to his neck, feeling the spike of bristles against her tongue. 'I don't want a coffee,' she murmured.

Sebastian shut his eyes as her tongue stroked magic over his skin, whispering illicit promises into his pulse points. He resisted the urge to let his head fall back, give her unlimited access. Just.

'Callie,' he groaned, opening his eyes as her lips trekked towards his shoulder. 'I don't think this is a wise idea. There's obviously something troubling you...and using sex to obliterate issues isn't a very good way to handle things.'

Callie smiled against his collarbone. The poor man was really trying to do the right thing. But pressed into her pelvis she could feel how hard he was for her, and the convulsive clutch of his hands at her hips spoke volumes.

'Relax,' she murmured. 'I promise it won't hurt.'

Sebastian chuckled. 'That's not what I'm worried about.'

Callie smiled again, the rumble of his voice tickling her lips as she returned her mouth to the strong column of his throat.

He pulled back slightly and felt her lips leave his skin. 'I'd hate you to regret this is the morning.'

Callie sighed. His honourable streak was commendable. She didn't know too many men who wouldn't take instant full advantage of what she was offering. 'I'm a big girl, Sebastian. I know what I'm doing.'

She rubbed his collar point between her thumb and forefinger. 'Or is it that a sexually aggressive woman threatens your masculinity?'

Sebastian regarded her seriously as she morphed back into Callie from the bridge. Bolshie and defiant. A man could get whiplash trying to keep up with her Jekyll-and-Hyde act.

Curiouser and curiouser.

Which one was she? The man in him found the challenge irresistible. And looking down at her moist lips and blazing amber eyes, he had to admit it'd be fun finding out.

He smiled. 'Not me. I'm exceedingly evolved. I love sexually aggressive women. In fact...' he pushed a lock of her hair off her shoulder '…I think they should take over the world.'

Callie laughed. 'Interesting thought.'

Sebastian joined her. But it was hard to concentrate when their bodies were pressed together so intimately and just her laughter was enough to cause a delicious friction between them.

He sobered. 'I need you to be sure, Callie.'

She sucked in a breath at the intenseness of his gaze. It took her right back to the bridge and the instant magnetism she'd felt. 'Would you like me to sign a disclaimer?'

He shook his head. 'Let's just seal it with a kiss, shall we?' And then he lowered his head.

Callie felt the flash of heat erupt down low the second his lips touched hers and she groaned, raking her fingers into his hair. She could hear his ragged breath loud in her ears and revelled in his no-holds-barred kiss.

Finally he was kissing her without reservation. Like she was a full-blooded, passionate woman. Not a fragile one. Not an about-to-fall-apart one.

And, man, did it feel good!

She broke off, her head spinning, pulse racing, breathing loud in the silence. *They really needed to get horizontal.* She looked around at the obviously half-unpacked apartment.

'You have got a bed, right? I'm getting too old for the floor.'

Sebastian smiled, took her hand and led her through a maze of boxes into his bedroom. 'Ta-da. A bed.'

Callie grinned. 'So it is.' More moonlight streamed through uncurtained glass and she walked in, sidestepping another two boxes. She sat on the edge and gave an experimental bounce. 'This will do very nicely,' she murmured.

He was lounging in the doorway, watching her with the same direct gaze from the restaurant. From the bridge. He was too far away.

'You're a long way away. And you're too dressed.'

Sebastian smiled. 'Hmm, whatever can we do about that?'

Callie looked at him for the longest time before leaning back on her elbows and crossing one leg over the other. 'Take off your clothes.'

Her husky request stroked feathers along his groin. 'You do like to be in charge, don't you?'

Callie rotated her ankle, one strappy black heel dangling from her toes. 'You've got to ask for what you want.'

Sebastian chuckled as he straightened and started on the buttons she hadn't managed to undo. Callie could feel her breath getting shorter as each button revealed glimpses of a magnificent chest, and she almost sighed out loud when he shrugged his shoulders and the shirt fell away to reveal the stunning breadth of him.

Just as she'd hoped, the events of the day evaporated.

His pecs and abs were taut and flat, smooth, framed by broad shoulders and very nice biceps. She could almost feel the weight of him crowding on top of her, pushing her into the bed, moving inside her.

Her gaze drifted south, wondering if what was below his zip was as magnificent as the rest of him. She forced her gaze back to his face. She used her foot to point to his jeans. 'And those.'

Sebastian had felt his breath stop in his lungs as her eyes had feasted on his chest and then dropped lower.

'Yes ma'am.' He saluted, a smile playing on his mouth as he reached for his button.

Thirty seconds later he had kicked free of his jeans and was standing before her, all but naked, watching her eyes roving over him. His thighs. His calves. His crotch. His breathing sawed in and out, in and out, waiting for her next move.

'Oh, my,' she murmured, pushing off her elbows into a sitting position and then rising off the bed. He looked incredible.

She just had to touch him.

She stopped in front of him, a centimetre separating them, his knowing, patient gaze boring into hers, dropping to her mouth then returning to her eyes. His clean male scent wafted towards her, making her nostrils flare.

She stroked a hand down his chest, holding his gaze, moving her mouth a little closer to his. His warm muscles shifted beneath her palm, hinting at their leashed potential. Her fingernail circled the hollow of his belly button and she felt the powerful contraction of his flat abdominals.

Dropping lower still, her hand brushed the hard ridge of his erection and she withdrew slightly before returning to trace the outline of it through his underwear. Callie smiled as Sebastian shut his eyes briefly.

When he opened them again Callie was looking directly at him. Her lips were a whisper from his. All he needed to do was move the barest amount and he could be plundering all their sweet plumpness. But he held himself in check, waited for her to make a move.

Callie could hear his ragged breath, could almost taste it as it mingled with her own. Her throat felt parched, her lips dry, despite her mouth watering at the thought of kissing him.

Her fingers stopped tracing the thick edge of him and wrapped around him, squeezing. She saw the bob of Sebastian's throat. 'Nice,' she murmured, and kissed his Adam's apple, brushed her lips across the flutter of the pulse either side then dipped to the hollow at the base of his throat before inching back to look at him again.

Sebastian didn't think it was possible to get harder, but he was wrong as their gazes meshed and her hand continued its firm grip around him. 'You have too many clothes on,' he croaked.

Callie smiled. 'Whatever can we do about that?' she mimicked.

'Take them off.'

CHAPTER THREE

SEBASTIAN'S husky command brushed against her sensitised skin as if he had actually touched her.

Callie stepped away slightly, swallowing, her hands trembling as she reached for her buttons. Sebastian's gaze was firmly locked on their action. She felt her stomach clench and her nipples become two painful points, rubbing erotically against her bra as she fumbled with the top button beneath Sebastian's stare.

She faltered for a moment.

She wasn't ashamed of her body. Being the tallest female by far growing up may have been a fault to focus on for a normal girl in a normal family, but things had been so far from normal at home that Callie had never had the luxury of worrying about what other people thought about her.

Including lovers.

But, undressing before his intent gaze, she felt a moment of doubt. Sebastian wasn't just any lover. Somehow he was different and every cell in her soul knew it.

And she wasn't twenty years old and stick thin. Not that she'd ever been stick thin. Unfortunately her large-boned genetics and size eleven feet would never put her in the waif group. And Sebastian looked like he was a man who could have any woman he wanted—especially the stick-thin ones.

Men liked stick thin, didn't they?

She couldn't even claim to be curvy. She was more straight up and down, long, strong limbs and athletic torso. She'd bet anything he had curvy women throwing themselves at him on a daily basis.

Men definitely liked curvy.

Sebastian saw her hands pause and a slither of doubt cloud her bright amber gaze. 'Callie?'

She looked at him, all honed perfect male, and looked down at herself, avoiding his gaze. 'I'm…' Her voice cracked a little and she shook herself.

This had never mattered before—she was a busy professional woman who was confident in her abilities, sexual and otherwise. She had no problems in asking for, and getting, what she wanted in bed. More than that, she was a take-it-or-leave-it kind of a girl. What you saw was what you got.

But this felt…different. Something about him, even after such short acquaintance, gave her pause. She'd never gone to bed with someone after knowing them for less than a day. How could a man who was essentially a stranger have had such a cataclysmic affect on her?

For someone who was used to being in control, that was more than a little scary. But perversely she also felt…safe.

She moistened her lips. 'I'm not twenty any more, you know?'

Sebastian was curiously touched by another seemingly uncharacteristic display. She was doing it again—changing before his eyes. From full-on sexually confident vixen to hesitant and doubtful. Almost shy.

Callie Duncan was one hell of a confusing mix.

'Well, thank goodness for that. Twenty-year-olds are vastly overrated.' He kept it light but it was one hundred per cent true—younger women tended to be clingy and needy and had way too many expectations.

Callie gave a half-smile. 'Still...'

'Callie?' he said softly. 'Does it look like I care?'

Callie's gaze dropped to the large bulge in his underwear. She smiled. 'If you don't mind me saying so, those things are not known for their fussiness.'

He didn't smile back. 'This one is.' He watched her hesitate further. 'Do you need a hand with that?'

Callie heard the silky challenge. He probably thought she was being *silly*. She lifted her chin. 'I think I can manage.'

And just like that she was back again.

Sebastian would have been dizzy had he not been so turned on.

Callie's fingers were surer as they popped each button and then quickly dispensed of her shirt. She wiggled out of her trousers in record time, thankful for the presence of the nearby wall. And then she was standing before him in her underwear, burning up from the heat in the slow, steady sweep of his appreciative gaze.

He lifted his hand and pointed to her bra. 'That too.'

Callie's eyes locked with his and she smiled as she reached behind her back for the clasp. Did she push her chest out a little more than necessary? Damn straight she did. The satisfying suck of his harshly indrawn breath made it worthwhile.

Sebastian felt air hiss out of his lungs as Callie's breasts swung free. They were pert, with large moonlight-kissed nipples that scrunched into tight berries as he stared at them. The bottom of her silver pendant brushed the swell of her cleavage. His mouth watered as he anticipated how they would taste.

He waited a beat or two then pushed out of the doorway and prowled the two paces separating them. He placed his hands on her shoulders and slowly ran them down her upper arms, his eyes glued to her breasts. He stopped midway and squeezed the firm warm flesh covering her biceps, pressing her arms closer to her body and pushing her breasts a little closer together.

'Oh, my,' he mimicked.

And then he turned her slightly, walking her a pace backwards until she bumped against the wall. He just caught her shiver as the cold paintwork hit her heated flesh before his mouth latched on to hers and all coherent thought was lost.

Callie opened to the demands of his lips, moaning against his mouth, winding her arms around his neck, revelling in the hard press of the wall behind sandwiching her against the lean, hard pressure of him.

She whimpered in protest as his lips left hers but moaned out loud when his hot mouth closed over one of her nipples a second later. She flung her head back against the wall, dragging in fiery air, twining her fingers into his hair, holding him there.

Another moan escaped as he sucked hard on the sensitive peak.

Sebastian pulled away, admiring the expressison of tortured ecstasy scrunching her brow. Her head was thrown back, her neck a tempting arc before him. Her swollen mouth had fallen open, her lips slack with passion and still moist from his ministrations.

She opened her eyes and he could see heat flaring in the amber depths and her dilated pupils as a mewed protest fell from her lips.

A surge of male pride rocketed into his system, ratcheting his craving to possess her even further. 'You're beautiful.'

The ragged whisper brushed sticky tentacles across her pelvic floor. Her breath hitched. She yanked at his head. 'Don't stop.'

Callie's knees almost crumbled when he complied, lavishing attention on her other breast. She gripped his shoulders, warm and solid beneath her palms, for purchase. The action pressed her closer still and she could feel the virile thickness of his erection as it rubbed against her.

She had to touch him.

Her hands drifted lower as he reclaimed her lips with a neck-snapping passion. She moaned into his mouth, and the muscles in his back rippled in response. When her fingers breeched the band of his underwear and she grasped his bottom, she felt the involuntary clench of his smooth gluteal muscles.

And when her hand sought and found the long hard length of him, squeezed him, his groan was soul-deep satisfying. He tore his mouth away, placing his forehead on hers, dragging in harsh breaths. Callie squeezed again, and he grasped her upper arms and growled, 'I think we need to lie down now.'

He caught her hand and dragged her towards the bed, somehow managing to step out of his underwear as well. And then they were tumbling onto the mattress and Callie's underwear was gone until all she was wearing was a silver necklace and two hoop earrings.

And then they were lapping at every inch of each other's bodies like they were covered in honey and neither of them had eaten for days.

'Now,' Callie cried, her hips rising off the bed.

Sebastian looked down at her. Her skin was flushed like an exotic jungle bloom, lush and open before him. He kissed her hard. 'One moment.'

Sebastian, his heart thundering in his ears, heard her mewed protest. He found his jeans, located his wallet, extracted a condom, and was back by her side in twenty seconds flat.

'Now,' he said, lowering his head further to drop a string of kisses around the base of her throat, his tongue tracing the line of her necklace, 'where were we?'

Callie felt the heat lick at her. 'Here,' she said, grasping the firm globes of his buttocks and rubbing herself against him.

Sebastian didn't need any further invitation. Her scent filled his head and it was the easiest thing in the world to slide into her, feel her tight around him, her fingernails pressing into his shoulder blades. And when she asked for more, he gave it, and when she wanted it faster, he picked up the pace, and when she cried out, his voice joined hers.

And when she went over the edge, he joined her.

It was quite some hours later they finally lay sated in a post-coital drowse among tangled sheets. Callie lay on her back, Sebastian's shoulder a perfect pillow. His arm crossing her chest was warm and vital and his fingers trailing up and down her arm kept the hum in her cells, the thrum in her blood on a steady burn.

'So...the bridge?'

Callie's eyes snapped wide-open, the malaise invading her bones and infecting her thought processes evaporating in a heartbeat. The hum and the buzz snuffed out.

'Sebastian.'

He regretted it immediately as her body tensed. All that languid warmth draped against him seemed to still and then tauten. 'Come on, Callie.' He ran a finger down her arm and felt her flinch. He stopped.

'Something happened back at the restaurant. If Gerri's to be believed, I think it has something to do with what happened on the bridge this morning.'

Callie vaulted up, pulling the sheet with her and leaving Sebastian exposed—not that she cared. She squirmed to the side of the bed, her feet finding the floor. She sat forward, her elbows on her bare thighs, her hands supporting her head. The only person who knew the story was Gerri. And that was the way she preferred it.

Her heart somersaulted in her chest at the mere thought of confiding in anyone else. 'Gerri should mind her own damn business.'

Sebastian rolled on his side. The golden skin covering the long column of her spine, the graceful arc where shoulder met neck, the dimples in the small of her back all tempted him. Sitting hunched over like this, as far away from him as possible, she looked so alone.

Still, she hadn't moved off the bed...

He reached out his arm and swept his palm down her spine. She didn't flinch this time and he dared to run it back up again and rest it on her shoulder.

'Maybe Gerri knows that sometimes talking to someone that you don't know very well is easier.'

Callie snorted. 'That's a nice euphemism for *virtual stranger.*'

Sebastian wasn't fooled by the sarcasm. He gave her shoulder a squeeze and dropped his hand to the bed. 'Okay. How about I guess?'

Callie shook her head. Couldn't he see she didn't want to talk about this? 'Just leave it, Sebastian.'

'I'm thinking that you lost a client on that bridge. Maybe recently? Maybe someone you were negotiating with at the time who decided to end it all anyway?'

Callie was horrified to feel tears pricking at her eyes as a sudden flash of her brother's anguished face flickered before her.

'Someone you couldn't help no matter how hard you tried.'

Callie heard Zack's little voice asking for his daddy and sucked in a breath. She *had* tried.

So hard.

'We can't be all things to all people, Callie.' On a deeply personal level, Sebastian knew that all too well. 'It wasn't your fault.'

She knew that. She did know it. But a familiar pain built in her chest anyway. And the pressure build-up behind her eyes was almost unbearable. A tear trekked down her face and the urge to unburden overwhelmed her.

For God's sake, she'd just shared the most intimate thing two human beings could share. She'd been as physically vulnerable as it was possible to be with a man. But to feel such an emotional connection, a compulsion to open up, had been totally unexpected.

Sebastian watched her closely. Was she trembling? 'Callie,' he murmured, stroking her back again, 'talk to me.'

Callie wiped at her face. His silky tone was so inviting. So soft. So understanding. If she didn't say something, say what was on her mind, she was going to burst. And in some strange way she couldn't understand, she trusted him. It was bizarre, she knew that. She barely knew him but she knew she could tell him this.

She shut her eyes as the stroke of Sebastian's palm encouraged her more. Somehow it was easier to say, to admit, with her eyes closed, in the dark.

'It was…my brother. Not a client. My brother committed suicide from that bridge eight years ago yesterday. I was there, talking to him, trying to talk him down, but…'

Sebastian's hand stilled. *This he hadn't expected.* He sat up and shuffled over to her, opening his legs, snuggling her into the V between his thighs. His powerful quads bracketed hers. His feet rested on the floor beside hers. He wrapped both arms around her waist and pulled her against him. 'I'm sorry.'

Callie opened her eyes and sagged against him as if she'd just had a ten-tonne bock of concrete lifted from her shoulders. She bit her lip. 'It was a long time ago.'

Sebastian nuzzled her neck and dropped a kiss on her shoulder. 'What was his name?'

Callie faltered. Tears welled in her eyes. Nobody involved in the case back then had ever been particularly interested in his name. He had just been a system failure. A chart number. And people who knew she'd been Zack's aunt and guardian had been too embarrassed or polite to ask.

She was curiously touched by the way he'd just humanised her brother.

'Andrew.'

Sebastian rested his chin on her shoulder. 'Did Andrew have problems or…?'

'He was a schizophrenic.'

'Ah.'

Callie drew in a ragged breath. It hurt to talk about

him. But it was nice to acknowledge his existence after years of avoiding the topic.

'In and out of psych wards from the age of sixteen. He was non-compliant with his meds and...transient... homeless for the last few years...'

The ugly scene at the restaurant came back to Sebastian and things clicked into place. 'That must have been difficult.'

Callie remembered those years of trying to help, trying to save him, trying to get him to see reason. Trying to be sister, mother and health professional, and failing at all of them. Learning the hard way that you just couldn't help someone who didn't want to be helped.

'The voices just got too much for him.'

'I'm sorry,' he said again. If anyone knew how mental health issues could affect family life it was him. Sebastian was quiet for a bit and they sat in a strange kind of solidarity that had little to do with the amazing sex they'd had for the last four hours.

After a while he moved back onto the bed and she followed him, turning into his side and draping an arm over his chest.

'Is that why you became a psych nurse?' he asked into the silence that stretched between them but some- how didn't feel unnatural.

Callie didn't answer for a moment, then she flipped over so she was lying on her stomach, her chin propped on his shoulder. She didn't know why she was telling him this. Any of it. She just knew it felt right.

'My mother was bipolar and Andy was diagnosed at sixteen. I didn't seem to be able to help either of them but I wanted to be able to do something. To try and help others. To...I don't know, understand, maybe.'

Sebastian used his forefinger to push back a lock of her hair that had fallen forward. Callie really had been through the wringer.

'What about you? Why'd you decide to become a psychologist?'

Sebastian searched her face. 'My father was a Vietnam vet. He was a prisoner of war for a brief time. He suffered severe PTSD. My mother was clinically depressed most of her life. Because of Dad mostly. Their marriage was certainly no bed of roses. So…' he shrugged '…I guess for the same reasons as you. To help. To understand.'

Callie nodded, liking the openness of his pale green eyes and the fact that he was some kind of kindred spirit. She shot him a slow smile. 'And what on earth are you doing in this neck of the woods? Community mental health is a little lowbrow for such a hotshot, surely?'

Sebastian chuckled but felt his gut tense. The answer to that one was complicated and a lot closer to home than the ancient history that was his family.

He played with a lock of her hair, rubbing its silky strands between his thumb and forefinger. 'I just needed a change of pace.' Callie was looking at him intently and he averted his gaze to what his fingers were doing. 'To try something different.'

Callie arched an eyebrow at his evasive answer. But she didn't say anything. His reluctance struck a chord, though, as she recognised her own behaviour in his avoidance. She didn't usually talk about herself either.

Instead, she leaned forward and kissed his very sexy, very understanding mouth. She lingered there as his tongue stroked her lips and desire squirmed through her belly. She smiled at him as she eventually pulled away and cuddled into his side again.

'So,' Sebastian murmured after the silence had gone on for an eternity. He'd been too wrapped up in the press of her breasts against his ribs and the slow, steady fan of her breath against his chest to speak.

And grateful that she hadn't insisted on knowing more.

'What I want to know is, how come you aren't married with a swag of kids by now?'

Callie laughed. 'You have to ask that? With my gene pool? Inflict that on some poor innocent child? You have got to be kidding!'

Sebastian smiled. 'You could have married,' he pointed out.

She shrugged. 'I haven't really found that one person, you know. I guess there have been a couple of guys over the years who I've had longish relationships with but… not for a quite some time.'

Not since Zack. There'd been nothing other than brief encounters while her nephew had lived with her.

'Let's just say I haven't found a man yet who's comfortable with my no-kids rule. Besides, I raised Andy's kid from two through to ten——I've done my mothering.'

Callie had spent a good part of her life caring for others. First her mother then her brother and then her nephew. All ending in heartache. Her mother's death, her brother's suicide had been harrowing, but saying good-bye to Zack had been like an emotional wrecking ball. She never wanted to be that vulnerable again.

'Raised? Past tense? Where is he now?'

Callie shifted, a spike of pain pushing her against the bed as she rolled onto her back. 'Back with his mother,' she said, staring at the ceiling.

'She wasn't always around?'

Callie shook her head. 'Zack's mother was a drug addict. And my brother wasn't capable of looking after him either. Aleisha's parents raised Zack until Andrew died and then...they couldn't cope any more. They didn't know if their daughter was dead or alive from one minute to the next and they were getting old, in their seventies. Too old to cope with an energetic two-year-old-boy. So I took him in.'

Sebastian could hear the emotion making her voice husky. He glanced at her. She had her eyes closed. 'But he's back with her now?'

'Yes.' She swallowed as the pain intensified. 'She's clean. Has been for two years. She's married to a good guy—very stable with a great extended family—and she has a great job. She wanted her son back.'

Sebastian didn't have to ask to know that giving her nephew up had been gut-wrenching for Callie—her soft, tremulous voice said it all. 'I'm sorry,' he whispered, rolling up on his elbow and dropping a kiss on her shoulder.

Callie nodded, squeezing her eyes together tight. 'It was the right thing to do.' She drew in a ragged breath. 'And it's working really well. He lives nearby, goes to the same school, has the same friends. He adores his stepfather. He's happy, that's all that matters.'

Sebastian kissed her shoulder again.

Callie knew she'd break into a million pieces if they kept talking about Zack. She took a deep breath and opened her eyes, staring directly into his. 'What about you? Do you have kids?'

It occurred to her that she didn't know much about him personally. They'd talked shop at the restaurant—professional history. Prison systems. Government policies.

His recent year-long secondment to the Department of Defence, counselling Australian military personnel.

But nothing personal.

She flicked a glance at his left hand. No ring mark.

'This, by the way, would be a very bad time to tell me you have three. And a wife waiting for you back in Melbourne.'

Sebastian chuckled. 'Oh, no, not me. No wife. No kids. Same reasons as you, really. Another bad gene pool and my parents' train wreck of a marriage led to my own no-kids policy.'

And he'd seen so much in his life, particularly this last year—so much violence and hate and suffering—he wasn't sure he wanted to bring an innocent child into such a screwed-up world.

'And let me tell you there aren't *any* women out there comfortable with that.'

Except Callie.

'Because women think you're going to change your mind. That they'll be the ones to make you see that you actually really do want babies. But…I don't think some people were meant to have children. Me included. Or at least some people shouldn't.'

Callie understood totally. 'Amen to that.' She rolled on her side and kissed him. Hard and deep. Grateful to have found the only man on earth who appeared to share exactly the same views she had.

Even if it was just for one night.

'Anyway,' she said, pulling away, sitting up, scooting to the side of the bed 'I'd better be off. I've got to work tomorrow.'

It was a well-practised manoeuvre for Callie. She never stayed the night. It was a rule she'd adopted early in her dating life, a product of a chaotic and unsettled upbringing, and had been cemented when an impressionable child came into her care.

And even though Zack was gone, sleeping—actually sleeping—with a man was an intimacy she didn't want to invite.

Especially not with Sebastian.

Still, as she rose and searched for her clothes, she was surprised at how hard it was this time. Normally she walked away without a backward glance. But with Sebastian watching her every move through half-open lids as she dressed in the moonlight, the temptation to stay was intense.

He didn't protest. Or insist. He just watched her and by the time she was dressed she felt thoroughly examined and one hundred per cent ready to get back into bed and go again.

She looked at him lying amidst the tangle of bedclothes all rumpled and sexy, the sheet just covering his modesty and exposing everything else. His eyes, hooded in the gloom, followed her actions like a lazy cat, ready to pounce.

'You sure I couldn't tempt you to stay a little longer?' he mused.

Sebastian threw the sheet back and grinned when her amber eyes widened at his readiness. That she wanted to leave was no skin off his nose. He preferred to sleep alone anyway, especially since the nightmares, so this part of a date was always awkward.

But he'd never had a woman so keen to leave.

And, besides, he didn't feel quite sated enough. Not yet. Maybe not ever.

Callie shut her eyes briefly. How was he even capable of going again? She opened her eyes and pierced him with her best no-nonsense look. 'Some of us have to work.'

Sebastian sighed and covered himself up again. She was looking around the room, her gaze not meeting his. This was what he'd feared. 'You're regretting it, aren't you?'

The thought disappointed him more than the fact that she was leaving. Something so wonderful should never be regretted.

Callie looked at him and frowned. *Was he joking?* If she lived to be a hundred she'd never regret this night. Sure, she knew in a couple of days she was going to regret baring her soul to him, but the sex? Never.

'No.' Her gaze swept the floor again.

He propped himself up on his elbow. 'Callie, you can't even look at me.'

Callie almost laughed out loud as she lifted her eyes. 'I've lost my earring, that's all.'

Sebastian chuckled. 'Oh. Sorry.' His gaze fanned over the bed and caught a glint of metal amongst the sheets. 'Here it is.' He held the hoop up.

Callie grinned. 'Thanks,' she said, sitting on the edge of the bed and relieving him of it.

Sebastian watched her attempting to hook it in without a mirror. 'So how do you want to handle this from here?' he asked.

'What do you mean?' she asked, concentrating hard on finding the hole in her lobe.

'Well…we are going to be colleagues as of next week…'

The earring found its home and Callie turned to face him. 'We're not forty-year-old virgins, Sebastian, swept away by a night of fantastic sex. Was sleeping together the wisest course of action? Probably not. But we're both professionals. I can keep my work life and my private life separate. Can you?'

Sebastian nodded. She was warrior woman again, bolshie and direct. God, he wanted to kiss her now, more than ever. Tumble her against the mattress and start all over again. 'Absolutely.'

'We can't do it again, of course, not while we're working together. I don't think colleagues being sexually involved ever really works.'

He couldn't agree more. 'Usually totally disastrous.'

'Especially when you're only here for a year.'

He nodded again. 'Doesn't make any sense.'

Callie nodded back, satisfied they were both on the same page. But then she made the mistake of following Sebastian's movements as he rubbed at the stubble on his chin and her gaze dropped to his mouth.

Damn it. She was going to have trouble forgetting where that mouth had been.

'Good.' She leaned forward to give him a businesslike kiss. She only lingered a little. Just for a few seconds. Inhaling him. Savouring him for one last moment.

She pulled back a little dazed, liking the way his mouth was moist from her lips, a small smile making it utterly irresistible.

Callie pushed herself off the bed before she kicked off her shoes and pulled back that damn sheet. 'I'll see you next week,' she said briskly, picking up her bag and striding out the door.

Sebastian blinked as she disappeared. He ran his tongue around his lips, tasting her one last time. He smiled.

Callie Duncan was one helluva woman!

It was a pity really they were going to be colleagues.

Because in every other way she was perfect.

She didn't push, she didn't want to marry him or have his babies, and she didn't want to stay the night.

She was his ideal woman.

CHAPTER FOUR

CALLIE had spent all the intervening days and about every spare second of her time over the weekend trying not to think about Sebastian's imminent arrival at Jambalyn. But as she pulled her car into her parking space Monday morning right next to Sebastian's, it could no longer be ignored.

She *was* going to see him again. Today. And every other day for the next year!

A nervous tremor ran through her stomach and she placed her hand against it. Why, why, why had she opened up to him like that? Opening her body to him had been far less intimate in comparison to letting him inside her head.

She felt as if Sebastian—*Sebastian Walker, for Pete's sake*—had crossed some sort of line. One she'd never let a man over before. And now he knew. And frankly that scared the hell out of her. How had she confessed something so personal to someone she barely knew?

She may as well have stayed the night too!

She pulled down her sun visor, annoyed at herself and at her train of thought. Her reflection stared back at her as she gave herself a quick once-over. She fiddled with her hair, inspected her teeth for stray food and pouted at her reflection. She reached for some lip gloss she knew was stashed somewhere in her voluminous handbag and grabbed it triumphantly when she found it almost immediately.

She looked back up to the mirror, watching herself as her hand hovered just above her lips.

And then sanity returned.

For crying out loud!

What was she doing? Was she trying to look nice for him? No. She would not do that. They were not in a relationship and neither were they going to be. She would start as she meant to go on—treating him as a colleague and pretending what had happened hadn't happened at all.

She was thirty-eight years old, for Pete's sake! And he was just a man. They were there to work and work only. It was imperative that she acted like a professional and forgot all about that night and the pillow talk that was making her feel unaccountably anxious.

Hopefully he'd get the message that their one-night stand was off-limits. And if he didn't, she'd just have to make it crystal clear.

Callie pushed the door open, got out and slammed it shut for good measure, before marching into the building.

Sebastian looked across the room as Callie—fierce, proud, warrior-woman Callie—strode into his new place of work with her head held high. She was wearing the same sort of clothes she'd worn on the bridge that fateful day. Loose-fitting jeans and roomy T-shirt in a rusty-brown that set off the honey highlights in her hair.

While there were no uniforms in community mental health, an ID tag hung from a lanyard around her neck and bounced against her breasts. Sensible flat shoes and a large black bag completed the picture.

She looked every inch the professional. Poised and confident, ready for another day at the coal face. A far cry from the sexy clothes she'd worn to the restaurant and which had ended up scattered all over his floor.

As she approached, her bag swung hypnotically against her hip, drawing his gaze lower and distracting him from Geraldine's fascinating explanation of the appointment system.

He had kissed that hip. Those thighs. Those long legs had locked around his waist. His gaze travelled up again, her necklace peeking out from the V of her neckline. Moonlight had glinted off that pendant as he had pounded into her.

Callie halted before Sebastian and Geraldine, her face warm, feeling stripped bare. And she didn't like it.

Hadn't she already bared enough?

'Good morning, Sebastian,' she said briskly, folding her arms across her chest, pleased to hear her voice was firm and strong.

He nodded, ignoring the way the action emphasised her breasts. 'Callie.'

'I see our new grandmother's giving you the tour?' Tahlia had given birth to a baby boy three hours after Gerri had left the restaurant.

'Not any more she's not.' Gerri grinned, tapping her watch. 'I have a breakfast meeting with the government community mental health advisor.' She walked the two paces to her desk to gather some files. 'Can you show Seb around? Take him out with you later today too. The sooner he gets to know the local area the better.'

And then she was gone.

Callie wanted to say no. She damn well couldn't show

him around. He kept looking at her like he wanted to undress her and that was not how she wanted this to pan out.

Plus he was in trousers and a long business shirt again, like the first day she'd met him—all buttoned up—which only seemed to emphasise what she knew lay hidden beneath.

Twelve months stretched ahead of her endlessly and her anxiety level kicked up another notch.

Instead she said, 'Seb, huh?'

He shrugged. 'Most people call me Seb.'

Not her. She'd cried his name so many times the other night he'd always be Sebastian to her.

She blinked at the rather possessive thought and felt a surge of irritation. She frowned at the buttons on his crisp white shirt. 'You might want to think about going a bit more informal,' she stiffly. 'I'm sure a man with your reputation must have a debonair image to maintain, and in your private practice your clients probably expect spiffy. But, trust me, in the community there are no expectations and most of our clients find it easier to relate to casual dress.'

Sebastian looked her up and down again, lingering on her thighs and breasts, unfazed by her prickliness—it was just part of the puzzling patchwork woman in front of him. 'Casual. Check.'

Callie swallowed. Okay. This couldn't go on. 'Don't look at me like that,' she said crankily, lowering her voice even though they were the only ones around.

Sebastian gave a half smile. 'Like what?'

Callie glared at him. 'You damn well know like what.'

He chuckled. 'Sorry. I'd forgotten how…great you look.'

Callie sucked in a breath at the slight emphasis on *great*. He didn't look sorry at all. She took a deep breath, flicking her eyes around the room, checking they were still alone. 'Don't, okay? Just don't. Don't look at me like that and don't think about the other night. You and I are going to pretend it never happened. Okay?'

Sebastian shouldn't have been surprised by her hushed outburst but he was. It was after all classic Callie hiding behind her mask. She was obviously running scared and this professional-boundaries front was her attempt to claw back control.

Sebastian regarded her quietly for a moment. 'You do know that what happened, the things we did and said, are private between us. Right? I would never break your confidence.'

Yes, but you know, she wanted to say. *You know.*

'But if you think I'm going to forget about that night—the things we did, the things we talked about—you're wrong. I know how hard that was for you, Callie, and I understand that at work you need to be able to put that side of you away and be the bolshie professional. And I also understand that it's not going to happen again. But I'm not into denial and I will not pretend it didn't happen.'

His tone held an unmistakable air of command and he was looking at her with calm authority—like he had when she'd mistaken him for a cop, all brooding and serious in his flak jacket. Like he did in his author photo on the back of his book, which she'd looked at obsessively the last few days.

His quiet words hit her in the chest with an impact that belied their volume. She should have known after their altercation on the bridge that Sebastian wouldn't be pushed around easily.

Damn the man!

'Fine,' she huffed. 'I'll pretend for both of us.' She brushed her hands together briskly. 'Let's just get on with our jobs, shall we?'

Sebastian nodded. At least they both knew where they stood now.

'And this is Donna's office. Your office,' Callie said, opening the door and striding over to his desk. She bent forward and tapped at the keyboard, bringing up his diary.

'When Rodney gets in he'll fix you up with a computer password and familiarise you with the system, but for now,' she said, hyper-aware of him standing behind her, peering over her shoulder, 'you have a couple of clients this morning...'

She paused, her gaze scanning the desk and locating the charts. She handed them to him. 'After lunch you have a group therapy session. I go out on my home visits at two.'

Callie straightened, her back brushing against his front for a cataclysmic second before she shimmied away from the desk.

'I'll...I'll leave you to it, then. I'll send Rodney in when he arrives.'

'Callie,' he chided, rolling his shirt sleeves up casually as he spoke, 'there's no need to be so jumpy. I do know how to be professional too.'

She watched the motion, mesmerised by his long fingers and strong forearms, remembering how they had looked against her body, how they had held and stroked her. A slow burn warmed her belly.

Sebastian's hands stilled as her body language communicated her internal struggle. Her mouth was saying professional but her eyes, her body were saying, *Shut the door and take me against it.*

He swallowed.

'Callie, if you want me to stop thinking about you and forget everything that we did and said and act like nothing happened between us, you really have to stop looking at me like that.'

Callie dragged her gaze back to his face and for a moment there was a flare of heat between them that was the sexual equivalent of a mushroom cloud.

'You can't have it both ways, Callie.'

His voice was soft but held an unmistakable edge. His face was grim and serious, the planes and angles uncompromising. He was giving her no quarter. Letting her know that he would hold her to the same standards she was holding him to.

Sebastian Walker was not going to be a pushover.

She gave an awkward nod. 'Rodney should be in soon,' she said, backing out of the room.

'So you go out most days, into people's homes?' Sebastian asked.

Anything to distract him from her alluring profile. He'd been yearning for a distraction since leaving the Gulf—something very different to do to fill his days and take his mind off the work he'd been doing there, the things that he'd seen. But Jambalyn was supposed to be the distraction. Not a woman.

He'd been sitting in the car with her on and off for the last two hours and her perfume was driving him nuts. It was the same one that permeated his sheets.

'Most days, yes.'

'By yourself?'

'No.' Callie shook her head. 'Always with another nurse.'

Sebastian nodded. *Good.* Working in the prison system and in several war-torn hotspots had made him especially attuned to safety issues. 'How big is your area?'

'Jambalyn staff cover mainly just the inner-city areas,' she said, grateful for something to take her mind off the bulk of his thigh in her peripheral vision. Since his gentle reprimand that morning she'd been exceedingly conscious of her every action around him.

But being this close was unnerving.

The department provided two cars for home visits. They weren't exactly spacious and Sebastian's size seemed to dominate the close confines of the vehicle.

'The health district we're in takes in all of northern Brisbane but there are several centres dotted around to break up the workload. Jambalyn is just one.'

Callie pulled up at a traffic light. She riffled through a pile of charts wedged in the centre console, grabbed one and handed it to Sebastian.

'The next client is twenty-four-year-old Ginny Carpenter,' she said. Sebastian's thigh flexed as he moved and she hastily averted her gaze.

The light turned green and Callie slammed the car into gear a little more firmly than required. 'Ginny has suffered from agoraphobia and severe depression since she was in her teens. She's been well controlled on medication and cognitive-behaviour therapy the last few years. She has a part-time job and got married almost a year ago now.'

Sebastian nodded. 'So this is a routine house call?'

'Yep,' she confirmed. 'Just a hi-how's-it-going kind of thing.'

Having accomplished the remainder of the journey in silence as Sebastian flicked through the chart, Callie pulled up at Ginny's house five minutes later and practically leapt out of the car. She really needed to get a grip here—she had another twelve months of this.

How the hell was she ever going to concentrate on her job if she was constantly distracted by his overwhelming physicality?

And then Ginny opened the door, her face tear-streaked, and Callie's professionalism trumped her hormones. 'Ginny? What on earth's the matter?' She stepped into the house, popping an arm around her client's shoulders.

'I'm… I'm…' Ginny led them into the house, her shoulders heaving, fresh tears streaming down her face. She led them into her bedroom and picked something up off the bed. 'I'm pregnant,' she wailed, holding up a home test kit with a little pink plus sign in the test window.

'Hey, hey,' Callie crooned as Ginny dissolved into more tears. She sat her down on the bed and took a seat next to her. She had to admit to a certain amount of relief. For an awful moment she'd thought Ginny might have been having a relapse of her symptoms.

'It's going to be okay, really, it is.' She put her arm around her client's shoulders again and rocked her slightly.

'Why don't I make us all a cup of tea?' Sebastian asked.

'A cup of tea would be fabulous,' Callie agreed, and watched as Sebastian left the room.

After a couple of minutes Ginny's weeping seemed to have settled to a few spasmodic, hiccoughy breaths. 'Let's go and have that cuppa, huh?' Callie suggested.

Ginny nodded. She rose from the bed and headed to the kitchen, followed by Callie. Sebastian had his back to them as he opened cupboards, looking for mugs. Callie was amazed at how he commanded attention, whether on a bridge, in a bulletproof vest, on the back of a book, or in a kitchen, making tea.

He dominated the small area.

Sebastian turned and smiled at them as they entered, and Callie made the introductions while Ginny took over, fussing around, putting a tablecloth on the table and pulling out a packet of biscuits.

There was silence as they all sat and sipped at their tea.

Callie flicked a glance at Sebastian before stirring another spoonful of sugar into the enormous mug. 'So, you…don't want a baby?' she asked tentatively.

Ginny immediately recoiled from the question, her hand sliding to her belly. 'Of course I want a baby, but…'

Sebastian looked from one woman to the other. 'But?' he prompted.

Ginny's upper lip wobbled. 'I'm not fit to be a mother.'

'Oh, no, Ginny. No, no, no,' Callie hastened to assure her, plonking her cup of tea down.

'It's true,' Ginny insisted. 'I've already been taking drugs that have probably harmed it. I've been on the internet all afternoon. The meds for my condition have been known to cause birth defects and low birth weights, even prematurity.'

Ginny started to cry again, her hand tightening on her abdomen. 'And I can't go off them, Callie, I just can't. I can't go back to the way I was. It'll kill me. I won't be any kind of mother if I can't even take my little girl for a walk in the park or down to the shops for an ice cream. And what kind of mother does that make me, huh?' she demanded, getting more and more wound up.

'The best kind, I'd say,' Sebastian interrupted.

Ginny stopped abruptly at his deep calm voice. 'What…what do you mean?' She hiccoughed.

'You're already thinking like a mum. Worrying about your baby. Putting its needs first. That's what the best mums do.'

Ginny rallied a little at his words for a moment or two. Callie just listened in awe—it had been the absolutely perfect thing to say.

'How far along are you, do you think?' he asked gently.

Ginny sniffled and shook her head. 'My periods are always so erratic. I just don't know.'

Callie watched the doubts return. Ginny turned beseeching eyes on her. 'If I go off my meds they might even…take my baby away from me.'

Callie squeezed her hand. 'That's not going to happen, Ginny. It's not going to happen.' She flicked a glance at Sebastian as she prioritised what needed to be done for her client. Ginny needed some facts, she needed to be checked out medically but, first and foremost, she needed her main support person.

'Where's Brad? Does he know?'

'At work. He didn't know I was taking the test.'

'Right.' Callie stood. 'Firstly I'm making an appointment right now for you to get an ultrasound.' She flipped open her phone. No reception. 'I need to go outside. While I'm doing that, Sebastian's going to talk to you about pregnancy and managing your condition.'

She looked straight at him all businesslike and he

nodded imperceptibly before she strode out of the house.

'I'm so sorry,' Ginny murmured. 'You must think I'm stupid.'

Sebastian shook his head. 'Not at all.' He sipped his tea. 'Okay let's talk facts, yes?' He watched Ginny nod and then continued. 'Generally there's not a lot of data about drugs in pregnancy because obviously no pregnant woman would volunteer for clinical trials. But for the type of medication you're on, we actually know quite a bit.'

He paused to make sure she was following him. 'There is one drug in particular that's been linked with minor heart defects in babies but...' he tapped her chart '...you're not on that. On the other things—the premature birth and low birth weights—there is some evidence around these in a couple of studies but usually only in women who also drink and smoke while on their medication.'

Sebastian paused again to give it time to sink in. The internet was a wonderful tool and he had no doubt that patients were more informed these days because of it—which was a good thing. But there was a maze of information out there that could be very confusing too.

He picked up a biscuit. 'Your chart says you don't drink or smoke.'

Ginny nodded. 'Never touch either of them.'

Sebastian smiled. 'Good, then.'

'But what about breastfeeding? Will I be able to do that on my meds?'

Sebastian nodded. 'Yes, quite safely. Only a very small percentage of the drug crosses into the breast milk and there are numerous studies reporting no ill effects from the medication you're currently taking.'

He smiled again and Ginny returned it, albeit rather tentatively.

Callie traipsed back into the house, pleased to see her client smiling. She glanced at Sebastian, who was pushing the last of a biscuit into his mouth. He smiled at her and she watched as he sucked residual chocolate off his fingers and flicked at some crumbs with his tongue.

Oh, dear God. Chocolate-covered biscuits and Sebastian. What would he taste like right now?

She blinked. 'Right, then.' She quickly dragged her eyes from his lips. 'I have an appointment for you in half an hour.' She strode to Ginny's fridge and pulled out the two-litre bottle of water she knew her client always had in the door.

'Wow! That was quick.'

Callie smiled at Ginny as she plonked the water on the table. 'I have my sources.' She tapped her nose twice. 'Now, drink up. You need a full bladder.'

Her gaze skittered towards Sebastian and his lips again before skittering away. 'We'll take you. You can ring Brad from the car.' She turned to Sebastian. 'You ready to go?'

Sebastian grinned. He'd caught the brief glazing of amber eyes as they'd dropped to look at his mouth. He drained the last of his tea. 'Me?' He stood. 'I'm ever ready.'

Callie's brows drew together as she was transported back to his bed She didn't grace him with a response as her pulse spiked. Was he trying to goad her into a reaction? Instead she turned to Ginny, who was drinking from the bottle. 'Let's go.'

* * *

It was only about a ten-minute drive from Ginny's to the local hospital but they were heading into peak hour so heavy traffic made the going slower. Callie drove while Sebastian talked some more to Ginny about managing her condition and the pregnancy. He explained it might be possible to reduce Ginny's medication and that they would see her more frequently during the following months to monitor the situation.

By the time they arrived, Ginny was actually smiling. She was obviously feeling much more positive about the unexpected twist her life had taken and with her ability to be a mother.

Callie, on the other hand, was not doing so well. She'd spent the entire time trying not to think about an ever-ready Sebastian sans clothes and smeared in chocolate biscuit.

She'd tried to concentrate on the services and strategies she could put in place to support Ginny—child health clinic, community midwives, a lactation consultant. She'd made a mental note to take Sebastian to the psych unit at the hospital to introduce him around. She'd even recited the twelve times table.

But the lull of his voice had washed over her as she'd driven and she couldn't banish the image of him reclining naked on his bed, the sheet pulled up over his hips, his chest beckoning.

'I'll wait outside,' Sebastian said as Ginny was shown straight in.

'Oh, no,' Ginny said, placing her hand on his sleeve. 'If its okay, I'd like you to be there. I'd like you both to be there.'

Callie nodded, even though she'd rather stick a poker in her eye than have to share such an intimate thing with Sebastian.

They'd already been intimate enough!

It was good—great, she supposed—that Ginny had taken so well to Sebastian but it really was the last straw in a very long day!

'Hi, Blake.' Callie greeted the sonographer. 'I really appreciate you fitting us in on such short notice.'

Blake grinned. 'Anything for you, Cal.'

Sebastian raised an eyebrow at the wolfish leer. He looked from Callie to Blake and back to Callie again, wondering about their relationship. Had they been lovers? Their familiarity, the nickname certainly hinted at a level of personal closeness that was more than collegial.

Callie laughed at something Blake said and swatted his sleeve playfully.

Sebastian wasn't amused.

In fact, he was downright irritated.

Which irritated him further.

'Okay, Ginny, climb up here, my lovely,' Blake said, holding out his hand to help Ginny onto the narrow couch. 'Are you ready to see your baby?'

Sebastian ground his teeth, his irritation ratcheting up another notch. Of course Blake was a thoroughly nice guy.

The ultrasound got under way and Ginny reached for Callie's hand. Callie gave Ginny's hand a reassuring squeeze but she was aware only of Sebastian standing to one side and slightly behind her. She could feel the heat radiating off his body and smell the rich, earthy tones of his aftershave, which seemed to be imprinted on her DNA.

All she needed to do was lean back and she'd be pressed along the length of him. Then it'd only be a small move to turn in his arms, press her face into his neck, feel his stubble scratching her cheek.

Blake pressed a button and the room filled with the steady *whop, whop, whop* of a tiny fluttering heart. It dragged Callie out of the haze miring her body and she actually took in what was on the screen for the first time.

'Isn't that a beautiful noise?' Blake grinned at them.

Ginny burst into tears and Callie squeezed her hand again. The fuzzy image squirmed and from nowhere a lump of emotion rose in her throat as tears pricked the backs of her eyes.

Callie blinked hard to dispel them. This was ridiculous! She'd sat through dozens of these. Unfortunately lack of sexual inhibition and promiscuity often went hand in hand with unmedicated mental health conditions, so she'd done this very thing with too many clients over the years.

She'd never, *ever* got weepy over the sound of a baby's heartbeat!

But there it was on the screen. All fuzzy and black and white with a fluttering movement right in the centre. It was rhythmic and utterly entrancing.

'She's beautiful,' Ginny whispered, touching the screen.

'Oh, you think it's a she, huh?' Blake grinned. 'Well, I think we'll need to wait until your nineteen-week ultrasound to know that one for sure.'

Callie didn't really take in what Blake and Ginny chatted about over the next few minutes. She was too caught up in the image flickering on the screen.

And for the first time ever a tiny worm of regret wriggled inside her.

'Well, according to my calculations,' Blake mused as he input his final data and pressed a button, 'you are twelve weeks along.'

'Twelve weeks?' Ginny squeaked.

Blake grinned and patted the large metal machine like it was a favourite shaggy dog. 'The waves don't lie.'

Ginny's startled exclamation snapped Callie out of the strange twilight zone she'd been stuck in. She moved away from Sebastian to Blake's side, avoiding her colleague's gaze. She did a quick calculation. 'That makes you due in September,' she said, helping Ginny adjust her clothes and aiding her into a sitting position.

'September twentieth, according to the waves,' Blake confirmed.

Ginny shook her head. 'I can't believe it.'

Sebastian crossed to the other side and held out his hand, joining with Callie to help Ginny down off the high couch. 'You'd better believe it. You're going to be a mum.' He smiled.

Ginny thanked the sonographer and Sebastian guided her out of the room as she chatted away. He looked back to see if Callie was following. She wasn't. But he did see her standing quite close to Blake, laughing, raising her face towards the other man just before the door swung shut.

Was Callie about to kiss him?

Was she in there now, kissing him?

Sebastian felt a strange but very immediate urge to kick the door down and drag her away.

But then Ginny's phone rang, distracting him. She pulled it out of her bag and by the time she'd answered it Callie was there looking like she hadn't just been kissed. Sebastian felt a weird sort of satisfaction. At least when he'd kissed her, Callie Duncan had looked thoroughly kissed.

'Is that Brad?' Callie asked. When Ginny nodded she said, 'Tell him to meet us at the cafeteria.'

They spent the next half-hour in the cafeteria, talking to Ginny and Brad about the baby and how to manage the pregnancy and Ginny's condition without compromising either.

'I'm worried that I'll be so anxious about the baby that it's...you know...okay that I might have a relapse of my anxiety,' Ginny admitted.

Callie grabbed her client's fidgety hands and squeezed, stilling their nervous plucking movements. 'I'm going to set you up with a community midwife service that'll see you every week, and if you're still worried—ever—you can come to Jambalyn. We have a hand-held Doppler there and I even know how to use it.' Callie grinned. 'You can listen to the baby's heartbeat every day if you want.'

Ginny looked at her uncertainly. 'Really?'

Callie nodded. 'Really.'

Callie was quiet as they walked to the psych ward a little while later. Brad had taken Ginny home so there was just the two of them. She was thinking about that strange moment again when the sound of the foetal heartbeat had filled the room and tears had threatened.

What had *that* been about?

'So, is he an ex-lover?' Sebastian asked, trying for casual.

'Hmm?' she asked distractedly.

'Blake. I'm guessing he's an old flame?'

Callie frowned as his question sank in. She glanced at him as they moved into dangerous waters once again.

'Why on earth would you think that?'

'Ah…I saw you kissing him.'

Callie laughed. Her and Blake? 'We're friends. Old friends. We went to uni together. He married another uni friend of ours. They have three children. I'm their godmother.'

Come to think of it, she was godmother to a lot of her friend's kids…

Always the godmother, never the mother.

She narrowed her eyes. She shouldn't ask the question but she couldn't help herself. 'Why?'

Sebastian blinked. Good question…why did he care? Except he did. Care. A lot. He shrugged. 'Just curious. It's the psychologist in me. People, their motivations are endlessly fascinating.'

And if it sounded like a lame explanation that was because it was. The truth was he didn't have an adequate reason for feeling like he did. But the thought of another man doing things to her that he had done just didn't sit right.

Not at all.

CHAPTER FIVE

THE plane hit an air pocket and Callie grabbed convulsively for her armrests. Unfortunately Sebastian's arm lay along their shared one and she felt the delicious rub of masculine hair against the pulse point at her wrist before she snatched it away.

'Nervous flyer?'

Sebastian's low murmur at her ear almost caused her to jump again. 'I prefer to be on the ground,' she said, her jaw tense, her pulse bounding madly. If only she could be sure it was from the turbulence and not the illicit brief contact she'd avoided for the last two months.

'Relax,' he urged, stretching out his legs. 'You know more people by far die in car crashes than plane crashes.'

She rolled her head to the side and regarded his profile. He'd shut his eyes and she looked her fill. Strong jaw cleanly shaven, straight nose, fringe flopping across his forehead. Long brown eyelashes casting shadows on a prominent cheekbone. And a mouth that still haunted her dreams.

'I like my chances of surviving a car accident more than I do should this plane suddenly go hurtling to the ground.'

Sebastian chuckled and opened his eyes, rolling his head towards her at the same time. She averted her gaze and he sobered slightly. Even after a couple of months the thing between them was still there. Sure, they'd both done a passable job of ignoring it but in unguarded moments they both knew it hadn't gone away.

That it was always there, simmering beneath the surface. Just waiting for a moment to erupt. Biding its time.

'Excuse me, sir, would you like something to drink?'

Callie opened her eyes to find a blonde, pixie-faced, well-endowed air hostess batting her eyelashes at Sebastian.

Oh, please!

Sebastian smiled at the very attractive woman offering him a beverage and, if the message in her eyes was correct, a hell of a lot more than that. 'I'd love a coffee, thank you.'

'Certainly, sir.' She poured some percolated coffee into a fine china cup. 'Are you going to Melbourne for business or pleasure, sir?'

'Business, I'm afraid. We're attending a weekend seminar.'

The air hostess, whose name badge proclaimed her to be Megan, pouted prettily, not even faltering at Sebastian's *we*. 'Oh, what a shame,' she murmured, passing him his coffee, her gaze firmly trained on him.

Callie rolled her eyes. 'I'd like one too, thank you,' she interrupted, a little more tartly than she'd expected.

'Certainly, madam.' Megan nodded, reluctantly dragging her flirty gaze from Sebastian to grace Callie with a cool, professional one.

Callie shook her head in disgust as Megan moved

on. 'Does every woman on earth flirt with you?' she grouched.

Sebastian smiled at her annoyed face. A little frown line formed between her brows when she was cranky that was actually quite endearing. It also formed when she was deep in thought and when she was determined. 'I don't know what you're talking about.'

Callie snorted. 'I thought she was about to offer you the chance to join the mile-high club.'

Sebastian chuckled. 'How do you now I'm not already a member?'

Callie faltered, her mind filled with an image of her and him going for it in the squashed confines of an aeroplane loo imprinted itself on her brain. For God's sake, with his height and width and her less than elf-like figure they'd probably maim each other.

Still, the idea fascinated her…

Intrigued despite herself, she asked, 'You…you're not, are you?'

Sebastian raised his eyebrows at her. 'A real man never kisses and tells.'

She watched as he took a calm sip of his coffee and her heartbeat skittered madly.

'Anyway, as I was saying,' she continued, desperate to dispel the powerful image, 'the woman at the check-in desk practically had her tongue hanging out on the counter.'

'Hey,' Sebastian chided, 'we got upgraded, right?'

Callie blinked. 'Oh, my God. You always get upgraded, don't you?'

Sebastian shrugged. 'It's the red hair.'

Well, didn't that figure! Callie spent her flying hours shoehorned into an economy-class seat, her legs up around her ears as the person in front invariably reclined their seat, and usually ensconced next to an inconsolable baby or a rotund gent with major sleep apnoea. While Sebastian used his charisma and his glorious hair to swan around in business class!

And what a luxurious experience it was—large comfortable seats of soft leather and enough room for her to completely unfold her long legs and stretch out. Discreet but attentive—perhaps too attentive—service. And not a crying baby in sight.

'So,' Sebastian asked as he drained the dregs of his coffee, 'are you nervous about your paper?'

She shook her head, pleased for a change in topic. 'No. I've presented a lot of papers over the years—more interesting ones than this, that's for sure.'

'The study findings are important, though. It'll garner a lot of interest.'

Callie shrugged. She knew he was right but she found presenting facts and figures and reams of stats very dry. 'Yeah, I know. Yours sounds much more interesting.'

Sebastian regarded her. He too was no stranger to presenting but this one was the closest to his heart. 'Well, let's hope everyone else will think so too.'

Callie frowned. He seemed a little uncertain and she was taken aback. She'd never seen him anything other than one hundred per cent confident. On the bridge, confronting an oaf in a restaurant, with Ginny and the numerous other clients she'd seen him with.

In bed.

It was the first time she'd seen even the briefest flash of doubt in his usually assured gaze and she almost reached out and put her hand on his sleeve.

Dangerous. Very, very dangerous.

She'd fought hard to put their night of passion behind her and something told her this was not the moment to test her resolve. This wasn't a dirty weekend away together. It was work. Business.

'Headphones, sir?'

Megan was back and this time Callie was actually grateful. 'I will thanks,' she said, reaching for one. Anything—*anything*—to occupy her for the next ninety minutes.

The plane touched down at Tullamarine in the early afternoon, and despite her luxurious ride Callie was pleased to be away from Sebastian's sexual orbit. Going away with him hadn't seemed like such a big deal back at her desk at Jambalyn, where their business-as-usual veneers were well practised. But suddenly, away from the safety net of work, she wasn't sure it was that simple.

Megan was at the door to see them off as they disembarked. She smiled at Sebastian. 'If you change your mind, sir, I have the next few days off,' she murmured, and out of the corner of her eye Callie saw her discreetly pass him her card.

She also saw him pocket it.

It put an itch up her spine and a frown on her face and she strode ahead of him, wanting suddenly to be far away.

Sebastian followed her at a more sedate pace, watching the way her auburn hair swung with the purposeful strut of every long-legged stride and how her black tailored trousers clung to the swell of her bottom.

He put his hand in his pocket and retrieved the card Megan had given him. He hadn't been on a date since before leaving for the Gulf. Sebastian tried to conjure up a mental image of the cute little blonde he'd left not even five minutes ago and failed miserably. All he could see was Callie.

He tossed the card in a nearby bin.

Thirty minutes later, after a very quiet taxi ride, they were standing in the classically elegant foyer of the Langham Hotel. Dominated by a grand, sweeping marble staircase and cascading fountains crowned by magnificent chandeliers, it gave off an aura of hushed, timeless luxury.

'We'd like to check in, please,' Sebastian requested the elegant older woman behind the desk. 'We're attending the C.M.H. conference.'

The woman looked up over half-moon glasses with a fixed pleasant smile that she'd no doubt honed over the years to greet customers. She looked close to retirement age, with steel-grey hair tucked into a sleek chignon. It was obvious she'd in the business for many years—she had brisk and efficient written into every well-concealed line in her face—and would scare the living daylights out of any new staff that put a foot wrong.

She certainly didn't look like she suffered fools gladly.

'Oh,' she said, and stared for a moment or two longer than was decent. And Callie could have sworn she actually saw a swathe of red bloom in her cheeks.

Oh, for crying out loud! Was there no end to Sebastian's effect on the opposite sex?

'Most certainly, sir.' She practically preened. 'Has sir booked a double or maybe a suite?'

'No!'

The woman glanced at Callie fully for the first time, a little startled by her vehemence, loud in the muted marble surroundings where the only noise was the trickle of a nearby fountain. Callie was beyond caring. It was bad enough that Rodney had booked them on the same flight. Same rooms were out of the question.

'There are two rooms booked,' she said, a little more controlled this time. She had double— *triple*—checked.

The woman eyed her for a moment longer, glanced at Sebastian and then back at her. Callie saw a fleeting *But why?* in the woman's gaze before she nodded graciously over her glasses. 'Certainly, madam. If you would both please fill out a registration form,' she said, pushing one each over to them.

She tapped on her computer keyboard as Callie and Sebastian scribbled their details on the proffered forms. 'Same floor be okay?' the woman asked.

Callie opened her mouth to say no. That she wanted to be as geographically distant from him as possible. But both of them were looking at her with curiosity, obviously waiting for her to object again, and she decided she wouldn't give either the satisfaction.

'That's fine,' she said briskly, handing her completed form back.

The woman spent a few more minutes completing the formalities and handed them their keys. 'Eleventh floor.' She tapped the numbers. 'They're opposite each other.'

Sebastian smiled at her. 'Thank you...' he paused, reading the woman's name badge '...Marion.'

Marion pinked up again and Callie gave a mental eye roll as she turned away, but not before she heard the older woman's breathy 'My pleasure, sir'.

Sebastian caught up with her as she entered the lift. She looked cross, her amber eyes flashing at him, daring him to say something. He held her glittering gaze as the door shut behind him. 'Are you okay?'

'Fine.' Except she wasn't. She was…frustrated as hell. She'd spent two months on a relatively even keel after a wonky start with Sebastian and now they'd left home turf her body had taken leave of its senses!

Outside Jambalyn it was like he'd lost his 'off-limits' force field and she was being dragged into his gravitational pull again. And watching every other woman in his vicinity being sucked in too—even shrewd grandmothers who should know better—was not helping.

Sebastian gripped the handle of his pull-along suitcase. 'You don't look fine.'

The lift dinged and Callie sagged against the wall in relief.

'Saved by the bell,' Sebastian murmured as Callie strode out ahead of him.

Callie's heels sank into the luxurious carpet, muffling any sound as she quickly located their rooms. She turned her back on his door immediately, preferring not to be reminded that for the next three nights only the width of a hallway and two doors would be separating them.

With a bit of luck she'd be in her room before he made it this far down.

But, alas, it was not to be as Callie's key-card chose that moment to be recalcitrant. She was cursing it under her breath as she jammed it repeatedly in and out, watching desperately for the little green light, when Sebastian drew level with her.

He stepped in close and put a stilling hand over hers. 'Allow me.'

Callie wanted to object but the touch of his hand, his clean male smell and the sheer utter breadth of him wrapped her in sticky tentacles. She bit her lip to stop herself from whimpering. 'Bloody things,' she said with an unsteady voice. 'I always get the dodgy ones.'

Sebastian chuckled. 'It's easy when you know how,' he murmured. 'You just have to be patient. Gentle. Slide it in slowly...'

Callie watched mesmerised as he held her hand fast on the card, entwining their fingers and inching the thin piece of plastic into the slot. Her stomach clenched.

'Wait for a second,' Sebastian continued, his gaze gliding from the lock and their joined hands to her face. He heard the slight click, knew the light would be green, but her attention had returned to his face and he couldn't look away. 'And then slide it slowly out.'

He pushed down on the handle and the door gave a little but neither of them noticed. Her gaze was fixed on his mouth and, heaven, help him, he dropped his to hers as well.

He'd dreamt about that mouth.

Callie felt as if she was sinking in quicksand and couldn't break away. This was crazy. She had to do something. Move or say something. Let him know where they stood.

She swallowed. 'I'm not going to sleep with you while we're here, Sebastian.'

Sebastian's mouth quirked at her bravado. 'Until now I was under no illusion that you would.'

'Just because I'm across the hall from you does not mean I'm...available.'

Sebastian flicked his gaze to her eyes simmering with naked desire before returning to her lips. He wanted to taste her so badly he had to grip the handle harder.

'You're doing it again, Callie,' he murmured. 'Don't tell me one thing with your mouth...' Sebastian lifted

a hand and rubbed his thumb along her bottom lip
'…and another thing with your eyes.'

Callie clamped down on the whimper that rose in
her throat and dropped her eyelids, shuttering the heat
she couldn't disguise. She felt as if her eyeballs were
burning two holes in her head.

With a monumental effort Sebastian dropped his hand
and dragged his gaze from her mouth. 'I'm not going to
play games with you, Callie. We're both adults here.' He
pushed her door open for her. 'I'm just over there…' he
inclined his head '…if you change your mind.'

Callie was damned if she was going to sit around in her
hotel room all afternoon until the black-tie fundraiser
this evening, replaying Sebastian's scintillating challenge over and over.

She was in Melbourne, for goodness' sake. She loved
Melbourne! The Langham was situated along the renowned Southbank Promenade overlooking the tran-
quil Yarra River. Right outside the hotel's doors waited
a fabulous world of shopping, boutiques and alfresco
cafés.

She would walk and shop and drink coffee and just
enjoy being anonymous in a big vibrant city.

Two hours later Sebastian was prowling restlessly around
South Bank, trying to ignore the *I'm not going to sleep
with you* echo in his head. He'd met an old colleague for
a drink, which had helped, but he knew he didn't want
to return to his room, knowing she was so close.

And yet so far.

So hard was he concentrating on not thinking about
her that he rounded a corner and careened straight into
a woman who had stopped in front of a shop window.

'Whoa! Sorry,' he apologised, grabbing hold of her body, trying at the last moment to lessen the impact and save her from falling.

Callie staggered, grateful for the man's hold on her as his body collided with hers. It took a moment for the world to come back to an even keel and for her to realise the identity of who exactly had almost knocked her flying. 'Sebastian?'

'Callie?'

Their simultaneous recognition was comical as they stared at each other dumbstruck for a moment.

'I'm sorry,' he apologised again. 'I wasn't paying attention.'

Callie nodded slowly, her pulse tripping along, her skin tingling where he'd touched her. Her arm, her waist. It hadn't meant to be sexual, she knew that, but its fiery wake was igniting a heat down low in her belly. If only she hadn't spent the last two months avoiding his touch, she might not be acting like a Victorian virgin now.

'What are you doing, standing in the middle of the footpath anyway?' he joked as he fought to bring his reactions under control. He could still feel the imprint of her waist against his palm and the press of her side down the length of him.

Callie dragged her thoughts back from where they'd been mired and turned her attention to the shop window and the most gorgeous dress she'd ever laid eyes on. It was so beautiful it had stopped her in her tracks.

'The dress,' she murmured.

Sebastian followed her gaze. He didn't pretend to know much about women's dresses. Except how important they were to the female of the species. And how easy they were to get off. But even he gave a long low whistle at the creation in the window.

Callie smiled. 'Exactly.'

'So, are you going to get it?'

Callie looked at it longingly but the facade of the trendy little shop reeked of money and she knew she'd never be able to afford the price tag. She sighed. 'No.'

Sebastian heard the unmistakable note of yearning in her voice. She wanted it. And he wanted to see her in it—and peel her out of it—too.

'You need a dress for tonight, right?'

Callie nodded. 'Yes, but I brought one with me.'

'But you want this one,' he said patiently, watching as Callie's teeth sank into her bottom lip, her gaze trained on the window. 'Come on.' He grabbed her elbow and tugged her towards the door. 'Let's go and try it on.'

Callie resisted for a moment then let him drag her into the shop.

The elegant shop assistant, who could have been Marion's twin sister, gave Callie a polite, perfunctory smile and then leapt to attention as Sebastian swept in behind her, commanding that the woman find a size twelve in the window dress as Callie would like to try it on.

Callie watched bemused as the boutique owner fawned over Sebastian. He was ushered to a plush leather lounge outside the spacious fitting room as the owner hung the dress in a cubicle for Callie. She made him a coffee and furnished him with a newspaper.

Ensconced in a cubicle she could have thrown a party in, it all felt surreal. Like she was in a scene from a movie.

Callie stared at the dream of a dress, touching it with shaking hands. Wanting it but afraid to ruin its crisp perfection by putting her body inside it.

Still, it called to her and she couldn't resist.

The second it floated down over her head, Callie had to have it. The deep purple fabric was satiny cool against her skin, close fitting but moving and stretching with every flex and twist of her body. The strapless bodice was ruched over her breasts but plain at the back.

It emphasised the thrust of her chest in a way she'd thought only screen sirens from the 1940s had been able to perfect. The fabric clung to her hips and her long legs and the contours of her butt and draped to the floor, the ruffled hem flaring slightly and pooling in a slight train behind her.

It was simply the most stunning thing she'd ever worn.

'You're not going to make me come in there, are you?'

Sebastian's voice brought her out of her daze as she stared at herself in the mirror. Her belly heated at the thought of him seeing her in it. It was a dress a woman wore for a man. Sexy. Slinky. Suggestive.

One shimmy of her hips and it'd pool at her feet in a tempting puddle of purple.

She looked at the tag and sighed. 'It's too expensive.'

Sebastian felt anticipation curl inside his gut. 'Some things are worth it.'

Callie rubbed her hands along the silky fabric.

It's just a dress. It's just a dress.

Maybe if she recited it enough she'd actually start to believe it.

'It's just a dress,' she said. Out loud this time.

'Why don't you let me be the judge of that?'

Callie was temped. Very tempted. After all, she was never going to buy it, but admiring herself in the mirror there was a tiny female part of her that yearned for someone else to see her in it too.

Yearned to see a man's reaction.

She took a breath, opened the door and stepped out.

Sebastian's heart almost stopped in his chest. Callie looked sensational. The deep purple suited her colouring and the dress hugged and flared in all the right places. She looked like a movie star on a red carpet or a model poised at the end of a catwalk.

He'd seen her in jeans and T-shirts, in tailored trousers and silky blouses—hell, he'd even see her naked—but this Callie was something else again. Yet another facet to the woman who seemed to have many.

Girlie Callie.

And girlie Callie was a sight to behold.

He stood. 'Wow.'

Callie flushed as his thorough gaze travelled all over her, lingering in all the places he already well and truly knew. Her nipples hardened at his frank gaze and the memory of them and, predictably, in a dress that clung like a satin glove, their arousal didn't go unnoticed.

His gaze zeroed in on her breasts and her breath stuttered to a halt.

'It's four hundred dollars,' she said into the growing silence.

Sebastian was a hair's-breadth away from telling her he'd pay for it. But he stopped. Deep in his bones he knew it would be a very bad move. A woman who'd just told him she wouldn't sleep with him certainly wouldn't let him pay for an expensive dress.

Sebastian licked parched lips. 'It'll be the best four hundred dollars you ever spent.'

Callie watched the flick of his tongue and tried not

to think how it would feel on her painfully tight nipples. 'It's…frivolous,' she protested half-heartedly, before she totally lost her mind.

He shrugged. 'What's wrong with frivolous?'

Callie held his gaze, immersing herself in the heat and hunger she saw there.

What indeed?

She turned to the shop assistant. 'I'll take it.'

Sebastian knew the minute he walked into the function that night that Callie was already there. He couldn't see her but the hairs on the back of his neck were standing to alert, just as they had that afternoon when she'd emerged from the fitting room.

And then the crowd seemed to part and he caught a flash of purple and there she was, her head thrown back, laughing in that all-out way of hers at something someone in the little crowd around her was saying.

And his heart practically stopped for the second time.

That afternoon in the boutique she had looked amazing. Tonight, with her eyes heavily kohled and her hair loose around her shoulders rather than bunched in a hastily constructed ponytail, she looked sensational.

The dress caressed her every line and angle. It moved interestingly against her body as each word in the animated conversation she appeared to be having, each sip of the champagne she was drinking rippled flesh and muscles.

She tipped back her head again and laughed, as he watched, one hand at her throat absently toyed with a chain of sparkly baubles glistening in the magnificent crystal lights overhead. Chandelier earrings also dazzled in the light and drew his gaze to her neck, her bare shoulders, the expanse of flesh above her cleavage.

Her cleavage.

As at the restaurant that first fateful night, people turned and looked, and Sebastian could see more than casual interest in several appreciative male glances.

A sharp nudge to his ribs bought Sebastian back to his surroundings. Brent Cartwright, an emergency physician at the Royal Melbourne and one of his oldest friends, handed him a beer.

'She's a bit of all right.'

Sebastian looked at Brent, who went through women as though the Apocalypse was upon them, and thought, *Over my dead body.* 'She's not your type.'

Brent hooted and clapped him on the back. 'Oh, and what *is* my type?'

'Younger, blonder. More party, less…'

Brent raised an eyebrow. 'Less?'

Sebastian looked his friend straight in the eye. 'Substance.'

Brent laughed, not remotely insulted. 'I don't know, Seb, old man, that dress has *party girl* stamped all over it.'

Sebastian frowned at the naked appreciation in Brent's eyes.

That dress has Mine *stamped all over it.*

'Callie is *not* the party type.'

Brent eyed him speculatively. 'Callie, huh?'

Sebastian shrugged. 'She's the colleague of mine I was telling you about this afternoon.'

'Ah,' Brent said dramatically. 'Curious you never mentioned how gorgeous she was.' He drained the dregs of his beer. 'Come on, introduce me.'

Sebastian resisted Brent's urging. 'I thought some hot babe gave you her room number this afternoon?'

Brent winked. 'You know I never pass up an opportunity to meet a beautiful woman. Unless...' Brent raised an eyebrow '...I'm trespassing?'

Sebastian thought how furious Callie would be to be talked about like she was some chattel to be traded. 'For God's sake, Brent, she's not a piece of land,' he said, more sharply than he'd planned.

Brent regarded his friend seriously. 'All righty, then, I'll take that as a yes. Now I definitely want to meet her.'

Sebastian followed him reluctantly, snagging another beer from a passing waiter—he was going to need something to get him through watching Brent unleash his not inconsiderable charm on Callie. He hadn't met one woman yet who'd been able to resist the whole tall, dark and handsome thing Brent had going on.

Callie knew Sebastian was approaching even before his arm brushed hers. Some strange sixth sense she had around him had her on high alert.

He was in a tuxedo and, as Victorian as it sounded, she almost swooned. The dark suit emphasised the breadth of his shoulders and the lush brilliance of his hair. She wanted to reach out and brush non-existent lint off his shoulder just so she could feel all that coiled strength she knew lay beneath the jacket.

He had one hand buried in a pocket, which pulled his jacket aside slightly to reveal a nice flat abdomen beneath the crisp white fabric of his shirt. He'd looked tall and commanding, a standout in a room full of black tuxedos.

Confident. Assured.

With a touch of arrogance.

Just as he had been on the bridge.

'Excuse me, Callie,' Sebastian interrupted the conversation. 'I'd like you to meet an old friend of mine, Brent Cartwright.'

Callie smiled brilliantly at the newcomer—anything to avoid looking at Sebastian. 'Pleased to meet you, Brent,' she said, sticking out her hand.

'My pleasure,' Brent murmured, shaking the proffered hand. 'Seb tells me you work together.'

Callie nodded, still avoiding looking at Sebastian. She could feel his gaze boring into her and she suddenly felt awkward. His very sexual attention in the boutique this afternoon, when they'd been by themselves and caught in a moment, had been one thing. But his hungry eyes in a room full of their colleagues was another thing entirely.

This was, after all, work. Business.

So she spent the next fifteen minutes chatting with Brent, her gaze firmly trained on the charming doctor. It wasn't that hard, really. Sebastian's friend was witty, exceedingly easy on the eye and made her laugh.

Even Callie, who'd never been into those tall-and-dark movie-star looks had to admit Brent was something else. It was a pity really that it wasn't him causing her pulse to skitter madly in her veins and her blood pressure to elevate.

Instead, it was the broodingly intense Sebastian watching her every move through heavy lids that made it difficult to concentrate.

She was hyper-aware of him in her peripheral vision—every time he shifted, every time he took a sip of his beer, every time he breathed. Callie was just about to tell him to go and brood somewhere else when they were called to dinner and she almost sagged against Brent in relief.

Having already agreed to sit at a table with interstate colleagues, Callie had hoped that would be an end to the tension. That she'd be able to relax and enjoy the evening. The surroundings were sumptuous and the company was entertaining. And she was looking forward to it.

She was sorely mistaken.

Sebastian's table was opposite and every time she looked up, he was in her direct line of sight. Looking at her. All broad, brooding male looking at her like she was naked. Or that he wanted to get her that way.

It was unnerving. Crazy. And a total turn-on.

Business, she told herself.

Business. Business. Business.

Sebastian listened only vaguely to the MC's prattle as the evening progressed, his attention straying a little too often. When the auction commenced he bid on everything because it gave him something to do with his brain and his hands that didn't involve trying to get Callie out of that dress.

But every now and then a glint would catch his eye and he'd look up. A twinkle of an earring, a glimmer at her neck as the flame from a table candle caused the jewellery to flash like a beacon. Their gazes would lock and he had absolutely no doubt from the flare in her amber eyes that her thoughts were running to naked too.

Callie tried to concentrate on the surroundings rather than Sebastian's incendiary stare. The ballroom was, after all, magnificently decorated. It had been transformed into a teeming jungle complete with greenery and live, lush tropical blooms. Myriad fairy lights amidst the foliage gave it an other-world feel.

No expense had been spared.

The table centrepieces alone would have cost an arm and a leg. Wound around a large central dish full of submerged flat, black stones were delicate orchids. Frilly, like her hem, their fragrance was heady in an atmosphere already charged more than enough for her liking.

Candles added to the mix, their light shimmering in the pristine water and refracting off the highly polished glassware. The whole table seemed to glitter and Callie felt like it was raining diamonds around her.

But by the time dessert was served she could stand Sebastian's stare and the twist in her gut no longer. She stood and excused herself. She needed to get far, far away from Sebastian and his tuxedo.

Or her assertion that she wouldn't sleep with him would be blown to pieces.

She made it to the lifts outside the ballroom before Sebastian caught up with her and grabbed her arm.

'Are you okay?'

She punched at the button wildly, giving him a tight smile, too afraid to loosen even that much lest she give in to the utter maleness of him. 'I have a really bad headache,' she lied.

Sebastian's thumb brushed the pulse fluttering at her wrist. 'I have some medication in my room.'

Callie's stomach clenched at the husky query in his statement. They both knew he was inviting more than that.

'I'll be fine,' she dismissed, punching the button again.

Sebastian sucked in a breath. 'Let me come with you.'

Callie shut her eyes. She wasn't here for this—she didn't want this. They'd made the decision to be work acquaintances only. It would be stupid to go back and undo two months of collegiality.

The lift dinged.

'Callie.'

She felt a slight pull on her arm. 'Don't,' she whispered. 'Please don't.'

She took advantage of the slackening of his hold and fled into the lift.

CHAPTER SIX

CALLIE heard the amplified calls of a coxswain setting the pace a minute or so before the slap of oar against water could be heard and a rowboat came into view. The sun was barely up and it was chilly in the early morning along the banks of the Yarra, but the river was alive and, even at this hour, the city pulsed around her as she walked along the boardwalk.

She'd given up on sleep about an hour ago. Her king-size bed was the ultimate in cloud-like comfort but its sheer size conjured up pictures of rolling in the sheets with a lover.

It was an image that had not been conducive to sleep.

Her blood had thrummed loudly through her veins all night, and she'd tossed and turned, trying to ignore its insistent call. Eventually she'd just had to get out.

'Hey.'

Callie startled as Sebastian's voice came from behind her. She turned to check she hadn't just conjured him up. Nope. There he was in full Technicolor festooned in jogging gear that exposed a lot of his superb body covered in a fine sheen of sweat. His shorts exposed muscular thighs, the quads lengthening and contracting with each footfall.

Last night in his tuxedo she'd thought she'd never seen him look more magnificent.

She'd been wrong.

She turned back, afraid she'd start to drool. 'Hey, yourself.'

Sebastian slowed and drew level with her, pulling the cool morning air into his burning lungs. He'd been running like the devil was after him this morning, thinking about Callie in that damn dress. And while her jeans, jacket and ponytail were a far cry from last night's purple sensation, his body didn't seem to know the difference.

'I didn't know you jogged,' Callie said.

Sebastian grimaced. 'I don't. Not really. I love it along here, though.'

They walked on for a few moments, their gazes tracking the rowing boats gliding through the water.

'How's the headache this morning?'

'Fine.'

'I thought you'd still be tucked up in bed, sleeping it off.'

Callie snorted. 'I couldn't sleep.' She regretted it instantly. He didn't need to know that. A smart man like Sebastian would be easily able to join the dots.

Sebastian raised an eyebrow. 'Neither could I.'

He'd lain awake half the night, torturing himself with images of that dress discarded on his floor in a purple puddle or draped at the end of his bed, a vibrant splash, like a parrot's wing, amidst the snowy-white bedclothes.

It was deeply satisfying to know she'd been lying awake too.

Callie picked up the pace as the brisk morning breeze carried his earthy male scent towards her—clean sweat and toothpaste. It was intoxicating and she had a crazy urge to stop and bury her face against his throat.

She searched for something to say to dispel the craving. 'How long have you known Brent?'

'Since uni.'

'He seems like a real jack-the-lad,' she mused.

Sebastian nodded. 'He wasn't always. He was engaged at twenty to this girl from uni. He was besotted with her, wanted the white picket fence and two-point-four children, the whole catastrophe. She broke his heart.'

'Twenty?' Callie's mind boggled. How could you know at that age that you wanted to spend your entire life with one person?

Callie looked back to herself at that age. She'd been in the middle of her nursing training and trying to keep her family together. Life had been chaotic. She couldn't even begin to fathom being so sure about anything, let alone a happily-ever-after.

But she guessed that's what normal adults in their twenties did—she'd just never had the luxury.

They were back at the hotel now and Sebastian nodded to the doorman as they entered the lobby and walked up the magnificent marble staircase. They made their way to the lifts.

'Are you ready for today?' Sebastian asked as he pushed the button for the lift a couple of times.

'Ready as I'll ever be,' she replied, concentrating on the day's programme and not the way his bicep bunched as he gave the button a third push. 'You?'

'Yep. Are you on before or after lunch?'

'Before.'

'Same here. Maybe we should do lunch afterwards—compare notes?'

Callie hesitated. Lunch was usually a stand-up affair

with finger food. It was supposed to be for networking and mingling. Not for cosy lunches for two.

But, oh, with perspiration making his shirt cling to flat abdominals, she was so tempted!

The lift arrived and Sebastian watched the little frown appear between her eyebrows. 'It's just lunch, Callie.'

The doors opened and she was grateful for the reprieve as they entered an already crowded lift. Momentarily, anyway. Until she found herself herded to the back by the other bodies and standing very close, too close, to Sebastian. He asked for someone to push the button for floor eleven and Callie tried not to groan at the row of lit buttons she could just see through a gap between arms and bodies.

Like it or not, they'd got a slow ride.

The doors closed and several people carried on their conversations while Callie feigned interest in the carpet. But the heat from Sebastian's arm rubbed against hers and as more people got in and the passengers shifted to accommodate them, she was pushed closer until her breasts were brushing against his side and her nostrils were full of his healthy male animal scent.

No amount of carpet gazing could negate the fact that she was in an enclosed space squashed up against a sweaty, muscular man at the mercy of her raging hormones.

When they reached their floor Callie pushed through the people in front and practically leapt out. She was almost at her door when Sebastian caught her up.

'I'll see you later, then?' he said.

'Yep.' Callie nodded as her lock clicked and she pushed open the door. 'Good luck today.'

Sebastian inserted his key and looked over his shoulder to return her good wishes but her door was closing and she was gone.

He stared at her shut door for a few moments and smiled.

Callie had no idea if Sebastian was in the audience when she presented her paper on the latest clinical drug trial Jambalyn had been involved in. The lights on the stage were too bright to see anyone from her vantage point and she hadn't noticed him in the audience prior to the session commencing.

Despite knowing that several other sessions were running concurrently—most way more interesting than hers—she couldn't quash a streak of disappointment.

None of the audience questions had come from him—not that they would, seeing that he'd been heavily involved in the trial too—and he wasn't around afterwards either. She felt curiously flat about it as she helped herself to fresh muffins at morning tea and chatted with interested delegates about her paper and the anti-psychotic's practical applications in a community setting.

And then it was Sebastian's turn. Brent gestured to her when she entered the room and Callie made her way over, sitting down when he patted the seat beside him. It was a few rows back but quite central with a great view of the stage.

Sebastian was busy talking to the tech guys and didn't see her but it didn't stop her gaze wandering to him as Brent kept up a running commentary of witty observations on the rest of the audience.

Sebastian crouched down to accept a hand-held microphone from one of the tech crew and she couldn't help but notice the tempting pull of his trousers across his truly fabulous backside. She sighed.

'Earth to Callie,' Brent called.

Callie dragged her gaze away. 'I'm sorry.' She smiled to cover her confusion. 'What were you saying?'

Brent opened his mouth but was interrupted by the chairperson calling the audience to order. He chuckled. 'Never mind.'

Sebastian was introduced. And an impressive introduction it was. She knew about his work in the prison system and his negotiator role with the police and that, prior to coming to Jambalyn, he'd been seconded to the department of defence and been overseas.

But she'd had no idea he'd spent the last year counselling defence personnel in such danger zones as Iraq and Afghanistan. Her heart thudded, thinking about him in such risky environments.

If she'd hadn't known from that first day on the bridge that he was utterly impressive, she certainly did now.

And if that wasn't extraordinary enough, he smiled and then started to talk and commanded the attention of every single person in the room from the second he opened his delectable mouth.

And it wasn't just the women.

His presence dominated the stage and the audience hung on his every word. Like a Shakespearian actor or an ancient Greek orator—captivating, compelling, charismatic.

He spoke for an hour, presenting his paper, 'The Shadows of Vietnam: Forty Years On', and Callie doubted whether a single person moved a muscle throughout. His voice and the subject matter were mesmerising and Callie was totally drawn into the complex issue.

Stats, clinical research and observations of the

continuing effects on family units of psychologically damaged soldiers who'd fought a lengthy, controversial war were outlined. Sebastian talked about another generation of children growing up in the shadow of the Asian conflict as grandchildren of veterans suffered the long-term consequences of having a parent grow up in a dysfunctional family unit dominated by PTSD and other attributable psychological conditions.

The speech was made all the more poignant because Callie knew he spoke from the heart. As a child born into a family unit completely broken by mental illness, she could tell that this wasn't just distant clinical observation and conjecture.

There was a depth of honesty in his words that couldn't be garnered from research and clinical practice alone. Listening to him, it was evident that he truly understood the subject matter. That he was intimate with it in a way that clinicians who hadn't lived it weren't.

For Sebastian, this was personal.

Callie could barely breathe, thinking about the type of things Sebastian must have witnessed, must have had to deal with growing up. Things a child shouldn't ever have to confront. Things that rob children of their precious carefree years. That could irrevocably damage them.

The mere thought of a bewildered red-headed boy—vulnerable, worried and old beyond his years—clawed at her gut.

It was always the children that suffered.

Tears burned the backs of her eyes and she shut her eyes hard to deny the moisture an outlet.

Later that afternoon Callie stood in her hotel room, her hand on the doorknob in mid-twist. She hesitated.

Dropped her hand. Then changed her mind and reached for it again. Then dropped it once more as her heart galloped in her chest.

She should just leave it alone. Keep things the way they were. On an even keel. Crossing the hallway and knocking on Sebastian's door would be a stupid move. She was too emotional at the moment. His presentation had really struck a chord and affected her.

But try as she may, she just couldn't get the image of that little red-haired boy out of her head.

Except the Sebastian in the room opposite was far from a little boy.

She turned away. Took a step or two back towards her bed and then stopped again. Completely indecisive. Her gut was telling her to seek him out. Her head was telling her to stay put.

And then fate interfered. A loud knock rattled the door and her heart leapt in her rib cage. She turned and walked slowly, almost in a trance. She knew who it was even before confirming Sebastian's presence through the peephole. Callie placed her forehead and the flat of her palm on the door for a moment, gathering her nerve.

Then she pulled the door open, a smile plastered on her face. 'Sebastian.'

She faltered. He was lounging against the doorjamb, his jacket and tie removed and the top two buttons of his shirt undone. His sleeves were rolled up and he had bare feet. He looked tired. Exhausted. And she had an overwhelming urge to step into his arms and lay her cheek against a broad pectoral.

He held up two long-necked beers with wedges of lime jammed into their openings. 'I felt like a beer.'

Callie hesitated again, tempted beyond belief. She shouldn't. She really, really shouldn't. Being alone in her room with him would really blur the professional boundaries they'd both worked so hard at keeping in place.

Her gaze dropped from his earnest expression, centring on a tempting stretch of throat where the knot of his tie should have been.

'I think you have a better view than I do.'

Callie swallowed. *She certainly did now!*

Knowing she didn't have it in her power to deny him, not when he looked so worn-out, she reached for her beer then stood back. 'Come through.'

Sebastian exhaled and pushed his lime wedge into the bottle neck with his thumb. He took a swig and pushed off the shoulder shoved against the doorframe. His arm brushed hers and a heat wave rippled outwards from the point of contact, down his arm and up to his shoulder and chest.

He made a beeline for the balcony. The king-size bed taunted him as he went past it. A brief image of tumbling Callie onto it mingled with the fragrance she wore and he sucked in a perfume-laden breath. For a second he even felt a little dizzy.

This was crazy. He didn't know why he was there. But she'd made it perfectly clear last night from her Cinderella act that she wanted to keep the status quo so he needed to push any images of her and him and the king-size bed firmly out of his mind.

He felt restless after the unexpected emotion of his presentation, that was all. He hadn't expected to feel so drained. And after a couple of hours of being with people who all wanted a piece of him, wanted him to be *the* Sebastian Walker, it was bliss to be with someone who had gone to great pains to not be with him.

Even if it was just sharing a beer and talking.

And when she'd opened the door and his gaze had taken in her silky, electric-blue blouse, the one she'd worn while presenting her paper earlier that day, he'd been lost.

His steps faltered as his gaze fell on another item of clothing. The purple dress was draped over the arm of a plush old-fashioned winged chair placed near the sliding door.

Bloody hell, was the woman trying to kill him?
With clothes?

Unable to help himself, he ran his finger over it as he passed. It wasn't quite how he'd imagined getting his hands on the dress but it felt cool and glossy against the pads of his fingers.

And beggars could not be choosers.

Watching him, Callie felt as if he'd stroked that finger along her belly and she too touched the chair as she passed to steady wobbly legs.

They sat at the small table on the balcony and for a few moments allowed the sights and the sounds of the river absorb them. The Yarra looked like mercury in the afternoon light, the setting sun throwing dark shadows and gilding the water silvery black.

Callie shifted her gaze to his profile, watching the bob of his throat as he tipped his head back and swallowed a mouthful of beer. She knew how he smelt there, how the spike of his stubble felt against her tongue.

She cleared her throat. 'I wanted to congratulate you on your paper,' she said. 'You were… It was magnificent. It was very well received. I couldn't get near you earlier to tell you…'

Sebastian had taken question after question and been swamped with colleagues afterwards.

Sebastian regarded her for a moment. He had known

Callie long enough to know she was nervous—her gaze was everywhere but on him. Which was just as well as he tried to distract himself from thoughts of how soft her blouse would feel beneath his fingers.

'Thanks. You were pretty good yourself.'

Now, that got her attention. Callie's heart performed a little leap inside her chest as their gazes met and held. 'You were there?'

She heard the breathless note in her voice.

She should probably have cared.

She didn't.

Sebastian nodded. 'Of course.'

She'd been marvellous. And, of course, the way her silky blouse had caressed the thrust of her breasts had been pretty damn good too.

It took Callie a few seconds to realise she was staring at him as his pale green gaze held her enthralled.

'So,' he said, breaking their connection, which seemed to be getting steamier by the second, 'which sessions are you down to see tomorrow?'

Callie breathed again as Sebastian steered the conversation to a safe subject. They chatted about the merits of the different sessions on offer the next day for quite a while as the late afternoon sky passed into the muted hues of twilight around them.

She actually relaxed as their chatter was kept strictly on track—business only. It didn't stray into personal territory but stuck to conference-related topics only. She even went to her bar fridge and got them both a second beer.

'What time's the dinner tonight?' Sebastian asked, looking at his watch, surprised to find it was nudging six-thirty.

Callie consulted her own watch. 'Seven-thirty.'

Except she didn't want to go. She wanted to sit on this balcony overlooking the Yarra, talking to Sebastian, for ever. Her initial misgivings had been unfounded and after two months of ignoring him it was bliss to be far away from work, cocooned in this little bubble, and be able to relax and enjoy his company.

Listening to him give his paper today had given her insight into the man behind the person on the bridge in the bulletproof vest. Had shown her a glimpse of the unhappy little boy.

The unhappy little girl in her, the one who had also lived through constant upheaval, was grateful to just be with someone who truly understood how she ticked.

Sebastian watched as Callie raised the long-necked bottle to her mouth and pressed it against her lips. He almost groaned out loud. Watching her drink was torture. There was something exceedingly sexual about it and despite the fact that this was just supposed to be two work colleagues enjoying some downtime, the catch in his groin every time she sipped had started a fever pounding through his blood.

She was staring out over the river in quiet contemplation and he was afraid that if conversation didn't continue between them soon, he might just haul her into his lap and start kissing her. 'What are you thinking about?'

Callie dragged her eyes back from the lights dancing on the darkening river. 'Your father.'

Sebastian paused, the bottle halfway to his mouth. 'My father?'

Callie turned to look at him. 'Your paper… I couldn't help but feel it was deeply personal for you. I know what its like to grow up with mental illness and I was listening to you talk and…' She shrugged. And what? What was she trying to say? 'I felt for you. I wondered if you were ever as scared and confused and worried as I used to be. I wondered if he was…violent.'

Sebastian placed his beer on the table between them. Like the lights reflected in the polished glass surface of the Yarra he could see the empathy shining in her eyes. It wasn't a subject he often talked about. People didn't really understand. But he knew she did. And after talking about it already today, albeit in an abstract kind of way, he felt strangely compelled to tell her more.

'No,' he murmured. 'He wasn't violent, just…dysfunctional. He had bouts of crippling depression and suffered from night terrors. He was severely agoraphobic. He couldn't work. He had chronic indigestion. He smoked and drank too much. But he wasn't a nasty drunk. If anything, I was probably…ignored. It was as if I was…invisible a lot of the time.'

Callie grimaced. 'I'm sorry.'

He shrugged. 'It could have been worse. And my mother did the best she could but she didn't know how to cope with any of it.'

Callie nodded. Why would she? No one handed out manuals at weddings, and wedding vows just didn't cover the prisoner-of-war contingency. 'I notice you didn't draw any parallels in your paper between the Vietnam experience and your own more recent experience overseas.'

Sebastian dropped his gaze. 'I didn't want to dilute the paper's focus. But rest assured, PTSD is alive and kicking among our military personnel.'

He picked up his beer and turned back to face the river as he took a deep pull. The skin on his scalp and at the back of his neck crawled as an image of an explosion flashed in his mind's eye.

He gripped the bottle tighter.

Callie watched Sebastian's profile, saw his jaw clench and his knuckles whiten. Being right in the thick of things had obviously affected him.

'Don't the defence forces have their own psychs? I didn't think they outsourced.'

Sebastian kept his gaze firmly planted on the Yarra. 'They do.' His lips twisted into a bitter smile. 'But my reputation preceded me.'

Callie frowned. 'Sebastian?' She reached out her hand and covered his. 'Are you okay?'

Sebastian shut his eyes. 'I'm fine,' he dismissed.

'You know,' Callie said as she absently rubbed her thumb over his knuckles, 'someone very wise once told me that sometimes it's easier to talk to someone you don't know that well.'

He looked down at her hand. A hand that had touched every part of his body. A hand that knew him pretty well. Each pass of her thumb felt like a stroke to his belly. 'Really. I'm okay.'

Callie didn't think so but she let it go. 'It must be a bit of an anticlimax, working at Jambalyn, after all that adrenaline.'

Sebastian felt his breath grown thicker as her touch continued. Working at Jambalyn had been a godsend. Just what the doctor had ordered.

'Jambalyn has been a fantastic experience. After the Gulf I needed...I wanted...to be somewhere where positive outcomes were tangible. To see that mental illness can be managed and people can go about their lives. I didn't want to be *the* Sebastian Walker, PTSD guru. I wanted to get back to the basics.'

Callie nodded. It seemed like a very reasonable aspiration to her and the yearning in his voice was real.

But something told her there was more to it. 'It isn't always a picnic in the community,' she murmured.

Sebastian was mesmerised by the circular motion of her finger against his skin, his gaze glued to the action. 'No, I know that. But it's good to see, to know that there is hope.'

Where he'd just come from, hope just hadn't existed.

She nodded, absently stroking the pad of her thumb down his fingers now. 'It can be very rewarding,' she agreed.

Sebastian almost groaned out loud. He was trying really hard here but a man had limits. 'Callie...'

The thick plea in Sebastian's half whisper, half groan scorched right through to her womb and brought her attention to the liberties her thumb was taking.

What the hell was she doing? She'd moved this into personal territory. Sebastian had been perfectly content talking about the conference and she'd gone and dragged them in to murky waters.

Talking about his father and then his stint overseas.

She was touching him, for God's sake!

Callie withdrew her hand as if she'd been rapped on the knuckles. She stood abruptly. 'You better go.'

Sebastian stood too. 'No. Wait.'

'No, really,' she said as she reached the door. 'I have to get ready for tonight. Wash my hair. Do my...' She stepped inside the room, faltering momentarily as the bed beckoned. 'Nails.'

'Callie.'

She headed towards the door, desperate to get him out. 'I guess I'll see you there,' she threw over her shoulder as she flayed herself mentally for such a serious lapse in judgement.

Just because she could empathise with him, it didn't negate the facts of their non-relationship.

Sebastian lengthened his stride and caught up with her at the bar fridge. He snagged her arm and spun her round to face him, dragging her up hard against his body.

'I don't want to go,' he said, before swooping his mouth down to claim hers.

Callie was stunned for two seconds before her body ignited and she opened her lips to him on a strangled moan, clinging to his sleeves for dear life.

Sebastian pulled away and looked into her flushed face, her amber eyes glittering with reckless desire. 'I want to stay. I want you.'

He didn't wait for her consent, returning to ravage her mouth. He groaned deep in the back of his throat when she opened to his hot, demanding tongue, matching his intensity with her own.

His hands found her waistband, tugging at her blouse, uncaring now how silky it felt in his rush to get it off. And then he was lifting it over her head and off, his hands cupping her breasts, his head lowering to suck her nipple through the smooth see-through fabric of her bra. And when she whimpered his name he yanked her bra aside and took her breast into his mouth.

Callie's head spun as she was sucked into the wild tumult of their desire. As her fingers fumbled with the buttons on his shirt his hands were at her waist, pulling at her button and zip, pushing at her trousers and knickers, pushing them down, pushing them off.

She tore her mouth from his as his smooth chest was finally bared to her hands, pressing kisses down his throat, across his pecs, against a flat male nipple. Her hands roved over the tautness of his belly and grabbed at his belt, unhooking it with fingers that shook in her eagerness to touch the thick erection pressing against her.

He groaned when she finally freed him and she smiled triumphantly as she palmed the length of him. So hard. Like a rod of steel packaged in the finest silk.

Sebastian shut his eyes as she explored him, stars exploding. When her hand crept lower and cupped him he growled, 'Callie,' before claiming her mouth again, bending her head back, one hand buried in her hair, the other unclipping her bra.

How he managed that one-handed he had no idea. It must have been primal instinct. Because the rasp of her breath was in his ears and the smell of her hair, her skin was in his nostrils and her lips tasted like sugar, her mouth like beer and lime, and he couldn't think of anything else other than being buried in her, making her moan.

Callie let go of him to shrug out of her bra and then he was walking her backwards as she reached for him again, their mouths still attached as he fumbled in his pocket for his wallet, kicked out of his trousers, ditched his shirt. And then he was pushing her down, following her as they landed on the bed and his mouth was at one breast, teasing the nipple and then the other, and she was gasping for breath, for mercy, for more.

'Sebastian, please,' she cried. 'I need you in—'

Sebastian cut her off with a kiss that had her whimpering, clinging to his shoulders. 'I'd forgotten how great you tasted,' he murmured, nuzzling her neck, his hand stroking over her hip.

'I want to taste you all over.' He moved lower, his tongue trekking to her breast, his hand straying to her inner thighs, his knuckles brushing ever so lightly against where she tingled and burned for him most.

'And then I want to start again,' he said against her puckered nipple, before sucking it into his mouth and stroking a finger between her legs.

Callie almost arched off the bed as she cried his name. But the gentle teasing of his finger was stoking a fierce need. She pulled at his head, her nipple impossibly peaked, engorged from his attention and sensitive to the sudden rush of cool air.

'Later. If you're not inside me in the next five seconds I think I'm going to die.'

Sebastian chuckled and kissed his way back up to her. 'Well, we'll have to do something about that, won't we?'

He reached for his wallet, discarded on the sheet nearby.

'Hurry,' she urged.

Sebastian laughed again as he pulled the foil packet out. 'Patience, patience.'

Callie glared at him as he teased her with a leisurely fingering of the packet. She reached down, grasped his erection in her hand and squeezed. Sebastian groaned and his eyes practically rolled back in his head. She was satisfied to see him rip open the packet with his teeth and sheath himself in a matter of seconds.

And then he was lifting her leg, propping it on his shoulder then leaning over her on his elbows and pushing deep into her, so deep she almost screamed it was that good.

'Oh, God, yes,' she cried as he pulled out and pushed back in again.

'Callie!' He shut his eyes as her tightness gripped

him, caressed him, massaged him. She was so hot and smooth and right, so right.

'More,' she gasped. 'More.'

And he gave her more and more and more until she was moaning and yelling and scratching at his back as she came, and when he joined her, shuddering and jerking, his fingers branding her hips, she wrapped her legs around him, gathering him closer as she came again.

'So,' Sebastian said, the tray in front of him littered with the debris of his meal. 'What say you and I keep this thing going?'

Callie raised an eyebrow, trying to play it cool. They hadn't talked about what happened next. They hadn't really had time.

Was it a thing?

He'd left her room in the wee small hours and returned early with room service for two. And had then persuaded her that a day in bed was much more preferable to anything the conference programme had to offer.

In fact, so thorough was he in his persuasion that they'd nearly missed their plane. After a mad dash to the airport they'd just managed to make their flight.

'We have a thing?'

Sebastian chuckled. 'This is the first time we've been out of bed since eight o'clock this morning. We played hooky from the entire last day of the conference. And I don't know about you but I'm not done yet.'

Callie was torn. She wanted to—God knew, she wanted to. But it warred with all the reasons why she shouldn't.

'Even now all I can think about is touching you.' He lifted the armrest between them out of the way and brought her hand to his mouth. 'Kissing you,' he murmured, his lips against her skin as he dropped a kiss on her knuckles.

The shiver travelled all the way to her core and she pulled her hand away. The denim of his jeans pulled tautly across his thighs and crotch, and even though a tray hid most of his lap she could see the thickening beneath his zipper.

She was pretty sure he was as turned on as she was.

She blinked hard. 'I'm not in the market for a relationship. I like my life the way it is now,' she said, keeping her voice low. 'I can do what I like when I like and not have to consult someone else or put someone else's needs first.'

As much as she missed her nephew and would have him back in a heartbeat, her life had certainly been a whole lot less complicated without him around twenty-four seven.

'Who said anything about a relationship?' he asked, moving in to nuzzle her neck now the armrest barrier had been removed. He heard the suck of a ragged breath and smiled as his tongue touched the lobe of her ear.

'The way I see it, this thing is so intense it's bound to fizzle out as quickly as it started.' He caught her hand again and brought it to his chest as he dropped light kisses down her neck. 'Look at it as pure sexual attraction.'

He moved her hand lower and felt his abdominals contract. 'Something that needs to be acted on.' He settled her hand beneath the tray resting on his erection. 'Exorcised. We're adults, Callie. We're allowed to act on our urges.'

Callie was sure everyone on the plane could hear her

breathing. Involuntarily she opened her hand over him
further, feeling the contours of the thick ridge beneath
her hand, and without a second thought she squeezed.
Sebastian moaned lightly in her ear and her nipples
beaded.

'Do it again,' he whispered.

Callie swayed closer to him, his voice hypnotic, a
swell of desire blooming in her chest and suffusing heat
southwards. But still she glanced around at her fellow
passengers. Could they see what was happening beneath
that tray?

She crossed her legs, giving them further privacy.
Yes, Sebastian had the window seat and the tray was
in the way, but she didn't want to be caught out like a
horny teenager.

'Callie…' The guttural groan in her ear was full of
ache and want.

She ran her hand up and down the length of him this
time and shut her eyes as his breath hissed out in her
ear. 'This is mad,' she muttered as her head spun.

'This can work, Callie,' Sebastian sighed, fighting
the urge to thrust into her hand. 'Let's just ride it till the
end.'

Callie flattened her palm against him, pressing down
hard as his mouth continued to create havoc and his
hand stroked her thigh. 'I can't concentrate when you
do that,' she whispered.

Sebastian smiled his lips at the angle of her jaw.
'Come on, Callie. You know you want to.'

'You're not playing fair.'

He chuckled. 'No. I'm not. I'm playing to win.'

Intractable as ever, giving no quarter, just as he'd been
on the bridge that day. All magnificent male, dominant
and authoritative and sexy as hell.

I'm right and we're doing it my way.

Thankfully the captain's voice came over the intercom, announcing some mild turbulence, and pulled Callie out of the sexual trance she'd been in. She let go of Sebastian, sat up straight and looked ahead, her cheeks pinking up at her behaviour.

Sebastian groaned. *So close.* 'Callie?'

'Shh,' she said, shutting her eyes. She'd never been more grateful for turbulence in her life. 'Don't talk. Just don't talk.' She rolled her head to look at him. 'I need to think.'

And think she did. A lot.

Would having a fling with Sebastian be that bad? She'd had a couple of short-term flings before and had come away unscathed. Burnt off some sexual energy— just as Sebastian was suggesting. And they'd been light and fun and she'd enjoyed them while they'd lasted.

And she was free now to do it again. So why not?

Because, a little voice said. Because.

When the plane landed she still wasn't any closer to a decision. But as they were walking out the terminal doors towards the car park, orange streaks bleeding into a magnificent sunset, Sebastian held out his hand and said, 'Come with me.'

Callie hesitated. She looked at his hand then back at him. 'We always go home to sleep in our own beds.'

Sebastian nodded. 'I wouldn't have it any other way.'

She took his hand.

CHAPTER SEVEN

Two months later Callie waved at Ginny as she pulled out from the kerb. Her seven-months-pregnant belly was on proud display in the form-fitting dress and she looked better every time Callie saw her—blooming, in fact. She was doing so well with her reduced medication and looking forward to the arrival of their baby girl.

Ginny had joked that Callie had better get a move on or she'd be too old, and Callie had laughed. But even standing there, with Ginny's belly round and firm in front of her, Callie had felt nothing.

Sure, she'd felt happy for Ginny and Brad but there had been no crashing urge to join the club. No desire to have her own belly full with child. Zack had been her one chance at experiencing motherhood, albeit it second-hand, and she was perfectly okay with that.

She must have been hiding behind a door when maternal instincts had been given out.

Still, despite this apparent flaw, Callie was deep-down-in-her-bones happy. The sun was shining, it was Friday afternoon, her patients were well.

What more could she ask for?

She certainly couldn't ask any more of Sebastian. Things were working out better than she had ever imagined. Somehow she and Sebastian seemed to have the work/personal balance right. She'd fretted that things would be awkward at work or that seeing so much of each other would be a recipe for disaster.

But she'd been wrong. And maybe the fact that they always went home to their own beds, that they weren't spending twenty-four seven with each other, had been the key.

One thing was for sure, things certainly hadn't fizzled out, as Sebastian had suggested on the plane. If anything, their appetite for each other seemed to be increasing.

Burning out of control, actually.

She'd worried that their colleagues would treat them differently if/when they found out, or would disapprove of such a potentially disastrous match. A few years back two of Jambalyn's staff had been involved in a tempestuous relationship that had come to a messy end and they'd all spent months walking on eggshells around the office.

But everyone had been blasé about it and Geraldine had announced, 'Thank the Lord for that,' when they were sprung one afternoon after work in Sebastian's office, stealing a kiss.

Sebastian had been right, it seemed. They were perfect for each other. They were both in it for the same reasons—to have fun and enjoy each other without the expectations of a formal relationship. Neither of them wanted marriage or kids so the pressure wasn't on to make anything more of it than it was.

And what it was was sex.

Lots and lots and lots of truly amazing, fabulous sex that just kept getting better and better.

Callie was going to miss it when Sebastian went back to Melbourne. She was going to miss it a lot.

Along with the other things. Like the laughter. And the dining out—for a change. The movies. Sunday

drives after sprawling out on her deck, eating pastries
for brunch and reading the weekend papers.

She was still smiling as her mobile rang and she
pushed the button so she could talk hands free as she
drove along.

'Callie?'

Callie's smile broadened at the voice that was as familiar to her now as her own. 'I was just thinking about
you.'

'That's nice.'

The smile slipped. Sebastian sounded tense. 'What's
wrong?'

'I've just taken a call from Frank Jessop's wife. He's
agitated and she's concerned.'

Frank was a Vietnam vet who suffered from PTSD
marked by severe flashbacks. 'You want me to divert
there?'

'Please. I'm on my way but you're closer and with
this afternoon traffic I could be half an hour.'

She nodded. 'That's fine. I'm only a few minutes
away. See you when you get there.'

'Callie…'

She'd been about to hang up but the strained note in
his voice stopped her.

'Just be there, for June, okay? If you think he's close
to the edge, leave the house with her and ring for an
ambulance… Don't engage him, okay?'

It was on the tip of her tongue to tell him she knew
what she was doing but Callie could hear tension in his
voice and guessed that this had to be hard for him. That
he'd probably faced this situation not only professionally
but personally.

'Of course,' she murmured, and rang off.

* * *

When Callie arrived at the Jessops' she was greeted by Frank's wife as if she was a floatation device and June was drowning. A small bird of a woman, she looked frantic and had obviously been crying.

'Are you okay?' Callie asked, surreptitiously running her gaze all over June to check she hadn't been harmed. 'Has he hurt you?'

'No, no, no,' June dismissed. 'He hasn't…he never would. I just…' She pressed her hand to her mouth. 'I haven't seen him like this in a long time.'

Callie reached for June's hands and smiled. 'It's okay now. I'm here and Sebastian's on his way.'

'Thank you,' June whispered. 'Thank you.'

Callie smiled again and squeezed the woman's hand. 'I might just pop in and check on him, okay?'

June nodded. 'Would you, please? I'm so worried.'

Callie's heart went out to June. Her love for her husband, even in his disturbed state, was inspirational. 'Of course.'

Callie followed June into the front lounge room. Frank was sitting on one of the chairs, the leather cracked and worn, staring at the floor. He was rocking slightly and muttering to himself. An image of Andy rose in her mind and she quashed it.

'Hello, Frank. Do you remember me?' Callie approached slowly and stopped a few feet away. 'Callie Douglas? One of the nurses from Jambalyn.'

Frank looked up at her, still rocking. He frowned and it was as if he was looking straight through her before he returned his gaze to the floor.

'Okay. Well, I'm going to have a cup of tea with June while we wait for Sebastian. Can I get you one?'

Frank curled his lip at her. 'No tea,' he barked. 'No shrink.'

Callie nodded. 'Okay. I'll just be out in the kitchen with June.'

June burst into tears when they reached the kitchen and Callie put her arm around the tiny woman and ushered her to the table. She busied herself making tea while keeping one ear on the occasional mutterings from the lounge.

She kept up a constant stream of inane chatter. She should have been trying to establish the events that had led to this breakdown but June seemed too raw and Callie knew she'd have to go over it enough times today as it was.

Sebastian arrived within twenty minutes and she greeted him at the door. He looked tall and capable and commanding coming up the path and her heart skipped a beat or two. She filled him in on her appraisal of Frank and the situation as they walked to the kitchen.

He sat down next to June and put his arm around her shoulders, murmuring to her in a low voice, asking the questions Callie hadn't and telling her everything was going to be okay.

Sebastian stood. 'I'll go and say hi,' he told them.

Callie nodded and she and June followed but waited at the doorway.

'Hello, Frank,' Sebastian said as he walked slowly towards his client. 'Not feeling so good today?'

Frank's head snapped up as if he'd been struck with a cattle prod. 'I said no,' he roared and leapt off the couch, lunging at Sebastian.

Sebastian stood his ground. Frank was surprisingly strong for a man in his seventies but he was no match for a fit forty-year-old. Sebastian gripped the older man's biceps hard, preventing any upward swing, holding him stationary while he railed and struggled.

June gasped and Callie's heart leapt into her throat as Frank's wild eyes chilled her. And then, as she watched, Frank stopped struggling and started to cry, crumpling against Sebastian.

Sebastian held the older man as he sobbed. He glanced at Callie, who looked pale, her bottom lip caught between her teeth. He smiled at her. 'Take June outside for a cuppa, will you, and ring for an ambulance? Code two will be fine.'

Callie, her heartbeat still roaring in her ears, returned a wobbly smile and nodded. She couldn't remember ever seeing him braver. Or more sexy. Not standing on a bridge in a bulletproof vest, confronting an arrogant fool in a restaurant, or presenting an important paper in front of hundreds of colleagues.

But holding a distraught man who was at the end of his tether, gently and reverently, brought a king-size lump to her throat.

'Come on, June,' she said. 'Frank's going to be fine now.'

Two hours later they were driving in silence back to Jambalyn. A grim-faced Sebastian was looking out his window as Callie navigated the heavy traffic.

She pulled up at a red light and glanced at him. He looked exhausted, the lines around his eyes and mouth more pronounced, his usually erect frame slightly less so.

It was the first time she'd seen him looking every one of his forty years.

But more than that, he looked…alone and she couldn't bear it. Not when she was right there beside him. She slid her hand onto his thigh and gave a gentle squeeze. 'Tough day for you.'

Sebastian dragged himself back from echoes of his childhood and rubbed a hand across eyes that felt gritty. He gave her a half smile and covered her hand. 'Tougher for Frank.'

Callie nodded. The light turned green and she removed her hand, watching as Sebastian returned to his silent vigil out the window. She wanted to pull over, crawl into his lap and just hold him. She wanted to wrap him up until the events of the day drifted away for ever. He looked so untouchable at the moment, so distant, she just wanted to bring him back. To her. Use her body to ground him in the here and now, snatch him back from wherever it was he'd gone to.

But at the moment he looked too far away, too far gone. He certainly didn't look like he needed anyone and the one drawback of being in a 'relationship' where the two people in it completely avoided defining it as a relationship was that she wasn't sure how much she could push. They were in it for 'better' after all, not 'worse'.

And she couldn't bear for him to reject her.

So she drove on and it wasn't until she shut off the engine that Sebastian even acknowledged that they'd arrived at Jambalyn.

Callie undid her seat belt and groped for the door handle.

'No,' Sebastian said, placing a stilling hand on hers. 'Go home. I'll do the paperwork and follow you.'

Callie was surprised how much it hurt to have him dismiss her. She sucked in a breath. 'Sebastian, I don't mind hanging around. I could—'

'No, really,' he interrupted. Sebastian could see the confusion in her gaze and squeezed her hand to reassure her. 'I think I need to… It's been a long day and I really want to get things straight in my head.' He smiled at her. 'I can never think straight around you. I think I need to just be alone for a bit.'

Callie smiled at his little joke, even though tears scalded the backs of her eyes and she felt as if a huge fist had been rammed into her heart. He was pushing her away and it hurt. She knew she had no claim on him or any right to expect anything from him but, still, she wanted to be there, wanted him to want her to be there. To reach for her, not push her away.

'Of course,' she said, forcing a note of professional courtesy into her voice as if he was merely someone she worked with. She buckled up her seat belt again. 'No problems. I'll see you when you get home.'

Sebastian inserted the key into Callie's door. He felt old and weary and he wanted her. Needed her. After a harrowing afternoon he needed to get lost in her, to take him away from the memories that had dogged him since their call out to Frank's place.

His father. His childhood. The Gulf.

To look forward, not back.

To affirm that life was good and right and decent.

'Callie?' he called as he threw his keys on the hallstand.

He didn't get an answer so he called again as he walked into the empty lounge. He heard water running and headed towards her bedroom. 'Callie?'

Her 'In the shower' drifted towards him and his pulse quickened. He toed his shoes off as he entered the bedroom, stopped to strip off his socks and kept walking towards the en suite bathroom.

He walked through the open doorway that connected the two rooms and there she was, gloriously naked, her head tipped back, her eyes shut as she washed shampoo out of her hair. Soapy water sluiced down her long, strong body, over her breasts and the curve of her belly and down her thighs. Bubbles clung to her nipples.

He hardened instantly and reached for his top button. She opened her eyes and stared directly at him with soft eyes that seem to see right inside him, and he got harder. Their gazes locked as he stripped off his shirt, undid his belt, pushed off his trousers and underwear.

He didn't ask permission, just opened the shower door, stepped inside and reached for her.

Callie went eagerly, plastering her wet body against all his hardness. He looked tired and a restless kind of desperation shadowed his normally clear peridot eyes. She could see how much he needed her and she could no more have said no to him than flown to the moon.

He devoured her mouth, pushing her back against the wall, trapping her body against the cold tiles, and Callie met his ardour with startling equality. Her breasts were squashed against him, her nipples painfully tight as his hard chest abraded the sensitive tips. His erection pushed into the apex of her thighs, butting against her as they ground their pelvises together.

His mouth abruptly left hers and lowered to capture a nipple, a hand moving to the other breast, squeezing, the thumb circling and flicking. She held his head and cried out as he sucked hard and his teeth grazed the tight bud in his mouth.

Her body flooded with sensation and she rocked against him, wanting more, wanting to be closer, wanting to be part of him. But most of all grateful that at last he *was* turning to her, reaching for her. He wasn't pushing her away now. He wasn't closing himself off.

She reached down for him, feeling his thickness,

hot and ready for her, slippery from the water and the soap, and she angled it to her entrance as he lifted her buttocks, lifted her feet off the floor, lifted her up and anchored her against the wall with his chest, her legs automatically circling his waist.

'I want you,' he groaned as her breasts swayed in front of his face and he took full advantage by flicking his tongue over each puckered nipple.

His erection nudged against her where the heat and tingling intertwined to excruciating proportions. 'Oh, God, Sebastian, now, please now.'

Sebastian heard the desperation in her voice, felt it deep inside him too—the urge to drive into her, to claim her, overwhelming. Her slick heat caressed his throbbing hardness and it took all his willpower to resist her urgent demand.

He placed his forehead against her chest and took a couple of calming breaths. 'Callie, we can't, I didn't bring a condom in the shower with me.'

No, no, no. No barriers. Not tonight. She shook her head violently, grasping his head, pulling it up to look at her. 'No,' she said. 'I don't want any barriers between us tonight. I want to feel you, truly you. All of you. I don't want anything between us.'

Sebastian was breathing hard as a bloom of some emotion he couldn't identify played havoc with his common sense. He wanted it too. Wanted to feel her around him, flesh on flesh. To be closer to her than he'd ever been. Just this once.

'Please, Sebastian,' she murmured, squirming against him.

Sebastian's eyes grew large and he hissed out a breath as their gazes locked. Her heat and slickness surrounded him and he wanted to go further. One push of his hips into all that slippery tightness and he'd be buried to the hilt.

She squirmed again, feeling a little more of him enter, and she moaned. She was desperate for still more, to feel him stretching her completely.

'More,' she whimpered. 'More.' Then she claimed his lips, pushing her tongue deep into his mouth, mimicking what she wanted him to do lower down.

Sebastian groaned and on a surge of high-octane lust gave her all of him. Hearing her cry spoke to something primal inside and he fought the urge to roar. It felt good. So damn good, skin on skin, her tight heat gripping him with shocking intimacy. He dug his fingers into the flesh of her buttocks hard as the sensation nearly crippled him.

The movement rocked her head back against the tiles and he latched on to the curve where her neck met her shoulder. She scratched at his back but he didn't even notice as he repeated the motion over and over, ramming into her, pounding and pounding and pounding, as the water drummed on his back, mingling with her cries and the desperate need to cleanse away the events of the day and reaffirm life.

Callie knew she was coming almost from the first full thrust hitting exactly the right spot, but she didn't want to let go, let it consume her just yet. Sebastian needed this, she knew it as surely as she knew he was holding back too.

But if anyone needed to let go, it was Sebastian. Only in his release would he find some kind of purging of the emotions that had built up over the day.

It was impossible to keep everything inside when you were breaking apart.

'Sebastian,' she panted. 'Let go.'

Sebastian, his head burrowed in her neck, rammed in hard and grunted, 'No.'

Callie bit her lip as the ripples edged out from her centre. 'Yes,' she demanded. 'Yes.'

Sebastian shook his head, straining to push the delicious sensations back. 'You,' he gasped, rocking in and out of her, 'first.'

Callie groaned. Stubborn man. But if that was what it took…

She stopped fighting it, letting the sensations rush out at her, giving the ripples free rein, feeling herself clamp down hard on him and his corresponding moan.

Then he sucked a nipple into the hot cavern of his mouth and the wave swept over and she cried out, flinging her head back as her orgasm consumed her. Sebastian's shoulders shook and she cried out, 'Yes, yes,' as a guttural groan was torn from his throat and he joined her.

The shower battered down on them like cool rain as his hot seed pumped into her and there were no words or thoughts as their bodies moved to a rhythm as old as time. Just him and her and the vortex of pleasure that swirled and twirled and cascaded down on them.

It seemed like an age before either of them moved. Callie's head lolled against his and they stayed forehead to forehead for a long time, the shower bathing them, cooling heated blood and soothing sizzling skin as their breathing slowly settled.

Callie stirred first, lifting her head and flopping it back against the tiles. The spray misted against her lips and she opened her mouth to moisten a parched throat.

'I think I just died and went to heaven,' she murmured,

half smiling as the feel of hard muscle beneath her hands came into focus.

Sebastian kissed her neck, malaise invading every cell, never wanting to move from this place. He pulled back slightly to look at her. 'Me too.'

Her brain felt as if it was operating in first gear at Sebastian's steady gaze. She could still feel him hard inside her still. Water droplets clung to his browny-blond lashes and beaded on his lips. She leaned forward, kissing his eyes gently, lapping at the drops.

It would be so easy in the aftermath of such mind-bending passion to let herself be swept up in believing that there was way more to this than two people having a good time.

Sebastian shut his eyes, the flutter of her lips there strangely innocent despite their very carnal position. He dropped a kiss on her mouth. Nuzzled her throat.

'This is nice,' he murmured as the water sluiced over his shoulders and ran in rivulets over her breasts.

They stayed for a while longer until Callie squirmed and he roused himself from the sweet line of her neck. 'Sorry,' he apologised.

'It's okay,' Callie said, her arms holding him closer.

'I'm squashing you,' he protested, pulling away.

His hands tightened momentarily where the backs of her thighs met her buttocks before he eased away from her and supported her as she slid down the tiles. Her legs buckled slightly and he held her tight, letting her lean into him for a moment.

'I'm okay now,' Callie whispered as her jellied legs regained strength. Even though she wasn't sure if she'd ever be the same again.

Sebastian let her go but grabbed her again as she swayed a few seconds later. He held her around the waist as he shut off the taps with his other hand then swept her up in his arms.

Callie laughed, hanging on around his neck. 'I *can* walk, Sebastian.'

He kissed her nose. 'I know.'

He carried her into the bedroom and laid her gently on the bed, joining her moments later, gathering her to his side and enjoying the press of her and the way her head automatically found his shoulder, her arm his chest.

It didn't matter that they were both dripping wet. Towelling seemed like such a vigorous activity in his post-coital languor and the wet sheets would dry. The only thing he wanted to do now was to lay Callie back and explore every inch of her body.

Really slowly.

Make her moan and sigh and quiver all over and then when she was begging for him, he wanted it to be deep and slow. Not frantic Neanderthal sex like in the shower. He wanted to make it last.

And he would. In a moment. As soon as the marrow returned to his bones and his brain cells organised themselves into some semblance of normality.

Soon.

Callie woke with a start. It was dark and something had yanked her from slumber that had come over her unawares.

The warm, bony pillow beneath her cheek twitched, rocking her head a little, and she realised Sebastian was muttering to himself. It took a moment to work out what was happening. She didn't know where she was or what time it was.

She half sat up, her hand still on Sebastian's chest.

Her bedroom came into focus as her eyes adjusted to the darkness. The luminous figures on her bedside clock pronounced it just after midnight.

'No.'

Callie startled as Sebastian's unexpected word frightened the life out of her. He shook his head from side to side as if he was fighting something and uttered, 'No!' again, but this time it was louder, more panicked, and he vaulted up in bed, displacing Callie entirely.

Callie's heart leapt to her throat. 'Sebastian?' She laid her hand on his shoulder and he jumped, twisting to look at her with wild eyes that, for a moment, didn't seem to recognise her.

She sat back, her shoulder blades scraping the bedhead. She removed her hand, her heart fluttering wildly in her chest. 'Sebastian?'

Sebastian sagged as his surroundings entered his consciousness and pushed away the dusty roadside and the smell of burning metal. 'Callie,' he said on an exhalation. 'I'm sorry, I'm so sorry.'

'Hey,' she murmured, opening her arms and gathering him close. 'It's fine. Just fine.'

She didn't know how long they sat there. Long enough for the tremble in his arms to settle and the mad pulsing of his heart against hers to return to its normal rhythm.

'Is it your father?'

Sebastian shook his head. 'No.'

'Do you want to talk about it?' she asked into the darkness when his grip around her waist eventually slackened.

Sebastian roused himself, the shocking realism of the nightmare receding. Surprisingly, he did want to talk about it—and he definitely owed her an explanation.

He turned in her arms, his back to her front. She slid her arms over his shoulder and cradled him against her. He placed his palms on her shins, needing to ground himself.

'I was travelling with a supply division to get to another base. There was a roadside bomb.' He stopped. 'The vehicle in front was blown to smithereens. I'd just been talking to the driver a few minutes before we left. He was supposed to be going home a month later.'

'Did he…?'

Sebastian stared into the darkness, his mind awash with flames and the desperation of men trying to save their comrades. 'He didn't make it. None of them did.'

Callie hugged him tighter, wrapping her legs around his stomach, linking them at the ankles. 'I'm so sorry,' she murmured, dropping a kiss on his shoulder. She couldn't even begin to imagine something so horrible.

Sebastian nodded, enjoying her embrace for long moments. 'I know.'

'Do you have nightmares often?'

'No, not really. Not any more. Only when I'm really tired, I guess.'

It was no surprise, then, that it had happened tonight. He'd come to her from Frank already totally exhausted. And then there'd been the sex. Sex that, for the first time, had been about more than physical gratification.

For both of them.

It had pushed emotional boundaries that had touched her more profoundly than the earth-shattering orgasm. And she didn't need to ask or be psychic to know it had touched him too.

'Have you seen anyone about it?'

He grimaced. 'Ironic, isn't it? The foremost expert on PTSD suffering from it himself?'

Callie rubbed her chin against his hair, her hands palming the skin of his abdominal wall. 'No. It's just life.'

'I have talked to someone about it. An army psychologist. It was him actually who suggested I ease back into work. That I should take a break from anything to do with post-traumatic stress altogether.'

'Well, he sounds very smart,' she murmured.

Sebastian chuckled. 'Yeah. He is.'

They sat locked together for a long while, neither saying anything. Just touching. Nothing sexual. Trailing fingers. Dropping a kiss. Rubbing a cheek. Not wanting to move, to disconnect.

Sebastian liked the weight of her legs wrapped around him, the feel of her breasts squashed to his back. But when he glanced at the time it was almost one and he stirred, knowing he had to go.

Talking had been cathartic and the last thing he felt like doing was getting out of Callie's bed.

But they were *their* rules.

'I'm sorry,' he said, easing out of her embrace, rubbing the fatigue from his eyes. 'I should go. I didn't mean to fall asleep.'

Callie felt an immediate sense of loss. She'd been enjoying the solid pressure of him against her, the steady, even expansion of his rib cage pushing into her belly.

She put her hand out, touched his shoulder. Slid it along the ridge that thickened into his neck then trailed it down his back. 'No.'

She didn't want him to go. They'd shared a deeper part of themselves tonight. Let down their defences. Crossed lines they'd sworn not to.

He'd fallen asleep in her bed because it had felt right.

It still felt right. She didn't want to send him away tonight. Any night.

'Stay.'

Sebastian stilled. Her hand was warm against his back. He turned slightly. She knew him, this woman. Callie. She knew more about him than he'd ever let another woman know.

He wanted to leave her bed about as much as he wanted to drill a hole in his head but she had to be sure. If they were going to do this—it would be the point of no return.

'Are you sure?'

Callie nodded and opened her arms.

'Here you are.'

Sebastian had woken the next morning to find the bed empty. He'd finally located Callie on her deck, staring out over the rooftops of suburbia. She was dressed in a pair of brief knickers that rode up high on the cheeks of her bottom and a T-shirt that didn't quite meet her underwear, leaving a tempting circle of skin bare.

Callie looked behind her and smiled. 'Here I am.'

Wearing only a towel slung low on his hips, he padded across to her and stopped directly behind her, placing his hands on her shoulders. It was gratifying when she leant into him, turned her face slightly so she could rub her cheek against his hand.

'Having second thoughts?' he murmured.

Callie shook her head. 'No.'

He nuzzled her neck. 'Why so pensive, then?'

Callie's gaze flicked back to the houses and greenery of her neighbourhood. 'I guess I'm just wondering what this means now.'

After all they'd shared last night, the thought of him

leaving one day, of this having to stop and to never be with him like this again, was increasingly disturbing.

Sebastian couldn't help but smile at the bewildered look on her face. 'I think it's time to face it, Callie. We're in a relationship. Just because we've been too wrapped up in each other to define it doesn't change the facts.'

Relationship.

Before last night Callie would have shrunk from the word. It was a big word. With a lot of expectations.

But it was suddenly very tantalising too.

An adult relationship with a man she liked, whose company she enjoyed and who could make her laugh.

Who shared himself with her.

Who could touch her body and make her see stars, who didn't let her hide and who understood, better than anyone else, the things from her past that had shaped her, that defined her.

She turned in his arms. He looked irresistible in his towel, his broad naked chest so sexy that even now in the middle of this momentous discussion she wanted to relieve him of the towel and give her neighbours a show they'd never forget.

'The thing is, Sebastian, we've never really talked about us in any kind of future terms. I thought we were just living in the moment?'

'I think we transcended that last night, don't you?' He used a finger to lift her chin slightly. 'I think we should keep this thing going. Even when I go back.' He shrugged. 'Melbourne's only a two-hour plane trip.'

Her breath caught in her throat. *A long-distance relationship?* It was a shocking thought. One she'd never entertained. But one, even now, despite the suddenness, was insidiously entwining itself in her grey matter.

'Sure, why not?' he insisted. 'We're having a good

time. We're both adults who are free to come and go with no commitments to other people. Who says we have to follow conventional rules? I can fly here or you can fly there. Or we can fly somewhere else and meet in the middle. There's weekends and holidays. Why not?'

Callie chewed her lip as temptation knocked. Why not indeed?

Her in Brisbane, doing what she loved. Still around for Zack and still being there for her clients.

Him in Melbourne, doing what he loved. Being famous and important.

Then meeting somewhere to do what they both loved together.

The best of both worlds.

The more the thought sat with her the more it excited her. The more enticing the possibilities.

But. Experience told her that men often wanted more and more. Things she just wasn't prepared to give.

She took a deep breath. 'I'm never going to want a baby.'

Sebastian blinked. He hadn't expected that. He'd been waiting for her to say something, something big, watching as the thing she grappled with flitted shadows through her amber eyes. But this was unexpected. 'Of course.'

She shook her head and blasted him with a serious look. 'I mean it, Sebastian. I'm not going to change my mind. I'm perfectly happy with my life. I don't need to experience motherhood to have a fulfilling existence. I've had Zack and that was wonderful enough for me. But I've been here before. Sooner or later, it always gets down to babies.'

Sebastian returned her gaze with a steady one of his

own. He slid a hand along her jaw, cradling it as his fingers speared into her hair.

'You don't have to worry. I'm with you on this, one hundred and fifty per cent.' He rubbed his thumb gently back and forth across her ear. 'I fully understand where this comes from. I have no desire for a child either and I would never ask that of you.'

Sebastian lowered his head and kissed her gently on the mouth. 'I promise.'

Callie sighed and smiled, her heart feeling as big as a basketball in her chest. 'In that case,' she whispered against his lips, 'I'd love to keep this thing going.'

And she reached for his towel and pulled.

CHAPTER EIGHT

THE steady, rapid rhythm of a foetal heartbeat filled Sebastian's office and Callie smiled down at Ginny, who was reclined on the couch, her shirt pulled up to expose her taut eight-and-a-half-month pregnant belly.

It was a noise that Callie had heard very regularly over the last five months. Luckily it hadn't affected her again the way it had the first time she'd heard it during the ultrasound.

Ginny's eyes filled with tears. 'I'm so sorry to be a bother.'

Callie smiled at Ginny as her client wiped away an escaping tear. 'It's no bother,' she reassured her as she switched off the hand-held Doppler.

'It's just that I've been so busy getting everything ready for the baby since I finished work and now everything's done and... What if something goes wrong? I keep thinking of all the things that could go wrong and I then I saw this documentary the other day about ana—anaceph...oh, I don't know how to pronounce it.'

'Anacephaly?'

Ginny nodded vigorously. 'That's it.'

'But, Ginny, your little girl has a perfectly formed head. You've had three ultrasounds—one of them 3D—and she has a beautiful head.'

Ginny sighed. 'I know. I know that. I guess I'm just…
What if I'm…going nuts again, Callie?'

Callie reached for a tissue on the nearby coffee table
and wiped at the gel she'd applied low down on Ginny's
belly then she picked up her client's hand.

'You are going through exactly the same thing that
thousands of mothers go through towards the end. You're
anxious—'

'Anxious?' Ginny interrupted, half sitting, alarm in
her voice.

Callie smiled and squeezed Ginny's hand. 'A lot of
mothers-to-be are anxious. What you're going through
is normal.' She squeezed again. 'Perfectly normal.'

Ginny relaxed back and even gave a half smile. 'I
suppose so. I guess when I realised that I hadn't felt her
move for a couple of hours I just panicked.'

'Remember what the midwife said?' Callie reiterated.
'Decreased foetal movements are common in the last
few weeks. There's not much room to move inside that
belly at the moment,' Callie joked, giving the round
expanse a gentle poke.

The baby, obviously objecting to the nudge, kicked
back and Callie watched the corresponding belly movements as the baby seemed to roll from one side to the
other.

'Of course she's been moving around like a jumping
jack ever since I walked in here,' Ginny said, absently
rubbing her belly. 'I should have waited.'

'No.' Callie shook her head. 'It's good to be in tune
to these things and if you do ever feel that she's not
moving as much then come here or ring the community
midwife.'

She pulled Ginny's shirt down and helped her into a
sitting position. 'It's better to be cautious.'

Ginny left five minutes later, much calmer than when she'd arrived. Callie stood in the doorway, watching her client leave. She smiled as Sebastian, who was in the glass-panelled group therapy room, waved at Ginny on her way out.

Her gaze stayed with Sebastian as he ran his teen group therapy session. He was in blue jeans and an olive T-shirt that complemented his eyes and the red-gold of his hair and sat snugly across his biceps and pecs.

He was leaning forward, both feet planted firmly in front of him, his elbows on his knees, his hands, loosely interlinked, hanging between his legs. Even from across the room she could see his absolute focus as he engaged Bree, a fifteen-year-old anorexic.

Callie glanced at the painfully thin teenager who was smiling shyly at Sebastian. A nasogastric tube used for night feeding was taped to her cheek and marred features that would have been pretty had they not been so gaunt.

Bree hated the tube. She hated the sessions. She especially hated the weekly weigh-ins. Or she had anyway. But for the tenth week in a row she'd gained weight and she taken delight in the progress instead of seeing it as a failure and another reason to hate herself and her body. She had a spring in her step and a smile on her face instead of her usual sullen frown.

Callie didn't doubt that Sebastian was a large part of the teenager's recovery.

Sebastian's focus shifted to Eric, the fourteen-year-old boy beside Bree, who had been referred for self-harming. But Callie kept her eyes glued on the girl. Prior to her turn-around Bree would sit in these sessions with the typical fidgety movements of those suffering from profound anorexia nervosa.

She'd tap her toes repeatedly, jiggle her thighs and drum her fingers against her crossed arms. Exercise in any form was important to anorexics—even seemingly passive they could increase their metabolic rate and burn fat. So movement, any movement, was good.

Being idle was the enemy.

But now she sat still, listening attentively. She laughed, smiled, joined in the conversation and even engaged the newcomers who were reluctant to join in.

Callie spied Bree's mother flicking through an ancient magazine in the central waiting area. She wandered over and sat opposite. 'Hi, Anita. How's it all going?'

Bree's mother glanced up from her reading and smiled at Callie. 'The bad days are getting fewer, thank goodness.'

Callie nodded. The smile couldn't erase the extra years Bree had added to her mother's life. Anita looked ten years older than when they'd first met two years ago after Bree's diagnosis.

They both glanced over at the session, which was drawing to a close. 'I can't thank Sebastian enough. He's just connected with her. Mind you...' she smiled '...I can't say I blame her. He's very easy on the eye, isn't he?'

Callie laughed as Anita openly ogled Sebastian. She quashed the urge to say, *You should see him naked.* 'That he is.'

'Seriously, though.' Anita sobered, looking back at Bree. 'Since her father left a few years ago she's been lacking a strong male role model. Sebastian has been such a godsend. You should hear her at home—Sebastian said this, Sebastian said that.'

Callie reached out and covered Anita's hand with

hers. 'It's good to see her coming out the other side. Don't forget, though, she's still got a way to go.'

Anita patted Callie's hand. 'I know. I know. It's just been so nice to see. So nice to not feel so utterly helpless for a change.'

Callie nodded. 'Of course.' She looked back at the room. 'Looks like they're done. See you next week?' she asked, rising from the lounge.

Anita nodded and winked. 'Wouldn't miss it.'

Callie had a smile on her face as she wandered into the staffroom a couple of moments later. Sebastian had caught her eye as she'd passed and given her that *have I got plans for you tonight* look.

Their transition to spending their nights together had been a natural progression once the *R* word had come out into the open, and Callie felt a small trill of excitement every time she thought about sleeping with him.

'Coffee's here,' Geraldine announced, walking past her with a laden four-cup cardboard tray from the coffee shop over the road.

Callie took hers and sat at the table. She removed the lid and inhaled the rich, earthy fragrance of her double-shot espresso, waiting for the delicious buzz as it hit her olfactory system.

It was a shock when a powerful surge of nausea took hold instead. Callie pushed the cup away violently, the liquid sloshing over the sides and onto the table. 'Ugh.' She clapped a hand to her mouth, relieved that it vanished as quickly as it appeared. 'That smells awful.'

Geraldine raised an eyebrow and lifted the mug to her face. 'Smells like coffee to me,' she murmured.

Callie shuddered. 'Must be that bout of food poisoning I had last week. I still feel a little delicate and things seem to taste different.'

Geraldine blew on her coffee, watching Callie over the rim. 'You sure it was food poisoning?'

Callie nodded. 'Sebastian was ill too. We think it must have been something in the take-away we'd had the night before. He got over his quicker than me, though.'

Geraldine took a sip. 'Funnily enough, I couldn't stand the smell of coffee when I was pregnant with Tahlia. The merest whiff and I was throwing up like there was no tomorrow.'

There was something in Geraldine's voice that made Callie's eyes narrow. 'Gerri,' she warned.

Gerri shrugged. 'I'm just saying.'

'Well, don't.'

Gerri sipped again. 'You and Seb being careful?'

Callie rolled her eyes. 'Of course, Mother.'

Except that once… *I don't want any barriers between us tonight.*

'Hmm,' she said, placing the cup on the table and crossing her arms over her ample bosom. 'And you've had a period lately?'

Callie did not like the speculation in her friend's eyes. 'Yes. Last week.'

'Yep, that can happen. I had my period until I was five months pregnant with Damon.'

'Gerri.'

'Tired?' she persisted, ignoring the note of warning in Callie's voice. 'Peeing a lot? Sore boobs?'

Callie stood. 'I am not pregnant, Geraldine Russell. So get that thought right out of your head.'

Rodney walked in, oblivious to the conversation. He placed his lunch on the table and lifted the plastic lid on his regular curry from the Indian take-away, also across the road. The aroma of coriander and all-spice wafted upwards and he inhaled appreciatively.

'I don't know what we're going to do if The Raj Palace ever closes down,' he mused. 'I might have to actually make my own lunch.'

Callie felt the nausea return with a vengeance but this time it didn't settle. Instead, it became all-consuming and she knew that there was definitely going to be follow-through.

'Excuse me,' she gasped, praying that she'd make it to the staff toilet in time.

Rodney blinked as he watched Callie gallop off. He looked down at Gerri, concern in his eyes, only to find her grinning like an idiot. 'What's so funny?' he asked.

'Life is, Rodney.' Geraldine laughed. 'Life.'

Callie felt so rough she popped into Sebastian's office to let him know she was taking the afternoon off and cancelling their movie plans.

'Of course,' he said, dropping his pen and rising from his chair. 'I'll drop by after work and check on you.' He reached her side and pulled her into an embrace.

'No, it's okay.' Callie dropped her head against the pillow of his chest. She was so weary suddenly she felt like she could sleep for a week. 'I'm having a shower and going straight to bed.'

'Okay.' He kissed her forehead. 'You do feel a bit warm,' he murmured. 'I think you should see your doctor. This food poisoning thing has been dragging on a bit too long.'

Callie nodded, pushing Geraldine's theory firmly from her head. 'Tomorrow.'

'Come on. I'll drive you home.'

'No.' Callie roused herself. 'You have your private session with Frank Jessop in five minutes. I'll be fine.'

Callie left soon after, the drive seeming to take an eternity. Long enough for her thoughts to turn back to Gerri's preposterous intimation.

Preposterous!

Gerri, better than anyone, knew Callie's stance on children and how she'd spent her entire fertile life trying to avoid pregnancy. Why on earth would she even put forward such a ridiculous idea?

But that night in the shower replayed in her mind. Her insistence that they have no barriers between them.

Surely not…?

Surely she couldn't be that unlucky?

Once—just once in her life…

Of course it was possible, she castigated herself. She was a nurse, for crying out loud, she knew that one time was all that it required.

But…surely not?

No. No, she'd had a period. Just last week. A little late but her cycle was getting longer as she moved towards her forties. And, okay, it had been quite light but it had happened in the middle of the whole food poisoning incident and she had figured that her body was giving her a break.

She refused to give Gerri's Damon anecdote any thought.

Callie swung into her drive and switched off the engine, wishing she could switch the thoughts off as easily. The prospect of going into an empty house with only Gerri's insinuations for company was daunting.

But her shower and her bed beckoned and within

twenty minutes, despite the ridiculous thought of pregnancy hanging over her head, Callie was sound asleep.

She awoke the next morning feeling much better. Rested and ready to face a new day. It was odd, though, to wake up without Sebastian next to her and she slid her hand over the cold sheets beside her. It felt wrong to wake alone.

Her stomach still felt a little delicate and the coffee she'd started to make was soon abandoned, but a piece of toast and a cup of tea seemed to settle things down and she left the house with a spring in her step.

'Morning,' Geraldine greeted her. 'And how are we feeling today?'

Callie ignored the probing gaze, breezing past her boss. 'Fantastic. Slept like a baby. Ready and raring to go,' she said as she entered the staffroom and stashed her bag in her locker.

Geraldine followed. 'Now, some would say that was a Freudian slip.'

Callie frowned. What on earth was Gerri on at the moment? 'What?'

Gerri raised an eyebrow. 'Slept like a baby?'

Callie turned and smiled sweetly at her colleague. 'I'm officially ignoring you.'

Rodney breezed past them with a bakery bag. 'Morning, ladies. Hot cinnamon rolls, baked fresh.' He plonked the paper bag on the table and ripped it down the centre decanting them onto a plate.

The room filled with a warm yeasty fragrance. Callie felt a surge of nausea as Rodney offered her one, the sweet, sugary aroma engulfing her. She dared not look at Geraldine as she tried not to recoil from the offering and excused herself to walk rapidly to the toilet.

She just made it in time as her stomach revolted and discharged its paltry contents in great heaving spasms that seemed to go on for ever. Afterwards she pulled the lid down and sat on it, elbows on knees, cradling her head in her hands. Her legs were shaking. Her hands were sweaty.

She wanted to die.

It couldn't be. Surely?

A knock pulled her out of her misery. 'Just a moment,' she said, taking a couple of deep breaths and standing gingerly. She reached for the lock and opened the door.

Geraldine was there, holding up a pregnancy test kit. 'I think you should do this.'

Callie looked at the packaged item that they always had in stock in their storeroom. Then she looked at her friend and shook her head.

'Humour me,' Gerri said. 'If you're so sure its negative, what have you got to lose?'

Callie swallowed. Somehow the mere thought of doing the test gave credence to this whole crazy thing. It gave it legitimacy—and that scared the hell out of her.

'This can't be happening to me.' To her horror she felt tears prick her eyes.

Geraldine passed the test to her. 'Maybe it isn't. There's only one way to find out.'

Callie reached for the packet. 'I don't want this.'

Geraldine nodded. 'Sometimes you don't get a say, Callie. And sometimes things happen that seem like a complete disaster at the time yet they turn out to be the best thing that ever happened.'

Two minutes later, a little pink plus sign swimming before her eyes, Callie's worse fears were realised. She opened the door to find Geraldine waiting. Callie walked straight into Gerri's open arms and promptly burst into tears.

'I can't do this, Gerri. I don't want this.'

Gerri listened silently as Callie sobbed and ranted and choked out incoherent words and jumbled, half-formed thoughts. She didn't say anything until Callie had run out of steam.

'Go home. It's Friday. Take the weekend. Don't make any rash decisions. Talk it over with Seb—'

'Oh, God!' Callie wailed. 'Sebastian. He wants kids even less than I do.'

So much for continuing after he left to go back to Melbourne. She'd be lucky if he actually spoke to her for the rest of his term. What on earth had possessed her to have unprotected sex that night? Where had her brain been?

'This is a mess. A damn mess,' Callie sniffed.

'Maybe he might surprise you,' Gerri offered.

Callie shook her head. 'We've talked about this. He...' She couldn't stop herself thinking about the moment she'd insisted on not using a condom. This was all her fault.

Her fault.

'He'll be pretty angry.'

'You have to talk to him some time, Callie.'

Callie avoided the frank look in her friend's eyes. 'I know. I know. I just need to think first. I need to...work out what I'm going to do.'

Gerri nodded. 'Sure. But don't forget, it's his baby too.'

Sebastian's baby. She was pregnant with Sebastian's

baby. It was too big. Too momentous to even comprehend. 'Can you tell him that I called in to say I've gone
away for a few days and that I'll see him on Monday?'

'Callie...'

'Please, Gerri, please. Just this once, okay? I *will* tell
him but I need to figure out how to do that. I need time
to think.'

Gerri sighed. 'Okay.'

Callie hugged her friend, her colleague, her boss.
'What would I do without you?'

Gerri patted Callie's back. 'You'll never have to find
out.'

Sebastian narrowed his eyes at Gerri. 'I don't believe
you.'

Gerri shrugged. 'That's what she said.'

Sebastian jammed his hands on his hips. 'So between seven this morning when she texted me that she
was feeling better and that she'd see me at work and
now...'

He paused and checked his watch. 'A quarter past
nine... She's just decided to take off for a few days?
Without rhyme or reason? Without telling me?'

Geraldine drew herself up to her very impressive
height. 'Hey, don't shoot the messenger.'

Sebastian was sure that Gerri's regal matriarchal
glare, unwavering in its intensity, scared the pants off
most people. But he was not most people. And he'd be
a pretty lousy psychologist if he couldn't see that Gerri
was lying.

Although he had to admit she was fairly con-
vincing.

Had he not worked in the prison system for the last
decade, she might even have got away with it. But he was

trained to read nuances and Gerri's subtle jaw clench gave her away.

And besides—the whole thing just didn't make sense.

Employing a stare of his own that had broken hardened criminals, he dropped his voice. 'Don't bullshit me, Geraldine.'

Gerri regarded him for a moment with pursed lips. 'Okay.' She caved in. 'She hasn't gone away. She's at home.'

Sebastian nodded, no triumph in his success. 'What's wrong with her? Is she okay? Is this something to do with her seeing the doctor?' A hundred worst-case scenarios whizzed around his brain.

Gerri shook her head. 'Oh, no, you don't. I'm not telling you anything else. Go and ask her yourself.'

Sebastian picked his keys up off his desk where he'd not long thrown them. 'Fine. I have every intention of doing so.'

Gerri held up her hands in the universal signal to stop. 'If you want my advice, you'll give her some breathing room. Don't hare over there now. Wait till after work. Give her a chance to… Give her some space.'

A chance to what? Some space for what? But Gerri had gone before he could form the questions.

He threw the keys back down in disgust and snatched up the phone receiver, punching in her home number. It went to her answering machine. 'Callie? Callie, it's Sebastian. I know you're there. Pick up the phone.' He waited for five seconds. 'Callie please, I'm worried about you.' More silence followed. 'I'll be round tonight after work, whether you like it or not,' he growled as he banged the phone down.

He sat in his chair, drumming his fingers on the desk.

He reached for the phone again and dialled her mobile. It went straight to her message bank and he cursed under his breath before leaving another similarly terse message.

Sebastian steepled his fingers and brooded, staring into space. What in God's name had got into her? Had he done something wrong? Had she really wanted him to come over last night with a bunch of flowers and some hot chicken broth? Had she set him some kind of a test that he'd failed, and now she was sulking?

No, that wasn't Callie. It just wasn't.

God knew, he'd known women like that. Women who constantly tested their men. Tried to trap them into doing something wrong to prove them unworthy. Irrational women. Women who liked to play games.

Which was one of the best things about his relationship with Callie—no games. No artifice. No lies. Just two adults enjoying each other's company. Respecting each other.

He clenched his fists. *Or so he'd thought!*

By the time Sebastian arrived at Callie's it was nearly eight o'clock. A last-minute crisis at Jambalyn had seen him tied up at the hospital, organising an emergency admission to the psych unit.

He was tired and had a knot of tension between his shoulder blades as big as his fist. He wanted nothing more than to curl up with Callie, lose himself inside her and forget about the entire day.

Walking up the front steps, looking at the darkened house, that particular fantasy didn't seem very likely.

He raised his hand and gave three hard raps against the wood of the front door. He waited for a minute and rapped again. Another minute passed.

'Callie,' he called, knocking for the third time. 'I know you're in there.'

More silence greeted him and Sebastian felt a most unnatural urge to rip the door off its hinges. He thumped at the wood instead, pounding his fist on it.

'Goddamn it, Callie. Open the door!'

Callie, who was lying on the couch in the same spot she'd been sprawled all day, frowned as the noise finally penetrated the strange cocoon she'd been wrapped in.

Sebastian? *No, no, no.* It was too soon to talk to him. She sat up. 'Go away,' she croaked. She cleared her voice and tried again, stronger this time. 'Leave me alone!'

Sebastian placed his palm flat against the wood. Her voice sounded feeble and the worry that had been gnawing at his gut all day intensified. 'No. I'm not going to go away,' he yelled. 'I'm not going to leave you alone. You can push me away as much as you like but I'm still going to be here. Now, open the damn door or I *will* use my key.'

Callie felt a moment of panic snap her fully out of the twilight zone she'd been hovering in all day. Geraldine's *You'll have to talk to him some time* taunted her. But now?

She wasn't ready. She hadn't worked out what to say.

But, then, was she ever going to be ready for one of the hardest conversations of her life? It was right up there with begging Andy not to jump and having to break the news to Zack that he was going to go back and live with his mother.

Another thundering pound on her door. Another desperate 'Callie!'

She stood, her legs weak and wobbly, her stomach lurching at the sudden movement after hours of complete idleness. 'Coming,' she called, lest Sebastian decided to knock her door down in preference to using the key.

He certainly sounded mad enough.

Sebastian heard her weak response and clenched his fists by his sides as a huge well of relief made him feel light-headed. The outside light above his head flicked on and he heard the lock being sprung and then the door opened.

He didn't know what would greet him but he wasn't prepared for the wan-looking woman before him. Her amber eyes were dull, her hair was lank and her eyes had dark rings beneath them

'Oh, my God!' he exclaimed, stepping closer. He had a strong urge to hug her, to infuse some of his strength into her. She looked wretched. But she shrank back from him into the shadows of the house, which appeared to be in complete darkness, and he stopped.

He pushed his hands into his pockets to prevent a repeat performance. 'Callie, what's the matter? You look...awful. Is there something you're not telling me?' His heart pounded as he thought of all the terminal and degenerative diseases he'd come across in his career.

'Are you...are you sick?'

Callie snorted. 'Not much of a catch now, hey?'

A spike of undiluted rage hit Sebastian's bloodstream and he was pleased his hands were firmly ensconced in his pockets as the urge to shake her took hold. 'You think I care about that?' he snapped. 'I just want to know what's wrong, damn it!'

'I'm pregnant.'

Callie hadn't meant to blurt it out. She really hadn't. But in the absence of a better plan it just fell out of her mouth.

She watched his face grow very still as the news

sank in. The light from above shone on the golden high-lights in his hair and eyebrows. It danced off his lashes, pooled in the hollows beneath his glorious cheekbones and caressed the twin curves of his lips.

She couldn't bear the growing silence. Couldn't bear the thought of never kissing that mouth again. 'You can go now,' she said, and turned on her heel.

Sebastian didn't move for a moment or two. Pregnant? She was pregnant. He shut his eyes. That night. After Frank. The shower. His desperate need for her, for life. Her desperate need to feel all of him—no barriers. Him wanting it too.

Oh, hell.

He rubbed a weary hand across his eyes and opened them. Pregnant. Callie was carrying his child.

With his heart in his mouth, he stepped into the house.

He found her sitting on the lounge, her legs tucked up beneath her, staring at the flickering, silent television. She looked up as he entered.

'I don't know what to say,' he said, raking a hand through his hair. 'What to think.'

Callie regarded him steadily. 'How about that I trapped you into this by insisting that you not wear a condom that night?'

Sebastian clenched a fist. 'You didn't put a gun to my head, Callie. I wanted it as much you did,' he said sharply as he sat down beside her.

Even now he remembered how liberating it had been to be inside her and to really feel her for the first time. 'I know this news is as much a shock to you as it is to me.'

They both stared at the television for what seemed

like an age, caught up in their own thoughts. 'Where do we go from here?' Sebastian finally asked.

Callie shrugged. 'I don't know. I just don't know.'

'Do you...do you want the baby?'

Callie recoiled at Sebastian's tentative question. The one she'd been avoiding all day. 'I don't know,' she repeated, ignoring the jab of pain that kicked her in the centre of her chest every time her mind drifted to the issue. 'Do you?'

Sebastian ruffled his hair for the umpteenth time, surprised to find he had any left. 'I...don't know. This is a shock. I'm sorry, I just don't know what to think or say.'

Callie nodded. 'Yeah, well,' she said rising to her feet, 'That makes two of us.'

Sebastian frowned. 'Where are you going?'

'To bed,' she said, not bothering to look at him. 'I've done nothing but think about this all day. I just don't want to think any more.'

Sebastian let her go. She was obviously still in shock, functioning mechanically and seeking solace in sleep rather than the reality of the situation.

That was totally understandable. He was pretty shocked himself. He, on the other hand, having only just found out, wasn't likely to get any sleep.

Maybe ever again.

He kicked off his shoes and lay back on the couch, the television casting an eerie pall over his churning thoughts.

Sebastian wasn't sure what time it was when something woke him from a sleep he'd not long slipped into after an interminable night of staring into the dark, alternating between castigation and indecision.

The noise, like that of a wounded animal, came again and he became fully aware of his surroundings. He was on a couch, Callie's couch, and the noise was coming from their bedroom.

Her bedroom.

He vaulted up and stumbled through the house. Callie wasn't in the bed and the noise was coming from the en suite bathroom. His feet were on the cold tiles in four long strides.

Callie was hunched over the toilet bowl, retching. 'Callie,' he murmured, crouching beside her.

Callie, already feeling wretched, felt her misery intensify as Sebastian witnessing her vomiting. 'Go away,' she cried, pushing at him distractedly, her eyes shut tight as she tried to mentally will the nausea away. Hot tears scalded her eyes and slipped out from behind her lids to course down her face.

Sebastian rubbed her back. 'I'm not going anywhere.'

'Please. Sebastian, please, just go,' she sobbed. 'I don't want you to see me like this.' Then another bout of retching took over and she couldn't talk any more.

Sebastian ignored her, continuing to rub her back. When the retching settled he stood, wetted a washcloth and gave it to her.

Callie took it gratefully, pressing the coolness to her mouth. She must look a mess. Her eyes were red and streaming, her nose running. She sat back against the wall. 'I'm s-so s-sorry,' she said in hiccoughy sobs, fresh tears taking the places of the ones she'd scrubbed way. 'I can't s-seem to s-stop crying.'

Apart from her howling episode with Gerri, she hadn't cried at all yesterday. She'd just stared at the television all day, feeling numb inside. But this, throwing up first thing in the morning, made the whole thing seem very real—more so than the pregnancy test—and the enormity had hit her again.

'Hey,' Sebastian murmured, sliding down the wall as she dissolved into a flood of tears. He hauled her into his lap and held her against his chest as she wept.

'It's such a b-big m-mess,' she bawled.

'Shh,' Sebastian soothed. 'It'll be okay. You'll see. We'll work it out. Shh.'

Callie wasn't sure how long she clung to him. All she knew was that his voice was soothing, saying all the right things, and the scratch of his red-gold whiskers against her hair as he rocked slightly was a strange sort of bliss.

She never wanted to leave the shelter of his arms. Here she was just Callie. And she adored it.

Except she wasn't just Callie any more.

She was Callie plus one.

And therein lay the problem.

CHAPTER NINE

CALLIE was still feeling numb when she drove to Jambalyn on Monday morning. She was tired of the same thoughts turning over and over in her head and was looking forward to the distraction of work. Eight hours of something else to concentrate on other than the fact that Sebastian's baby was growing inside her.

Her stomach was still delicate and she'd spent half an hour that morning in and out of the toilet. Of course, it didn't help that it was also churned up at the thought of seeing Sebastian again.

Sebastian had wanted to stay the weekend but she'd needed to be alone. It was too hard to think with him there. Her affection, her sexual attraction to him became all jumbled up in the seesaw of emotions inside her and just muddied the issue further.

So he'd gone. Almost eagerly, she'd thought. But how could she blame him? He'd just had this momentous news dumped in his lap too; why wouldn't he also need time to think things through?

He'd looked like hell when he'd left. Unshaven. Haggard. The lines around his eyes and mouth more pronounced. He looked like he had that night after Frank and a part of her had wanted to call him back. Hold him tight. Tell him it was all going to be okay, as he had assured her earlier on the bathroom floor.

He would have stayed—she had no doubt of that. Had she asked. But something had stopped her.

The shock pregnancy news had thrown up some sort of shield between them. A physical and mental barrier. It was like they suddenly didn't know what to say to each other. How to act. There was an awkwardness that had never existed between them. Not even in the beginning.

And she wanted it back the way it had been.

Before the baby.

'Hi.'

Callie stopped in the staffroom doorway in mid-stride as Sebastian pulled up beside her. Her stomach did its usual funny dip thing, which did not bode well in her current state.

Her gaze ate him up. He was clean shaven but his peridot eyes lacked their sparkle and there was a certain grimness to a smile that didn't quite reach his eyes. 'Hi,' she murmured back.

Sebastian drank her in too. She looked…peaky and he could just make out the shadows below her eyes beneath heavier than usual make-up. It looked like neither of them had got much sleep. Out of habit he raised his hand and stroked the back of his palm down her cheek and along her jaw before dropping his hand.

'How are you feeling?'

Callie felt her stomach clench at the huskiness in his voice. She gave him a half-smile. 'Delicate.'

Sebastian nodded. 'We need to talk.'

Callie's heart boomed in her chest. 'Yeah, I know.

We will. I just need a little more time...to get my head around it.'

Sebastian regarded her for a few more moments. 'Okay. But soon. I'm not going to wait for ever.'

Callie watched him walk away, his shoulders back, his head with its glorious crown of red and gold held high. He looked like a man who'd made a decision. Who knew what he wanted.

Trepidation squirmed through her already unsettled belly.

Thankfully the morning was frantic and Callie didn't have time to dwell on things too much. Sebastian was scarce and Geraldine, sensing Callie's need for space, didn't push her on anything, even though Callie could tell that her boss was dying to talk to her about it.

Unfortunately, due to the way Rodney had booked appointments, Callie found herself doing community visits with Sebastian in the afternoon. Four hours of being trapped in a car with him stretched ahead of her and her stomach shifted uneasily.

They made it through two of the four visits, sticking to safe subjects—the clients and other work-related matters. Then Sebastian dropped his bombshell.

'Just so you know,' he said as he pulled the car out into traffic, 'I do want the baby. Very much.'

Callie, who'd been sucking on a lolly to keep the nausea at bay, almost choked on it. 'Wh-what?' she asked, bewildered, after the coughing fit settled.

'The baby,' Sebastian repeated, his eyes on the road. 'I've thought about nothing else since you've told me. You asked me the other night whether I wanted it or not, and it was all too enormous to take in back then. I know that you're still at that stage too, but…I'm not. I *do* want this baby.'

Callie was stunned. That she hadn't expected. 'But I thought you didn't want children.'

'I didn't.'

'You said that some people in this world shouldn't have them and that you were one of them. *Me included*, you said.'

Sebastian pulled up at a traffic light. He turned to face her. 'And I still believe that not everyone is equipped to handle the responsibility of a baby. But not wanting a baby when there isn't one is completely different to not wanting a baby when there is one.'

He put his hand on her knee and gave it a gentle squeeze. 'Circumstance may have forced my hand, Callie, but I'm in. Fully in. And I want to be a part of my child's life.'

Callie's head started to spin. She could hear the words but nothing seemed to make any sense. *Part of my child's life?* What did that mean exactly? A life with her too? Or just him and the baby? The baby she wasn't even sure if she wanted.

Her brain was full. Just too full of startling information to comprehend.

'So what does that make me? Some kind of unnatural freak, some kind of…anti-woman because I'm still grappling with this while you're painting the nursery?'

Sebastian touched her face again as he had that morning in the doorway. She flinched and he dropped his hand. 'Oh, Callie,' he murmured. 'It makes you human.'

A car behind hooted and Sebastian turned his attention back to the road as Callie looked out the window. He'd shocked her. Hell, he'd shocked himself. But one thing had become crystal clear over the weekend—his child was growing in Callie's womb, *his child*, and he would do anything to protect it.

'What if I don't?' Callie asked, looking back from the window. 'What if I don't want this baby?'

Sebastian felt the slow, steady thud of his heartbeat kick up a notch. She had that bolshie tone he knew so well. 'Then I guess we have a problem,' he replied with steel in his voice. 'Because I will fight for this child.'

Callie looked away again from the grim determination she saw on Sebastian's face. She'd seen that look on the bridge.

He'd been adamant then.

He looked immovable now.

'My mother was bipolar,' she said, staring out the window. 'My brother was schizophrenic. Both of those are familial mental illnesses.' She turned back to face him. 'Are you prepared for that?'

Sebastian slowed and stopped for another red light. Her voice had been tight with fear. A fear that he, probably more than most, understood. He knew what it was like to have the sword of mental illness hanging over your head. 'It's okay to be scared, Callie.'

'Well, that's good,' she said, a hitch in her voice, ''cos I'm terrified.'

Sebastian heard the tremor lacing her words. He wanted to haul her into his arms until the fear went away, but she looked like she'd shatter at the lightest of touches.

'Well, I'm not. Everything's going to be okay. I'm going to be here for you, Callie.'

'Except for when you disappear off back to Melbourne.'

He shook his head. 'I'm not going anywhere.'

Callie blinked. 'What?'

'I'm going to stay in Brisbane. Or you could come to Melbourne. But I figured you'd want to stay close to Zack. Either way, I don't care. I think we should get married.'

Callie gaped at him. 'What?'

Sebastian faltered as he mentally caught up with the words that had fallen unchecked from his mouth. They hadn't been part of what he'd planned to say. He should have been horrified. He should have been recanting. But somehow they just seemed...right.

'Sure. Why not? We were going to have a long-distance relationship, so why not this?'

Callie put a steadying hand against the dashboard as the light turned green and the car moved forward. The whole world suddenly seemed topsy-turvy. 'Oh, I don't know. What about love? I think that's kind of vital, don't you? You don't even love me, Sebastian.'

Sebastian frowned. 'Yes, I do.' The words tumbled out, again without prior warning, but again he knew they were right. He loved her. He knew it as surely as he knew he loved their baby.

'You love me?' she said, shaking her head like someone had just struck her on the face. Had she heard correctly? Had he taken leave of his senses?

Since when?

'Just like that, huh? Suddenly I'm pregnant and suddenly you love me,' she said with scathing disbelief.

Her tone rankled and her insinuation was insulting. But he took a deep breath as his knuckles whitened around the steering-wheel. It *was* a lot to take in. 'I know it's sudden.'

'Sudden!' Callie could hear the note of hysteria edging into her voice. 'You think?'

Sebastian kept a tight rein on his temper. 'I guess sometimes it just happens that way.'

Callie snorted. 'So we've spent months and months pretzelled together in either your bed or mine and there's been no mention of the *L* word. But today you've had a sudden revelation?'

Sebastian nodded. She'd pretty much nailed it. Love hadn't been on his agenda. Love hadn't been on either of their agendas. In fact, they'd painstakingly avoided talking about the boundaries of their relationship since the beginning, preferring to just enjoy the ride without any of the normal relationship pressures.

Love was certainly not something they'd ever discussed.

But it had happened anyway. For him at least. Without his knowledge or consent.

'Pretty much,' he agreed.

Oh, God. Her head spun. As if it could possibly spin any more! *How could he be so calm?* She turned away from him, totally exasperated. Now she was faced with not one bombshell but two.

'Do me a favour and just don't talk any more, okay?'

Sebastian gripped the gear lever so hard he was afraid he was going to have the numbers permanently tattooed to his palm. But he kept his eyes firmly on the road. 'Sure.'

They completed the rest of their visits in relative silence. Sebastian didn't push. He knew that he'd shocked her and that she was going to need time to process what he'd said.

Hell, he'd even shocked himself. But he wasn't sorry that he'd said it. Any of it.

He hadn't really given his thoughts any coherent voice until just now and it had felt good to articulate them. Felt good that he'd been honest about his feelings about her and the baby.

As shocking as they were.

At least he'd declared himself. Callie needed time to sort out her thoughts and her feelings, he understood that. He'd just dropped an awful lot in her lap. But at least now she had all the facts to consider.

He daren't think about what would happen if Callie couldn't get past her fears. If she never loved him back. His life stretched in a long bleak road ahead of him at the very thought.

She just needed time.

And time he had.

'Could you drop by Ginny's?' Callie requested when Sebastian started the car after their last appointment for the day.

They were the first voluntary words she'd spoken to him since his startling announcements and even they grated. She was still shocked, her emotions churning. And she was angry. Angry at him. At the situation. At herself.

His declaration of love and spontaneous marriage suggestion played over and over in her head. He appeared to have it all worked out. Whether she liked it or not.

He loved her? What the hell? They'd not long decided they'd try the long-distance thing, for crying out loud. And there'd been no mention of the *L* word then.

It was ironic really. In another time, under a different set of circumstances, his admission would have been like music to any girl's ears—even hers. But hot on the heels of their pregnancy surprise, how genuine could it be?

A woman would be a fool to be swept up in words spoken on the coat-tails of such a life upheaval.

'Sure. Is Ginny okay?'

'She's fine.' Callie wanted to explain herself about as much as she wanted to be in the car with him but all she had between her and total breakdown was her professional facade. 'I've taken to dropping in with the Doppler if I'm nearby.'

Sebastian nodded. 'Okay.'

They pulled up at Ginny's five minutes later and Callie scrambled out of the car in relief. He was too near, too close inside the small interior and the things between them too big. She couldn't breathe.

She longed to be able to turn back the clock to a few days ago when the only thing large between them had been their desire.

Sebastian also exited the car and it was more than she could stand. He'd been dogging her every step that afternoon. 'You don't have to come.' Callie waved him away. 'I'll only be five minutes.'

The very last thing she wanted was Sebastian in the same room as a heavily pregnant woman. The waters were already muddied enough!

Sebastian shut his door, ignoring her dismissive wave. 'I'm coming,' he said, capturing her gaze.

Callie shivered at the determination glittering in the clear green of his eyes that took her straight back to the day they'd first met, his flak jacket like armour between them. She watched him as he strode past her, command in every line of his body.

'Let's go.'

There was nothing left for Callie to do other than take a deep breath and traipse after him.

Ginny was happy to see them both and insisted they have a cup of tea first and some of her home-made lamingtons. Callie was about to decline but when Sebastian said, 'That would be lovely,' and Ginny beamed at them, Callie found herself following him again.

'I've been cooking all weekend.' Ginny chatted away as she waved off their assistance with a look that said, *I'm pregnant, not an invalid.* 'And cleaning.' She laughed. 'Brad's been reading these maternity books and reckons I'm nesting.'

'That sounds normal,' Callie murmured, her face aching from keeping a smile on her mouth and her gaze averted from the taut basketball shape of Ginny's belly.

'You're looking great,' Sebastian added.

How would Callie look heavily pregnant with his child? Would she rub her hand across her stomach in the way Ginny was, like she was subconsciously soothing the babe inside? Or somehow trying to connect through the layers of skin?

'Liar.' Ginny laughed. 'I was up half the night and then I couldn't get comfortable in bed because my back's been aching something fierce the last few days and I've been cleaning all day.'

Callie frowned. Ginny did look tired. 'I hope you're not overdoing it. You're supposed to be using this time to rest. You won't get the chance after the baby comes. It's only two weeks away.'

Ginny waved her off again. 'I know, that's what Brad says, but I just want to get everything shipshape for the baby. Actually...' Ginny patted the table '...I'm pleased

I've got you both here. I'd really like a second opinion, if you wouldn't mind.'

'Sure,' Sebastian said.

Ginny grinned and hauled herself up from her chair. She took a moment to stretch out her back, grimacing. 'Ugh! I tell you,' she joked, waddling towards the doorway to the hall, 'backs weren't meant to carry so much extra weight out front.'

They followed her into a room at the end of the hall. Callie should have known it was the nursery from the pink glow that intensified the closer they drew. She approached reluctantly. She didn't want to look at pretty pink frilly baby things—stuffed toys and teddy bears and musical mobiles.

Not today. Maybe not ever.

The room was exactly what she'd expected. Varying shades of pink on the walls, the ceiling painted with white fluffy clouds. A wooden cot, varnished to a high dark gloss, stood ready on one wall made up with a pink sheet. A mobile of fuzzy candyfloss sheep attached to the headboard hung over the cot, just waiting to spin around to the music.

And abutting its end a large change-table with a quilted plastic cover sporting green frogs in pink tutus. There were pots of things lined up neatly on its surface against the wall and a bag of pink disposable nappies stood at the ready. Two fluffy white towels were folded to one side and three piles of tiny pink and white clothes, looking soft and perfect, sat on top of the towels.

With white wooden shutters open to the streaming afternoon sun, the picture was complete. Even the smell of the room somehow evoked the essence of baby. That strange concoction of fragrances unique to tiny bundles of humanity.

Powder and soap. Sweetness and light.

Callie hovered in the doorway, uncomfortable with where her thoughts were heading. She was more than ready to give her opinion and leave. Sebastian, however, looked right at home, one shoulder shoved against the doorjamb, lounging lazily.

How was it possible for a man to look so lethal, so manly, surrounded by so much pink?

Sebastian watched as Callie took in the room, her hand on her belly. Hope bloomed in his chest. His own itched to join hers. Of course there would be nothing to feel now but he wanted to be there for every change, even the slightest nuance. He wanted to feel his baby move inside her.

'So we can't decide between the yellow ducks and the pink unicorns.'

Sebastian dragged his gaze from Callie's. Ginny was holding up two samples of what looked like a wallpaper frieze. She turned and faced the wall, placing each one against a different section of pink. 'What do you think?'

'Ducks,' they answered in unison, and then glanced in surprise at each other.

Ginny looked over her shoulder at them and gave a rueful smile. 'Yeah, yeah, too much pink, I know.'

Sebastian chuckled, returning his attention to Ginny. 'Pink is a very calming colour. Your little girl is going to be very laid back.'

Ginny laughed. 'My little girl is going to be spoilt rotten.'

Callie, agitated by the pink room and the talk of babies and agreeing on yellow ducks, said, 'Are you ready to have a listen to the foetal heart now?' She just wanted to do what had to be done and get far away from the stark reality of her potential future.

Ginny nodded. 'You bet.'

Sebastian watched from the doorway of the nursery as Callie and Ginny headed to the main bedroom. He turned back to the baby's room. Shoving his hands in his pockets, he took a couple of steps inside, swivelling his head to look all the way around. He moved in farther until he was looking down at the cot.

Dust motes swirled in a stream of sunlight that pierced the centre of the mattress like a beam from on high, like a sign from something not quite earthly that this was his path.

Fatherhood.

A chance to give life. To love unconditionally. To prove that the legacy of his own childhood ended with him.

And to share it all with the woman he loved.

He reached for the cot side as the enormity of it nearly brought him to his knees. The smell of baby surrounded him and the possibilities seemed endless.

He just had to make Callie believe in them too.

'Sebastian?'

Callie stood in the doorway. She'd called him twice already and he hadn't heard. Then he turned and the longing in his eyes was paralysing. It called to something primal in her. Something she couldn't control with rational thought or total avoidance.

'Let's do this, Callie.'

Callie didn't know what to say. Just do it? Just like that? Her hand pressed low on her abdomen. Was it really that simple? 'Come on,' she murmured, 'its time to go.'

Ginny had wrapped up some lamingtons in plastic

film when they arrived back in the kitchen and handed them over. 'For morning tea tomorrow at Jambalyn.'

'What makes you think they're going to make it that far?' Sebastian joked as he accepted them.

'I'll tell Geraldine to expect them.' Ginny laughed as she led them to the front door.

She reached up to release the lock and stopped abruptly, bending over and clutching her hand to her abdomen, crying out.

'Ginny?' Callie placed her hand in the small of her client's back and bent forward too. 'What's wrong?'

'I think my waters just broke,' she said, straightening a little and looking down.

Callie and Sebastian looked down too at the rapidly growing puddle on the polished floorboards.

'I think you may be right,' Sebastian agreed.

Ginny looked at them with wild eyes that quickly turned glassy. 'But…it's too early. Too early,' she said, clutching at her belly with one hand and tugging at Callie's sleeve with another.

'Nonsense,' Sebastian dismissed. 'You're nearly thirty-nine weeks. That's not early. Your little girl just can't wait to see her pink room.'

'What are we going to do?' Ginny wailed as tears spilled down her cheeks.

'We're going to take you to the hospital,' Callie stated matter-of-factly. The last thing they needed was for Ginny to become hysterical. 'Are you having contractions?'

Ginny thought about it for a second. 'No,' she sniffled, wiping at the tears. 'I don't think so.'

'Good. So we've got plenty of time. What did those books tell you about first labours?'

'That they go on for ages.'

Callie smiled. 'Okay, then. No need to panic. Let's get you organised. Have you got some things packed?'

Ginny nodded and pointed to the small overnight bag standing near the door. 'Right there.'

'Good. Perfect,' Callie said. Used to crises, Callie was an expert defuser of fraught situations. She knew that if she stayed calm that Ginny would also. 'Sebastian is going to stow it in our car. Then he's going to ring Brad and ask him to meet us at the hospital.'

'Check,' Sebastian said, smiling at Ginny, admiring Callie's unruffled composure.

'Brad.' Ginny's chin wobbled slightly.

'It'll be fine.' Callie patted Ginny's hand. 'He'll be at the hospital in a jiffy. We all will. Now, while Sebastian does his thing, we're going to get you changed and then we'll go, okay?'

Ginny sniffled. 'Okay.'

Ten minutes later Callie had helped Ginny into a fresh set of clothes and thrown some towels from the linen closet on the pool of fluid sitting in the hallway. Sebastian was waiting for them at the front door, holding it open.

Ginny made it halfway to the door when she stopped abruptly and screwed up her face.

'Contraction?' Callie asked.

Ginny bit her lip. 'Yeah.'

'That's fine. We'll wait till it passes.' She motioned to Sebastian to time it with his watch.

The contraction was long and painful and Callie rubbed Ginny's back as the mother-to-be panted. When it passed they started towards the door again but after two paces Ginny had to stop again.

They were nearly at the door when the third contraction hit and Ginny cried out, 'I need to push.'

'No!' Both Sebastian and Callie said it together. Callie had studied birth during her nursing training and seen a few babies being born—twenty years ago. But even she remembered that the urge to push was a sign of very advanced labour.

'Oh, God,' Ginny wailed, her eyes bulging in her head, reaching for both of them for support. 'The head, it's there, I can feel it. It's right there.'

Callie's heartbeat thundered in her ears at Ginny's calamitous statement. It was so urgent, so desperate that Callie didn't doubt the truth of it for a moment.

She glanced at Sebastian, who raised an eyebrow at her over Ginny's downcast head and sucked in a calming breath. 'Okay. No problem. Change of plan. Let's go into the lounge and see what's happening down there.'

'No, no,' Ginny wailed. 'We need to go to the hospital. I need Brad. The baby's coming now. It's coming now,' she sobbed.

'Ginny,' Sebastian said, his voice firm and calm, 'it's not safe to take you in the car. Callie's going to be with you and I'm ringing the ambulance. They'll be here pronto and will be able to get you to the hospital much quicker and more safely than we can. Then I'll ring Brad and let him know the change of plan. Just don't push, okay? Do not push. Do you understand?'

It worked, his voice carving through Ginny's rising hysteria. She nodded. 'Yes.'

'Come on,' Callie directed. 'Let's get you comfortable.'

They went left through an archway into the lounge room and Callie positioned Ginny on the couch. A brief examination revealed that Ginny was indeed right. The head was there, just starting to stretch the vaginal opening. Another contraction hit and Callie urged Ginny, 'Pant, pant, pant.'

Which she did—splendidly. Despite the overwhelming dictates of her body telling her to *push, push, push*. But at the end of it more head was revealed and Callie knew that the arrival of Ginny's baby girl was imminent.

Sebastian entered the room. 'Ambulance ETA is eight minutes,' he announced.

Callie looked at him. She didn't have to say a word for him to know that they probably didn't have eight minutes.

'What do you need?' he asked.

CHAPTER TEN

'I HAVE gloves in my handbag. A stack of clean towels from the linen cupboard in the hallway. Something from the nursery to wrap the baby in.'

'No, no, no,' Ginny moaned. 'I can pant. I promise I'll pant.'

'I know, Ginny,' Callie soothed, rubbing her palms up and down Ginny's arms as Sebastian left the room again. 'You're doing so well and the ambulance will be here soon but I don't know if they'll make it before the baby. I just want to be prepared.'

Sebastian was back in record time and despite the turmoil of the last few days, she'd never been more pleased to see him. She donned the gloves he gave her and placed several thicknesses of towels beneath Ginny, covering as much of the lounge as she could.

'Where do you want me?' he asked.

Callie nodded at the arm of the lounge. 'Slide in behind her, give her something solid to lean against.'

Personally, right now, she'd kill for that solid wall of muscle behind her too. Someone to lean on as the events unfolded. It was a strange sensation. She'd learned from an early age to be independent, to rely only on herself. To have his calm, commanding presence was a surprising windfall.

To actually want it was a miracle!

How would it be to have it for ever? Joined in marriage. To be able to rely on someone else for a change?

Sebastian positioned himself as requested, Ginny's back propped against his front, his hands resting against her sides, where the swell of her belly began, her arms linked over his, her elbows resting on his thighs.

Ginny shifted a little, her back aching, her body and mind restless. She looked at Callie. 'Have you delivered a baby before?'

'Nope.' Callie wished she could quantify that somehow to make her denial more palatable to a labouring woman.

Nope, but. Nope, but I've assisted at several. Or, nope, but it's a special-interest area for me and I'm really well read on the subject and up on all the latest practices.

Because the truth was her interest had been exactly zero. She'd never been interested in any of it. Not babies or the birth process or whether pink unicorns trumped yellow ducks.

Zack had come to her as a two-year-old; the mechanics of how he'd got there hadn't been something she'd had to worry about.

Ginny looked over her shoulder at Sebastian. 'Don't suppose you have either?'

Sebastian shook his head. 'Sorry.'

Ginny looked like she was about to lose it so Callie pulled back from her own thoughts and hastened to reassure her. 'Look, Ginny, these babies, these home deliveries you hear about on the news, they practically deliver themselves.'

'I don't want a bloody home birth,' she cried. 'I want to be in a hospital where there are doctors and nurses.

People who know what they're doing. And epidurals. I want drugs. Lots of drugs.'

Sebastian smiled over Ginny's head and winked at Callie. Callie was not amused. Witnessing labour at first hand like this, in an uncontrolled environment, she couldn't blame Ginny for wanting the security of obstetric professionals and some pharmaceutical back-up. She'd want nothing less for herself.

Callie sucked in a breath. No, no, no. This was *not* about her!

'I understand that,' Callie soothed. 'I know this isn't what you planned. But your body knows what to do, Ginny, it's already doing it. I'm just here to catch should it happen before the ambulance arrives.'

'No.' Ginny shook her head. 'I don't know what to do,' she wailed. 'It's too hard. I can't do it.'

'Yes, you can,' Sebastian assured her hastily. 'Your body is doing an amazing thing, Ginny, a truly won-drous thing. And Callie's right, a woman's body knows. It knows what to do.'

Callie glanced at him and knew the words were not for Ginny alone. His gaze captured hers for a moment, seared right to her core, and it was as if there was just the two of them there.

'Why is this happening to me?' Ginny's wailed demand broke the connection between them. 'I've done everything right, everything. I've read all the books, I've eaten all the right stuff, I've been diligent with my meds.' Her face crumpled. 'I haven't even done the ducks yet.'

Sebastian rubbed his hands up and down her arms. 'The ducks can wait,' he soothed.

But it got totally lost in Ginny's 'Oh, God, oh, God,

oh, God' as she dug her elbows into his thighs and braced for another contraction.

'Just try and breathe through it, Ginny,' Callie murmured as a little more of the head was exposed.

She tried not to think about what would happen if the baby got stuck or Ginny tore or if she haemorrhaged.

The ambulance was coming and Callie had faith that they'd be able to deal with any complications.

But mostly she tried not to think about the baby she was carrying inside her. And the man who'd put it there being calm and composed as his quads had two elbows ground into them and he mastered a situation that'd test most men's mettle.

Ginny gritted her teeth as she grabbed the backs of her thighs with her hands. 'It so…bloody…hard,' she grunted.

'I know, I know,' Sebastian urged. 'Keep panting. You're doing really well.'

Callie glanced at Sebastian. His eyes were downcast as he spoke to Ginny. Her head was tucked in under his chin and somehow, even with her enormous belly on display, she seemed tiny surrounded by him. His reassuring words, his solid presence and supreme calmness was utterly sexy.

He looked like he helped labouring women every day. At the moment he looked like he could leap tall buildings in a single bound.

Was this how he would be with her? When she went into labour?

He chose that moment to look at her and Callie swallowed. His clear green gaze was unwavering. He'd looked at her a thousand times. At home, at work, at play. Had stared straight into her eyes, nose to nose when they'd been joined as intimately as two people could possibly be joined. But she'd never felt it reach right down inside her. Not like now.

It was a gaze that was sure and gentle at the same time. It projected possession and truth. It was a gaze that told her he wasn't going anywhere. And he had all the time in the world.

Oh, help.

Ginny sagged back against Sebastian as the contraction passed, drawing Callie's attention back to the problem at hand. She looked down, knowing as if she'd been a midwife for the last twenty years that the head would deliver with the next one—this baby wanted out.

'It's coming, isn't it?' Ginny asked.

Callie looked up, trading a glance with Sebastian. Ginny's mood was all over the place at the moment. How would she react to the news? She wanted Ginny focused for the hardest part—not hysterical. He gave her an imperceptible nod and she didn't even question that he was on the same page as her.

She shifted her gaze slightly to Ginny and smiled. 'Yes, I think you're going to see your daughter very soon.'

Ginny nodded, twin tears trickled down her face as she choked on a sob. 'Brad's going to miss it. He so wanted to see his little girl come into the world. I wanted him to be the first face she saw. So they'd form an instant bond too. Fathers miss out on so much and I want her to know right from the get-go how much her daddy loves her.'

Ginny stopped for a moment, more tears threatening to spill. 'He wanted to cut the cord.'

Callie swallowed, touched by the longing in Ginny's husky voice. In the middle of everything, intense pain and overwhelming emotion, Ginny was thinking about her husband. About her baby.

So that was love.

'He might still make it,' Sebastian said gently. 'He wasn't that far away when I phoned him.'

'I hope so,' Ginny sniffled. 'He'll be devastated that he wasn't here for it.'

'Trust me,' Sebastian said. 'He'll just be pleased you and the baby are okay and that you've been in good hands.'

Ginny nodded. 'That's true. Imagine if you guys hadn't been here…' Ginny shivered. 'I would have been here all alone and…the baby… What if—?'

'But we are here,' Callie interrupted. Ginny's eyes had grown wider and her voice had picked up speed. There was no point in letting Ginny get carried away with what-ifs. 'And everything is going to be fine.'

Ginny gave a strained smile. 'I know. I know. I can't thank you enough.' She twisted her head round to look at Sebastian. 'You too, Seb.'

Sebastian grinned. 'Pleased to be of assistance.'

Ginny's return smile died almost before it even started. 'Oh, no.'

'Another one?' Sebastian asked.

Ginny nodded, turning back to face Callie. She grabbed Callie's gloved hand. 'Please tell me again that this is going to be fine.'

Callie gripped Ginny's hand hard. 'It. Will. Be. Fine.' She let go of the hand. 'Now, let's meet this little girl who's in such a hurry.'

Ginny's face screwed up as the contraction intensified. 'Oh, God,' she groaned, gripping the backs of her thighs.

The wail of a distant ambulance siren penetrated the

intense little circle. 'Hear that?' Sebastian said. He had
so much adrenaline in his system he didn't even feel
the pain as his quads were pulverised beneath Ginny's
elbows. 'The cavalry are almost here.'

Callie would have cheered out loud had she not been
totally focused on the action. Ginny's loud prolonged
bellow combined with the agitated trampling of her feet
against the lounge cushions heralded the fully crowned
head, which popped out completely in a matter of
seconds.

The sight took Callie's breath away. It was a miracle.
A beautiful, amazing miracle.

Ginny collapsed back against Sebastian with a loud
'Oof.' She sucked in a couple of gasping breaths, recovering from the mammoth effort. 'Is it out? Is it out?' she
asked frantically, reaching down to feel.

'Yes,' Callie said, watching as Ginny's hand ran over
the contours of her baby's head.

Ginny started to cry again and tears filled Callie's
eyes at the reverence of Ginny's touch.

The front door banged. 'Ginny?'

Ginny rallied instantly. 'He's here,' she said to no one
in particular. 'He made it! Brad? Brad! In the lounge.'

Brad strode into the room and threw himself down
beside the couch. 'Oh, my God,' he whispered as he
gazed down at his daughter's head. 'Are you okay?' he
asked, pressing kisses to Ginny's face.

Ginny half laughed, half choked on a sob. 'I'm better
now.'

Callie averted her gaze from what should have been a
private moment between a husband and wife sharing one
of the most intimate things it was possible to share.

She clicked back into nurse mode, only vaguely hearing Sebastian, Brad and Ginny's voices. The baby's head

was out. The shoulders came next. But what did she do while they waited for the next contraction?

Suction.

In the couple of births she'd witnessed they'd immediately suctioned the nostrils while the baby had still been in the birth canal.

Hmm. Well, that wasn't going to happen. Callie took a calming breath. While she'd kill for a portable suction unit right now, that just wasn't possible. But the siren was louder now. Closer. The ambulance would have one for sure.

Next.

What was next? Think, think, think.

Cord. Check for the cord.

With her heart rate rocketing and no idea what she was doing, she inserted a finger, feeling for the neck. When it came into contact with something rope-like she almost had a heart attack.

No, no, no.

Her head snapped up, her gaze colliding with Sebastian's. 'What?' he mouthed.

'Cord,' she mouthed back.

Sebastian felt his shoulders tense and his own pulse kick up a notch at the panic in Callie's eyes. Her gaze was wild and she was chewing on her bottom lip. She needed to stay calm.

'You'll be fine,' he said, pleased that Ginny and Brad were too wrapped up in each other to be paying attention.

Would she? Callie felt frozen for a second. She was a mental health nurse, not a midwife. Or a magician. She sucked in a calming breath. She'd seen a delivery that had involved the cord being wrapped around the neck.

The midwife had very calmly slipped the cord over the baby's head before the shoulders were delivered.

She looked at Sebastian and he gave her another encouraging nod, shaken by his level of confidence in her. With her heartbeat sounding almost as loud in her ears as the nearby squealing siren she took a deep breath and with a trembling hand she felt for the cord again, running her finger along it.

It appeared to be wrapped only once and didn't seem to be too tight. She manoeuvred her finger under it and slowly worked it loose enough to pull it up and over the baby's head. She closed her eyes briefly as the success of the procedure sank in.

She opened them again, her gaze colliding with Sebastian's. His smile lifted her heart and she smiled back.

'Okay, Ginny, let's not wait till the next contraction.' Callie had no idea if the baby would be compromised because of the cord problem but she didn't want to delay in case. 'Let's get this baby out, okay?'

'I can push?' she asked.

Callie nodded. 'With all your might.'

Ginny looked at Brad. He kissed her head. 'Hold my hand, babe, you can do this.'

So with Sebastian supporting her from behind and Brad holding her hand, Ginny's shut her eyes, screwed up her face and bore down, bellowing loudly as the baby was completely expelled from her body in one smooth, slippery movement.

Ginny was crying as she slumped back against Sebastian. Brad was pressing kisses to her temple, saying, 'You did it, you did it.'

Callie's heart thumped madly as she held the blinking newborn in her hands. The baby girl was the most beautiful thing she'd ever seen and an emotion she'd never known before bloomed in her chest. A giant mushroom cloud welling up and up and up. Making it hard to breath. Hard to move.

She knew in that instant that she would love and protect the fragile life inside of her for ever. She glanced at Sebastian. Just as she would love the man who had given her such a precious gift.

'Why isn't she crying?' Ginny asked. 'Callie, what's wrong?'

Callie dragged herself back from the overwhelming emotion of the moment as the siren was switched off and vehicle doors could be heard slamming.

'N-nothing,' she said, reaching for one of the bunny rugs Sebastian had given her earlier. 'She's just a little stunned, that's all,' she murmured, rubbing the towel vigorously over the baby's face, pinching her nostrils hard and sweeping downwards to clear any mucus.

She rubbed the fabric briskly over the baby's torso and blew on her face, just as she'd seen a midwife do all those years ago. A long, sharp, angry cry pierced the air just as the paramedics tramped up the steps and Callie passed Ginny's bawling daughter, umbilical cord still attached, up to her.

It was the sweetest thing Callie had ever witnessed. A mother and father meeting their child for the first time. There was a reverence in their movements as they gazed at the newborn, who'd hushed as if instinctively knowing that these two people were important.

A tiny fist waved in the air and the profound wonder on Ginny and Brad's faces was humbling. It was as if neither of them could believe they'd actually created this amazing complete miniature human being.

She glanced at Sebastian, who had eyes only for her.

'You did it,' he mouthed, and Callie choked back the thick clog of emotion lodged in her throat.

'She has your eyes,' Brad murmured, stroking his daughter's cheeks as the paramedics entered the room.

'Well, well, well,' the first one said. 'Looks like someone was in a hurry to be born.'

And then it was action stations as the paramedics took over. Sebastian slipped out from behind Ginny and Callie relinquished her post, and they stood watching the proceedings. One of paramedics double-clamped the cord and let Brad cut between the clamps, and the other slipped a saturation probe onto Ginny's finger and took her blood pressure.

Neither Callie nor Sebastian said anything to the other but Callie was hyper-aware of him. His biceps occasionally brushed hers, the feather-like touch coursing electricity through her entire body until it was practically humming. And his male scent blasted towards her on the waves of heat radiating from his body, intoxicating her already elevated mood further.

How had it taken her so long to figure out what was now patently obvious? Had determination alone so blunted her to the possibility of falling in love that she hadn't even recognised it when it had slapped her in the face?

She could pinpoint the exact moment it had happened. That night in the restaurant. Facing down a superior yuppie to champion a homeless man.

Her hero.

No wonder she'd gone home with him.

Although maybe it had happened even before that. Earlier that day, on the bridge. There had been an unmistakable connection as they'd clashed. An instant awareness of him that she'd never had with another man. It had been easy to dismiss as irritation given his steely resolve that day but maybe, even then, deep down she'd known something in her gut.

The baby protested as it was taken from Ginny to be snugly wrapped by one paramedic as the other expertly sited an intravenous cannula in the back of Ginny's hand.

Callie slipped her hand over her abdomen. Deep inside her, beneath her palm, her own baby grew.

Their baby grew.

Another, more intimate connection with Sebastian.

And her love for him intensified again. She'd only been aware of it for the last ten minutes but just like that it had doubled...trebled.

She'd been so busy pretending they were having an adult relationship that didn't need romantic, messy things like love and happily-ever-afters to define it that she hadn't realised she'd gone and fallen in love anyway.

Deep, foolish, messy love.

'Okay, let's rock and roll,' the paramedic said as they helped Ginny onto the trolley and strapped her in. Brad passed the swaddled baby to Ginny and she took the bundle as if she'd just been handed the secret to eternal life and the Holy Grail combined.

'What are you going to call her?' the paramedic asked.

Ginny looked at Sebastian and Callie. 'Well, I think after all that's happened we're going to have to name her after our impromptu midwives, Seb and Callie.' Her gaze switched to her husband and she held out her free hand to him. 'What do you think about Sallie?'

Brad took her hand and smiled. 'I think that's really pretty.'

Ginny smiled. 'Sallie it is. Is that okay with you guys?'

Callie nodded because the lump in her throat had also trebled and she didn't think she could speak without bursting into tears. Sebastian grinned. 'It's perfect,' he said.

'Congratulations, you two,' the paramedic said as he slapped Sebastian on the back. 'You've just been immortalised.'

Sebastian chuckled. 'We'll try not to let it go to our heads.'

'Rightio, let's shake a leg.'

Callie and Sebastian followed the procession to the front door. 'Would you mind locking up?' Brad asked, absently handing his keys over, eyes only for his wife and daughter.

Sebastian took them. 'Of course. Go, don't worry about it. We'll bring the keys up in a bit once your girls are settled.'

Brad looked at Sebastian then at Callie. 'My girls...' He shook his head. 'I'm a father,' he said, his voice full of wonder and pride.

Callie smiled. Both Ginny and Brad were sporting that strange mix of exhaustion, astonishment and elation, like they were the only two people in the world to have ever performed such an amazing feat.

'Go,' she urged as Ginny and the baby were loaded into the back of the ambulance.

Brad didn't need any further encouragement and Callie and Sebastian watched as he practically ran to the waiting ambulance.

Sebastian laughed. 'That is one proud daddy.'

Callie smiled. 'I'm so happy for them.'

The paramedic shut the back door and Callie turned

to go back inside, her gaze falling to where the neatly packed hospital bag had been before.

'Sebastian,' she said urgently. 'The bag. It's in our car. She'll need it.'

Sebastian nodded and took the stairs two at a time. Callie laughed at him this time, her heart overflowing with love and all the beautiful things she had witnessed today.

She could hear her phone ringing from inside the house and she dashed into the lounge room to get it but it rang out just as she picked it up. It was Geraldine's number. Callie threw the phone back into her bag—she'd ring her boss in a bit.

The couch area looked like a war zone and Callie set about picking up the packaging the paramedics had left strewn around. Donning another pair of gloves, she gathered the soiled linen. She could hear the low rumbling idle of the ambulance and saw Sebastian chatting to one of the paramedics through the window.

She picked up the towels in the hallway as well and made her way quickly to the laundry. Now the excitement was over she was nervous and activity gave her something else to do other than think about Sebastian and his wild promises from earlier today.

And the baby.

Callie threw the towels into the washing machine, added soap powder she found in a cupboard and started the washing cycle. She made a mental note to remind herself to let Brad know that the towels would be waiting for him when he got home.

After that was done she gathered the linen that hadn't been used and put it back in the linen cupboard. One item remained. A soft baby-pink muslin wrap. Callie looked down towards the end of the hall to where the pink glow beckoned.

She turned towards it, the wrap clutched to her chest, her feet not under her conscious control. A mere hour ago she'd wanted to flee the nursery so badly she'd practically run from it when she'd had the chance. But now it called to her.

Like a homing beacon.

She reached the doorway and hesitated for a moment before tiptoeing into the middle of the room. It was so… pink. Yet what had seemed too much an hour ago suddenly seemed just right. The perfect room for a perfect baby girl. Even the pink unicorns didn't seem over-the-top now.

Callie lifted the muslin to her face and inhaled deeply. The soap and powder smell was intoxicating and she dragged in another enormous lungful of pure baby essence.

'Smells good, doesn't it?'

Callie startled, dropping the wrap as she whirled to face the door. 'Sorry, I didn't hear you.'

He crossed to her and bent to pick it up. He put it to his own nose and sucked in his own lungful before handing it back to her. 'It's been a big day,' he murmured.

Callie turned back to face the cot. All during Ginny's labour she'd deliberately tried not to think about the baby. Their baby. But standing in this pink room, next to this man, looking at the cot, it was impossible not to.

Sebastian watched as Callie's hand fell to her belly, the fingers spreading down low. He moved closer until he was standing behind her. 'Are you thinking about the baby?'

Callie dragged in a breath. It would be easy to play

dumb and pretend that Sebastian was talking about Sallie but they both knew what he meant.

Callie nodded. 'I think she's going to be tall.'

Sebastian, who had been holding his breath, let it hiss out. 'She?'

Callie pressed her hand against her belly harder. 'I know it's strange but somehow I just know it's a girl.'

Sebastian's heart thumped so loudly he felt sure that Callie must be able to hear it. He didn't move; he barely breathed, for fear that Callie might scare. 'I'd love a little girl,' he said quietly. 'She'll have your amber eyes.'

Callie swallowed and swayed. It was easy to lean against him, the emotion of the day combining with the baby fragrance to cocoon them both. 'And your gorgeous hair,' she whispered.

Sebastian shut his eyes as her body settled against his, lightly at first and then with more confidence. His heart thumped hard against his ribcage—surely she could feel it against her back?

'I thought…' Sebastian didn't know what he'd thought. He hadn't dared hope. His fingers itched to slide around her waist. He could see down her front to where her hand absently caressed her belly and he wanted to join his hand with hers, cover their baby together. 'What happened today?'

Callie heard the roughness, the uncertainty in his voice. She smiled. 'We delivered a baby.'

Sebastian tensed, opening his eyes as her closeness had a predictable effect. Pinned close like this, he wanted her very badly but he wanted all of her, not just the bits she was prepared to give.

There was so much at stake.

'Yes, we did,' he said cautiously.

Callie felt his heat seep into her back. His fragrance

joined the baby powder aroma to make a potent, irresistible mix. 'And I fell in love.'

Sebastian was mesmerised by the slow stroke of her fingers against her abdomen. 'With our baby?' he asked.

Callie nodded. 'And you.'

Sebastian didn't move for a moment. He didn't think. He didn't speak. He didn't breathe. It seemed like an age before he released the pent-up breath on a slow husky exhalation.

Even then it was a while before bodily function returned. 'May I?' He moved his hand tentatively around her waist.

Callie lifted her hand eagerly, bringing his around, pressing it low down against her belly and covering it with her own. 'We won't be able to feel anything for ages,' she murmured.

Sebastian tightened his hand for a moment as a massive surge of emotion took hold. Earlier in the day, driving with her in the car, he'd known he loved her in his bones. Known it automatically. In that logical male way.

But standing here with her now, their baby living and growing beneath his hand, it was more than knowing. It swelled in his heart and bloomed in his chest.

Now he *felt* it.

'I love you,' he whispered, dropping a kiss in her hair.

Callie felt an answering well of emotion as tears pricked her eyes. 'Are we being crazy? Is this just about the baby?'

Sebastian shook his head vehemently. 'No. Absolutely not. It was the bridge for me. You were so damn pushy.' He smiled and dropped a kiss on her temple. 'I know hardened criminals that wouldn't have dared speak to me the way you did. But you were so...ballsy. I'm just sorry it took me so long to figure out.'

Callie smiled. She had been pretty annoyed that day. 'It was the restaurant for me. The homeless man. It was such an ugly scene and you were so...heroic that night. But I guess I just wasn't wired to think like a normal woman. I was comfortable with being on my own. It never occurred to me that I'd find my one...my soul mate so late in life. It was easier just to think of you as a sexual attraction thing.'

Sebastian grinned. 'Hey, no complaints from me.' He turned her, kissing her forehead, her eyes, her nose and finally her mouth. 'And just think,' he murmured against her mouth, 'we wouldn't have our little girl if you hadn't ruthlessly exploited the sexual attraction thing.'

He pulled away from her slightly, his hand returning to cradle her stomach again.

Callie swallowed at the sight. His big hand gentle against her. 'I think actually, deep down, that was the main reason I avoided getting involved in relationships. Because I knew that eventually I'd want the whole shebang. A wedding ring, suburbia, a white picket fence and babies.'

She looked at him, his face so concentrated on their baby it took her breath away. 'And I couldn't disregard my family legacy. My mother being bipolar, Andy's schizophrenia... How could I expose a tiny baby to all that potential?'

Sebastian returned his gaze to her. 'Does it still worry you?'

The thought tore at her heart. She would never want a child of hers to go through the rigours of mental ill-ness. 'Of course,' she whispered. 'Looking after Zack all those years, worrying if he's got more than his father's athletic ability...it frightens the hell out of me.'

Sebastian's hands crept to her face, cupping her jaw, his thumbs stroking the hollows beside her mouth. 'Don't,' he murmured. 'We wipe the slate clean. You and I.'

'But what if—?'

'Shh.' Sebastian placed a thumb against her lips. 'There are no guarantees in life, Callie. You and I both know this child could get any number of horrible ill-nesses. So could we. But we can't live our lives like that—in constant fear. We just love our kids and we love each other and we hope like crazy it all works out. And no matter what, we'll deal with whatever life throws us.'

Callie's hands came up to grasp Sebastian's wrists. He was right, of course he was. Life was for living—they both knew that, probably better than most. 'I love you,' she whispered.

Sebastian smiled, using his thumbs to tilt her jaw back. 'I don't think I'm ever going to tire of hearing you say that.'

'Good,' she murmured, ''cos I'm not ever going to tire of telling you.'

Sebastian dropped a kiss on her upturned mouth. And then another. And another, until they melded into one and they were clinging to each other and their harsh breathing and low moans were the only sounds in the room.

'Just promise me one thing,' he said, pulling away while he could still think coherently.

Callie sucked in a breath, her head spinning from the kiss. 'Anything.'

He looked around. 'Can we not have a nursery quite this pink?'

Callie laughed. 'Actually, it's kind of grown on me.'

Sebastian groaned. 'Well, can we at least have yellow ducks?'

She nodded. 'It's a deal.'

And sealed it with a kiss.

NAVY OFFICER
TO FAMILY MAN

BY
EMILY FORBES

MILLS &
BOON

All the characters in this book have no existence outside the imagination
of the author, and have no relation whatsoever to anyone bearing the
same name or names. They are not even distantly inspired by any
individual known or unknown to the author, and all the incidents are
pure invention.

First published in Great Britain 2011
Harlequin Mills & Boon Limited,
Eton House, 18-24 Paradise Road, Richmond, Surrey TW9 1SR

© Emily Forbes 2011

ISBN: 978 0 263 88573 6

Harlequin Mills & Boon policy is to use papers that are natural,
renewable and recyclable products and made from wood grown in
sustainable forests. The logging and manufacturing process conform
to the legal environmental regulations of the country of origin.

Printed and bound in Spain
by Litografia Rosés, S.A., Barcelona

Dear Reader

This book is my fourth linked tale—I seem to be developing a habit! You might recognise my heroine Juliet from my last book, DR DROP-DEAD GORGEOUS. She was the heroine's sister, but she was having her own interesting experiences and was demanding that I tell her story too. I have never started a book knowing it's going to be the first in a series, but somewhere along the way my secondary characters develop to a point where I can't abandon them. So it was with Juliet.

She has had a rough eighteen months. A divorce, surgery and chemotherapy have taken their toll on her, and now she's a single mother to two young children and about to undergo more surgery. Juliet would love to turn the clock back a few years—wouldn't all thirty-something women?—but she knows that's impossible, and she's just hoping for a brighter future. I wanted Juliet to have that bright future, I wanted her to be happy, but the trouble was I'd already divorced her from the love of her life. Could I help her to find love a second time, or had her luck expired? Answering that question became my goal.

Juliet and Maggie are the second pair of sisters I've written about. That is no surprise to me, because I am lucky enough to share a close bond with all my siblings, including two sisters, and I enjoy giving life to characters who share that same relationship. It's a fabulous thing to have a person in your life who loves you unconditionally, and I hope that everyone reading this has someone—be it a sister, friend, daughter, cousin or mother—you know will catch you if you fall or will let you catch them. This story is for all the women of the world.

Best wishes

Emily

Emily Forbes began her writing life as a partnership between two sisters who are both passionate bibliophiles. As a team Emily had ten books published, and one of her proudest moments was when her tenth book was nominated for the 2010 Australian Romantic Book of the Year Award.

While Emily's love of writing remains as strong as ever, the demands of life with young families has recently made it difficult to work on stories together—but rather than give up her dream Emily now writes solo. The challenges may be different, but the reward of having a book published is still as sweet as ever.

Whether as a team or as an individual, Emily hopes to keep bringing stories to her readers. Her inspiration comes from everywhere: stories she hears while travelling, at mothers' lunches, in the media, and in her other career as a physiotherapist all get embellished with a large dose of imagination until they develop a life of their own.

If you would like to get in touch with Emily you can e-mail her at emilyforbes@internode.on.net, and she can also be found blogging at the Harlequin Medical™ Romance blog—www.eharlequin.com

Recent titles by the same author:

DR DROP-DEAD GORGEOUS
THE PLAYBOY FIREFIGHTER'S PROPOSAL
WEDDING AT PELICAN BEACH

Dedication

This book is dedicated to two women without whom this book would still be just an idea in my head. Belinda, my sister, and my editor Lucy

CHAPTER ONE

JULIET entered the courthouse, passing through the security screening area and into the foyer. Her unfamiliar heels clicked on the marble floor, echoing in the space, as she strode towards the notice-board on the opposite side of the atrium. She rarely wore heels any more, not since she'd given up a career in law for a career as a university lecturer, but she knew adopting a power-dressing approach would give her some much-needed confidence today. She'd deliberately chosen one of her old suits—she'd barely worn it and hoped it still passed inspection—and she'd teamed it with the confidence-boosting heels. At five feet two inches she needed all the help she could get in the height department and a couple of extra inches immediately improved her self-assurance.

She checked the list of the day's cases pinned to the board, looking for her name and case number. She found it, about a third of the way down. Today she was nobody special, just another number. She headed for courtroom number three, making her way towards the waiting area.

The waiting annexe was sombre, dull and outdated, depressing. Gone was the imposing decor of the entrance foyer, the marble floor and chandeliers giving way to stained carpets, fake wood wall-panelling and a mismatched collection of chairs, some plastic, some scratched timber and some with faded upholstery. She wasn't inclined to sit down.

Juliet knew she was being ridiculous with her silent criticism; the dull room was perfectly suited to her mood, but she wasn't used to feeling depressed and she wanted the room to lift her spirits, not contribute to the feeling of finality. She wanted the room to instil in her a sense that she was doing the right thing but all it was doing was making her feel worse. It exacerbated her loneliness and increased her sorrow.

But there was no turning back, despite her sister's parting words as she'd dropped her off at the courthouse earlier. Juliet had come this far and she wasn't changing her mind now. There had been times where she could have backed down, where she could have stopped this day from coming, but not now. Not any more. The decision had been made.

Juliet had always been stubborn and that hadn't changed. She sighed and chose a seat on the right-hand side of the room. While she sat waiting for her case number to be called she looked at the other people scattered around the room. Mostly they looked tired and worn out and their demeanour did nothing for her mood either. All of them were in everyday clothing, none of them had bothered to smarten up their attire, and the contrast between their outfits and hers flattened her confidence a little.

The weak winter sunlight struggled to penetrate the grimy windows, the glass surfaces were smeared with dirt, too high up to be easily cleaned and it looked as though no one had bothered for years. Juliet was watching the floating dust motes as they wafted through the sporadic beams of light, pushed about by the invisible breaths of air as people moved about the room. A large gust of air disturbed the dust as someone pushed open the door and the movement drew Juliet's attention. A stray shaft of sunlight illuminated a man as he entered the room, tall, smartly dressed and familiar.

It was Sam.

The love of her life. Her husband.

Soon to be her ex-husband.

But circumstances weren't enough to stop the tingle that surged through her every time she saw him. In her eyes he still looked as good as the day she'd met him.

He paused just inside the doorway and Juliet took a moment to admire him, knowing she didn't have long before he would find her in the small room. He was wearing his white naval officer's uniform, the crisp, clean colour even more eye-catching against the dirty, dull tones of the room. But, then, she'd always been a sucker for Sam in his dress uniform.

He was tanned from his time spent on the ocean and in the sun, his olive skin contrasting with the white fabric of his clothing. His thick blond hair was slightly longer than usual, long enough to be showing a little of its natural curl as it brushed the nape of his neck.

His eyes scanned the room and settled on her. He moved towards her, smiling his crooked smile. She'd never been able to resist his smile. It started on the right side of his mouth, that corner always lifted first, before the smile spread across his lips, revealing a row of perfect, white teeth, until it reached the left corner, by which time Juliet always found she was smiling too. Even now his smile was working, lifting the sombre mood, lifting her spirits, if only temporarily.

In a few steps Sam had reached her side. He sat beside

her on an upright wooden chair and leant across to kiss her cheek.

'How are you?' he asked. His voice sounded calm and controlled, completely the opposite to how she felt. She was apprehensive and nervous, plus she'd been unable to sleep soundly for several nights and now she was exhausted. But she told him none of this.

'Good,' was her reply. 'And you?' She sounded so polite, almost as though she was talking to a stranger, not to someone who had shared her bed for a third of her life.

Up close she could see that Sam had a few more wrinkles at the corners of his green eyes and a few strands of grey in his blond hair. Neither detracted from his looks. He was still a handsome man and Juliet imagined he would always be. He would age well, she thought. She wondered how they looked to the other people in the room. What did they think she and Sam were there for? Would anyone guess they were about to get divorced? Would anyone else care?

'How long until it's our turn?' His voice interrupted her thoughts. If he had any trace of concern he was hiding it well, sounding relaxed and completely unfazed by the situation. She could imagine him in a crisis on board a naval vessel, directing sailors, getting people to do what he wanted without having to yell. Nothing much ever seemed to rattle him and it looked as though today was no exception.

'I'm not sure,' she answered. 'I think there are still a couple of cases before us.'

She felt Sam's arm brush against hers and the contact made her look down. He was pinching the crease in his trouser leg, a crease she could see was ironed to within a fraction of perfection. Juliet could see the outline of the muscles in Sam's thigh straining against the fabric. His leg was too close to hers, making her feel an unfamiliar sense of unease. He was too close. She wished he'd left a seat between them, kept some distance, then maybe she would have been able to calm her nerves.

Sam looked fit, healthy and full of life. A huge contrast to the rest of the crowd and probably a huge contrast to her. She felt tired, a feeling she was getting used to and had attributed to life as a single mother. Sam, on the other hand, looked as energetic as the day they'd met. Thirteen years ago.

She kept her gaze focussed on her lap. She didn't want to look at Sam, couldn't face seeing him there. All it did was remind her of everything she was losing.

How had they come to this?

Her sister Maggie had suggested that she could still stop this process but Juliet felt they'd tried everything they could and still they were in front of the magistrate. She'd tried, they both had, but in the end they'd run out of options. A marriage couldn't work without compromise.

Her hands were shaking. She grabbed her handbag from the chair beside her, pulling it onto her lap, holding it firmly in an attempt to stop the shaking. Her engagement ring caught the light, shooting sparks over the floor in front of her, small bright spots glistening in the dirt. She hadn't removed her rings as in her mind she was still married. For a little longer anyway. She sneaked a sideways glance at Sam's hands. He still wore his wedding ring too.

'How are the kids?' Despite Juliet's less than enthusiastic responses, Sam continued to attempt to make conversation and Juliet thought she'd better make an effort to hold up her end.

'Fine,' she answered honestly. 'They're doing fine.' It was true too, but, then, they were used to their father being absent for long periods of time. Even when he had lived with them he could spend months at sea. They thought it was normal.

Juliet hadn't wanted it to be their normal circumstances. She'd wanted them to have a father who was around. She and Sam had planned for that to happen but their efforts had failed. She'd failed. And now the kids would have a father who was more absent than ever. She wondered if they'd forgive her when they were older and realised what they'd missed out on.

Would they forgive Sam for putting the navy first or would they blame her for not compromising?

Would they realise their father could have compromised too or would they take his view and agree that he'd been asked to make sacrifices, not compromises?

'Is it okay if I take them out for dinner tonight? I'm only on leave until tomorrow.' Sam's question interrupted her musings.

'You've only got twenty-four hours?' Sam nodded. 'Why did you come?' Juliet asked. 'You didn't have to, you know. We don't have to be here in person.'

'I know. But I wasn't going to pass up my last opportunity to see my wife.'

'What do you mean?'

Sam turned slightly on his chair so he was facing her more directly. 'This is it, Jules. We're getting divorced. Next time I see you you'll be my ex-wife, and I know I've missed a lot of things in all the years we've been together but I'm not about to let our marriage end in my absence.'

She wanted to stamp her feet and yell and scream. If only Sam had been prepared to make more of an effort to participate when they had been married, perhaps it wouldn't have come to this.

'So, can I take the kids or do you have plans?'

Juliet wanted to say, no, he couldn't take the kids. She wanted to make it difficult. She wanted to remind Sam that it was his choice to be a part-time father but she knew that would achieve nothing.

'We don't have plans. They'd love to go with you.' And they would. There was no reason for them not to spend time with their father. She wasn't going to become one of those single mothers who denied children time with their father out of spite. She wasn't spiteful and she was to blame for this situation as much as Sam. They'd both been too stubborn to back down. That's what had brought them here.

'Taylor versus Taylor.' The bailiff called their case.

Sam and Juliet stood and followed the bailiff into the courtroom to stand before the magistrate.

The courtroom was in marginally better condition than the waiting area but still small and unimpressive. Juliet wasn't sure what she'd expected but something a bit grander, a bit more official in appearance would have suited the occasion better in her opinion. If it weren't for the raised bench where the magistrate was sitting, one could be forgiven for thinking they were in a school classroom circa 1980. At least the magistrate in her robes lent some formality to the occasion but the room itself was far from grand and in Juliet's opinion it was diminishing the event. Not that she wanted the event celebrated but she wanted to be able to look back on their twelve-year marriage with positive thoughts and this sombre, dull, drab room was taking the gloss off those years.

The magistrate nodded at them before saying, 'State your names, please.'

Juliet opened her mouth to speak but no words came out. She heard Sam's rich voice beside her—'Samuel Edward Taylor'—and that gave her the courage to state her own name, although her voice quivered with nerves. 'Juliet Ann Taylor.'

'You're filing for divorce?'

'Yes, Your Honour.' To Juliet's relief, Sam answered. She'd done about as much talking as she was capable of. Her knees were weak and she wasn't sure how long she'd be able to hold herself up. Her palms were sweaty and her mouth was dry.

'It says in your petition there are two minors. Have satisfactory custody arrangements been made for the children?' the magistrate asked.

'Yes, Your Honour.' Sam repeated his words.

'All right. Your application is granted. Your divorce becomes absolute one month and one day from now and the paperwork will be posted to you. Next case.'

That's it? Juliet was dumbfounded. Twelve years of marriage, dissolved in fewer than one hundred words. Sam turned and started walking away from the magistrate. Juliet followed him, feeling completely disoriented.

Sam walked the length of the courtroom and kept walking until he'd passed through the waiting chamber and into the corridor. Only then did he stop and turn to her.

'Is it always that quick?' he asked.

'I don't know,' she said. 'It's the first time I've got divorced.'

Sam smiled and her stomach trembled in response. 'I thought she'd ask a few more questions.'

Juliet shrugged. Now that she thought about it there wasn't any reason for discussion with the magistrate. 'She's not a counsellor. As far as she's concerned, as long as we've filled in the application properly and made arrangements for the kids, she doesn't care. We're not contesting anything. She was probably glad to have a straightforward case.' She was irritated with herself over her reaction to Sam's smile and her annoyance had made her respond abruptly. But it wasn't Sam's fault she still found him attractive and she attempted to tone down her snappiness. 'But I know what you mean. It doesn't feel real, does it?'

'I guess it won't until we get the paperwork,' he replied.

Juliet didn't believe that would make any difference. So much of their day-to-day life would remain unchanged, continuing as it had for the past year, if not longer. She'd missed Sam when they'd been married and she expected to still miss him. She didn't expect much to change. The children would probably see just as much of him as they always had but she'd wanted him around more. That was what had started this whole process but now all that would change was that he wouldn't be coming home to her.

She knew that, at least initially, she'd be the only one who'd feel like something was missing. Sam had his career, his whole other life, and the children were still young enough to be oblivious to all the grown-up worries surrounding them. It was fair to say that Juliet didn't feel as though this situation had turned out quite as she'd planned.

Sam started walking, heading for the main foyer and the exit. 'Do you need a lift? I'm going to grab a taxi to the hotel.'

'No, thank you. Maggie will pick me up, I just need to call her.'

He stopped and turned to her. 'I'm sorry, Jules. Sorry it's come to this.' He leant down and placed his hand on her forearm as he kissed her on the cheek. His hand and lips were warm and her skin burned where he touched her. 'I'll see you around five-thirty when I pick up the kids.'

Juliet nodded, the lump in her throat preventing her from talking.

Sam left her then. Left her standing in the foyer, alone. Juliet watched him go and only once he was out of sight did she let her composure slip. She collapsed onto a nearby bench and let all the day's emotions pour out of her in a torrent of silent tears. She'd felt close to tears all day but she'd refused to let anyone see her cry. Not the children, not her sister, and especially not Sam. She searched her handbag for the packet of tissues she knew was in there as she wondered what had happened to their dreams, their plans for the future. But she knew what had happened. Sam had changed the rules and she had gambled and lost. She'd have to learn to live with that.

CHAPTER TWO

'DAD's here, Dad's here.'

Juliet could hear Edward yelling. He'd been sitting at the front window since five o'clock, waiting for Sam to arrive—he'd never sat still for that long in his life. Now Sam was here and Edward was running around the house like a maniac. Thirty minutes of inactivity was obviously far too long for a five-year-old boy!

Juliet answered Sam's knock at the door. He'd changed out of his uniform and was now wearing jeans and a pale green polo shirt. Juliet didn't recognise the shirt and she wondered when he'd bought it. Sam never shopped, he spent so much time in a uniform he said he didn't need many civvies so Juliet had always bought his clothes for him. Who was choosing them for him now? The shade of green was a perfect foil for Sam's tanned skin and highlighted his green eyes. Juliet couldn't imagine Sam choosing the shirt deliberately so he either got lucky with the colour or someone else bought it for him. It wasn't her business any more but she couldn't stop the flash of jealousy that raced through her.

She stepped back to invite Sam in just as Edward hurtled past her, launching himself at Sam like a little blond rocket. Sam caught him easily, scooping him up against his broad chest and carrying him inside. Juliet had been wondering whether or not to greet Sam with a kiss on the cheek but Edward's body formed a wall between them, taking that option out of the equation. Had they just set a precedent for all future greetings?

'Where's your sister?' Sam asked Edward.

'Dunno.'

'She's in her room,' Juliet replied, and Sam veered right, carrying Ed into Kate's room.

'Here's my gorgeous girl—are you ready for dinner?'

Juliet followed behind them, stopping in the doorway. Kate was still getting ready—aged eight, she already spent more time in front of the mirror than Juliet did. She was sliding a clip into her brown hair and Juliet smiled, Kate had been doing her hair for the last ten minutes, trying out different styles with varying accessories—clips, headbands and bows—but Sam's arrival seemed to have sped up the process. Kate finished her hair and grabbed her swing coat before crossing the room to greet her father with a hug and a kiss.

'Where are we going?' Edward asked.

'Sofia's.'

Juliet's throat was tight and hot tears stung her eyes. Eating at Sofia's Italian restaurant was a family tradition and it hurt to find that the tradition was going to continue without her. She blinked back tears, desperate to stop them from spilling over onto her cheeks. She couldn't believe she was still so wound up, she would have thought she'd cried enough earlier in the day to last her a while.

'Yay! Can I have *gelati*?'

Sam laughed and punched Edward lightly on the arm, immediately starting a play fight. 'Spaghetti first and then *gelati*.'

Juliet let Edward wrestle his father for a minute before

calling a stop to the physical stuff. 'Okay, enough, guys,' she said. 'Time for dinner.'

'Your mum's right, champ,' Sam said as Edward started to complain that their game had been halted prematurely. 'The taxi's waiting.'

Juliet hadn't considered how Sam had got to their house but as she herded them through the front door and into the driveway she saw a cab parked behind her car. 'You can take my car if that's easier. I don't need it.'

'Aren't you coming with us?' Kate picked up on Juliet's wording.

'No, darling, this is Dad's treat.'

Sam stopped, extending her an invitation. 'You're welcome to join us, Jules.'

'Thanks, but there's some stuff I want to do here. Let me get the car keys.' She turned away from Sam, not wanting him to see the lie on her face. She grabbed her keys from the hall table and returned to find Sam had sent the taxi off. She handed him the keys and kissed her children goodbye. She watched them climb into her car and waited as they waved to her before they disappeared down the street.

She turned, picking up a stray football that was lying in the front garden, and took it inside with her, the vision of Edward's fair head stuck in her mind. He was the spitting image of Sam to look at, a little ball of muscle. They were both bundles of energy and Ed was already mad about ball sports, although, living in Melbourne, he preferred Aussie rules football over Sam's choice of rugby union.

Juliet had grown up in Sydney where rugby was the main winter sport, and although she hadn't been a huge fan she now had a soft spot for rugby as that was how she'd first met Sam. She moved through the house, tidying up bits and pieces as she let her mind wander.

She was still finding it difficult to reconcile herself with the idea that Sam was no longer her husband. He would always be part of her life, connected to her through their children, and she needed to work out how they were going to deal with that. After twelve years of marriage she couldn't expect to accept that it was over without some regrets but she knew she had to get past that.

The house was quiet, too quiet, but she had to be prepared to be alone. She wasn't exactly looking forward to having the house to herself but she thought the solitude might at least give her a chance to make some sense of the day.

In some respects twelve years seemed to have passed in the blink of an eye. Mostly, if it weren't for the changes she saw in her children and for the strands of grey appearing in her dark hair, changes that made it hard to ignore the passage of time, she wouldn't believe she was nearer forty than thirty.

Other days she felt all of her thirty-six years. Today was one of those days. She felt tired, physically and mentally. She wasn't surprised to be emotionally exhausted. It wasn't every day one had to appear in court to get divorced but if she was honest with herself she'd have to admit that she was often physically tired by early evening. Realistically she knew it had nothing to do with being a single mother, she'd been a single mother for long stretches of time when Sam had been away on naval exercises, but she hadn't been able to pinpoint any other change, except perhaps stress. She should probably go and get a check-up, she thought, she couldn't afford to get sick.

She took some clean laundry into her room. Her bed was freshly made, the pillows plumped and inviting. The house was still. It couldn't hurt to lie down for a few minutes, could it? Maybe a catnap would lift her spirits.

She lay down, trying to remember what she'd looked like thirteen years ago when she'd first met Sam. It was easier to recall exactly what he'd looked like. A gorgeous, blond Adonis, and it had been lust at first sight. She'd been twenty-four and had moved from Sydney to Canberra, the nation's capital, to do her Master's in international law at the Australian National University. Her flatmate, Stella, had dragged her to a rugby game between the engineering faculty of the ANU and a team from the defence force academy. It had been an annual event, a huge social day with the rugby match followed by a party, and Stella had been chasing one of the university players, so Juliet had been her moral support. Juliet had expected to help Stella meet her man, she hadn't expected to find one for herself.

Canberra, 1995

Juliet was standing with Stella and a group of friends on the boundary of the rugby pitch when a man, a glorious, blond man, raced towards them, flying down the wing. He had the ball tucked under his right arm and his rugby jumper was moulded to his body. Juliet could see the outline of his biceps and deltoid clearly defined by the contours of his top. She was a sucker for good arms and there was no doubt that this guy had them. She watched as he fended off an opposing player with his left hand, a quick shove to the chest upsetting his opponent's balance, and he was away, strong legs pumping as he headed for the try-line. He goose-stepped over a diving defender, his quick movements belying his size. He had to be at least six feet of solid muscle but he moved with the agility of someone much lighter.

Juliet could see the last line of defence, a pair of opponents, blocking his path, lining up to double-team him. She saw him look around quickly, assessing his options. He had a teammate coming up on his outside. He didn't slow his pace but ran in a slightly diagonal line towards the centre of the pitch, straight towards the oncoming defenders. Juliet held her breath, willing this glorious stranger safely past them. She couldn't see how he could possibly manage to evade them—as solid as he was, the others were bigger again and there were two of them. They had the typical build of rugby players—massive limbs, thick necks and take-no-prisoners looks on their faces. They looked like two enormous tree trunks in the middle of the field.

Juliet waited, expecting to see the blond demigod attempt to dodge around the opposition—she was convinced he'd be fast enough to get around them but he kept running straight at them. She watched him drop his left shoulder and spin to his right as the full backs crunched into him, slamming him into the ground. Even on the soft grass the thud of bodies colliding was loud and painful. Her hands flew to her mouth—somewhere under that man mountain lay the most divine male she'd seen in a long time—how many pieces was he going to be in when the dust settled?

She felt someone bump against her, the crowd around her was screaming and yelling, people were jumping up and down. She saw the ball come sailing backwards, arcing through the air. Had he managed to release the ball before he'd been crunched?

The diagonal path he'd chosen, the path that had led him straight into danger, had given his teammate a chance to gain some ground and Juliet watched as the ball landed securely in the teammate's hands. He was ten metres from the opposing try line with no one to beat.

Juliet celebrated the try with the crowd, caught up in

the moment, caught up in one man. She nudged Stella as the celebrations continued. 'Do you know who number fourteen is for the defence force?'

Stella shook her head. Juliet wasn't surprised; Stella was there to cheer for the university side—she had no allegiance to the defence academy. But that didn't mean Juliet couldn't adopt the defence force team as hers.

'Can I have a look at the programme?' she asked.

Stella handed over the paper she'd been holding and Juliet scrolled down the page. Number fourteen—Sam Taylor. It wasn't much, but it was better than nothing.

Juliet spent the rest of the half with one eye on Sam and the other on the crowd, trying to determine if anyone seemed to be following Sam particularly. There were plenty of supporters yelling for him whenever he got the ball, which seemed to be a frequent occurrence, but it was hard to tell if any of them were as focussed on Sam as she was. In the end she gave up and spent the rest of the time enjoying the spectacle and vowing to introduce herself to him after the match.

The spectators gathered in the university rugby club bar at the end of the game and wasted no time before ordering drinks. Juliet was careful to stay in control. The rugby players had all gone to shower and change and she wanted to be prepared for Sam's return. She was going to make sure she made a good first impression, for reasons she didn't fully understand but which seemed vitally important.

She and Stella positioned themselves between the band and the bar and kept an eye on the doors. The players were beginning to drift in now. They were easy to pick out of the crowd as most still had damp hair from their showers. The university boys were in civvies but the defence force boys were in their dress uniforms. In Juliet's opinion the defence force boys had an unfair advantage over the university boys. Dress uniforms trumped casual clothes any day.

Sam came through the doors, his white uniform immaculate. She'd always been a sucker for a man in uniform. He was six feet of muscle impeccably dressed. His hair was damp from the shower so it was a darker blond now, thick and wavy. Juliet wondered if there was a regulation about hair length in the navy. Sam's hair looked longer than most, although it stopped short of his collar. His shoulders were broad and straight and he looked like a perfect gentleman, strong and protective, chivalrous. Juliet knew he might be none of those things but he could certainly sell the illusion.

She scanned the room, waiting to see if anyone went to claim him. A couple of his companions broke away to meet their girlfriends but Sam continued walking. From her spot on the far side of the room she could see him sweep his gaze across the crowd. Was he looking for anyone in particular? He hadn't stopped scanning the room and she was concentrating so intently on his movements that she was unprepared when his gaze swept her side of the room. Before she had a chance to look away their eyes locked. She tried to relax. After all, he couldn't know she'd been watching him ever since he'd stepped inside, and she thought she'd pulled it off until he winked at her. She felt herself blush and was tempted to dive behind Stella, but at least he'd noticed her. That was a good thing, so she smiled at him before looking away. She still had time to play it cool and work out her plan of attack.

She waited until he was at the bar then offered to fetch Stella another drink.

'Excuse me, would you mind if I squeezed in here?' People were packed tightly together along the bar, giving her the perfect excuse to cram herself in beside Sam.

'Not at all,' he said, moving over to make space for her. He smiled at her and Juliet felt her heart skip a beat. She'd always thought that was just a saying but there was no other way to describe the effect of his smile on her. If he was gorgeous when he was running around a rugby field, he was absolutely superb when he smiled. His smile was wide and white and started at the right-hand corner of his mouth before spreading to the left and finally reaching his eyes. Crinkles appeared in the corners of his eyes, but they didn't detract from his looks. He looked like a man who smiled often and easily. The moment his smile lit up his face Juliet knew she was in big trouble. Sam had to be hers—there were no two ways about it.

Her eyes were still locked on his as she thanked him for making room. 'I enjoyed the game. Congratulations on winning.' She paused for a fraction before deciding nothing ventured, nothing gained. 'It's Sam, isn't it? I'm Juliet,' she said, holding out her hand.

He shook her hand and Juliet had the strangest sense of déjà vu. His touch was familiar but she knew that was impossible, yet she could sense a memory, almost as though her skin had felt his touch before. It was slightly unnerving but Juliet couldn't force herself to remove her hand.

'Have we met before?' Sam asked. He was frowning and a crease appeared between his eyes.

'No.' Had he felt the same strange familiarity or was he only asking because she'd used his name? She could explain one reason but not the other. 'I looked you up in the match programme after that first try. I wanted to know who everyone was cheering for.' Juliet let go of his hand.

He smiled again, his right-to-left smile, and said, 'What about you? Who were you cheering for?'

'No one really...not for the first fifteen minutes anyway. I came with a girlfriend to cheer for the uni team but I might have swapped allegiances.' She gave him a sideways glance, hoping he'd pick up on her invitation.

'So you don't have a boyfriend on the uni team who's going to get upset if I buy you a drink?'

'No boyfriend.'

And that had been it. Somewhere along the way Juliet had remembered to give Stella her drink and had been relieved to find her in a group that included the boy she was keen on, but after that Sam had been the only one who had held any interest for Juliet.

They'd had such passion and she still found it hard to believe that it hadn't been enough to sustain them. Hard to believe they hadn't made it.

She'd only ever had eyes for Sam but passion was no match for reality.

The sound of the front door opening brought Juliet out of her reverie. Initially she thought Sam and the children were home but then she heard Maggie calling her. Her sister had gone for a run and was now probably wondering where everyone had disappeared to. The house was in darkness as Juliet hadn't turned any lights on and it probably seemed abandoned.

'In here, Mags,' she called out, letting Maggie know she was home.

Maggie stuck her head into Juliet's room. 'What are you doing?'

'Nothing,' Juliet said as she sat up.

'It's very quiet. Are the kids already in bed?'

'No, Sam's taken them out for dinner.'

'He's still in town?'

'He goes back tomorrow,' Juliet said.

'And then what?' Maggie crossed the room and sat on the bed beside Juliet.

'I'm not sure. That's what I've been thinking about. Where do I go from here? On one hand nothing's changed but on the other...'

'Everything's changed.'

Juliet nodded.

'You could have gone with him.'

'I could have but moving every three years or, worse, every six months wasn't the right thing for the children, especially Kate. Regardless of her issues, moving constantly once we had a family wasn't our plan and I thought that given the childhood Sam had he'd want to keep his family together. I thought it would be important to him. But the navy was more important and Sam couldn't, or wouldn't, give it up.' Juliet picked at the quilt cover as she spoke. 'I made him choose between the navy and us, and I lost.' She shrugged. 'No point sitting here feeling sorry for myself. I'll just have to get on with things.'

Maggie hugged her. 'You know I'll always be here if you need me.'

'Thanks, but I can't expect you to jump on a plane and fly down to Melbourne at the drop of a hat. You're here now and I do appreciate that but I'm an adult, and I should be able to manage on my own.'

'You can manage but there will be times when it's tough to do that and Sam won't always be able to help you with the kids in a crisis—he could be on the other side of the world. I'll only be in Sydney so if you need me, I want to know. You've done it for me and I'd be upset to think you wouldn't call me. Okay?'

Juliet nodded. 'Thanks, Mags.'

Maggie squeezed her shoulders. 'No probs. Now, can I make you a cup of tea before I jump in the shower?'

'No, I'm fine really. The kids should be back soon. Have a shower while there's still some peace and quiet.'

Maggie disappeared into the guest bathroom and was still in there when Sam and the children returned. Juliet met them at the door and Sam handed her the car keys and a pizza box. 'We thought you probably hadn't eaten. It's a Margherita.'

'Thank you,' she said as she took the box from Sam's hands. Margherita was her favourite. Sam had always been good at the little things but it was the big things that had torn them apart. He could remember her favourite pizza topping and how she liked her tea but couldn't understand why she didn't want to move house every three years for the rest of her life.

Let it go, she reprimanded herself, *it's over.*

She took the pizza into the kitchen and she could hear the children asking Sam to tuck them into bed before he left. She let Sam help them brush their teeth, change into their pyjamas and read them a story while she ate a couple of slices of pizza, leaving some for Maggie. When the children were ready for bed she stood and watched as Sam kissed them goodnight, amazed as always that she and Sam had created two incredible little people. Two miniature versions of themselves.

But the similarities between her and her daughter were physical rather than psychological. Kate, with her thick dark hair and bright blue eyes, was the spitting image of herself at the same age but she was far more reserved than Juliet had ever been. Juliet was stubborn and headstrong and prone to making quick decisions; Kate was far more measured and in control of her emotions, even at the age of eight. Juliet sometimes wondered if Kate's dyslexia had influenced her personality. Had she learned to take her time with her responses to ensure she made fewer mistakes or was she simply less volatile than her mother?

Edward and Kate were as different as chalk and cheese, both in looks and behaviour. Edward had inherited his father's looks and much of his personality. They were both adrenalin junkies, both attracted to danger. She was constantly on the lookout around Edward because he was still too young to assess risk. Sam liked order and routine, he liked to follow the rules and would never make a rash judgement. Juliet hoped Ed would develop some of his father's sense as he matured but she was worried because she suspected Sam might have always had that slightly sensible gene and that healthy regard for the rules may have been reinforced by his defence force upbringing. Sam's love of order and routine had certainly helped him to cope with the frequent moves that he'd been exposed to as a defence force brat. From what he ate for breakfast and how he read the paper to the system in his wardrobe and in his bookshelves, Sam was a creature of habit. Even the kids' bedtime routine had been started by Sam. And now Juliet had taken away some of that.

She followed Sam's lead, kissing the children goodnight as an unwelcome thought burrowed its way into her head—other than their children, they hadn't made much of a success of their life together.

CHAPTER THREE

August 2008

JULIET was rushing around the house, trying to get several last-minute jobs out of the way before fetching Edward from kindergarten, when she was interrupted by a knock at the door. A postman waited with a letter, registered mail. She showed the postman her driver's licence as identification and signed for the envelope with a shaky hand. She knew what the envelope contained— it could only be one thing. It had been a month and a day since she and Sam had been in court.

This was it. Her self-imposed D-Day.

She'd been delaying a whole host of things, things she couldn't put off any longer. She hadn't set a date exactly but she'd decided that once the divorce was final and she had the paperwork that said so, she would have to face facts.

She took the envelope to the kitchen and slit it open with a knife.

It had been a month and a day since she'd seen Sam, one month and a day since they'd been in court. Her divorce was absolute. It was there in black and white in front of her. She was now officially a divorcee.

Before she could procrastinate again or let herself be

distracted by the children, she did the two things she'd been avoiding. She slid her wedding and engagement rings off her finger and slipped them onto her right hand. It was a slightly tighter fit but she wasn't ready to be without them totally, though she also had no cause to still be wearing them on her left hand. The rings felt heavy on her right hand and her thumb automatically fiddled with the bands. She supposed she'd get used to the sensation.

One more task to do. She picked up the phone but hesitated before dialling. She put it onto the kitchen bench while she deliberated. What if she didn't need to make this phone call after all? She palpated her left breast with her fingers, hoping, once again, that maybe the lump had disappeared. But it was still there, about the size of a small walnut. She retrieved the phone and made a long-overdue appointment with her doctor.

'Good morning, Juliet,' Dr Wilson said as she called her into the consulting room. 'What can I do for you today?'

'I've found another breast lump,' Juliet said as she sat down. She had a history of benign nodules and she'd had various tests done in the past but thankfully they'd all come back negative for any malignancy.

'When did you notice this one?'

'A few months ago,' she answered honestly.

'Any changes in this one?'

'I think it's got bigger.'

Dr Wilson looked at her with one eyebrow raised. 'Any reason why you haven't been in to see me sooner?'

Juliet knew that the change in the size of the lump should have sounded warning bells. It had, she just hadn't had the time or energy to deal with it. Part of her had also tried to pretend that this lump was just like all the others and they'd been fine, hadn't they? But she knew that this lump wasn't the same—it had kept on growing.

'Sam and I got divorced. I had a lot on my plate.'

'I'm sorry to hear about the divorce—that must have been tough.' Dr Wilson paused before adding, 'Do you want my lecture on how important it is not to neglect your health now or should I save it for later?'

Juliet shook her head. 'Save it. I know I owe it to my children to look after myself, that's why I'm here.'

'Fair enough. Let's have a look at this lump, then, shall we?'

Juliet undressed and was poked and prodded for the first of what would become many times over the course of the next few days. The lump was tender but no worse than the others had been.

'How big was it when you first noticed it?' Dr Wilson asked.

'About the size of a pea,' Juliet recalled.

'Just under a centimetre, then. It's now between three and four. When did you notice that it had got bigger?'

'Probably five or six weeks ago,' Juliet estimated. It had been around the time she and Sam had gone to court, which was one reason she'd ignored it. It hadn't reached the top of her list of priorities yet.

'I think we need to check this out further. You can get dressed and then I'll take some blood, and I'm also going to send you off for a mammogram. You haven't had one before, have you?'

'No, only ultrasounds.'

'It can be a bit difficult to get a clear picture with a mammogram in the under forty-five age group because your breast tissue is still quite dense, but I want to do that so we can get a look at the size and shape of the lump and a clear idea of its position. I'm going to refer you for a biopsy as well but those results will take a little longer to get back.'

Juliet was dressed now and sat in the chair beside Dr. Wilson's desk, extending her left arm, ready for blood to be drawn. The needle stung as it entered her arm and she watched the dark red blood fill up the vial, wondering what sort of nasty things her blood was harbouring.

'I want you to have the mammogram this afternoon, and I'll make some calls and see if I can get you in for the biopsy tomorrow,' Dr Wilson said as she capped and labelled Juliet's blood. 'Is there someone who can help you with the children if the appointment times clash with school pick-ups? It might make it easier to get appointments for you if you can be flexible.'

Juliet nodded silently. She didn't have a clue who to call but she was sure she'd think of someone once her brain had time to process all the other stuff Dr Wilson was talking about. Mammograms, biopsies, blood tests. She hadn't actually said the word yet but Juliet knew what she was thinking. Cancer.

Juliet was struggling to get past that word. The word was stuck in her head, making it very difficult to concentrate on everything else Dr Wilson was telling her. The word was also stuck in her throat, making it difficult to breathe. Perhaps she'd feel better if that word was out in the open.

'You think I have cancer?'

Saying it out loud didn't improve matters much. She was breathing now but the tightness in her chest had been replaced by nausea.

Dr Wilson's reply didn't ease her fears. 'I think this

lump is different from the fibroadenomas you already have. It's presenting more like a tumour because it's growing rapidly and I don't like that. I think we need to get as much information as we can to determine what we're dealing with but, remember, not all lumps are malignant.'

Juliet nodded but nothing else changed—she still felt nauseous, she still had a new lump in her breast.

'Do you want to call someone now? Get someone to drive you to the breast-screening clinic?' Dr Wilson asked.

'No, I'm okay, I'll drive myself,' Juliet replied, thinking that she needed to get through the mammogram as quickly as possible to make sure she was in time to collect the children from kindy and school.

'Okay. But can you arrange for someone to drive you to the biopsy? Your chest is likely to be quite sore once the local anaesthetic wears off and you'd be wise not to drive.'

Juliet nodded and left Dr Wilson's surgery with referrals for the mammogram and the biopsy and a follow-up appointment for two days hence. The receptionist would ring her with a time for the biopsy.

The mammogram was not the horrific experience she had been anticipating, judging from comments she'd heard from other women over the years. It was uncomfortable but in the scheme of things it was bearable.

Maybe she was in shock, numb to what was happening around her. She felt as though she was in a nightmare. The whole day had a surreal quality to it and she half expected one of the children to wake her up at any minute. Trying to take on board everything that she was being told was proving difficult when she felt as though she was wading through thick fog. Nothing was making sense. Was it really possible that she had cancer?

She tried to think through the situation but it was virtually impossible, partly because she had no facts yet and partly because she couldn't believe it was really happening.

She got dressed after the mammogram and hoped she was giving all the right responses as the technicians gave her more information, but her mind had already moved on to the next day and to the arrangements she would have to make. There was a message on her phone with the appointment time for the biopsy. Who would drive her to her next appointment? Perhaps she should take a taxi. Who could she ask to collect the children? She knew that this might only be the beginning of a host of favours she could need from people. If there was bad news then Dr Wilson was right—she was going to need support. Where was this going to come from?

She put those thoughts to the back of her mind while she drove to the kindergarten to collect Edward, focussing on the road and on getting there safely.

Edward's face lit up with a delightful smile, Sam's smile, when he saw her waiting to collect him—it was as though her presence was a big surprise. She wondered who would collect him if something happened to her and then quickly pushed that thought to the back of her mind as she hugged Ed to her when he arrived at her feet at full speed. He was closely followed by his best friends, Jake and Rory—they'd met on their first day of three-year-old kindergarten and were almost always together, like the three musketeers. Their mothers, Anna and Gabby, had become good friends of Juliet's by association and she wondered if their friendship would stretch a little further if she needed their help.

She saw Gabby arriving to collect Rory, running late as usual. Gabby waved and came straight over to Juliet. 'Hi, how are you? Rory was wondering if Ed would like to come for a play. Would that suit you?' Gabby asked, not pausing for breath. She always did things at a fast pace and was always busy, and Juliet sometimes wondered if she ever slept.

'Is there any chance you could have him tomorrow instead?' Juliet hated asking but if Gabby was offering to have Edward surely she wouldn't mind if it was tomorrow and not today? 'I need to have some tests done and I'm not supposed to drive afterwards.'

The boys, sensing that their mothers weren't in a hurry to leave, had made a beeline for the playground adjacent the kindergarten. Gabby and Juliet wandered in that direction too.

'Are you having eye tests?' Gabby asked.

Juliet knew that eye tests often involved eyedrops that dilated pupils, making driving difficult. She wished it was something that simple. She supposed she should explain; she would end up telling Gabby at some point anyway as she was sure to need her help. 'No. I have to have a biopsy. I found a lump in my breast.'

Juliet heard Gabby's sharp intake of breath and saw her eyes widen. 'When did this happen?'

'I noticed it a while back but I was at the doctor today.'

'And you're straight in for a biopsy?'

Juliet knew Gabby was considering the timeline, recognising the sense of urgency. 'I had a mammogram today. My GP wants the information as quickly as possible.'

'Have you got any info yet?'

Juliet shook her head. 'No, the mammogram results

will go straight to my GP and to the surgeon for tomorrow.'

'How are you getting to tomorrow's appointment?' Gabby was firing questions at Juliet, once again barely pausing for breath.

'I'll catch a cab.'

'Why don't I drive you? I'll make sure you get home and then I'll pick up the boys and Kate and bring them home later.'

'What about work?'

Gabby waved a hand, dismissing Juliet's protests. 'Finn's around. I'll just tell him he'll need to manage the gallery—it doesn't need both of us there.'

Gabby and her husband owned an upmarket art gallery and travelled frequently. Juliet started to protest and then stopped herself. As much as she didn't like to ask for help, she would have to get used to it, just as she would have to get used to accepting help when it was offered. 'If you're sure, that would be fabulous. I'm a bit apprehensive.'

'Of course you are, anyone would be, but I'm sure it will all be fine.'

Juliet wished she could be so certain. She was expecting bad news, she could almost feel it coming, but she didn't comment. She called to Edward, told him they needed to collect Kate, and then gave Gabby the details of where and when the appointment was, and agreed to be ready an hour before.

The next week was a whirlwind of appointments. Juliet saw the specialist and had a core biopsy under a local anaesthetic; she had a follow-up with her GP and then went back to the specialist. It was all she could do to keep track of which doctor she was seeing on which day, which hospital she had to be at and which forms she needed to take with her, without having to worry about the routine things like feeding the children. Fortunately Gabby was fabulous. She stepped in and basically ran Juliet's life for her, taking over all the general household chores and giving Juliet time to deal with the doctors and to hug her children. Over the next week Gabby alternated between being Juliet's taxi service, nanny, personal shopper and cook, but even Gabby couldn't stop the downward spiral that was Juliet's medical condition.

Seven days after the mammogram the specialist delivered the diagnosis and it was just as Juliet had feared. The lump she'd been ignoring for several months was a malignant tumour.

She had breast cancer.

Juliet's world was crumbling around her. She had two small children and she was on her own. She was divorced. She had breast cancer.

She wanted her old life back. She wanted her health back. She wanted Sam.

Gabby was supportive. Once again she cooked dinner for Juliet's children on the night Juliet got her diagnosis and she offered to cook for Juliet too, but she couldn't eat. She couldn't imagine that she'd ever feel like eating again.

Gabby did what she could but she wasn't Sam.

She'd offered to stay, had offered to keep Juliet company after the children had been put to bed, but Juliet had said she wanted to be alone.

She'd lied.

What Juliet wanted was Sam.

Sam was her rock. He had got her through her first crisis, her first two crises. She remembered how Sam had been there for her nine years ago and she knew she wouldn't have managed without him. Who would be her rock now?

Darwin, 1999

Juliet carried the last of the shopping bags into the house. It was a humid, steamy day, typical Darwin dry-season weather, and she could feel the beads of sweat trickling down between her breasts. She unpacked the groceries, putting the things that had to go into the fridge away before deciding to leave the rest until after her swim.

She and Sam had moved directly from wintry Canberra to the tropics of the Northern Territory. It had taken her a while to acclimatise to the tropical Darwin weather but she'd finally learned to slow her pace to suit the climate. Things moved more slowly in the north. It was something the rest of the country always commented on and Juliet could understand why—it was impossible to maintain a hectic schedule in these hot, moist, stupefying temperatures.

They'd lived in Darwin for nearly three years now and because of the city's transient population they were almost considered locals. Being part of the defence force had made the transition relatively easy. Defence force personnel were accustomed to people coming and going and were generally a sociable, welcoming group of people. They had settled easily into the city. Juliet had completed her Master's in international law in Canberra and had gone on to complete a diploma in education as well. She was teaching at the law school at the university and through this network and the defence force they had a wide circle of acquaintances.

There was always something happening—a barbeque,

a game of tennis, drinks for someone who was leaving or to welcome new arrivals—and Sam and Juliet had an active social life, but what Juliet really loved was when it was just her and Sam, together, their own little unit. They'd moved here as virtual newlyweds and Juliet still cherished the rare occasions when she had Sam to herself. It was an idyllic lifestyle and they existed in a state of euphoria and contentment. Only a few weeks ago, their little bubble had expanded when Juliet had got a positive result on a pregnancy test. She now had everything she'd ever wished for.

She finished putting away the groceries and went to find her bathers. It was an afternoon ritual for her to meet Sam at the swimming pool on the naval base for a late-afternoon swim and a game of tennis or a drink with whoever was around in the officers' mess. The base was only a five-minute drive from their married quarters and the trip was worth every second in this hot and humid climate.

Juliet found her swimsuit and changed out of her sundress. As she stepped out of her underwear she noticed some spots of blood. Just small spots, but surely that wasn't normal. Beside her bed was the bible of expectant mothers and, slightly panicked, Juliet grabbed the book, searching for information. What did the book say about spotting? Was there anything in there to reassure her?

Chapter two said some women got spotting in the first month of pregnancy around about the time their period would normally be due. The advice was to rest and see if the bleeding stopped. But Juliet was eleven weeks pregnant. She flipped through the book, frantically searching for more. Chapter seven talked about bleeding in the last few weeks of pregnancy but there was nothing in between. She found nothing that set her mind at ease. Swimming was obviously out of the question if there was bleeding. Rest seemed to be the answer. She lay on her bed and continued scouring her book for any more information as she willed herself to stay calm and relaxed and prayed for the bleeding to stop.

It didn't.

Calm and relaxed turned into stomach cramps. Juliet was almost too afraid to check but she had to know. She went to the bathroom. The bleeding was heavier and the blood was bright red. That wasn't good.

She phoned Sam and he was by her side within ten minutes. Fifteen minutes after that he'd whisked her off to the emergency department at the Darwin Hospital and she was being taken into a cubicle for an ultrasound scan. Sam held her hand as the technician started the consult and stayed beside her when the technician went to call for the doctor. Juliet felt her pulse increase its pace with nervousness. She wanted the technician to show her an image of the baby on the screen, not fetch the doctor. She'd read enough of her pregnancy book to know she should be able to see her baby on the monitor. The only thing that kept her from panicking, that prevented her from screaming and yelling and demanding to know what was wrong, was Sam's calming presence. She knew if he let go of her hand she would lose control. Somehow Sam knew that too and he held his position, comforting her with his solid, dependable presence. Maybe, just maybe, she thought, things would be okay as long as Sam was there.

The female doctor was young, too young to be completely reassuring, but she had a calm and confident manner that helped to put Juliet at ease.

'How far along are you?' the doctor asked as she moved the ultrasound over Juliet's abdomen.

'Eleven weeks.'

The doctor nodded and then pointed towards the ultrasound monitor. There was a little arrow that moved about the screen as she manipulated the mouse. 'Can you see that circle?' she asked. 'That's the foetal sac.'

Yes, Juliet thought, that's better. The doctor will be able to show me my baby. Maybe the technician was just having trouble finding it. But the doctor hadn't finished.

'I should be able to see a heartbeat within the sac but there's nothing there. Your baby hasn't developed.' The doctor removed the ultrasound transducer from Juliet's abdomen and wiped the gel off her stomach. 'I'm sorry.'

Juliet had no words of reply.

Sam wasn't quite as stunned. 'You're sorry? What do you mean, you're sorry? We had a positive pregnancy test,' he said. A frown creased his forehead and Juliet knew he was trying to understand what the doctor was telling them. It wasn't making much sense to her either.

'You were pregnant but the pregnancy hasn't progressed,' the doctor explained.

'You're telling us there's no baby?'

The doctor nodded.

'What happened?' Sam asked.

'We never really know,' the doctor replied. 'It's impossible to tell at this stage—the foetus just stops developing. One in three babies don't make it. It's not uncommon, it's just that people don't talk about it much. Give yourself some time to heal and grieve and then you can try again. Most of the time there's no rhyme or reason for losing a baby, just like there's no reason to think things will go wrong next time.'

Juliet didn't say a word. She couldn't think about the next time, all she could think about was this baby they'd just lost. The doctor had called it a foetus, but it hadn't been a foetus, not to her. It had been their baby.

Sam took her home and put her to bed and held her while she cried, held her while she mourned their child. He didn't try to tell her everything would be okay. It was too soon for that and Juliet loved him for being able to feel her loss. He felt it too.

A baby had been the next step in their life together. Juliet doted on her sister's children. Maggie had married and had had her children at a young age, and while Juliet loved her niece and nephew she'd never had a burning desire to have her own family until she'd met Sam. Everything had changed for her then. She'd found the man she wanted to spend the rest of her life with and that included the man who she wanted to be the father of her children. She'd been ecstatic to discover she was pregnant and now that had been taken away from her with no warning.

Sam had been just as excited. He was an only child and his mother had died when he'd still been quite young. While he was close to his father Juliet knew he loved the idea of creating his own family and she knew he was upset too. But Sam made it his priority to look after her and for the next few weeks Sam was her rock.

He organised sick leave for Juliet and took time off work himself and they flew to Ubud on the Indonesian island of Bali, where they spent a week in the mountains. The villa Sam rented came with a housekeeper and a cook and Juliet regained her appetite on a diet of fresh fruit, lean meats, fish and salads. They walked every morning and spent the afternoon lying by their private pool.

Juliet still cried herself to sleep but Sam was there for her and after a few days Juliet's spirit started to recover. After four days Sam's crooked smile returned and that lifted Juliet's spirit even further.

After five days they ventured down the mountain into the hustle and bustle of beachside Kuta. Juliet had been apprehensive about the crowds but no one knew her and no one knew she'd just lost a baby. She looked no different to any of the other tourists and no one gave her a second glance. No one except the hawkers, but they weren't targeting her specifically, they targeted all the foreigners.

She found the hawkers overwhelming at first after the more relaxed shopkeepers of Ubud but Sam protected her from their frenzied persistence and Juliet eventually embraced the noise and the colour and, to a lesser extent, the crowds. The smells were a little harder to embrace but even those she eventually got accustomed to. She could have hidden away from the overwhelming vibrancy, she could have insisted that Sam take her back up the mountains, but instead, with Sam beside her, she absorbed the energy and felt it restore some life into her soul. With Sam beside her she survived the streets of Kuta and that felt like a major achievement. Not only had she survived but she was starting to come back to life, and Juliet knew she would be okay, knew that, as long as she had Sam, things would be all right.

They were back at their villa in time for dinner. Sitting beside the pool, surrounded by the scent of frangipani and dining by candlelight, they began to talk about the future again, to discuss their hopes and dreams for the family they would surely have. Slowly Juliet started to trust that their dreams were not over, just delayed.

A couple of days further on and she was ready to return to Darwin. She felt rested and, if still not fully recovered, at least able to face her life. She understood that there wasn't always a reason for things and she trusted that children would be part of their lives when the time was right. Sam had given her comfort; he'd known how to help her heal, and while she never forgot this pregnancy she was able to get past the loss.

What she didn't know as she boarded the plane in Denpasar was that the miscarriage would be the first test of her resolve that year, but not the last.

One week later she received a call from her father. That in itself was unusual—her mother normally phoned and her dad would speak briefly once she and her mother had finished gossiping. Juliet immediately anticipated bad news and assumed it involved her mother. Why else would her father call? He reassured her that her mother was fine and he was calling about her brother-in-law, Maggie's husband, Steve.

Steve was a policeman in Sydney and he'd been called in as part of reinforcements when riots had broken out at a Sydney beach. Juliet had seen images on the evening news the previous day—temperatures were soaring in an early summer heatwave and some longstanding cultural differences had spilled over from verbal sparring into physical violence. Juliet had called Maggie to check on Steve and had been told he'd sustained a head injury but had been discharged from hospital. She'd relaxed and she relaxed again now—she'd only spoken to Maggie a few hours ago, she could reassure her father that all was well.

But her father had more recent news, and was calling

to tell her that Steve had been readmitted to hospital during the night. He'd had a large subdural haematoma and had died before the neurosurgeon had reached the hospital.

Her sister Maggie was a widow.

Juliet and Sam were on the next flight to Sydney.

Sam had been worried that Steve's death would stretch Juliet to breaking point but for Juliet, Steve's death put things into perspective. Her loss paled in comparison to Maggie's. Thanks to Sam, Juliet had been able to escape to the sanctuary of Bali where she had been able to hide from her life until her sorrow over the miscarriage was able to be tucked away in her heart. It was no longer completely overwhelming and all-consuming.

Maggie had lost her husband and she was left with two young children to comfort, explain to and care for. There was nowhere for Maggie to hide and despite Sam's concerns Juliet was able to embrace the responsibility of being the one to support and comfort Maggie.

She stayed in Sydney when Sam went back to Darwin but when she returned to Sam she was her old self, determined to move forward. They had each other and they would be okay, she'd make sure of it.

Throughout all of this, Sam had supported her and she knew she would never have made it through to the other side without him. He'd been her rock then but who would be her rock now?

CHAPTER FOUR

September 2008

IT HAD been several days since she'd finished having all the tests and since the oncologist had given her the bad news. It had taken Juliet a few days to get it all straight in her own head and some time to work out the best way to inform her family of the situation. She needed to make sure she had all the facts and information clear in her own mind before she attempted to explain it to others. She needed to make sense of the diagnosis, treatment and prognosis, and she felt it was important that she have control over who was told when.

Everyone who needed to know, other than the children, was in New South Wales—her parents, her sister and Sam. The best plan was to arrange a weekend visit, organising it as just a weekend away with no other agenda. There would be time for explanations when she arrived.

She phoned everyone and made arrangements. They would stay with Maggie for two nights and Juliet would tell her first. She was a nurse and Juliet expected her to cope best with the news. Sam was free on the second night and Juliet arranged for him to take the children out and that would give her a chance to see him. The next morning Maggie would drive Juliet and the children down to Bowral, where they would all spend the weekend with Juliet and Maggie's parents. Juliet wanted Maggie there for emotional support.

Maggie's weekend was the first that Juliet ruined but Maggie was stoic and more than happy to give Juliet whatever support she needed in whatever form. Juliet had expected nothing less from her older sister but it was comforting to know that Maggie would be there for her. Now it was Sam's turn to hear the news.

Sam opened Maggie's gate and walked up the narrow path to the front door. Maggie had lived here for as long as he'd known her. He knew that originally Maggie and her husband Steve had planned to buy something bigger as their children got older, but that had been before Steve had died. Maggie hadn't wanted to move after that; she'd wanted to stay where her memories were. Sam was pleased—there were lots of happy memories for him here too. He and Juliet had spent plenty of holidays and Christmas times here with their children and their cousins and Sam didn't have any regrets about that. Just walking through the gate put a smile on his face, and knowing he was about to see his kids for the first time in several weeks made the walk even sweeter.

He knocked on the door and waited to hear the sound of children's footsteps running up the passage, echoing on the wooden floorboards. But the steps he heard were quieter and much more even. The door opened and Juliet was standing there. Just Juliet.

He frowned. Where were the kids? The house was small so he should have been able to hear their noise.

'Hello, Sam, come in.'

'Juliet.' He was distracted by the silence and just

managed to remember to return her greeting. He looked past her, searching for the children, but there was no sound and no movement.

Juliet stepped aside, making space for him to enter the house, and he looked properly at her for the first time as he moved through the doorway. She looked different. She was tiny, almost a foot shorter than him, and the top of her head barely reached his shoulder. She was barefoot, which made her seem even smaller, but her height wasn't the difference as she'd always been little.

Had she changed her hairstyle? He didn't think so—her thick chestnut hair still fell past her shoulders and framed her petite, heart-shaped face. She had delicate features and the most amazing blue eyes, and those were as striking as ever.

He followed her down the passage to the kitchen at the rear of the house. Had she lost weight? Was that the difference? She'd never been fat but she was normally curvy and she looked thinner than he remembered. From behind she was still the same hourglass shape, her bottom still round and firm, but she was definitely thinner.

He listened for the sound of the children as he walked. Nothing but silence. He frowned. He had the right day and time, he was certain of that. 'Where are the kids?'

'Maggie's taken them to a movie. They'll be back in an hour or so.'

Sam was annoyed. He'd made a promise to himself that he'd be easygoing when it came to arrangements concerning the children in the hope that Juliet would always allow him to see the kids when it suited him as his schedule was often inflexible, but Juliet had arranged this visit so the least she could have done was make sure the children were there. 'You could have phoned me, I would have come later. I'm leaving on a training exercise tomorrow, there're a thousand things I've got to do still.' He'd told her that already, which was why they'd made plans for him to see the children today because tomorrow he wouldn't be in Sydney. He'd be sailing north and would be gone for six weeks.

'I know,' Juliet replied. 'But there's something I needed to talk to you about and I didn't want the children to hear so I asked Maggie to take them out.'

'Why didn't you tell me on the phone?'

'I wasn't quite sure what to say. I thought it would be easier just to leave it all until we were face to face.'

She'd met someone. That was the first thought that ran through Sam's mind. The idea made him feel slightly nauseous. While he knew that was probably inevitable, he'd avoided ever thinking seriously about that possibility and he certainly hadn't expected to be forced to deal with it so soon.

Juliet sat down at the kitchen table, motioning for him to do the same. 'I have to go into hospital for surgery.'

Sam let out the breath he'd been holding. That announcement hadn't been what he'd expected and he felt a strange sense of relief. 'Right…good.'

'Good? What do you mean by "good"?' Juliet's tone was incredulous.

'If you're having surgery then I assume that whatever is wrong can be fixed,' he explained. 'That's got to be good.' Yes, he thought, surgery sounded better to him than the alternative—that she'd found herself a boyfriend. That was much better than having to be pleased for her about her ability to move on with her life without him. Surgery he could deal with, he could help, he could be useful. He could do something to assist her.

'What do you need me to do? Do you want me to have the children for a few days?' Excellent. He was able to be easygoing, relaxed and generous, he thought as he offered his help. There was no need for any ill-will. He just hoped she wasn't booked in too soon, and that it could wait a few weeks until he was home again.

'It's a bit more complicated than that. The whole process is going to take a bit longer than a few days,' Juliet said.

That didn't make sense—what surgery took longer than a few days?

Juliet seemed to be able to follow his train of thought. Not surprising really, she knew him better than anyone. 'Surgery is just the first step. I'll have to have some follow-up treatment afterwards and I'm not sure how I'll manage with that,' she explained.

Treatment, not rehabilitation. Sam's relieved state disappeared with that one word. Ongoing treatment didn't sound quite so good.

'What sort of treatment?' he asked.

Juliet's eyes were fixed on his, locked and unwavering. 'Chemotherapy.'

'Chemo? But…' Chemo meant cancer, that couldn't be right. The nausea was back.

But Juliet was nodding. 'I have breast cancer.'

'Bloody hell.' Now what? Sam was a man; he liked fixing things but he was completely out of his depth with cancer. He needed some details, some facts. There had to be something he could do, something to make him feel useful. 'Are you sure it's cancer? You've had other lumps and they've always been fine—why is this one different? Do you think you should get a second opinion?'

'I've seen my GP and two oncologists, I've had blood

tests, a mammogram and a biopsy.' Juliet was reeling off words as if she was reading a shopping list, and Sam was having trouble following her. 'I've had plenty of opinions and they all agree. I have cancer.'

Most of the words made no sense to him. It was as though Juliet was speaking a foreign language. All he really heard was 'cancer'. What was he supposed to say now? What was he supposed to do? He searched for the right words, something, anything to show that she could depend on him, but it was hard to offer support when he had minimal understanding of what was going on. 'So what happens now?'

'I'm booked in for a mastectomy in ten days.'

Ten days—in ten days he'd be on a ship in the Timor Sea.

'Mastectomy?' He knew what that word meant. 'You're having the whole breast removed? Can't they just remove the tumour?' Surely, with all the advances modern medicine had made, that should be possible. Or was the tumour too big?

'One option was to just remove the lump but I tested positive for an abnormal gene, which increases my risk of developing more tumours in the breast tissue. I'm choosing to have all my breast tissue removed to decrease the risk. I don't want to give the cancer any chances to come back.'

She sounded very matter-of-fact but he was struggling to process all the information. 'What do you mean, "all your breast tissue"?'

'I'm having a double mastectomy.'

'Double?' Had he heard her correctly? 'Both of them?' he clarified.

Her breasts had always been large, a CC cup, which on Juliet's tiny frame had always been noticeable, and

Sam couldn't imagine her without breasts. He didn't want to imagine her that way.

Juliet nodded. 'I want the odds in my favour. This is the best option. I'll start chemotherapy after the surgery.'

Things were going from bad to worse. He couldn't believe that just ten minutes ago he'd thought that Juliet having surgery was a better option than Juliet announcing she had a boyfriend. Now he desperately wished her news had been that minor. In reality he could have dealt with a boyfriend—one way or another. He was completely out of his depth with this announcement but he was determined to get a handle on the situation and do whatever she needed.

'If the doctors are taking all your breast tissue, why do you need chemo as well?'

'There's always a chance of tumours developing in the small amount of breast tissue that may remain behind after the surgery. The oncologist recommends chemo for pre-menopausal women with this type of tumour,' Juliet said with a shrug of her shoulders. 'It decreases the chance of anything further developing. If he's recommending it, I'm going to follow his advice.'

Sam took a deep breath, trying to organise his thoughts, trying to work out what he could do, how he could help. 'So what exactly does all this involve? What do you need me to do?'

'I'll be in hospital for a few days with the surgery. I'm having that done in the school holidays and I'm going to ask Mum and Dad to have the children. You'll be away.'

As usual. He could imagine Juliet wanting to add the accusation to the end of her sentence. He knew he was away a lot but she'd married a naval officer; he knew they'd had a plan but he'd tried a desk job and he'd hated it. In his opinion he'd done what he could to save their marriage and it hadn't worked. They were both to blame but now wasn't the time to look back. They needed to focus on the present. They couldn't change the past. Their marriage was over and he should be able to travel without feeling guilty, but he knew now that he wouldn't be able to. Not when Juliet was sick and his children were going to need him.

In the circumstances he decided it was best to ignore her comment. He didn't want to start an argument, especially one he wouldn't win because she was right. He would be away. But he wouldn't always be away and if he knew what the schedule was he should be able to be around for Juliet and the children at least some of the time. 'And then what?'

'Then I have chemo.'

'How does that work?' It was strange—cancer was such a common disease, everyone knew someone who'd been affected by it and everyone bandied around terms like chemotherapy and radiotherapy, but Sam really had no idea what any of it meant or how it worked. How exactly did the doctors target the cancer cells and what else got damaged along the way? How sick was Juliet going to get? Would she be in hospital for weeks at a time? Would she be able to manage the children? 'Chemo is what you see people having in the movies when they're hooked up to the drips?' he asked, needing clarification. He needed to make sure he understood.

Juliet nodded. 'It's not always given that way but Hollywood makes it look like that. Some of the drugs are given intravenously and others are in a tablet form—it depends what combination the medical oncologist decides to use. Whichever way I have the drugs, the usual process is four lots of chemo given about three weeks apart. The doctors expect me to be finished by Christmas.'

Christmas. Could this be her last Christmas? That thought burst into Sam's head before he could censor it. He couldn't think like that, he knew he needed to stay positive. Juliet needed support, not negativity. He'd stick to getting the facts first, deal with the things that were certainties. 'And how long does each session take? Do you stay in hospital each time?'

What would happen to their children?

'I'll have to go into hospital for a half-day on the first day of each cycle. Then I wait a few weeks and repeat the process.'

'What about the kids? Will you be able to manage them?'

Juliet shrugged. 'I hope so. It's a bit of a waiting game to see how I cope with the chemo. It affects people differently. I might have to call in some favours from friends but if I get really sick I'm sure Mum will come down to Melbourne.'

'You haven't told your parents yet?' Juliet's wording implied she hadn't given them the news.

'Maggie's going to drive us down to Bowral tomorrow. Maggie knows.' Juliet shrugged. 'She'll help me tell Mum and Dad.'

'And what about the kids? What have you told them?'

'Nothing yet.'

Sam frowned. 'What am I supposed to say to them?' He was used to Juliet telling him what to do when it came to organising their family. He was comfortable being in charge on board a naval vessel but when it came to working out domestic matters, he relied heavily on Juliet. As a single father he knew he'd have to work things out for himself, but he hadn't had to deal with anything this dramatic and he was at a loss.

'Nothing. I'll tell them over the weekend when we're at my parents'. Just take them out to dinner, that's what they're expecting. They won't pick up on anything if you behave normally.'

Behave normally! Hell, his wife—ex-wife—announces she has breast cancer and he's supposed to behave normally.

'Sam, I know this is a shock but there's a really good success rate with this treatment regime. I am going to beat this.'

'How can you be so certain?'

'I'm going to have everything that's recommended for me, I will do everything possible, and I'm counting on that being enough. I will do whatever needs to be done and that includes fighting this thing with every bit of strength in me. I am not leaving my children.'

And there it was, the thought that was on both their minds, out in the open. What was going to happen to their family—what was left of it? Even though the children seemed to be coping well with the divorce, he couldn't imagine how they were all going to get through Juliet's treatment, let alone what would happen if she didn't make it. How would the children cope? He knew what it was like to grow up without a mother and it wasn't something he would wish on anyone, especially not his own children.

Juliet knew what he was thinking. 'I understand that the idea of something happening to me, and what that would mean to the children, worries you. It was the first thing I thought of too. But your mum was killed in an accident— there was nothing that could be done to change that. I can be treated and that's why I need you to stay strong. I'm going to make sure the children are okay through this and the rest of my energy I'll use to fight this thing. I can't be worrying about how the adults are coping. I'm going to fight this and I'm going to win.'

Sam knew Juliet never said anything she didn't mean. She was tiny but so full of courage and determination. He knew she would fight with every last breath and, knowing Juliet, she would win.

Their conversation was interrupted when Maggie arrived home with the children in tow. Sam felt as though his heart would burst with love and pride for his kids but there was also a trace of fear and worry in there too. What would become of them all?

He tried to focus on the children but his mind kept drifting back to Juliet's health. He was still finding it hard to believe they were divorced but the fact that they were made it more difficult now—he would do anything and everything he could to help but how much help would Juliet accept, and realistically, what would he be able to do? He was about to spend six weeks at sea, something that was a regular occurrence and the very thing that had been at the root of their separation. He didn't even know when he'd next have a chance to speak to Juliet properly. Discussing things on the phone hadn't proved very satisfactory in the past and he didn't imagine it would be any easier now.

But she'd need help now. She'd need him.

No, he thought, she had her sister and her parents. Yes, she'd need help but she didn't necessarily need him. Her family was close, they would help her, he had no doubt about that. He was probably a long way down her list and that thought bothered him considerably. He wanted to be able to offer her support, wanted her to be able to rely on him, but realistically it wasn't going to happen. Not when he was going to be out of the country.

He took the children to the Sydney fish markets and the fresh, salty air helped to ease his fears slightly. Being near the sea always made him feel better. He'd missed it when he'd lived in Canberra and he'd missed it when he'd taken leave from the navy to try to save his marriage. He knew now that he needed to be near the ocean, he needed to know that he could get out on the water if necessary. The ocean helped to clear his mind and soothe his soul. He just wished he and Juliet had been able to work out how to have it all, but they hadn't made it.

He and the children walked around the pier before they went to choose their dinner. Dozens of boats were moored to the bollards and Edward had to inspect several of them as they bobbed gently on the waves. Watching Ed, Sam wondered if the love of the sea was a genetic trait. He had it, his father had it, and it looked as though Ed had the same fascination. The scene must have reminded Edward of Sam's father, a retired naval officer who still spent the majority of his time on his own boat, fishing, pottering about or just thinking.

'When are we going to visit Grandad?' Ed asked.

Sam wasn't sure how to answer that. He and Juliet had made tentative arrangements for the Christmas holidays. This was to be their first official Christmas apart; even last year when they'd been separated they'd still celebrated Christmas together, but this year would be different. Their plan had been that Juliet would spend Christmas with the kids and her folks and then meet Sam in Merimbula, on the New South Wales coast, where the children would spend a week with him and his dad while Juliet returned to Melbourne. Sam had no idea whether that would still be possible. But the kids knew nothing of Juliet's illness yet so he supposed explanations weren't necessary. As far as he could work out, those plans wouldn't need to change.

'I'm going to take you to see him after Christmas. We'll have a holiday at the beach.'

Sam still loved spending time with his dad. Sam was an only child and his mother had died when he'd been about Kate's age—which was partly why Juliet's news had freaked him out—and he'd been brought up by his dad and his dad's widowed sister. They'd been a close family, as close as it was possible to be when his dad spent weeks at sea, just like he himself now did. Sam knew what it was like to have an absent father but he didn't feel that it had affected their relationship. They were close and they had their shared love of the sea to bond them.

Sam still felt that Juliet had never really understood that the ocean was in their blood and he couldn't stand the thought of not being able to get out on the water. He imagined he'd be like his father when he retired and still spend his time mucking about in boats. He wanted to start teaching the kids to sail and he'd planned to get a little boat this Christmas that they could play around in and keep at his father's. Sam had fond memories of lazy summer days of his childhood spent on the water, learning to sail, and he wanted to create the same memories for his own children. He didn't want these plans to change. Somehow, they'd have to get to Merimbula.

CHAPTER FIVE

September 2008

SAM couldn't settle. He paced in his cabin, unable to relax, unable to keep focussed. He was almost wishing for an emergency. Wishing for something to happen that would distract him from his thoughts. He needed a crisis to demand his full attention because at the moment he had too much time on his hands. Too much time for thinking.

He'd been at sea for nine days with another thirty-three to go.

And Juliet was having surgery. Today.

He'd tried to be positive about the procedure, had tried to tell himself everything would be fine, but day by day the tension had slowly increased until he was edgy and stressed. He hated this feeling of helplessness, hated being so far away. He was starting to understand why Juliet had wanted to keep them all together. He wanted to be with his family too. For the first time in a long time he didn't want to be at sea—he wanted to be in Melbourne.

He left his cabin, unable to endure its confines a minute longer. Maybe the ocean breeze would clear his mind and settle his nerves. It usually did.

He nodded to the few sailors he passed on his way to the deck but didn't stop to engage in conversation. His mind was too preoccupied to discuss anything more detailed than the weather, but the fresh air didn't allay his fears. His thoughts followed him, colliding with each other inside his head just like the waves he could see crashing into the bow of the ship as he stood at the rail. All the different scenarios rolled through his mind, threatening to overwhelm him. What if the surgery was unsuccessful? What if Juliet didn't even make it through the surgery? What if he lost Juliet not through divorce but through death?

He hadn't considered the divorce to be a final, complete separation. He knew they'd always be connected through their children but the idea of losing Juliet altogether was devastating. The thought had been in the back of his mind since she'd told him about her diagnosis—had that really only been ten days ago?—but he'd managed to suppress it until now. Until she was undergoing surgery and he could no longer ignore just how serious this situation was.

He'd arranged for flowers to be delivered to her at the hospital. It had seemed important to him to let her know she was in his thoughts but now his thoughts were far from sunny and light, nothing like the flowers he'd sent. Now that seemed like such a minor, meaningless gesture. What good would flowers be?

He closed his eyes and let the salt spray fall on his face. There had to be more he could do. Juliet deserved more.

He should be there. He should be with his wife.

That thought confirmed his dilemma. He still thought of himself as married. He still thought of Juliet as his wife. She was still his responsibility and he should be

by her side. But instead of being there and supporting
her, he was thousands of miles away in the middle of
the ocean.

Juliet had been right. He had his priorities wrong.
He'd made the wrong choice.

He felt helpless. Devastated. Lost.

Would he have a chance to fix things?

Juliet sat on the hospital bed with her back to the doorway. It wasn't the door she was afraid to face but the
mirror beside it.

'Are you okay? You're very quiet.' Maggie was standing behind her, brushing her hair like she'd done years
ago when they had been children.

Juliet nodded. Maggie's strokes were long and rhythmical, almost hypnotic, and Juliet's mind drifted as her
hair was tended. She wasn't okay, far from it, but she
didn't really want to tell her sister where her mind had
drifted to—she had a feeling talking would make the
situation worse, not better.

'Shall I plait it for you?' Maggie asked. 'You'll have
to wear one of those paper hats in Theatre—tying your
hair up will keep it under control.'

Juliet knew she'd be going off for surgery soon and
as the time approached she found herself becoming
increasingly nervous. The surgery itself didn't bother
her and she'd made the decision to undergo surgery
without hesitation. In her opinion surgery was her only
option, but what if it wasn't enough? What if the cancer
was lurking somewhere else in her body? What if she
couldn't beat this?

Juliet could feel Maggie lift the weight of her hair in
her hands, separating its length into three strands before
twisting them together. Her chestnut hair was long and

healthy—it had always been one of her features that she'd liked and she'd looked after it. So far her hair looked like it always had if she ignored the odd grey hair—it was still glossy and thick. The rest of her also looked the same as she'd done for the past twenty years, give or take a few wrinkles. So far the only things about her that had changed were all on the inside but still she'd become wary of mirrors. She was wary of confronting her physical self. She knew she was trying to forget what she looked like so the new Juliet wouldn't be so much of a shock.

Today was the beginning of some major changes. And some big losses. She knew very well that her hair might not be with her for much longer but she also knew she could live without it. She was going to lose much more than her hair. Just as long as she didn't lose her life. As long as she could live she didn't care about her hair. Or any other parts of her.

'Did Mum ring this morning?' Maggie's question interrupted her ponderings.

Juliet nodded.

'How did she sound?'

Juliet had been dreading telling her parents about her cancer. She'd been far more nervous about giving her parents the news than she had been about telling Maggie and Sam. How did a daughter tell her parents she had a malignant tumour? What parent wanted to be told their child might die? But having Maggie's support when she'd made the trip to see them had helped immeasurably. And Juliet had been surprised at how well they'd taken the news.

Her mother had been shocked initially. Juliet had seen the shock roll across Harriet's face as she'd processed the news. She'd seen her try to compose herself, try to hide her thoughts, but she'd always been easy to read. But Harriet recovered well and started doing what she did best—organising her family. It was her way of holding things together.

Her parents had listened as Juliet had given them the information she'd had and then they'd taken over, planning the logistics of having their grandchildren to stay and organising support for Juliet. Juliet had wished her mother could tell her everything would be okay but she knew that wasn't possible. She knew her mum was waiting for someone to tell her the same thing but all Juliet had been able to do was give her the facts—she couldn't make any promises. But just sharing the information with two more people, two people who she knew would do anything for her, had eased her anxiety.

Telling her parents had been difficult but now that they knew she felt the burden had lifted. As always, her parents had the ability to make her feel better about the situation. Part of her wished she could ask them to come down to Melbourne with her but Kate and Edward would be better off in Bowral. They would benefit from John and Harriet's reassurance and Juliet really didn't want to expose her children firsthand to the events of the next few weeks. It would be much better for them to stay protected up there until she knew how things were going.

'I think she'd like to be here,' Juliet answered, knowing that was how her mum felt, even if she hadn't voiced that opinion. 'But I really couldn't cope with lots of people around,' she added honestly.

'Is that why you asked Mum and Dad to have your kids?'

'Partly. You know how Mum is. She's much better

if she's busy, and looking after the kids will keep her occupied, give her less time to worry.'

Maggie nodded in silent agreement. 'How were the kids?'

'Good. They've been yabbying and looking after the chooks and bottle-feeding the lamb the neighbours gave Dad.' She could picture the two of them, running amok around the farmhouse and the few acres that her parents had on the outskirts of Bowral. They would be enjoying their country holiday with their grandparents, oblivious to what was happening in Melbourne, and that was the way she wanted it. 'I think they've got plenty to occupy them and it's far better to have them busy up there.'

'What did you end up telling them about your surgery?' Maggie asked as she finished plaiting one half of Juliet's hair and started on the other side.

Juliet had found it difficult to know what to tell the children. She'd been worried about imparting more bad news so soon after the divorce and she'd discussed her concerns with Maggie.

'I was vague. Sam and I spoke to a child psychologist before we told the children about the divorce and she suggested that we tell them only what we thought they needed to know. She said to give them enough information so they could make sense of what was happening without overloading them. I thought that was good advice and something that would work in this situation too.

'I didn't think they needed to hear about the worst-case scenario,' she continued. 'I know they'll realise I look different so I've prepared them for that. I told them I found a lump in my breast and the doctor is going to take it out to make sure the lump doesn't grow. They know to expect my breasts to be smaller. I couldn't quite tell them they'd be gone altogether and I haven't mentioned chemo yet or the word *cancer*. I wasn't sure how much they would understand. I can give them more information as I go through the treatment.'

'I think they'll surprise you with how well they cope, especially if how they've dealt with the divorce is any indication,' Maggie responded, showing her support for Juliet's decision.

Their conversation was interrupted at this point by the nurse who bustled into the room and dropped a gown on the bed beside Juliet. 'Can you change into this for me? You'll be going to Theatre soon.' She barely paused to make eye contact before she hurried out again, saying she'd be back shortly.

Maggie snapped an elastic band around the tail of Juliet's plait. 'I'm finished. Do you want me to wait outside while you get changed?'

Juliet shook her head. 'I need to use the bathroom,' she said. It wouldn't have mattered anyway—she'd been stripped naked and poked and prodded in front of more people than she cared to think about over the past six weeks so undressing in front of her sister was no big deal.

She picked up the gown and went into the en suite bathroom. She stripped off her T-shirt and bra. Out of habit her fingers went to her left breast, palpating the lump. She wasn't sure when that had become a habit. Just as she wasn't sure if she was still hoping that one day, miraculously, the lump would have disappeared. But there it was. It was the size of a walnut in a shell but she knew that a few months earlier it had been the size of a pea.

The diagnosis had put her into a spin—the divorce had turned her life upside down but getting the diagnosis of breast cancer had sucked her into a vortex and the only way to stop her life from spiralling out of control had been to fight. And she was fighting with everything she had, starting with sacrificing her breasts. She was going to fight this disease and she'd keep fighting for as long as it took to beat it. That was the only way.

Today was step one. The mastectomy.

Her heart rate increased at the thought of it.

I am not scared, she told herself.

She wasn't afraid of losing her breasts. Her breasts were insignificant, inconsequential. They were nothing compared to her children. She wasn't prepared to leave her children without a mother, and if that meant letting someone take her breasts, it was a small price to pay. She'd chosen surgery without hesitation and once she made up her mind she very rarely changed it.

Saying she wasn't scared of the surgery itself was probably an understatement. She wasn't afraid of having parts of her removed. She didn't think she'd miss her breasts and she didn't imagine anyone else would either, but she was a little apprehensive about the risks associated with surgery. She had to get through it. Her children needed her.

Juliet turned her back to the bathroom mirror as she slid her arms into the gown and fastened the tie behind her neck. But avoiding mirrors didn't completely mean she could avoid her reflection. As she emerged from the bathroom she could see Maggie waiting for her. She knew how similar they were so she was still able to picture herself in Maggie's image. Maggie, older by four years, was taller and slimmer but their colouring was identical. Juliet always thought of herself as a rounder version of Maggie. Even now, with the weight loss she'd suffered, that was still the case. In their younger years

Maggie had always complained of being too skinny and had called Juliet 'curvy'. She'd been envious of Juliet's bust but, as was the way of teenagers, Juliet would have happily swapped her CC cup for Maggie's narrow hips. Maggie had an oval face and Juliet's heart-shaped face also made her seem slightly rounder by comparison. But while their physical shape was different, their identical colouring always identified them as sisters. They had the same chestnut hair, although Maggie's had a wave in it while Juliet's was heavy and straight, the same bright blue eyes, the same fair skin with a dusting of freckles across their noses.

Looking at Maggie now gave Juliet a teensy insight into what her body might look like after surgery—without the narrow hips. She had decided not to have a breast reconstruction immediately and she knew it would be strange not to feel top heavy, but she could cope with looking like her sister—at least until she decided what to do about new boobs.

'I brought you a present,' Maggie said as she handed Juliet a small, flat parcel. 'I'll make sure it's beside your bed when you wake up—it'll help to remind you that you're doing the right thing.'

Juliet unwrapped the gift. It was a photo of her children that had been taken at their grandparents' house on the weekend that Juliet had visited to tell them the news. Kate and Edward had been feeding the lamb and smiling up at the camera. They had been full of life and their sheer delight had been captured perfectly. Maggie was right, the children were the reason she was here. They were everything.

'It's perfect, thank you.'

Maggie hugged her just as the nurse came into the room to take Juliet to Theatre. 'It'll all be fine,' Maggie said as she kissed Juliet's cheek before putting the photograph on the bedside cabinet for her.

Juliet was wheeled off to Theatre still thinking about her children. They had taken the news of her surgery remarkably well considering they were probably still processing the reality of the divorce. Or perhaps she was projecting thoughts onto them. She liked to think that she'd told them as much as they needed to hear, but was it possible they were coping so well because they were still too young to really understand everything that was happening? So far the divorce hadn't really affected their day-to-day lives and they didn't know anyone who'd had major surgery so the idea of something going wrong would not occur to them. Cancer was also an alien concept to them and one Juliet was not about to mention at this stage.

She had explained the operation in very simple terms but she guessed that until they saw the post-op result, until they saw her in her altered state, the surgery wouldn't mean much. The rest of the treatment—the chemotherapy and any reconstructive surgery—she would explain later. One thing at a time, she'd decided. There was no point telling them about things that would happen months down the track—that was far too distant in their future.

She had reached the Theatre suites now and had been transferred to the operating table. The surgeon was in the room and she'd been connected to monitors. The anaesthetist had begun. The anaesthetic had been administered and the mask had been placed over her face. Juliet was counting down now. This was it.

Fourteen weeks to Christmas.

Thirteen years she'd known Sam.

Twelve weeks of chemo.
Eleven...

Juliet stirred. She was vaguely aware of being in a strange environment but what she was most aware of was pain. She was flat on her back and her chest was on fire.

'Juliet.' Someone was leaning over her, leaning into her field of vision. 'The surgery is all over, and you're in Recovery.'

She remembered now. The mastectomy.

'Have you got any pain?' The person leaning over her was a nurse. It hurt just to breathe and Juliet didn't dare move. Was the nurse serious? Of course she had pain. She tried nodding her head.

That was a mistake. Just that slight movement intensified the pain and she felt a wave of nausea wash over her. She must have looked as bad as she felt because the nurse reached behind the bed and grabbed a small green bowl. Juliet turned her head just in time, wincing as the pain carved through her chest, and vomited into the bowl.

It didn't help. She felt as though her chest was being split open, ripped apart along the seam that turning her head had created. The nurse waited until she'd finished then gave her something for pain and nausea, but the cycle continued for several hours. She vomited at regular intervals and she couldn't work out whether pain was making her vomit or whether the vomiting was giving her pain.

The consensus was she had reacted badly to the anaesthetic and that had caused the nausea, which had exacerbated the pain. Eventually the nursing staff got everything under control but by that stage Juliet was so exhausted she felt she could sleep for days. As the pain receded she sank blissfully into a state of oblivion.

Juliet opened her eyes and cautiously looked around the room. She saw that she was out of the critical care ward and back in a private room, but she had no idea how long she'd been there. She'd been vaguely aware of people coming and going around her bed but she'd lost track of the days. She remembered seeing Maggie but couldn't remember whether that was a before- or after-surgery memory. She supposed it didn't really matter what day it was, although she'd ask the first person she saw just to satisfy her own curiosity.

The first person to come into her room was one of the nurses, bringing a delivery of flowers. 'Aren't these gorgeous? Someone's thinking of you,' the nurse said as she handed Juliet the blooms. 'I'll just go and find a vase.'

Juliet held the flowers. Yellow tulips. They were her favourites. She knew who they were from without reading the card that was nestled in their midst.

Sam.

'What is the date?' she asked the nurse, before she could disappear from the room. It wasn't idle curiosity making her ask the question but a sixth sense suddenly telling her it was now important to know what day it was.

The nurse paused in the doorway. 'September the twelfth.'

'Oh.' Juliet slipped the card from the little plastic stick and opened it. It was hand-written in Sam's neat, precise script. That surprised her. She thought he would have just dictated a message over the phone to the florist.

My darling wife,
I hope you are recovering well and that these
tulips bring a bit of sunshine to your day.
I will see you soon, all my love, Sam.

Juliet read the card again. *My darling wife*—did
Sam have difficulty remembering they were divorced
too? Nearly three months after signing the papers Juliet
still thought of herself as married. When would that
change?

They would always be connected but at some point,
surely, she'd have to accept that she was single.

Accepting it wasn't the issue. In her head she knew she
was divorced but in her heart she still felt married.

Had Sam's wording been deliberate? Had he used the
word *wife* on purpose? Juliet could remember exactly
where she'd been thirteen years ago today. Did Sam
remember too? She counted the tulips—thirteen. He
hadn't forgotten either.

Whenever Juliet saw a yellow tulip she was instantly
transported back to Canberra in spring of 2005. Sam had
taken her to the Floriade flower festival on the shores
of Lake Burley Griffin. She closed her eyes as she let
her mind drift back.

It had been a glorious September day, with the sun
shining in a cobalt-blue sky. The water on the lake had
been unusually calm and everything about the world
had seemed right. She'd been able to smell freshly
mown grass and popcorn as they'd waited in line for
the Ferris wheel, standing among some of the thousands
of spring blooms that were specially planted for the
festival. Hundreds of visitors had wandered through
the acres of gardens but Juliet had only been aware of
Sam. They'd boarded the Ferris wheel and when their

carriage had reached the summit it had come to a stop. Looking down, Juliet had seen a carpet of yellow tulips spread our beneath them, blanketing the ground like a reflection of the sun. It was such a happy colour and it had suited her mood perfectly. Sam, however, had been more interested in looking at Juliet.

September the twelfth was the day he'd first told her he loved her, cuddled together on a seat at the top of a Ferris wheel. And on September the twelfth, thirteen years ago, above a sea of yellow tulips, Sam had proposed. Today was the anniversary of their engagement.

But thirteen years later everything had changed. The fairy-tale had unravelled. Juliet opened her eyes. Her dreams lay shattered at her feet in a million tiny pieces and her heart sat heavily in her chest, a leaden weight, immobile, stitched inside her skin.

Her body had failed. Her marriage had failed. She felt betrayed. Despite the tulips there was no gallant knight on a noble steed coming to rescue her.

The twelfth of September was now the anniversary of her surgery. It was no longer a celebration.

The mild perfume of the tulips suddenly made Juliet nauseous and she thrust them to the end of the bed just as the nurse returned with the vase. Juliet was about to ask her to take the flowers away but she hesitated, not quite able to part with them. The nurse picked them up, arranging them in the vase before placing it on the bed-side table. Juliet turned her head, watching the nurse's movements, and her gaze settled on the photograph of her children that Maggie had given her.

She would keep the flowers, she decided. Her marriage might be over but she still had a lot to be grateful for. She was going to concentrate on saving her future.

Her children's future. September the twelfth would be the anniversary of the beginning of the rest of her life. There was nothing to be gained by rehashing the past. The fairy-tale might be over but if she was lucky, her life wouldn't be. She had vowed to fight and she wasn't finished yet. Other battles had already been lost and she wasn't going to lose this next one.

The nurse picked up Juliet's chart. 'Do you need anything for pain?' she asked.

The pain of the surgery was bearable now, as long as she didn't move too much, and the nausea had settled almost completely, but Juliet's heart was hurting. She needed to rest and she wanted to sleep so she asked for the medication that was due.

Perhaps she shouldn't have because when she did drift off to sleep it wasn't restful. Whether it was the medication, the after-effects of the anaesthetic or just circumstances Juliet didn't know, but whatever it was it resulted in a dream that was far too realistic for her liking.

She was walking along the coast. She could feel the breeze in her hair, could smell the salty tang of the ocean, but she didn't recognise the beach. She did, however, recognise the figure walking a few hundred metres in front of her. It was Sam. He was wearing shorts and the green polo shirt he'd worn the night he'd taken the children to dinner at Sofia's, the night of their divorce. Where were they? And why were they there?

She called his name, hoping the wind would carry it to him. He turned. He'd heard her. He was smiling and Juliet's heart flipped in her chest, just like it did every time Sam's right-to-left smile lit up his face. He held out his arms, open and welcoming, and Juliet felt the last vestige of pain in her chest float away. But before she could move, before she could take another step towards him, Kate and Edward appeared from behind her and ran into Sam's embrace.

He hadn't been looking at her, she realised. His smile hadn't been for her, it had been for his children.

Sam waited for the children and then turned and kept walking, holding their hands. No one paid Juliet any attention. It was as though she was invisible.

Juliet was frozen to the spot, unable to move, as she watched her family walk away without her, without so much as a backward glance. They continued walking along the beach, every step taking them farther away from her. Didn't they know she was there or did they not care?

Just as Juliet thought she couldn't feel worse, she saw an unfamiliar woman walking up from the water's edge to join her family. The woman entered the tableau from the side so Juliet couldn't see her face, only her back. Juliet called out but if anyone heard her this time, no one turned around. No one stopped. She was helpless, immobile, trapped in a nightmare, and there was nothing she could do as the woman walked away with Sam, Kate and Edward. Her family.

It didn't matter that Juliet couldn't see the woman's face, she knew who she was. She was her replacement.

She woke with a start. She must have moved as she'd woken up because her chest was burning. The dream was so real, so vivid, and Juliet knew she wouldn't forget it easily.

She lay still in bed, waiting for the searing pain in her chest to subside as she thought about the dream. What did it mean? Had Sam remarried? Replaced her?

She'd been able to see everything. Had she been able

to hear them? Had they been able to hear her? It didn't appear so. A horrible thought hit her. Was the Juliet in the dream dead?

Would Sam want to give their children another mother? Someone who bought him green T-shirts that matched his eyes. Someone to plait Kate's hair just as she did now. Someone to cook pancakes for Edward.

Juliet had always been so terrified of Sam going off to war and getting himself killed. She'd been terrified of becoming a widow like Maggie. But what if she was the one who died?

She hadn't really wanted a divorce but her pride and stubbornness had led her down that path before she'd realised where she was heading, until all of a sudden there had been no turning back. Part of her still thought they could salvage the situation. If they couldn't, she knew they would make the best of the hand they'd been dealt, but what if she wasn't even around? She didn't want her children to need another mother. She didn't want someone else taking her place.

She wanted her kids to know she loved them. She wanted that to mean something.

She lay in her hospital bed, physically and emotionally bruised. The truth of the matter was that she loved her kids and she still loved Sam.

What a fool she'd been. How much damage had she done? Could she fix things? Thoughts whirled around in her head, colliding with each other, confusing her.

Should she try to mend things or was it just circumstances making her feel melancholy? Had there been an opportunity to save their marriage? Had they really tried as hard as they could have?

She shook her head in a physical attempt to stop the mental battering her thoughts were giving her. When they'd separated she had been adamant they'd done their best. She couldn't afford to have doubts now.

The fairy-tale was over. End of story.

2007

Juliet had told people that she and Sam couldn't agree on where to live, couldn't agree on what was best for the children, but it was more than just a disagreement over location. But she'd never spoken the whole truth to anyone.

They had left Darwin in 2000 and moved to Sydney. That had suited Juliet perfectly as she'd been close to Maggie who was still recovering from her husband's death. Kate had been born that year and Edward two years later. Life had been good for their little family.

In 2003 Sam had been transferred to Melbourne. That move had also been easy but they had begun discussing what they would do once the children started school. Juliet didn't want to move them every three years for ever—she didn't think it was fair. Sam had said it hadn't bothered him when he was growing up as a defence force kid but Juliet didn't want to point out that, after his mother had died when he had been just seven, he'd been dealing with bigger issues than moving house.

She also knew that while Edward would cope with frequent moves, Kate, with her more serious and introverted personality, probably would not. She wanted Kate to have time to settle into school and make friends. She didn't want to be uprooting her every few years.

At the end of 2005 they were looking at another transfer, this time to Adelaide. It was defence force policy to move their people every three years. This transfer didn't constitute a promotion for Sam, it was just a scheduled transfer and Juliet put her foot down. Kate was about to start school and Juliet wanted her transition to be as smooth as possible. Kate had been diagnosed with suspected dyslexia and Juliet wanted her to start school with her friends from kindergarten, not be moved interstate, as she thought Kate had enough to deal with. They had been working with a tutor and she and Kate had established a good rapport. Juliet wasn't prepared to disrupt that. She refused to move their family, and while she wasn't mean enough to make Sam leave the navy she did want him to explore other options. Sam, to his credit, did try to work with her demands, at least initially. He took a six-month leave of absence from the navy, something the defence force was always happy with. The navy figured it was better to give people leave than to lose them all together. The defence force human resource department even helped to find Sam a civilian position through their contacts. In this instance being magnanimous worked out perfectly for the navy—they looked like the good guys and within six months they had their officer back.

The job they found for Sam was with an oil company that had drilling operations in Bass Strait, south of Melbourne. It sounded ideal but the only problem was that he didn't get to go out to the oil rigs, he didn't get to go out to sea, he didn't get to fly in choppers. He was a desk jockey. His work was operational trouble-shooting and he was good at that. He'd had plenty of experience in planning, scheduling and problem solving, but there wasn't enough variety or physical work to engage him. He missed the danger and excitement of the navy.

He was bored. Bored and unhappy. He missed the ocean and he missed the diversity. While he loved routine in his home life, he discovered he hated it in his job. He was miserable at work and he brought that home with him.

He joined the country fire service, a volunteer emergency services organisation, looking for something to satisfy his need for adrenaline bursts. Endless meetings and training exercises took over his weekends and weeknights, not to mention the actual emergencies that took him away from the family too. Bushfires, storm damage, flooding, trees falling onto houses and across roads all seemed to need the services of the CFS. And Sam was always available. He needed the excitement.

To Juliet it seemed as though Sam was home even less than before. He couldn't get his fix of adrenaline from his work or his family and he got more and more involved in the CFS. His need for excitement and danger and the ever-decreasing time he spent with his family made Juliet suspect he was punishing her deliberately and she grew resentful and bitter. She couldn't believe he needed to spend so much of his time with the CFS and she started picking arguments. She could hear the accusations in her voice but she couldn't seem to stop herself. Their conversations became terse until they almost stopped conversing altogether. Eventually Juliet realised this life was never going to be exciting enough for Sam.

At the end of Sam's leave of absence he was offered a six-month secondment to Singapore on a training mission. The family could go with him and he thought that was a perfect solution.

'I'm not prepared to move the children every three years—what makes you think moving every six months is any better?' Juliet argued.

'We can stay together this way,' Sam countered. 'If

I was going off to combat, you couldn't come too. Isn't this better?'

'If you were going to war, we wouldn't have to move anywhere.' At that stage Juliet thought that sounded like the better option and the thought horrified her. She'd always been terrified that Sam would be sent to a war zone and never come back, and now she was thinking that was a better scenario. She must be mad.

'I've accepted the position.'

'You're going? We're not discussing this?' Sam had taken it without consulting her? 'I have given up everything to follow you—my home, my career—and you know why I can't keep doing this. If it was just me, that would be different, but this affects our children too. I can't believe you would do this to them.'

'I think you're being melodramatic. I haven't gone into this blindly. The schools are world class. Kate will be fine.'

'Melodramatic!' Sam hadn't been listening to anything she'd said. 'You want to move us to Singapore for six months and then what? Where will we be six months after that?'

'I can't tell you that.'

'Because you don't know, do you? It's all in the hands of the defence force.' It was obvious to her then that they needed a break. 'I'm not going to let the navy dictate our lives any more.'

Sam had a different opinion. He left for Singapore. Juliet knew he was eager to get back to navy life and that thought hurt her more than anything. She so badly wanted to be enough for him. Wanted their family to be enough, and she thought, hoped, that when he returned to the navy he'd realise he missed them, realise he was missing the opportunity to watch his children grow up.

In Juliet's mind it was a trial separation and she accepted that, confident that Sam would eventually return to them.

But things turned out differently.

The six months in Singapore was extended to twelve and, in hindsight, Juliet realised she should have gone with him, but she'd made such a big deal about keeping the children settled she couldn't then back down. Once again her stubbornness and pride got in the way. Her mother used to say that pride came before a fall, and she was soon to find that was true.

At the end of the year Juliet wanted him home. She filed for divorce, thinking it would make Sam realise what was important, but that backfired spectacularly. Sam chose the navy over his family.

That was her interpretation. Juliet knew Sam saw things differently.

CHAPTER SIX

October 2008, a Friday

JULIET was nervous. Her palms were clammy, she could feel every beat of her heart pulsing in her throat and her stomach was in knots. Her second round of chemo started today, she was due at the hospital in an hour, but that wasn't causing her nervousness.

Sam was back from his six-week exercise in the Timor Sea. He was flying into Melbourne this morning. He was coming to spend a weekend with the children and they were going to a beach house on the coast, but when he'd found out she had an appointment he'd offered to take her to the hospital. He was due to arrive at her house in fifteen minutes and she was getting herself into a right state.

He hadn't seen her since the surgery.

He hadn't seen her flat-chested.

He hadn't seen her since her hair had started falling out.

Juliet was scared of his reaction. She didn't expect him to vocalise his thoughts but she was terrified that she'd be able to see them reflected in his eyes. She was afraid she'd see herself reflected there and she was fear-ful of what that might look like.

Her own reaction had frightened her at first and she thought she'd been prepared. For twenty-three years she'd been an hourglass shape and suddenly she was a pear, all hips and no breasts. Her tops hung loosely on her frame, making it obvious, in her mind, that something was missing, almost accentuating her new shape. She hadn't done anything about buying special bras yet, ones that would give her a false profile because she hadn't thought it was a priority and her chest was still too sore to contemplate the idea of wearing anything firm against it. But now, with Sam's visit looming, vanity was getting the better of her. She didn't want to look different, not to him.

She stood in front of her wardrobe, wrapped in the comforting warmth of her old dressing-gown, as she tried to find something to wear. She grabbed a black shirt dress. She didn't want to wear anything figure hugging—that would only make things worse—and slipped her arms into the dress, fastening the buttons. The shape was okay but it made her look like she was going to a funeral. Not the look she was after. She took it off and threw it on the bed. She continued to rummage through her clothes, searching for something that made her feel confident.

The pile of discarded clothes on her bed grew higher. Sam would be there in five minutes. The next thing she found would have to do. She gave up looking through the clothes on hangers and searched the drawers. She found a light woollen top in a navy, grey and white argyle pattern. She grabbed it from the pile, hoping the pattern would cover a multitude of sins, pulled on jeans and a T-shirt and dragged the jumper over her head.

She glanced quickly in the mirror, still not completely comfortable with confronting her own image. The top wasn't a bad choice as the pattern did camouflage her flat chest to some degree. Anyway, it would have to do, she was out of time.

She cleaned her teeth and ran a brush over her hair, trying to ignore the strands of hair that clogged the bristles. In the last week her hair had started to fall out. Not enough that anyone looking at her would notice, but she was finding hair on her pillow in the morning, in the shower and in her brush. She consoled herself with the thought that at least the chemo was targeting cells and she just hoped it was getting the cancer cells too.

There was a knock on the door. Juliet took a deep breath. She'd had four weeks to get used to her new look and she still found it confronting. How was Sam going to react?

He wasn't sure what he'd been expecting to find when he saw Juliet. He'd expected her to look different but he wasn't exactly sure what changes might have occurred. He'd prepared himself to be surprised, shocked even, but she looked just the same. Her chestnut hair was still long and thick, framing her heart-shaped face. Her blue eyes were enormous in her pale face and her freckles were perhaps more prominent against her skin, but otherwise she still looked like his Juliet. She was still beautiful.

He stepped through the door and bent down to hug her. His greeting was automatic and it was then that he felt the difference, felt the change. She was skin and bone, the comforting softness of her breasts gone.

Juliet sucked in a breath, short and sharp, as he hugged her.

'I'm sorry, Jules, did I hurt you? I wasn't think-ing.' Had he hurt her? He couldn't believe he'd been so careless—being hugged was probably the last thing she wanted.

She shook her head as she pulled out of his embrace. 'I'm fine,' she said, but he noticed she avoided eye contact. What didn't she want him to see?

'We'd better go. Parking might be hard to find.' She turned round to grab her car keys from the hall table and Sam could see the change now. Juliet's familiar profile had been replaced by one he didn't recognise. The familiar swell of her breasts had disappeared and in their place was nothing. He'd known what a double mastectomy meant yet he still hadn't pictured the reality. Hadn't been able to imagine it. And now he didn't need to imagine any more; he could clearly see just what this cancer had done to Juliet. He had felt it and he'd seen it.

He tried to hide his surprise as she turned back and handed him the car keys. He hadn't expected such a dramatic change. And if the physical changes were so obvious, what about the emotional strain? How was she coping with that? He knew surgery had been her choice but were the changes worse than she had expected too? How was she managing on her own? Maggie was back in Sydney and Juliet was responsible for the normal family routine again. Was it too much for her? Did she need more support? He didn't really understand what was involved with regard to her treatment. He knew that the lymph nodes that were excised during the mastectomy had tested negative for cancer cells and that her first dose of chemo had gone smoothly, but he wasn't up to speed on the process of chemo or the potential side-effects. How much of an effect did the chemo have on her physical capacity?

Sam knew he had to do something, had to offer some

kind of support, but he hadn't been able to work out what to do or how to do it. He didn't know what Juliet needed or what she'd accept. He needed more information about what she was going through and how she was coping, starting with what happened today. He took the opportunity to ask questions as he drove her into the hospital.

'Do you see the surgeon today?' he asked as they waited at a red light at the corner of Swan Street and Punt Road.

'No. Dr Benson is the surgical oncologist, I've finished with him.' She paused. 'Hopefully. The medical oncologist is in charge of the chemo. That's Dr Davey.'

Sam had looked at various websites, trying to find information about chemotherapy, and he tried to recall what he'd read. He didn't suppose it mattered to him which doctor was which, he just wanted to know what they were going to do for, and to, Juliet. 'What does he do exactly?'

'One of the first things they'll do today is take some blood. It gets tested and once the test results come back, Dr Davey will see me and review my treatment.'

'What are they testing it for?'

'To see if my white blood cell count is okay. If it's too low, it lowers my resistance to infection and they'll send me home and give me some more time for my count to build up. But I've been feeling okay so hopefully I'll get my second dose. I don't want any delays, I want to get this all finished before Christmas.'

'Would you like me to come in with you? Keep you company?' he asked as he navigated the right-hand turn into Punt Road.

'I'll be at the hospital for the best part of four hours. You don't want to sit there all that time, do you?'

'I've got no commitments until Kate and Edward finish school and kindy.'

She didn't answer immediately. Would she rather be alone?

In his imagination Sam could picture Juliet sitting in a room full of strangers, everyone hooked up to various machines and monitors, all looking tired and ill. Juliet looked well—if he could ignore the fact she'd lost her curves. She was still gorgeous and he couldn't imagine her sitting alone in a group of sick people. He didn't *want* her to sit there alone. He wanted to be with her.

Should he have told her that? He wasn't sure. He didn't know if she would have felt obliged to let him accompany her and, as much as he wanted to go with her, he didn't want to put her in a situation that made her feel uncomfortable. He tried a different explanation. 'I'd like to understand your treatment—if the kids ask me questions about what's happening it'd help me if I've seen what goes on and it would help to clarify things for me.' He flashed her a smile. He knew how she felt about his smile and he just hoped that hadn't changed. He knew he wasn't playing fair, using the children in his bargaining, and hopefully using his smile to his advantage, but he wasn't sending her in there alone.

She shrugged and nodded. 'If you're sure,' was all she said in reply. Sam took that to mean yes.

Juliet directed him to the most convenient parking garage and then led him to the oncology unit. She was signed in and once the nurse collected her it was a slow but steady process through a battery of tests. Juliet introduced him to the nurse as her 'support person'. He noticed her slight hesitation before she clarified his position and he wondered what she'd been about to call him. He wasn't sure what he wanted to be but he supposed 'support person' was probably the best he could hope for at the moment.

Juliet's blood pressure, pulse rate, temperature, height and weight, even her respiratory rate were all recorded before her blood was taken and finally a bung was inserted into her elbow ready for the IV attachment. They were then sent back out to the waiting area.

'What happens now?' he asked.

'We wait. Once Dr Davey has reviewed my test results, I'll see him. There's a lot of sitting around.' Juliet pulled a book out of her handbag. 'Why don't you grab something to read from that magazine rack?' She indicated a stack of magazines and newspapers on the opposite side of the room. There wasn't anything else to do; they could hardly have a private conversation in a room full of people, so Sam perused the selection and chose something to flick through while they waited.

He'd read the same article three times by the time Juliet was finally ushered through to see Dr Davey.

Once again Juliet introduced him as her support person but this time Sam wasn't so surprised. If that description meant he got to sit in on all her consults, it was fine with him.

Dr Davey shuffled some papers on his desk. 'Your blood tests are all okay,' he said once they were all seated. 'I assume since I didn't hear anything after your first dose of chemo that you didn't have any adverse reactions?'

Juliet shook her head. 'No major problems at all.'

'No nausea, no constipation?' Dr Davey clarified.

'I kept my fluids up and everything was fine.'

'Well, we can start the second dose today. I'll increase

the dosage slightly and same rules apply—if you experience any problems, make sure you let the clinic know. Do you have any concerns at all before we begin?'

Sam waited for Juliet to speak first but she just said everything was fine. She might understand what was going on but Sam had lots of questions. But no one seemed to expect him to say anything—no one looked in his direction or gave him an opportunity to talk. Before he realised what was happening Juliet was standing, waiting for him to join her. Dr Davey wrote in Juliet's notes and saw them to the door. The appointment was over. It was all rather anti-climactic in Sam's opinion, done and dusted before he'd absorbed what had been discussed.

One of the nurses took Juliet's case notes and led them to a large room, which Sam would have called a ward except there were no beds. In the spots where he assumed the hospital beds would normally be were recliner chairs. It reminded him of a day surgery recovery area. Some of the chairs had the curtains drawn around them, others were in full view. Some were occupied and some were empty. The people in the chairs—the patients, he supposed—were all hooked up to drips. Some were sleeping, some were chatting, others were reading. He was surprised to see how relaxed everyone seemed.

Sam pulled an armchair up next to Juliet's recliner as a second nurse joined their little group. The two nurses double-checked Juliet's name, cross-checking it with the hospital name tag around her wrist, and then double-checked the medication order with the medications on the tray. Apparently everything was in order because Juliet was handed a tablet and then the nurse hung a bag on the dripstand and connected Juliet to it.

Juliet washed the tablet down with a drink of water before explaining what was happening. 'The Adriamycin is given through the drip. It blocks DNA production and kills cells. The tablet was Cytoxan. It stops cells from dividing so basically it stops new cancer cells growing. The Adriamycin won't kill all the cells in one go so if the doctors can stop cell division as well then the number of cancer cells will gradually decrease and there will be fewer cells to be killed each time. Does that make sense?'

Nothing about this made sense to Sam but as long as the combination of surgery and chemotherapy worked, he didn't care if everyone but him spoke Swahili. As long as they cured Juliet.

Juliet had chosen a chair at the far end of the room and at this stage the neighbouring chairs were all unoccupied. The medication could take a couple of hours to run through the drip and Sam was grateful to be away from the other patients, out of earshot. He needed to discuss some things with Juliet and didn't want the whole room to hear.

'How have the kids been coping with everything that's been happening? Is there anything I need to know before I collect them this afternoon?'

'Ed's doing fine. Nothing much worries him and I don't think he's really noticed any change to his day to day life. Kate's a little more clingy than usual. She's been fine until this past week. My hair has started to fall out and I think that's freaked her out a bit.'

Sam found himself giving Juliet's hair a closer look, it looked like it always had to him, thick and dark and glossy. 'Your hair doesn't look any different.'

'There's been quite a lot of hair on my pillow in the mornings. I've been trying to clean up the evidence before she sees it but she's been coming in to my room during the night so it's not always possible to hide the fact that I'm losing my hair,' she explained.

Sam knew a common side effect of chemo was hair loss but he had no idea to what extent it could be expected. 'Are you likely to lose all your hair? Is it going to cause problems for Kate, do you think?'

'The Cytoxan is causing the hair loss and it's quite likely I'll lose it all.' She shrugged. 'I'm telling myself that at least it means the drug is having an effect but I'll need to be conscious of Kate's reaction. I might need a wig. I have the number of a cosmetician and I'll make an appointment to see her. I think it would be a good idea if I can try and minimise, or at least disguise, some of the physical changes. It might lessen the trauma for the kids.'

Sam found the idea of Juliet losing all her hair quite disturbing. If that was his reaction, he could imagine how Kate might feel.

'I'm sure she'll be fine with you,' Juliet continued, 'but just expect her to stick a bit closer to you than normal. The weekend at the beach might be just what she needs. It might give her a chance to feel as though everything is fine.'

Juliet had read his expression, misinterpreting it slightly. Sam didn't correct her, choosing to follow her line of thought instead. 'You think that's still a good idea, the beach? You don't want us closer to home? What if you need someone?'

'I'll be fine, and Gabby and Finn are only a street away if I need something. I haven't had a lot of energy lately so it'll be good for the kids to have some fun.'

'Do you think they might want another beach holiday over Christmas?'

Juliet looked startled by his question. 'Why?'

'Edward was asking when he was going to see my dad. I sort of promised that we'd go to Merimbula after Christmas. I've taken leave and I thought a week at the beach would be nice.'

'You want to take them for a week?' Juliet's expression was flat and Sam wondered what the problem was.

'It was what we'd planned, remember?'

'I know, but a week's a long time.'

Sam frowned. 'It's not really,' he argued. 'I thought it might give you a chance to have some peace and quiet, some recovery time. I know you were going to go back to Melbourne but you could stay with your parents instead, have some time out.'

'I don't think I want time out and I don't want to be separated from the children for a whole week. That's too long.'

'You want me to take them for a shorter time?' Sam was a reasonable man but he wasn't about to miss out on time with his children.

'I'm not sure,' she replied.

'I have a better idea.' Another plan came to him suddenly and he wondered why he hadn't thought of it earlier. 'Why don't I drive up to Bowral on Boxing Day and collect you all.'

'You're inviting me too?'

Sam nodded. 'You can have your R&R in Merimbula. It might not be as peaceful as staying at your parents' but this way we can both have time with the kids. Dad and Aunt Helen would be thrilled—they'd love to see you as well.'

'Can I have some time to think about what I'll do

and let you know? Maybe I could come at the end of the week for a few days.'

'You decide and let me know but it's no problem for you to stay the whole week if you like.' He hoped she'd see the sense in joining them. The sunshine and fresh sea air would be a perfect tonic but he recognised that now was not the time to make an issue with it. He didn't want to be overbearing. He'd sown the seed of the idea and he hoped Juliet would agree to his whole plan.

The drip had run through and the nurse arrived to disconnect Juliet. She took a final set of obs before announcing that Juliet could go home. Sam waited while she went through the discharge summary with Juliet, explaining the anti-nausea medication to her and instructing her to drink plenty of fluids.

Watching Juliet being poked and prodded, seeing her being dwarfed in that huge recliner chair looking so tiny, fragile and pale, had brought out his protective instincts and he knew that he wasn't averse to the idea of her joining them in Merimbula. She needed looking after, that was obvious, and it would be so easy to look after her if she was by his side. If he could convince her that the ocean air would do her good then he knew, with the help of his dad and his Aunt Helen, they would be able to restore some of her spirit. The more he thought about his suggestion, the more he liked it. He'd keep working on her—it was in everyone's best interests for her to agree.

By the time Sam had driven Juliet home he had just enough time to gather the children's bags before leaving to collect them from school. He'd wanted to head straight to the beach, hoping to get out of the city before the weekend peak-hour traffic started, but he wasn't totally comfortable with leaving Juliet alone. Only after making her promise she'd call if she had any problems did he finally get into the car, but he was still uneasy. He checked in on her every hour for the rest of the day and first thing on Saturday morning. Each time Juliet insisted she was fine but it was only when she told him to stop bugging her and to enjoy his time with the children instead that he finally stopped checking up on her and did as he was told and relaxed and had fun with his kids.

October 2008, a Sunday

The setting sun was low in the sky and the clouds looked like tufts of pink cotton candy against a honey background as Sam turned the hire car into Juliet's driveway. He and the children had had a busy two days at the beach, body-surfing, playing beach cricket and collecting shells, and now Kate and Edward were both asleep in the back seat.

Sam left the children in the car. He'd get Juliet to open the door and then he could carry them straight to bed. He'd rented the cottage until tomorrow to give him a full day's access today, which had given him time to bathe and feed the children before returning to Melbourne. He'd wanted to make things easy for Juliet. It was something he could do and he was pleased with his planning. He knocked on the front door and was surprised when his knock went unanswered. He'd sent Juliet a text message telling her what time to expect them and he'd thought she'd be waiting at the door, eager to see her babies. He knocked again and tried the front door. It was locked and there was no sound from inside.

His bewilderment turned to concern. He pulled his phone out of his pocket, checking for messages. Juliet hadn't replied to his text. Was she out or had something happened? It was out of character for her not to keep in contact.

He stepped off the veranda and skirted the house. He stood on the rubbish bin and peered through the garage window. Her car was there. He tried the back door but it was also locked. He dialled the home phone number as he reached into the spot where they'd always hidden the spare key. Old habits die hard, he thought as he retrieved the key. He could hear the phone ringing inside, his call going unanswered. He didn't hesitate any further but slipped the key into the lock and opened the door.

The house was dark and quiet. 'Jules, we're home—are you here?' Sam stepped into the family room. This room and the adjacent kitchen were both empty and silent. His worry increased. 'Jules?' he called as he continued up the passage.

A noise made him glance to his right. Something moved on the bathroom floor. It took his brain a moment to process the picture. Legs and feet were just visible through the bathroom doorway.

'Juliet!'

Had she collapsed? He took two steps and was in the bathroom. Juliet was lying on the bathroom floor, her head cushioned on a bunched-up bath towel.

How long had she been lying there? Was she conscious? He could smell vomit. Was she breathing?

He squatted down beside her and put his hand on her wrist, feeling for a pulse. He felt it, weak and rapid. He touched her forehead. It was cool, no sign of a temperature. He moved his hand to her arm. That was cool too—shouldn't she be warmer?

'Jules? It's Sam. Can you hear me?'

She opened her eyes when he spoke and lifted her head at his touch. She attempted to sit up.

'Wait. Don't try to sit up. Tell me what happened first.'

'Nothing happened. I'm just sick.'

Why was she lying on the bathroom floor? 'You promised you'd call. Have you been vomiting all weekend?'

'No.' She shook her head weakly. 'Only this afternoon.'

Sitting up must have disagreed with her. She leant over the toilet bowl as she retched. Sam gathered Juliet's hair into a ponytail and held it away from her face as she heaved, but there was nothing in her stomach to bring up. He waited for the convulsions to stop before he let go of her hair. Dark strands of hair clung to his fingers. He shook his hand and the strands fell to the floor, gathering in clumps on the white tiles. He tried to block the picture from his mind. 'Tell me what I can do, Jules. What do you need? Shall I get those tablets the doctor gave you for nausea?'

Juliet shook her head. 'I've tried taking those but I just vomit them straight back up. Nothing's staying down.'

'There must be something we can do. Let me help you into bed and then I'll call the doctor. You can't stay lying here.'

He scooped her up in his arms, ignoring her protests and her assurances that she was capable of walking. If she was capable of walking, why had she been lying on the cold, hard bathroom floor? She was light and fragile in his arms and all his protective instincts rushed to the fore. He would sort this out for her, he would make sure she was okay, he wasn't going to leave her on her own in this condition despite her protests.

'Where are the kids?' she asked as he laid her down on her bed.

'They're asleep in the car. I'll bring them inside in a minute. They're okay for now. Let's get you sorted.' He fetched a bucket from the laundry and a clean towel from the bathroom. Juliet's dark hair was littering the bathroom floor, stark against the white tiles. He swept it up, removing all traces of it, conscious of Kate's potential reaction to the sight, and then brought the children in from the car. Once his family was all in bed he turned his mind to Juliet's predicament. He needed some advice; he had no idea what to do. He looked up the phone number for St Vincent's Hospital, hoping to find a twenty-four-hour helpline for the oncology department, but the best he could do was the emergency department. He was quite prepared to drive her to the hospital and he wouldn't hesitate to phone Gabby and ask her to come and mind the children, but the nurse who answered the phone suggested that he call a locum. That sounded like good advice to Sam, only he didn't know if Juliet's GP used a locum service. The nurse passed on a number and Sam was gradually able to get the situation under some semblance of control.

The locum doctor gave Juliet two injections, an anti-emetic for nausea and a sedative. 'That should settle things down for her,' he explained. 'Get her to take the anti-nausea tablets tomorrow but if she still can't keep anything down, you'll need to take her in to the hospital.'

By the time Sam had paid for the service and seen the doctor out, Juliet was asleep. Sam was relieved. Juliet needed to rest but his mind was whirling. He couldn't believe he'd found her prostrate on the bathroom floor. Alone. Why hadn't she called him? Why hadn't she called someone? What if she'd been home with the children? Would she have called someone then?

He hoped Juliet would have reacted differently if the children had been home. He was almost certain she would have—the kids were certainly the first thing she'd thought of when he'd arrived back; she didn't want them to see her in that state any more than he did. He had to assume she would have called somebody if she'd been home alone, even if it was only to take the children out of the house.

The questions that had been plaguing him for weeks ran through his mind. Was there anything he could do? Or should do? How many decisions could he make? How much input could he have? What did Juliet need? What would she accept? For weeks he'd had no answers but suddenly he realised what he needed to do.

He'd worry about the Christmas holidays and their trip to Merimbula later. Juliet needed help now and he would give it. He wouldn't wait until December, he would stay by her side right now. She wouldn't be able to argue with him as it was in the best interests of their children. He just needed to organise it.

CHAPTER SEVEN

JULIET slept solidly for twelve hours and woke early, feeling much better. She rolled onto her side and came face to face with Sam. The surprise made her gasp and whether it was that small sound or her movement it was enough to wake him.

He stirred and opened his eyes. His face was only inches from hers. The slightest movement would bring him within reach. Without thinking, she stretched out one hand and her fingers brushed his chest. She was disoriented for a moment, lost in the past, their past.

He wasn't wearing a shirt and his skin was warm and lightly tanned. His green eyes darkened with her touch and, suddenly realising what she'd done, she quickly withdrew her hand.

'Good morning. How are you feeling?' His voice was husky, thick with sleep. Juliet's skin tingled as a shiver of longing ran through her, reminding her again of the years before.

'Much better,' she replied as she fought to regain her equilibrium. Those years were over. They would now only be a memory. 'Have you been here all night?'

'Pretty much.'

'Oh.' Her stomach did a strange, slow, belly-flop.

Sam had been lying beside her, close enough to touch, all night.

'I was worried about leaving you on your own in case you were sick again.'

Any romantic notions she'd been harbouring were quickly dispelled.

'Are you hungry? Can I make you some toast?' He was all business.

Sam loved a project. A mission. Fixing things, problem solving was what he did best, and Juliet knew he saw her as a project. Something that needed sorting out, but she was fine. She didn't want to be seen as a problem that needed solving.

'I'm fine. You don't need to stay. Haven't you got a plane to catch?'

'I've changed my flight. The locum said to make sure you could keep something in your stomach today and I'm going to follow his advice. I'll leave when I'm sure you're okay.'

Even though she didn't want to feel like a charity case, she was grateful for Sam's concern. Despite saying she was fine she really didn't want to be alone after her experience yesterday and she wasn't convinced that she was one hundred per cent better.

'Toast sounds good, then, thanks,' she said, accepting his offer of help.

'No problem. You stay in bed and I'll bring it to you. I'll make breakfast for the kids too.'

The children! Were they awake? Had they seen Sam lying beside her? 'Have the kids been in?' Her heart was in her throat as she asked the question. She didn't want to have to explain the picture to the children.

'No. They're still sleeping but I don't expect that will last much longer.'

Sam rolled out of bed and stood and stretched. His back was to her and he was wearing only a pair of shorts. She let her eyes run over him, taking in his broad shoulders and lean trunk. She could see the muscles flexing over his shoulder blades as he stretched his arms, and she watched them ripple and move as he lowered his arms to his sides. He was a picture of health and Juliet was well aware of the contrast between his peak physical condition and her own. Any remaining fantasies she'd been harbouring about the night in a shared bed were now completely obliterated. She rolled onto her side as Sam left the room, turning her face away from the door.

She heard Edward getting up a few minutes later. As usual he went straight to the kitchen, always ready to eat the minute he woke up. Kate surfaced shortly after and Juliet lay in bed, expecting her to come into the room, as was her normal habit, but she bypassed Juliet. Had she been lured by the sound of Sam's and Edward's voices coming from the kitchen? Juliet lay in bed, alone, trying to decipher the muted strains of conversation.

Eventually the conversation came to her when Sam and the children brought her breakfast.

'Kate, can you get ready for school?' Sam said as Kate put a plate of toast beside Juliet. 'I'll drop you off this morning. And do you think you can help Ed find some clothes too? I want to talk to Mummy.'

Kate nodded but Juliet started to protest. 'I'll get up and help get them ready.'

'Kate can manage, can't you, sweetheart?' Sam interjected.

Juliet was about to argue before she realised that Sam was right. Kate was perfectly capable of doing the task and would probably enjoy the responsibility. She needed to let the children help in whatever ways they could.

She picked up her cup of tea as her children left the room. 'What did you want to talk to me about?' she asked Sam.

'I've got a proposition for you.' He sat on the edge of her bed. He looked worried. His forehead was furrowed and there were creases in the corners of his green eyes. 'You frightened me last night.' He sounded worried too and his concern made Juliet feel better. Just knowing he cared helped. 'What would have happened if I hadn't come back when I did? What would have happened if you'd been home by yourself with the children? Would you have called someone?' Oops, now he sounded annoyed.

'Of course I would,' she retorted. Defending a hypothetical situation made no sense but he seemed to expect an answer.

'Who would you have rung?'

'Gabby or Anna. I told you Gabby and Finn were in town—they would be happy to help.'

'They have their own families. Do you think it's fair to rely on them?'

'They've offered to help and I know they mean it. I'd do the same for them. What exactly are you getting at?' She knew he was building up to something, she could see it in his expression.

'I don't think you can cope on your own with the kids—'

'I've managed often enough on my own with the children,' Juliet interrupted. She was cross now. There had been plenty of times when Sam hadn't been around to help and she'd managed perfectly well. She couldn't believe he was going to criticise her now.

'Jules, let me finish.' Sam's demeanour was calm, in

contrast to her rising temper. 'I was going to say "just while you're going through chemo". I was on the internet last night, researching the drugs you're taking. Dr Davey increased the medication this time. What do you think will happen next time if you have a similar reaction?'

She shrugged. 'I don't know.' How was anyone to know? 'I'll speak to Dr Davey and see what he suggests. Okay?'

'I have a better idea. Why don't I take the children to Sydney to look after them there while you finish your treatment?'

'No. Absolutely not.'

'I didn't think you'd like that option. Which leaves option two. I will take leave until Christmas and move down to Melbourne to help you.'

Sam sounded as though the decision had been already made. Juliet wondered what his agenda was. 'Why?'

'Because I can.'

Juliet didn't respond. She just looked at him, waiting for him to elaborate. At this point it didn't sound like much of a reason.

Sam continued. 'I want to help. You're the mother of my children. We may be divorced but I still care about you and about how you're coping. I can run around after the children, take you to your appointments, do the cooking. It would make things easier for you if you had help.'

'I can pay for a housekeeper,' she retorted. '*You* can pay for a housekeeper if it makes you feel better. You don't need to take leave. I don't need full-time help.' As much as she'd appreciated his offer of help when it was for the day, the idea of having Sam around for the next few weeks was unsettling. She didn't want him to think she couldn't manage. She didn't want to think he might be right.

'But I can do it. I want to do it. Think of it this way if you prefer—wouldn't this arrangement be better for Kate and Edward too?'

'You'll take leave? Just like that?'

'I've been in the navy for twenty years. I think I'm owed some carer's leave.'

'I'm not sure it'll work.'

'It will. Tell you what, if I can prove to you how easy it will be, if I can organise leave by the end of the day, will you let me stay and help?'

'You want to stay here?'

Sam shook his head. 'I think that's a bit too confusing for everyone. I'll find something close by. A short-stay apartment should do.'

She knew she should argue, knew she should insist that she could manage, but the reality was that she could use the help and the kids would benefit from having Sam around. But it was only a temporary solution so would it make things more difficult in the long run? She wasn't sure and she really had no way of knowing.

Juliet stayed in bed and ate her breakfast as Sam got the children ready for school. Her mind was buzzing but eventually she decided that, until Sam had made firm arrangements, she didn't need to worry about hypothetical situations.

She waited until Sam had left to drop the children off before getting out of bed. She had intended to have a shower but a wave of dizziness threatened to overwhelm her, and sitting on the edge of the bath to clean her teeth was all she could manage before collapsing back into bed. She wouldn't refuse Sam's help, she decided, even if it was just for the day.

* * *

Sam came into her room when he got home. He had a bag laden with fresh fruit and vegetables in one hand and a paper bag from the pharmacy in the other. He handed the paper bag to Juliet.

Inside was an assortment of vitamin supplements. 'What are these for?' she asked.

'I rang Dr Davey to get his advice. He suggested you continue with the anti-nausea tablets and also take these. If you're not starting to feel better in another twenty-four hours, he wants to see you. Did you manage to keep breakfast down?'

She nodded.

'I've got some phone calls I need to make but why don't I run you a bath first?'

A bath had sounded appealing until Juliet faced the reality of her naked figure. She knew she'd lost weight but when she was dressed she could ignore the bony protuberances. Now the harsh morning light was exaggerating every angle in her normally curvaceous figure. Even her thighs were thin and floppy she noticed as she stepped into the bath. Her skin, although normally pale, had an unhealthy tinge of yellow and her chest was disfigured by scars.

Juliet slid quickly under the water, letting the bubbles hide her nakedness. She thought she looked ten years older and she felt it too. She closed her eyes, trying to picture something other than her flaws. All she could see behind her closed eyelids was Sam's smile. In her mind she turned him round and feasted her eyes on his naked back as she remembered how he'd looked when he'd climbed out of her bed that morning. He was perfect, his tanned, toned muscles contrasting dramatically with her own pasty, flabby flesh.

Tears rolled from the corners of her eyes. She

shouldn't care about how she looked. She should only care that she was alive but she couldn't stop crying. Being alive wasn't enough for her today. All she could think about was what she'd lost. Emotionally and physically.

She knew she was being pathetic, wallowing in self-pity, but she couldn't stop.

She sank under the water, letting her tears mingle with the bathwater. She stayed submerged until she ran out of air. Rising to the surface to breathe, she concentrated on filling her lungs. She wiped her face, removing the traces of tears and water, and climbed from the bath. She hurriedly towelled herself dry, keeping her back to the mirror.

When Sam came to check on her she was back in bed and she'd stopped crying, but she knew her eyes were still puffy and red.

'What's wrong?' he asked.

'Nothing,' she replied, trying to look as if she had her emotions under control. 'I'm just having a moment.'

'Are you feeling sick?' he asked as he placed another cup of tea on her bedside table, next to the bottles of supplements.

'No, I'm feeling like a failure.'

'What do you mean?'

'I thought I'd cope better than this. I had no problems with the first lot of chemo and I expected the same outcome this time, but you're right. I can't manage to look after the children like this. I can't even manage to look after myself.'

'That's why I'm here. It's my turn to look after my family. Think of all those times when I was away and the burden of responsibility fell on you—it's my turn now.'

'And what if I don't beat this? What then?'

'You will.'

'How can you be so sure?'

'Because you told me so yourself.' Sam's face lit up as he smiled at her. His green eyes were shining and his smile lifted Juliet's spirits a little. 'I know you—I know how stubborn and determined you are. You can do this but there's no reason to do it alone. Let us help you. Let *me* help you.'

She'd been trying so hard to keep things together, telling everyone she was going to beat this cancer, but even she wasn't convinced it was true. She knew that Sam's presence would ease the pressure on her—that was why she'd dissolved into tears in the first place, because suddenly she wouldn't have to be the one who was making sure things ran smoothly. She wouldn't have to be the one who worried about whether or not the children had clean uniforms and fresh food for their lunches. She wouldn't have to worry about ballet lessons and play dates. Sam's offer was terribly tempting and she didn't have the energy to refuse. 'Can you stay?' she asked. While the idea of Sam seeing her in a weakened, unattractive state was daunting, she did find the idea of having someone to share the burden appealing.

'Do you want me to?'

She nodded. If he was offering to help, she was going to accept it. Hopefully he'd seen her at her worst last night and she'd worry about the ramifications of having him back in her life later.

'Good, because I've organised leave. If everything goes according to plan, you have eight more weeks of treatment and I have eight weeks of leave. We're sorted. I just need to find some accommodation close by.'

A wave of relief rolled over her. Could she push her

luck a little bit further? 'About that…' Juliet hesitated. 'It would be easier if you stayed here, with us, if you're here to help.'

'Probably, but it's okay. I'll find something.'

'Why don't you make up the spare bed in the study? That would be the sensible option, wouldn't it?' If Sam was there in the morning, she wouldn't have to make sure she was up before the children, up in time to clean up any hair that had fallen out during the night before Kate saw it. It would be easier for everyone if Sam was close to hand, wouldn't it?

Sam wasn't sure if staying in the house was the best option. Did he want to be a guest in his old house? Would he feel like an intruder? But he had offered his help, and he'd been prepared to insist that Juliet accept his help so her suggestion was probably not worth arguing over. Juliet obviously wasn't well enough to look after the children and they were his responsibility. Staying in the house would make things easier, so he accepted with good grace and prepared to get on with caring for his family.

For the next two weeks he ferried the children around, shopped for groceries and cooked. Luckily the children were happy to exist on meals of pasta and barbecued sausages, but he was worried about Juliet. She was so thin and so pale and so tired. For the first week he was there she spent most of each day in bed. That was good; it was what she needed, but what bothered Sam was that he didn't have to insist that she rest. She didn't want to get up and that wasn't like the Juliet he knew. She would get out of bed in the afternoon when everyone was home but he could see the effort she was making and how taxing it was for her to pretend to the children that everything was fine. They ate dinner together as a family, although Juliet barely ate, existing on fruit and mashed vegetables.

By the middle of the second week things were improving. Juliet started to feel better in herself and Sam was relieved. While he understood the effects of the chemo he had struggled to come to terms with how harsh it was and the physical changes in Juliet were confronting. It was hard to watch the woman he loved suffer. He had done everything he could to ease the burden but it was a huge relief when she felt like getting out of bed again. When he got home from dropping the children at school one morning he was thrilled to find her showered and dressed and tidying the kitchen. He handed her a card that Gabby had given him that day at the kindergarten.

'What's this?'

'Gabby has invited us to dinner for her birthday.'

'Both of us?'

He nodded.

'What did you tell her?'

'I said I would pass it on to you.'

Juliet glanced at the invitation before dropping it onto the kitchen bench without comment.

Her lack of interest surprised him. 'What do you think?' he asked.

She shrugged.

He hadn't realised how much he'd been looking forward to going out with Juliet but perhaps she didn't want to go with him. 'Would you rather go on your own?'

'No, it's not that. I just don't feel up to going out.'

'I thought you were feeling better.'

'I am but I don't think I'm ready to get dressed up and make witty conversation.'

'These are your friends, Jules. No one is going to expect you to be the life of the party.'

'The death of the party would be more like it.'

'What do you mean by that?'

She turned to face him. 'Look at me.' She raised her hands to her shoulders and swept them in front of her down to her hips. 'I look dreadful.'

'I think you're gorgeous.' She was pale and too thin, a shadow of her former self, but in his eyes she was always beautiful. Her blue eyes were even more striking now, contrasting with the pallor of her skin, and her fragile appearance made him want to scoop her up and protect her from the world.

'And I think you're a terrible liar,' she replied.

But Sam didn't care what Juliet said because she was smiling and she hadn't smiled at him in days. She'd smiled for the children but it had been obvious to him that she'd been making an effort to keep up appearances, but now her smile was natural, unforced, and it was all the reward Sam needed.

'If you don't believe me, can I make a suggestion?' he asked. She looked at him warily, one eyebrow raised. 'Why don't I ring the cosmetician, the one the oncology nurses told you about? She might be able to suggest some things that might make you feel brighter.' He half expected his idea to be shot down in flames but Juliet actually acquiesced and fortunately the cosmetician had a free appointment. Sam wasn't certain that he would have got Juliet there on a different day.

He drove her to the appointment and although she wouldn't let him go in with her she seemed happy enough when he met her afterwards. He hoped the session had gone well. It hadn't occurred to him until she'd gone in that it could be too much for her.

'How did you go?'

'Good news and bad news,' she said. 'She showed me some tricks to put some colour back in my face and suggested I get a wig sooner rather than later if I'm planning on wearing one. She said it's better to start wearing it before my hair falls out. There's no point in waiting until it's all gone.'

That was what he'd been worried about. Would the cosmetician be too blunt? Would the conversation remind her of how she'd changed or help to boost her confidence?

'Is that what you want to do?' he asked.

'If I can find a wig that doesn't look too fake, I'll wear it. I think it would be better for the kids.'

'Did she tell you where to get one?'

Juliet nodded. 'There's a good wig shop in the city, that's the good news, but clothes are a different story. I wanted to get something that put a bit of shape back for me but the best shop is in Canberra. I guess I'll have to try online.'

'Why don't we start with your hair?'

'Now?'

Sam shrugged. He figured he was here to help so he might as well do this, and as Juliet seemed happy to embrace the idea of boosting her appearance he figured they might as well start today. 'Why not now? We've got time. I've always wondered what you'd look like as a redhead,' he said in an attempt to lift the mood.

Juliet tilted her head to one side, a slight frown on her beautiful face. 'Really?'

'Yep.'

'Okay, then.' It was her turn to shrug. 'But I'm not sure about a redhead. Don't blondes have more fun?'

* * *

'I don't think I'd be any competition for Marilyn Monroe,' she said half an hour later as she pouted at him from under a curly blonde wig.

'That's not so much Marilyn, more Shirley Temple.'

'Hey, be nice, this was your idea!' Juliet laughed and Sam absorbed the sound. He couldn't remember when they'd last laughed together. There hadn't been much to laugh about, and it felt good to share this moment. It felt like old times.

'Try this one instead,' he said, handing her a wig of long, straight auburn hair. He was sure the colour would complement her complexion. The blonde made her look washed out and she didn't need that at the moment.

She whipped off the blonde wig and exchanged it for the red.

'The colour's better,' he said, and it was a big improvement, the deep auburn shade a good foil for her pale skin and blue eyes.

'But I look about fourteen.'

He nodded. She was right.

'What about this?' The sales assistant was holding another auburn wig but this one was in a short, cropped style. Juliet's expression was dubious. 'It'll look better on,' the sales girl insisted.

Juliet held out her hand. 'All right, in for a penny, in for a pound,' she said as she swapped wigs.

'Wow.' Juliet looked amazing. Sam felt as though he'd had the wind knocked out of him and he was almost speechless. He would never have guessed a hairstyle could make such a difference but the transformation was incredible.

'You like it?'

'You look sensational.' He'd always liked Juliet's long hair but he had to admit she looked fantastic with this crop. She was small enough to get away with short hair and it suited her heart-shaped face. The sales girl knew her stuff.

'Really? I don't look like a boy?'

Sam shook his head. 'It's perfect.'

'What about the first one I tried on?'

The first wig had been a match to her normal hair in both style and colour. 'That was fine but this one is fantastic. If you're looking for something to give you a confidence boost, this is it.'

'I don't know,' Juliet wavered. 'You don't think this one is too extreme?'

He knew what she was really asking. Wouldn't it be better to look like her old self? Would a drastic make-over be too much for the children, Kate particularly?

'Why don't we get them both?' he suggested.

'What for?'

'So you have time to think it over. Or you can show the kids, see if they have a preference.'

Juliet allowed herself to be persuaded and Sam happily paid for both wigs. If it was going to mean she felt able to face an evening out with her friends, and with him, it was money well spent in his opinion.

Juliet was dressed, eventually. It had taken her ages to choose an outfit because even though dinner wasn't about her, she wanted to look good. She wanted to look healthy. She didn't want the focus to be on her and the better she looked the more people would treat her normally. She'd finally settled on a blue shirt with a ruffled front. She hadn't had time to do anything about her wardrobe but at least this shirt would disguise her flat chest.

Her hands shook as she snapped the back onto her

diamond earring. It was only a small group invited to dinner for Gabby's birthday and Juliet knew almost all of them well, yet she was still nervous. She hadn't been out for a while but that wasn't what concerned her. It was the fact that she and Sam were going together.

She adjusted her wig, staring at her reflection in the mirror. She was ready. She couldn't delay any longer.

Sam was waiting in the family room. 'You look fabulous, Jules.'

His gaze was fixed on her face and he flashed her a smile, his gorgeous right-to-left smile that made her toes curl.

His compliment made her cheeks flush and she touched the wig self-consciously as she paused in the doorway. 'Thanks.' She'd decided to wear the short auburn wig. She knew Sam liked it but it was Kate's influence that had finally persuaded her. 'Kate helped me.'

Kate was hovering near the kitchen bench and he winked at his daughter, making her laugh. 'Good job, Katie.' He turned back to Juliet. 'Are you ready to go?'

'Just let me make sure I've got everything.' Juliet made a show of checking in her handbag, using the time to regain her equilibrium. Sam's compliment had pleased and surprised her and his smile had thrown her further out of kilter. It had seemed more potent than usual or perhaps it was something in his eyes tonight. He looked like he had a secret and she was dying to know what it was.

But if he had a secret, it didn't seem as though it was one he was going to share with her. There was little time for any sort of private conversation. Gabby and Finn were both gregarious and so were many of the other guests. It made for a lively evening and Juliet found she was enjoying herself. People were glad to see her but after asking her how she was feeling they didn't question her at length about her cancer, and she was pleased to find that she was able to forget about it herself for a few hours and just enjoy the company. Particularly Sam's company.

He was very attentive, behaving as if they were a newly dating couple and not ex-husband and wife. She wondered if the others noticed Sam behaving any differently before realising that what she and Sam did was of little consequence to anyone else.

Sam was sitting on Juliet's right and on her left was Gabby's brother, Ben, whom Juliet had met for the first time tonight. She'd seen photos of him. He was one of Melbourne's most eligible bachelors, according to the social pages, and Juliet assumed it was to do with his status as heir to his father's publishing company. It didn't hurt that he was extremely good-looking—tall, dark, handsome and rich—not a bad combination, Juliet thought. She knew nothing about him really and assumed he was single by choice, but her curiosity got the better of her and she decided she needed more information. Gabby's seating arrangements were perfect—sitting next to a stranger meant that Juliet could pretend she was just like everyone else at the party, fit and healthy— without the stigma of cancer hanging over her head.

She was curious to know what Ben did for a living. 'Do you work in publishing, Ben?' she asked.

'No. I'm a doctor.'

'Really?'

'Yes. That surprises you?' He was smiling at her, obviously not offended by her faux pas.

'No. Yes. I—I guess it d-does,' she stammered, a little

embarrassed by her mistake. 'Funny how you make assumptions, isn't it? Sorry.'

'Don't apologise. It's a common misconception. But I do wonder why Gabby is allowed to be an artist but everyone expects me to work in the family business. Everyone except my parents.'

'What sort of doctor are you?'

'A plastic surgeon.'

'A cosmetic surgeon?'

'A cosmetic surgeon is a Hollywood thing. Technically I'm a plastic and reconstructive surgeon but I think plastics has become interchangeable with cosmetics in people's minds.'

'What's the difference?'

'Cosmetic surgery is a form of reconstruction but it's really just elective surgery—for people who want to change their appearance. Plastics and reconstructive work grew from a need or ability to repair deformities that were either congenital or following a trauma of some kind.'

Perhaps Gabby's seating arrangement wasn't accidental—Juliet wasn't sure if she was game to ask. 'So do you do any cosmetic surgery or do you only do serious things?'

'It's all serious.' Ben paused slightly. 'Well, it is to the people undergoing the procedure. Even if I think it's unnecessary, if my client can convince me that there's a good reason for the surgery, if it can be justified, I will consider it, but my passion is reconstruction work.'

'So is there a difference between breast reconstruction and breast augmentation, for example, or is it just semantics?' Juliet couldn't resist asking.

'Technically they are both cosmetic but augmentation is simply changing someone's appearance for the hell of it, whereas reconstruction is repairing, restoring if you like, someone's appearance. Mostly that's done just to make them look like they did before.'

Juliet hadn't really investigated the procedure, it hadn't been a huge priority, but meeting Ben gave her food for thought. She would consider it and if she wanted to look into it further, she now had a place to start. She would get Ben's details from Gabby if she needed them, she decided. A dinner party was probably not the appropriate place for a longer discussion about the ins and outs of breast surgery.

Dessert had been served and it was obvious the other guests were in for a late night, but Juliet was looking pale and, even under her make-up Sam could see the dark circles beneath her eyes. It was time to go. He thanked Gabby and Finn and bundled Juliet out to the car.

'Have you had a good evening?' Sam asked as he pulled into the driveway.

'It's been lovely but I am looking forward to climbing into bed.'

'Why don't you get ready for bed? I'll sort out the babysitter and bring you a cup of tea,' he offered. 'And you can sleep in tomorrow. I'll take the kids to the park.'

Juliet didn't argue.

Sam carried a cup of tea in one hand and an envelope in the other. Juliet was in bed. She'd taken her make-up off but was still wearing her wig. He put the cup on the bedside table and handed her the envelope.

'What's this?' she asked.

'A surprise. A good one, I hope.'

Juliet smiled. Her face was aglow. The colour of her

wig emphasised the blue of her eyes and they sparkled in the dim light. Sam felt a stirring of desire. Despite the circumstances his reaction to her was as potent as ever. She was still the only woman capable of taking his breath away.

Juliet opened the envelope and pulled out the sheets of paper inside. 'Plane flights to Canberra?' She looked up at him, a slightly puzzled expression on her face.

'I thought we could take the kids up there for a weekend. Show them some of our old stomping ground and maybe you could do some shopping.'

'The shop the cosmetician was telling me about?' She guessed his agenda.

Sam nodded. He'd seen how much difference the wigs had made to Juliet's confidence. He wanted her to feel as good as possible and he hoped this shopping trip could help. 'I thought it would be nicer to shop in person instead of online.'

'That's a brilliant idea. The kids will love a weekend away. When did you want to go?'

'I thought we could play it by ear a bit, see how you feel after the next lot of chemo and go then if you're up to it.'

'That sounds like a plan. Thank you.' She grinned and Sam enjoyed the feeling of satisfaction that spread through him.

'My pleasure. Now, drink your tea and get some sleep.' He kissed her gently on the forehead, savouring the creamy scent of her freshly washed skin.

He closed the bedroom door softly behind him.

He was pleased with the outcome. If he could prove to Juliet how much better things worked if he was around, how much more smoothly things ran with them working together, perhaps she would agree to give him another chance. Getting her to Canberra and boosting her confidence with an updated, tailor-made wardrobe would surely serve to further his chances.

He knew he still loved her; he had never stopped, and being together, even under such difficult circumstances, had made him question why he had given in to her before and hadn't fought against the divorce. She'd applied for it and he'd never denied her anything if he could help it. She had convinced him it had been in the children's best interests but now he doubted that.

He would be patient but he was going to get his family back.

But there were a few final hurdles. Baby steps, that's what they needed. Getting her to Canberra was step one, getting her through chemo was step two and getting her to agree to spend New Year in Merimbula with his side of the family was step three. Little steps to show her how much better things could be if they were together. A family again.

Who knew if there would be more? But if there were, he would get through them all. He wouldn't rest until they were together again.

CHAPTER EIGHT

December 2008

IT WAS early morning on New Year's Eve as Sam and his father headed out to sea, heading towards the rising sun. They travelled in silence, Sam's father steering the boat as he checked his electronic fish finder, searching for decent schools of fish, while Sam prepared the rods and lines. They were both completely at ease on the water and had spent hundreds of hours together fishing and many fewer hours talking.

Sam watched his father as he stood in the cabin. He was concentrating on the job at hand and unaware of Sam's scrutiny. Sam was looking for any signs that his father wasn't well but could see nothing untoward. At sixty-five years of age he still cut a fit figure. He was solidly built but wasn't carrying any excess weight. He was almost as tall as Sam, although he'd shrunk a bit in the last ten years. His hair was now totally salt and pepper with no trace of the dark blond it had been. Even his beard was shades of grey. His hair probably needed a cut, a tidy-up, as did Sam's, but this was a legacy of not having a wife to remind him it was time for a visit to the barber. With his tanned, almost leathery skin, erect posture and greying hair he looked like a movie version of a sea captain. His eyes were brown; Sam had inherited his green eyes from his mother, but there was no debating the fact that his father, Sam and Sam's son, Edward, were three peas in a pod.

The noise of the engine prohibited conversation so the two of them followed their usual routines, just as they'd done for over twenty years. Sam rigged the rods, checked the bait, tossed a few cockles to the seagulls who always followed the boat for the first few kilometres and then did a few running repairs. Conversation could wait until they were fishing. They would have a few hours to discuss anything they needed to, which was more than enough time on any day. Today, in fact, Sam did want a sounding-board. He needed a sensible ear and his father, with his carefully measured manner, could usually be relied on to provide judicious advice.

'We might get lucky here,' his father said as he cut the engine. 'Snapper could be biting.' Together they baited hooks and cast the lines. Sam's father cleared his throat as they settled into their rhythm, a sure indication that today's fishing trip wasn't going to be the usual, mostly silent affair with a bit of general discussion. Throat clearing always preceded a father-son chat, as Sam thought of them, and had done so since he'd been a little boy. Something in Sam's behaviour must have suggested to his father that he needed a listening ear. Out on the water was the perfect time to embark on discussions. They were both comfortable at sea but having something to occupy themselves with, ensuring they didn't have to maintain eye contact, also helped.

'Juliet seems to be in good spirits,' Bob said. 'She tells me she's going to be fine. Is that right?'

'I hope so but it's really too early to know. She'll have to continue having blood tests and regular checks but the doctors are pretty confident that they've got everything. Jules took up every option that they offered her in terms of treatment.'

'And what are your plans for next year? You're going back to Sydney? Back to the navy?'

'I have to,' Sam replied. 'I've been trying to assess my options but if I want to stay in the navy then I can't see any other alternative.'

'What if Juliet needs more surgery or more chemo or radiotherapy? How are you going to manage the situation from Sydney?' Bob got a bite on his line and he jerked it back, hooking the fish and reeling it in as he continued. 'Even if there's nothing you need to do for Juliet, you need to think about the children. Someone has to look after them and even though you and Juliet are divorced they are still your children, still your responsibility.'

'I know that, Dad. I'm trying to do the right thing by everyone, but it's not easy. I wish there was a way I could have it all but I can't see that happening.'

'All?' Bob had his head down as he unhooked his catch before throwing it into a container filled with sea-water, where it continued to swim around.

'Yes. I really don't want to give up the navy but I didn't want to give up my family either,' Sam said as he reeled in his line to check the bait. The bait was gone so he replenished it before casting out again, continuing the conversation as his hands stayed busy. 'I didn't want to get divorced but that's what I am, and I can't see how I can fix this.'

'You're not prepared to give up the defence force? Even now?' his father queried.

'The navy is all I know. It's what I'm good at.' Sam raked his fingers through his hair. 'I love my family, Juliet included, but I can't stand the idea of going to work for the next thirty years doing something I don't enjoy just to pay the bills. I need to be out at sea. I take after you there. Look at you, you're retired but you're still on the ocean almost every day.'

'Are you sure you're not using the ocean as an excuse?'

'An excuse for what?'

'Settling down, staying in one place. Are you avoiding family life? I would give all this up in an instant if it would bring your mother back. Once she died there didn't seem any reason not to stay with the navy. Your aunt Helen was happy to come with me and you were okay, but I would have preferred you to have had your mother.'

'I would have liked that too.'

'In a perfect world you would have had us both. Your kids can still have that.'

'But that's just it. I don't see how.' His father was watching him, he could feel it. Sam looked up from his line. 'What?'

'I'm just wondering what you'd do if, heaven forbid, Juliet doesn't make it. Would you drag your kids around the country then?'

Sam thought of Kate. She was coping well at the moment, and the time she was spending with both him and Juliet seemed to be easing her concerns. But if something else did go wrong he knew he wouldn't be able to move her without consequences. Juliet had been right about that. Kate needed constancy—she wasn't a child who coped well with change.

'No,' he replied.

'So why don't you look at what you'd do then? You don't have to wait for something else to go wrong if you can find a solution now.'

'But that's the problem. I can't think of any solutions.'

Juliet seemed to be doing so much better. Sam had thought about her not making it when she'd gone in for the mastectomy but since then he'd blocked from his mind the thought that it might not fix things. He didn't want to think about her not making it but maybe his dad was right. Maybe he could use that thought just as a hypothetical. He'd have to find a solution then.

'Can I make a suggestion?' Bob asked.

Sam nodded in response as he realised that this was what he'd been hoping for. He'd wanted another head to help solve his dilemma. 'Go for it.'

'There are jobs with the defence force that keep you in one place—'

'Desk jobs.' That was not what he wanted to hear. A desk job was not for him.

'They're probably desk jobs by definition,' his dad agreed, 'but they would allow you to be permanently placed somewhere. If you considered teaching or operational positions, you might still have a little time at sea but you wouldn't have to be away for long stints or move every few years.'

'How do you know about these?' Sam asked as he wondered why he hadn't considered that angle.

'Because I thought about it when your mum died but with Aunt Helen's help, and you being the type of child you were, we managed the moves. Not all children are cut out for frequent changes. Not all children are like you. It's an option worth thinking about.'

Sam finally hooked a fish of his own and he thought about his dad's suggestion as he brought the fish in. Despite Juliet's cancer, the best days of his year had been the two months when he'd been surrounded by his family. He knew if it wasn't for Juliet's cancer he wouldn't have had those times, and while he wished for Juliet to get her health back, he was also glad that he'd had an opportunity to spend that time with his family.

Having them all together had reminded him of how much he loved them, of how much he needed them and how much they needed him. He'd been trying to ignore how lonely he was going to feel after the end of this holiday.

He still believed, still hoped, that Juliet was going to be okay but a shore-based posting did have its merits. It would mean he could still be a part of the navy. The navy had made him the man he was, and he was reluctant to give it up if he didn't have to. Leaving the navy for a civilian life, even temporarily, had made him frustrated and angry and he didn't want to be that person again. He needed fulfilment in his career but this time he knew that if he had to sacrifice one or the other, this time his family would come first.

But what if he could find a shore-based position? It would mean he could be available if Juliet or the children needed him. And it could mean the difference between getting his family back or not. His dad was right—it was worth considering. It was his best option. It was his only option.

New Year's Eve, 2008

Juliet stepped out of the shower after rinsing the salt water from her skin. She wrapped herself in a towel and then squeezed the water from her bathers. She was slowly getting used to her naked appearance but she still preferred to avoid mirrors when she could. Once she was dressed it was a different story.

The surprise weekend shopping trip to Canberra that Sam had organised had been a chance to shop for bras, breast prostheses and swimming costumes. Juliet was happy with the results of her retail therapy session and although she hadn't been able to do much about her naked self yet, when dressed in a properly fitted bra and the right stuffing, she thought she looked okay.

The weekend in Canberra had been fabulous. Sam had been fabulous. The children had loved seeing the university oval where their parents had met, the Ferris wheel where Sam had proposed, the flat they'd first lived in. There had been a lot of good memories.

Juliet didn't know how she would have managed over the past couple of months without Sam's help and she'd agreed to spend this week in Merimbula with him as her way of saying thank you. She'd known he'd wanted her to join him and she'd had no reason to refuse.

They'd had five days in Merimbula already and the kids were having the time of their lives. How they were all going to cope when the time came to go back to Melbourne was concerning her a little, especially as they would be leaving Sam behind. His carer's leave would be finished and he was due to go back to Sydney.

But she had another two days before the trip was over and perhaps everything would be fine. She wasn't going to make a mountain out of a molehill and stress about things that might or might not happen. Reducing her stress levels had been part of the advice Dr Davey, the oncologist, had given her, and it was advice she was going to try hard to follow. Studies had shown that some cancers were stress related and she wasn't going to disadvantage her recovery by letting her imagination get the better of her and worrying about every little possibility.

She took a deep, calming breath, visualising all the pleasant things she and the children had been doing in Merimbula.

Bob's house was a gorgeous weatherboard cottage overlooking the sea about two kilometres from the centre of town. There weren't a lot of reasons in Juliet's mind to leave the cottage but they had ventured into town on pushbikes and pottered about down by the river that ran behind Bob's house. The children swam off the beach at Spencer Park, which was at the mouth of the river, while she rested in the shade. She had spent a fair bit of time eating the mangoes and strawberries that were in season and the freshly caught fish that Sam and Bob brought in most days. Sam had spent most of the time with them too, the only exception being when he went fishing with his father, but quite often he took one or both children too.

Juliet hadn't felt up to going fishing yet. She couldn't spend hours in the sun as the chemo had made her susceptible to sunburn and she didn't really have enough energy for fishing, but she'd been surprised to find how much she missed Sam's company when he was gone for a few hours. The time here was reminding her of the time they'd had in Bali all those years ago. She needed time to heal and with Sam's attention she could feel herself recovering.

She hung her towel on the rack and decided to dress for a celebration—it was New Year's Eve after all.

She had packed carefully for the Christmas holidays, including most of her purchases from Canberra, telling herself that if she looked as good as possible it would boost her confidence. She knew that really she just wanted to look good for Sam. This week in Merimbula together was all about the children and ostensibly to give her a chance to rest and regain her strength, but it wouldn't hurt to look good.

She chose a white dress—her fair skin for once was lightly tanned and the dress would show off her tan and emphasise her arms. It had a modest neckline that allowed her to wear her new prostheses and she teamed it with a headscarf in a blue-and-white pattern that she knew brought out the colour in her eyes. If she was going to dress up, she might as well give it everything. Kate had bought her the scarf, with Sam's help, and had given it to Juliet for Christmas. Her hair had completely fallen out and she found her wigs were much too hot and uncomfortable to wear out in the sun to the beach or the river. Kate's scarf was perfect. She knew Kate had bought the scarf because she couldn't stand the thought of a bald mother, and Juliet was careful to keep her head covered when she was around the children.

She tied the ends of the scarf and let them fall loosely down her back before applying some mascara and lip-gloss to make herself more presentable. Her eyelashes and eyebrows hadn't been affected by the chemotherapy drug, Cytoxan, probably because those hair follicles were slower growing than her head hair and she was grateful for some small mercies. Finally she was ready.

Sam had already taken the children down to the beach to get the bonfire started, and Sam's dad and aunt were celebrating New Year with friends so it was just the four of them having their own party on the sand. Juliet checked her reflection one final time and took another deep breath to calm her nerves as she remonstrated with herself about being foolish. She grabbed a warm coat, switched on a couple of lights and left the house to walk down the path to the beach.

* * *

Juliet had rested on the pillows Sam had carried down to the beach and watched him cook fish and potatoes in coals taken from the bonfire while the children had toasted marshmallows. For dessert Sam had split open bananas and filled their centres with chocolate before wrapping them in foil and baking them in the coals. They'd eaten these while they'd watched the nine o'clock fireworks display that lit up the far end of the beach. It had been an almost perfect evening.

It was nearing midnight now but it was still a glorious calm summer's night. There wasn't a breath of wind but the temperature had dropped slightly and the fire wasn't throwing any warmth onto them now. It had burnt right down and all that remained was a pile of glowing coals. The kids had fallen asleep. Edward was tucked in against Juliet's side and Kate was on her other side, curled between her parents. Sam had set up a groundsheet with cushions and quilts and had covered them all with blankets. Juliet could feel the cool air on her face but the rest of her was surprisingly warm and comfortable. She yawned.

'Have you had enough?' Sam asked, hearing her yawn.

'No. I want to stay up for the midnight fireworks. I want to see in the New Year.' She looked down the beach. The local surf lifesavers had handed out glowstick bracelets to revellers earlier in the evening and the beach was dotted with lights. At the far end, where the fireworks would be set off, a stage had been erected, a band was playing and the young adult crowd was partying in full swing.

'It's just another day. We should call it a night if you're tired.'

Juliet shook her head. 'It's more than another day.

It's the start of a new year and it's a chance to move forward. I can't wait to put 2008 behind me—it wasn't the best year of my life.'

'I guess not.' Sam paused and flashed her his familiar, lopsided grin that instantly made her feel like the world was a better place. 'I'm really glad you're here, Jules. You had me frightened for a while—I wasn't sure that we were going to have another Christmas.'

'I told you I wasn't leaving my children.'

'I know. I'm just glad you meant it. How are you feeling, honestly? Are you ready for the year?'

'I feel good. I'm getting stronger every day. I just want things to go back to normal.' She still wasn't quite sure what normal was but it sounded like the right thing to say.

'Are you going to be okay?'

'I think so.'

She knew what he was really asking. She'd grown used to having Sam around. The children had too and Juliet knew they'd take some time to adjust back to being a family of three again. Making this transition again was what she'd been worried about when Sam had first moved back with them but the past couple of months had been worth it. She didn't think she would have managed without him. Once again, he'd been her rock.

'You were right, you know. I wouldn't have managed the past couple of months without you. Thank you.' It was important to her that he knew she was grateful.

'I'm happy I could help. You would have got through but if I've made things easier then I'm glad. That was my intention and I want you to know that you can call on me at any time, for anything, and I'll do my best to help. The children are still my responsibility and, despite everything, I still feel I have a responsibility to you too.'

She nodded and watched him as he lay on his back, propped on his elbows, one knee bent. He was simply gorgeous and her heart flipped in her chest. He still affected her as much as he had on the day they'd met. There remained a physical pull of attraction every time she saw Sam—her body still ached for his caress, she still craved his touch. He was her addiction and she was finding that being under the same roof as him, to have him so close yet untouchable, was becoming more and more unbearable. How she wished his priorities had been different. How she wished he could have put his family first.

She had set him free, hoping he would come back, and he was back, but only temporarily. He was there out of kindness and compassion, and when things had settled down again, he'd be gone.

She'd spent a lot of time over the past year wishing things had turned out differently, but she was still finding it difficult to reconcile her heart with the facts, although she was beginning to accept that some things couldn't be changed. But as she lay on the blankets with Sam just inches away from her she let herself imagine, just for a moment, that they were still a couple. She imagined reaching out to stroke his arm. She closed her eyes and she could imagine the feel of his body under her fingers, the soft hair on his forearm, the warmth of his skin. She could picture his fingers joining with hers, holding her hand, and she could imagine his touch; she could feel the shivers of pleasure that would shoot through her as their fingers locked together.

In her mind his fingers were now trailing up her arm, imprinting his mark onto her skin, brushing the nape of her neck as he pulled her towards him, his breath sweet on her cheek, his lips soft against hers. She could almost taste him, could almost feel the thrust of his tongue against hers, could almost hear his soft moan of pleasure.

Just the image of him holding her, loving her, was enough to warm her soul. There would never be anyone else for her, not while Sam still lived and breathed. She knew that. She would never love anyone else the way she loved Sam.

'What are you thinking about?' Sam's voice interrupted her reverie.

She opened her eyes, ridiculously disappointed to find that she wasn't wrapped in his arms, to find he was still on the other side of the blanket. She couldn't imagine him wanting her back in his arms but that didn't stop her from imagining how it would feel. 'Nothing really.' It was ridiculous to reminisce like this. Imagining things didn't change their reality. It didn't change the fact they were divorced. It didn't change the fact that in two more days she'd be returning to Melbourne without him.

But, just for tonight, she would let her imagination run wild. There would be plenty of time for reality when she returned to Melbourne.

He stood and stretched. 'It's nearly midnight,' he said.

He was silhouetted against the stars and Juliet's breath caught in her throat. 'Where are you going?'

'I have something for you.' He rummaged through a bag and withdrew a parcel. He knelt beside her on the blanket and passed her the package.

Juliet unwrapped the present. Inside was a silver link bracelet and hanging from the links were two small, thin, silver circles. She lifted the chain from its bed of velvet. Each disc was engraved, the first with the word *Kate*, the second with *Edward*. It was delicate and gorgeous.

'It's not to remind you of what's important,' Sam explained, 'you know that as well as I do. It's to remind you of what we created together. I'm hoping the new year will be a year in which you'll be able to celebrate being well and I'm hoping that this bracelet will serve as a reminder of all the people around you who love you.'

'It's perfect. Thank you.' It was beautiful and it was almost perfect, but it was missing a disc. Juliet couldn't help thinking that there should have been a third disc with Sam's name on it. But she didn't say that, she just undid the clasp and passed the bracelet to Sam, holding out her hand for him to fasten the bracelet around her wrist. His fingers were warm on her skin as he held her arm steady, his touch gentle yet strong, disturbing her senses, just as she'd imagined it would.

As he snapped the clasp shut the first midnight firework exploded in the sky above them.

He grinned at her, his familiar smile lighting up his face. 'Happy New Year, Jules.'

'Happy New Year,' she repeated. Her voice was quiet in contrast to the noise of the fireworks but Sam was so close there was no need to shout. He was kneeling mere inches from her side and as she watched he leant towards her, closing the distance between them until it was no more than a finger's space separating them. No more than a breath. His eyes were shining, the hazel flecks in the green almost undetectable as his pupils dilated. The light wasn't reaching his eyes, their faces were so close that the light couldn't penetrate. Their gazes were locked. Juliet could feel the tension sparking in the air around them. She sat, motionless, too afraid to move in case she broke the spell.

She closed her eyes, wanting, waiting for Sam's touch.

She licked her lips. She could feel the breath coming out of her, could feel it being expelled from her lungs in short, shallow bursts, felt it move over her moist lips. Her respiration was rapid, matching her pulse.

Sam's breath was warm on her face.

She waited for his kiss, certain it was inevitable.

His hand cupped the back of her head and his fingers brushed the nape of her neck.

She gasped as he tilted her face up to his and his lips brushed over hers, soft and tender.

She heard herself moan and then Sam crushed her to him, the tenderness swamped by far more primeval emotions. Hunger, desire and passion took over. She parted her lips, welcoming him back to her.

She was home. She was back where she belonged. There was no other way to describe it. The light that had been missing from her life was back. Sam was vital. She knew now she could exist without him but she wouldn't be living. A life without Sam was a half life.

Her heart and soul went into the kiss and she felt Sam respond. Time stood still. No, it was better than that. Time reversed. It was as though all the things that had gone wrong in her life had been imagined. She could feel Sam breathing life back into her soul, restoring her.

She embraced the feeling of rejuvenation. Embraced Sam. She let him fill her heart and mind, her body and soul, until she was overflowing. She held tight to him; she couldn't let him go.

He tasted like chocolate, his mouth soft and warm

and sweet. She put a hand to his cheek. His stubble was rough under her fingers and his skin was hot to the touch. Sam pulled her down to the blanket, pinning her beneath him, his body hard and lean above her. She was vaguely aware of the fireworks continuing to explode in the sky; she could see the flashes of light through her closed eyelids and it felt as though the eruptions were keeping time with her heartbeat.

Sam deepened the kiss and Juliet forgot about the fireworks. Forgot about everything. For a moment it was just her and Sam, cocooned in a bubble, their own piece of time and space. She was shielded from the world, protected by Sam.

Gradually, though, the thin film of their bubble was penetrated by the outside world. The night grew silent and dark, the fireworks had finished. Voices carried to them, caught on the sea breeze, and Juliet remembered they weren't the only ones on the beach. The voices disturbed her, interrupted her and she pulled back, very slightly, as she became self-conscious.

'Time to go?' Sam asked.

Juliet wasn't sure. What was she going to? What would happen when they got back to the house? Would they continue where they'd left off? Should they continue? But one thing she did know was that they couldn't stay down on the beach all night. She nodded.

'I'll carry Kate up and come back for Ed.' In the heat of the moment Juliet had even forgotten about her own children, lying on the blankets beside her. Sam scooped up their sleeping daughter, carrying her easily back to the house before returning to douse the fire and collect Ed. Juliet carried the cushions and blankets and followed in Sam's footsteps. She used his depressions to make the trek through the soft sand easier, even though his steps were far larger than hers and she had to stretch right out to match his stride. Sam took Edward into his bedroom and Juliet waited on the veranda.

She couldn't go inside. She knew she'd feel hemmed in, contained, and she was worried that it would feel like the end of the evening. She wasn't ready for it to end just yet. She wasn't sure what she was ready for exactly so, for now, she leant on the veranda railing outside her room and took a deep breath, letting the night air fill her lungs.

Sam came back outside after carrying the children to their beds. Neither of them spoke. Sam stood beside her and his distinctive warm, spicy scent filled her nose, blocking out the smell of the sea. The beach in front of them was dark and the ocean stretched away to the horizon, blending with the sky. It felt as though they were floating in the night. They were surrounded by stars; millions of bright, glowing spots of light were strewn across the inky-black sky.

Juliet felt Sam reach for her and she turned, meeting him halfway. The light from the bedroom illuminated the left side of his face. Automatically she raised her hand, lifting her fingers to his face as she traced the lines in the corners of his eyes. She saw the right side of his mouth lift in a smile and her fingers moved to follow the movement of his lips.

Sam caught her fingers in his, taking them to his mouth and kissing the tips. Juliet closed her eyes as Sam took her thumb between his lips and slid it into his hot, moist mouth. A soft moan escaped from her as Sam sucked on her thumb. He lowered her hand and bent his head, covering her mouth with his, muffling her moans of pleasure. Juliet opened her lips, her tongue meeting his, joining with him, lost in the familiar and enchanting feeling of being in his arms again.

The evening air was cool and Juliet shivered as a light breeze blew across her back. Sam pulled away when he felt her tremble. He wrapped an arm around her shoulders and tucked her against his side, sharing his warmth. 'Let's get you inside.'

He took her hand and led her into her bedroom. The double bed was the dominant feature of the room but beside it was an old armchair. Sam skirted the bed as Juliet trailed behind him. He led her to the armchair and pulled her onto his lap.

Juliet didn't resist as Sam claimed her again, kissing her soundly. They had unfinished business and Juliet didn't stop to think where it might end. His hand was on her knee and she felt it slide under the hem of her dress, caressing the inside of her thigh and sending pulses of desire shooting up to the very centre of her soul. She could feel her body responding to his touch, feel herself getting moist; preparing to welcome him back.

Sam shifted Juliet's weight, moving her bottom farther into his lap, and she could feel his arousal pressing against her. Involuntarily she parted her legs slightly, ready for his touch, but his hand wasn't on her thigh now. She felt him reaching behind her, the fingers of one hand on the zip at the back of her dress. She looked down, watching as his other hand brushed over her breast. Except it wasn't her breast. It was only padding. She could see his hand touching the thin fabric of her dress but she could feel nothing. No desire. No spark. No fire. Nothing.

Nothing except a reminder of what had transpired. Of how she'd changed. Of what was missing. Of what had gone.

'Stop.' The word escaped from her lips before she had time to think about what she was doing. She stood up, almost leaping out of Sam's lap. She was aware of Sam's shocked expression. She watched his face, could see him trying to process what had happened. She took a step back, away from the chair, knowing he would reach for her.

'I can't do this.'

She turned and fled to the en suite bathroom. She shut the door, leaning against it before she turned the lock. She could hear Sam on the other side.

'Jules, what's wrong?' She felt the door handle jiggle behind her back and for a moment she panicked, thinking she hadn't locked it properly.

It held.

'Jules?'

She couldn't do this.

'Just give me a minute.' She stepped away from the door and leant on the basin, breathing deeply, trying to slow her racing heart. She glanced in the mirror. Her pale face stared back at her, her freckles dark against her skin, her eyes shiny with unshed tears.

'Come out and tell me what the matter is,' Sam pleaded. 'I can't help if I don't know what's wrong.'

'Wait. Please.'

'Open the door, Jules.' The door handle rattled again. 'You can't stay in there.'

Sam was right, she knew he was. She couldn't stay closeted in the bathroom. She was being ridiculous. But she couldn't go out there. Not yet.

She turned on the taps, splashing her face with cold water as she tried to gather her thoughts. She pulled a towel from the rack, burying her face in the soft folds. She knew he was right. They needed to talk;

they probably should have talked before they'd started making out like a couple of horny teenagers.

She dried her face and opened the bathroom door. Sam was sitting on the bed but stood and crossed the room in two strides. He stretched out one hand to wipe the traces of a tear from her cheek. 'I'm sorry if I pressured you. I didn't mean to.'

'You didn't.' Juliet took a step forward and Sam wrapped her in his arms, holding her to him.

'I thought we wanted the same thing.'

She couldn't blame him for thinking that—she'd certainly been a willing participant. To a point. 'That wasn't the problem.' Her voice was muffled against his chest.

'I need to know what you're thinking, Jules. I need to know what you want.' He moved back a pace, creating some distance between them.

'I can't...' She broke off. How did she explain what she'd been thinking, what she'd been feeling?

'Can't what? Can't be with me?'

She nodded.

She saw Sam glance at the armchair but he obviously thought better of sitting there again. He tugged her towards the bed, sitting down beside her, not quite touching. He was frowning. 'Why not?'

She hesitated, uncertain about how to phrase her answer.

'Jules, you need to tell me what's going on. We need to clear the air. Perhaps we should have had this conversation before now but we are going to have it before we make any more decisions. I need to understand what's happening, how you feel. I'm not going to make assumptions again—that didn't turn out so well for us last time.'

He was right. It wasn't his fault and he deserved to know that. 'I'm scared,' she said.

He was still frowning and his green eyes were dark. 'Of making love?'

She shook her head. 'Of being naked,' she whispered. 'I don't look the same any more.'

'What difference does that make?'

'All I can think of is you'll look at me and see all the bits that are missing. I don't want you to be disappointed.'

'Disappointed? You think I'll be disappointed?' He gathered her hands in his. 'My darling girl, all I can think about is how lucky I am to have a second chance. I can't believe we're here, together. Disappointed is not how I'd describe myself. Let me tell you what I see when I look at you.' He held both her hands in one of his as he tilted her face up to look into her eyes. 'I see the most beautiful woman. The woman I adore. And when you were on my lap, all I was thinking about was how lucky I was. I wasn't thinking anything more than that.' He smiled, and the frown lines disappeared and his eyes lightened.

'Trust me, I'm not taking inventory. I don't care about the bits of you that are missing—all I care about is you. All I want is you.' He traced her lips with his finger before bending his head to kiss her cheek. 'But I can be patient.'

Wasn't he going to argue? Wasn't he going to try and convince her to spend the night with him? Disappointment flooded through her but before she could feel the pain of rejection she realised she was partly relieved too. She knew she wasn't ready. She knew that in her fragile state Sam could be more than she was ready to cope with. She wasn't confident enough to take things further. Not tonight.

Sam's fingers cupped her chin and his thumb brushed over her lips. Her lips felt swollen and tender under his touch. 'This is just the beginning, Jules. You need to know that.'

'The beginning of what?'

'The rest of our lives. I want a chance to make things right again. I've made a New Year's resolution—I want my family back and I'm prepared to make the changes necessary to achieve that. I've learnt a lot about myself in the past year and you were right—our family does need to come first. I love our kids and I love you. So, if you can give me a little time I'm going to do what I can to repair things and then maybe we can have a future. What do you think? Will you give me another chance?'

She wanted to say yes. Despite her cancer and the chemotherapy, the past two months had been better than she could have hoped for thanks to Sam's presence and assistance. Having him beside her had been what she'd dreamt of, what she'd wanted all along, but she still couldn't imagine how it could all work out now.

She wanted to say yes but she couldn't see how things could change. 'I don't see how we can work this out.'

'Just say you'll give me another chance and I'll worry about the rest.'

She nodded. She said yes. She knew she would always love Sam and having him in her life felt right, but she hoped she wasn't making another mistake.

They had two more days together before their holiday was over, before she took the children back to Melbourne and Sam left for Sydney. There were a few

stolen moments—shared glances, a lingering touch of
Sam's hand, a few passionate kisses—but there was no
opportunity to take things further and Juliet was grateful
for that as she was wavering in her thoughts and feelings.
Not wavering exactly, more torn. When she was with
Sam, all it took was one of his lopsided smiles and the
touch of his fingers as he surreptitiously brushed her arm
or thigh to make her feel like throwing caution to the
wind. But when she caught a glimpse of herself in the
mirror or thought about the reality of taking her clothes
off, she didn't know if she could do it. She didn't know
if she'd ever be able to. And where would that leave
them? All Sam's planning would be pointless. She still
couldn't see how this was going to work.

As their day of departure grew closer she knew she
had some decisions to make.

She was worried now about returning to Melbourne
without Sam. She was worried about how the children
would cope. She had thought about this before, at the
beginning, months ago, but somewhere along the way
she'd become so caught up in the feeling of being part
of a couple again that she'd ignored the fact that it was
only a temporary arrangement.

Should she even be contemplating trying to repair
her relationship with Sam?

Was she making a mistake?

If she was going to have a relationship with anybody,
she needed some help. She would make an appointment with Ben McMahon, Gabby's brother, she decided.
Plastic surgery might resolve her fears.

That was the easy decision.

That decision was made and then she would concentrate on the future. Would that future contain Sam?
Could it?

CHAPTER NINE

IT TOOK them all some time to get used to being just the three of them again. Sam was back in Sydney, back to being a weekend father. Juliet was feeling good. The holiday and Sam's company had refreshed her but she was lonely. She knew she had to be careful. She missed Sam, she still had feelings for him, but even if he felt the same way, their circumstances hadn't changed and she couldn't afford to get carried away with the idea of salvaging their relationship.

She had to get on with her life.

She'd had an appointment with Ben McMahon to discuss reconstructive surgery and she had a date scheduled for the operation. She had promised Sam that he'd be the first person she'd call whenever she needed help with the children and, if he could, he would come down to Melbourne. It wasn't as good as having him in the same city but it was an offer that she would take him up on. She dialled his number and after some preliminary chat brought up the reason for her call.

'I was wondering if you could do me a favour?' she asked.

'Sure.'

'I'm going into hospital for more surgery—'

'What's happened?' Sam interrupted. 'Is everything okay?'

'Everything's fine,' she said, trying to allay his fears. 'I've decided to have a breast reconstruction and I need to know if you can come down to Melbourne for a few days to look after the kids while I'm in hospital.'

'When?'

'I'm booked in for January the twenty-seventh.'

'That soon?'

Juliet wondered why it mattered how soon the operation was. In her opinion, the sooner the better. 'Ben has agreed to squeeze me in, then.'

'What time would you need me in Melbourne?'

'I get admitted at seven in the morning so I'd need you here the night before, on Australia Day.'

'Jules, I can't. We've got a huge day on the harbour for Australia Day celebrations. The entire Sydney fleet will be out on the water. I'd never be able to get down to Melbourne then. Do you have to go in that day?'

'That's when Ben has a spot. I want this done.'

'Why now? Are you sure you're ready for more surgery?'

It was her decision—why was he debating this with her? Losing her breasts had become a constant reminder of what she'd been through and since the bedroom disaster of New Year's Eve Juliet had known that she would have to have reconstructive surgery. In her mind she needed the surgery to help her believe she was winning the fight and she also knew that if she was ever going to be able to have a relationship again, with Sam or anyone else, she needed to feel, and look, like a woman again.

'I want this surgery. I want to look like me again. It's important.'

'You look good now, Jules, but if you're going to have

the surgery, can't you wait a bit? I'm sure we can work out a date that suits us both.'

She didn't want to wait, she wanted the surgery done soon, she wanted to be put back together. She knew she needed it before she could move forward. And she'd wanted Sam's help but, as usual, there was a clash between his work commitments and his personal life and she knew work would triumph. She knew she was being unfair but she couldn't help it. She'd been spoilt by his attention before Christmas and it was difficult to come back down to reality with such a hard bump. Back to the days where work had been more important than family.

'Don't worry, I'm sure Mum or Maggie can help out,' she snapped at him. She could hear the bite in her tone but she couldn't help it. She should have known better and her foolishness made her angry.

'I'm sorry, Jules, but you know what the navy's like. Everything is planned so far in advance, I need a bit more notice.'

She did know what the navy was like. She knew very well. But that didn't make her feel any better. 'Sure. Forget I asked.'

She hung up the phone, feeling ridiculously annoyed and frustrated and angry. Sam had *asked* her to call if she needed help and stupidly she'd taken him at his word. She'd actually thought she might be able to rely on him, but all his platitudes about how important his family was had been just talk. Nothing had changed. Sam had learnt nothing from the weeks they'd spent together as a family last year. Already work was his number-one priority. Maybe he saw elective surgery as not important but she wasn't going under the knife without due consideration. It was about more than just her physical appearance. She needed this emotionally as well.

Her feelings for Sam had been a big influence on her decision to have this surgery and now she felt like a fool. Why had she thought this would make any difference? She should have known better.

27 January 2009

Once again it was Maggie who came to help and, even though she was all Juliet needed, when it came time to be admitted to hospital Juliet was still irritated that Sam hadn't made it.

She tried not to be disappointed, tried not to worry, but the feeling that he should be there was almost too strong for her to ignore. But there wasn't anything she could do about it. She had to get on with things, had to move ahead.

'Morning, Juliet, how are you feeling?' Ben McMahon stepped into her room. She'd been impressed with his knowledge and confidence and his natural, easy bedside manner at her first appointment and hadn't hesitated to choose him as her surgeon. 'I just thought I'd go over the basics with you once more, to make sure you've got everything straight in your mind.' He'd had a clear vision and understanding of what she needed and she was comfortable with her decision but still nervous about the actual operation. She knew that Ben had realised this and was there to try to set her mind at ease.

She greeted him and watched as he took the few steps he needed to cross the room. He was wearing a navy suit with a blue shirt that matched his eyes and he was smiling. He had a nice smile that framed a set of even, white teeth and he was tall, dark and handsome, if you went for that type. Personally she preferred her men tall, blond and handsome, with green eyes and a lopsided smile.

'Now, remember, this is just the first step. I'm going to implant the tissue expander under your chest muscle and the second step will start in a fortnight when we begin the weekly procedures to inject the saline solution into the expander. Depending on how easily your skin stretches, it may take between six and eight weeks before there's enough space to swap the expanders for the implants. You'll have little or no feeling in your breasts as this is purely cosmetic, and if you decide you want a nipple reconstruction I'll have to do that at a later stage. Is that how you understood the plan?' Juliet nodded. 'Do you have any questions?'

'I don't think so.'

'All right. The anaesthetist will be in to see you shortly. We've discussed your reaction last time and he's going to give you something for the nausea while you're under anaesthetic. I'll see you in Theatre.'

The anaesthetist came and the nurse came, but the constant checks just added to Juliet's feeling of disquiet. Her nerves were building and, to make matters worse, as she was being wheeled off for surgery she recalled the dream she'd had following the mastectomy—when she'd watched the faceless woman walk off with her family. Her replacement.

Her nervousness intensified but overriding it all was her irritation with Sam. His offers of help had been empty promises, his words worthless. At least she knew there was no point in trying to salvage their relationship. She had to move on, for her own sake. She needed to be independent. Thank goodness she hadn't done anything foolish while they'd been in Merimbula. The reality was she was still on her own and Sam, despite his promises, had still put work first. Nothing had changed and she was glad they hadn't taken things further.

Somehow now she even felt like blaming him for the dream she'd had. As if he'd put the idea into her head. She knew she was supposed to remain as calm as possible, she knew that the more stressed patients were before surgery the worse their recovery was, and she knew that was why Ben had stopped by earlier—he'd been trying to set her mind at ease. But nothing had worked. She was cross and concerned now and there was no time to calm herself down. She could almost feel her blood pressure rising and there was nothing she could do about it.

The light was incredible, as though the whole sky was glowing. Juliet looked up and was surprised to find it wasn't the sky but the air itself that shone. Almost as though each little oxygen particle had its own light source within it. The light was bright and reminded her of those hot summer days when, as teenagers, she and her sister had lain at the beach, sunbathing, and they'd had to close their eyes against the glare of the sun. But even with your eyes closed the sun still shone through your eyelids, as though your eyelids were made of gauze.

But this light didn't hurt her eyes—she didn't need to close them. This light was welcoming. This light was like a living thing.

She stretched out one hand, thinking she'd be able to touch it, but of course there was nothing there.

It was warm, though. Juliet hadn't realised how cold she was but she could feel the light landing on her skin, wrapping around her, enveloping her, warming her, and she knew she was safe. She walked into the light, wanting to feel its warmth on her skin. She turned round, letting the light warm her back.

Now she could smell fresh grass. Where was she? She had no recollection of being anywhere. She looked down, expecting to see grass under her feet, but there was nothing, just the light.

No, there was something beyond the light. People. They were busy, moving quickly. Coming and going around a central point like bees buzzing around a hive. What were they doing?

She frowned and looked up again, turning round in a slow circle. The light was all around her now but there was nothing else. No landmarks, no people, no sky, no ground. Nothing.

'Juliet. Juliet, can you hear me?'

The voice was coming from her left. She turned but there was still nothing to see. Nothing but the light.

'Juliet.'

She thought she recognised the voice now—it was her brother-in-law.

'Steven?'

She took a step towards him.

'No!'

She stopped and her brother-in-law spoke again. 'You can't do this, Juliet. Can you hear me?'

'Yes.'

'It's not your time yet.'

She frowned. He wasn't making any sense—her time for what? 'What are you talking about?'

'Juliet, not now. Your children need you.'

And then she remembered. Steven was dead, he'd been dead for ten years.

The shock went through her like a bolt of lightning.

The light, Steven's voice, this was what people talked about.

She looked down again. That was her in the middle of the circle of people. She was the beehive. All those busy people were buzzing around her. But while they were busy, she was still, lying on a table, immobile. She kept watching and saw one person lean forward as the others took a step back.

'This time, Juliet.'

She looked back towards Steven's voice as a second bolt of lightning hit her. She couldn't speak, couldn't breathe, and then the light faded to black.

He was gone and she was alone again.

'Juliet, can you hear me?'

No, she wasn't alone; he was still there. 'Steven?' She tried to open her eyes but her eyelids were too heavy.

'It's Ben, Juliet. You're in hospital. You're in the operating theatre. Everything's all right now.'

Ben? She didn't know anyone called Ben.

She was tired and cold. She just wanted to be warm.

27 January 2009

Sam was exhausted. The Australia Day celebrations had been a huge exercise—just the final details alone had taken up almost every minute of the three weeks he'd been back at work. But now it was over. He'd debated jumping on the first flight to Melbourne that morning to be at the hospital for Juliet but she'd quickly put an end to that, telling him Maggie would be there and she would let him know how the surgery went. He knew she was mad with him, he knew she'd expected him to be there for her. He couldn't blame her really. He had asked her to call him for help and the first time she'd done it he'd been tied up with work. Again.

But surely she could have delayed the surgery? It was only cosmetic after all.

Everything they'd achieved before Christmas had unravelled in the space of one conversation. They were back to square one, divorced and living in different cities.

He'd spoken to his captain about a desk job but he wasn't even sure if that would be enough.

The morning dragged as he waited for Maggie's call but when it came it wasn't the news he'd been hoping for.

He snatched his phone up as it buzzed on his desk.

'Maggie?'

'Hi, Sam.'

'How is she?'

'Um, there have been some complications.'

'What's happened? Is she okay?'

'She's okay now but apparently she had a reaction to one of the drugs.' Maggie paused. 'They had to resuscitate her.'

'Resuscitate her!' Oh, God. Sam was grateful he was already sitting down. He put his head between his knees. He thought he was going to throw up.

'Sam? Are you still there? Are you okay?'

He was perfectly okay. It was Juliet who wasn't. His father's words were repeating themselves in his head. *I'm just wondering what you'd do if, heaven forbid, Juliet doesn't make it. Would you drag your kids around the country then?*

He hadn't thought his father's words would be so accurate. But it sounded like he'd come within a whisker of being in exactly that situation. What would he do?

'What happened? Do you know?'

'Her blood pressure was quite high when she went into Theatre and they gave her something to bring it down. They gave her some anti-nausea medication as well to try to eliminate the nausea she experienced last time and they think she had a reaction to that, which further dropped her blood pressure. She's out of danger now and the doctor says she'll be fine. We have to believe him, we have no other choice.'

'Can I speak to her?'

'Not yet.'

'What about the doctor, Ben? Can I speak to him?'

'I'll ask the nurses to get him to ring you and I'll let you know if anything changes. I'll take care of her, Sam.'

He knew she would but he wanted to do it. Juliet was his girl. Even though they were divorced he still thought of her as his and he knew he always would. He had tried to do the right thing for his family by letting them stay in Melbourne but he should have stayed there too. He realised that now. Now more than ever.

He'd done it again. He'd let work dictate his life. He'd learnt nothing.

No. That wasn't true. He'd learnt but he'd been too slow.

He wasn't going to sit in Sydney any longer.

He was on the next plane to Melbourne.

He was going to get his wife back.

He hadn't counted on not being allowed to see her.

'I'm sorry, visitors are strictly limited in Intensive Care,' the nurse told him.

'But I'm her husband.' Sam struggled to keep his

voice down as he stretched the truth just a little. He hadn't come there only to be foiled at the last hurdle.

The nurse was flicking through Juliet's chart. 'You're not listed as her next of kin. You'll have to wait for the doctor. If he thinks she's up to an extra visitor then maybe you can see her.'

'Can you ring Dr McMahon for me? He's a friend of the family.' Sam stretched the truth a little more in the hope the nurse would be persuaded to do him a favour. He needed to see Juliet now.

'He should be here shortly,' the nurse said, her tone terse. 'If you have his number, you can call him.'

Sam's ploy had backfired. He didn't have Ben's number, he'd only met him once, so he had no choice but to sit and wait. 'If you're expecting him soon, I'll wait. No need to bother him unnecessarily,' he replied, not wanting the nurse to think she'd had the last word.

'Sam! Are you waiting to speak to me?'

Sam stood as Ben arrived and shook his hand. 'I'm actually waiting to see Juliet.'

'What's the hold-up?'

Sam inclined his head towards the nurses' station. 'I'm not listed in her chart—that makes me *persona non grata*. I need your permission.'

'She's doing fine. Just let me do a quick check and then she's all yours.' Ben disappeared into the intensive care unit with the battleaxe of a nurse trailing behind. Sam watched from the doorway, looking for Juliet's bed.

'She's pretty drowsy but you can have a few minutes with her,' Ben said as he came out.

Sam didn't need to be told twice.

She was so still. So tiny. Her head was bare, no wig, no scarf to cover her scalp, and Sam was momentarily surprised. He hadn't seen her without some sort of head cover and although her hair had started to grow back, regrowth was minimal and the soft cap of downy hair was barely noticeable. If he hadn't seen which bed Ben had gone to Sam doubted he would have recognised her. He double-checked the name tag above the bed.

He dragged a chair closer to the bed.

'Jules?'

Her hand was resting on top of the sheet. He covered her hand with his and she opened her eyes.

'Hi.' He squeezed her fingers.

She smiled and a tidal wave of relief rushed over him. His eyes were burning and he could feel tears gathering.

'You're okay.' He leant forward and carefully kissed her cheek, mindful of the tubes and wires connecting her to the various pieces of equipment.

He sat in the chair. 'I'm so sorry I wasn't here earlier. If I'd known…' How could anyone have predicted this? And what would he have done? His words tapered off. Juliet had closed her eyes and she said nothing. What could she say? The silence was broken only by the rhythmical *blip-blip* of the monitors.

Sam watched her, making sure she was breathing, watching the numbers on the monitor, waiting for her to speak. But there was nothing. Was she sleeping?

'I've let you down again, haven't I?' He spoke to the silence. 'I'm going to make up for it. I promise.'

Juliet's monitors started beeping. The *blip-blip* changed to a buzzing sound. What did that mean? Was it an alarm? Sam looked up at the screen but, of course, the lines and numbers meant nothing to him. But none of the numbers read zero so he supposed that was a good thing.

The nurse bustled in; she pressed a button that switched off the alarm as she checked the screen.

'You'll have to leave now,' she told Sam.

'Is everything all right?'

'She needs peace and quiet. She doesn't need any more excitement. She needs to rest.'

Sam didn't know where the nurse had got the idea that he was exciting Juliet. She seemed quite calm to him, but he knew the nurse was taking great delight in being able to evict him from the ICU. He wouldn't argue. As long as Juliet was okay, he wasn't going to make a scene.

He stood up and kissed Juliet again, aware of the nurse watching him closely. 'I'll be back and I'll do a better job next time, I promise,' he whispered to Juliet before he left the unit. Having seen her with his own eyes, he felt much better. The visit had reassured him and he knew the trip had been worthwhile. He could go now and if he got a chance he would come back again before he had to return to Sydney. The nurse had asked him to leave but she hadn't said he couldn't come back.

Sam had promised Juliet he'd fix things. He'd promised twice. But while he had put the wheels in motion he now needed to speed things up—he couldn't afford not to. He needed to speak to his captain again.

There were signs everywhere reminding visitors not to use mobile phones so Sam left the hospital building before dialling his superior's number.

'Sir, it's Sam Taylor.'

'Sam. What can I do for you?'

'I'm just following up on our conversation regarding permanent postings. I need to know about the next available position in Melbourne—whatever it is.' He had broached the subject when he'd returned from leave and had known it could take a while before something suitable came up, but that hadn't bothered him at the time. Now he wanted something, anything, as soon as possible.

'Why the rush?'

'Juliet's not well,' he said, then explained what had transpired in surgery. 'I need to be there. I need to be there soon.'

'I'll see what I can do.'

'Thank you, sir.' Sam knew his captain didn't want to set him up with a permanent posting. He didn't want to lose him and he'd told him that much in their first meeting, but Sam trusted him to keep his word and he knew the other man would do his best to find something. He just hoped it wouldn't take too long.

CHAPTER TEN

February 2009

SOMETIMES Juliet wondered if she'd dreamt Sam's visit to Melbourne when she'd been in the ICU. Her recollection was vague at best but Ben had confirmed that she hadn't imagined it. Sam hadn't stayed for long but he'd promised to return and now he was coming to Melbourne for the weekend. He was still promising to fix things but Juliet wasn't putting much stock into that. He was being very cagey about his plans, and had told Juliet he was sorting some stuff out and would explain when he got there. He was coming to watch Kate in a ballet recital but Juliet didn't know anything more than that.

All the progress Kate had made prior to Christmas had unravelled since Juliet's 'incident', as she thought of it. Kate had barely left her side and had refused to go to school on several occasions. Juliet had been forced to sit through numerous ballet rehearsals just to ensure that Kate would stay and it had been exhausting. Juliet understood that Kate was afraid but nothing she said seemed to ease her daughter's fears. Juliet was at a loss as to what else she could do.

Fortunately Maggie was still in Melbourne and

she'd borne the brunt of taking care of Edward's extra-curricular activities, but Juliet was hoping that Sam's presence would divert Kate's attention and give her some time to spend with Ed. She was looking forward to a break from Kate's constant shadowing and the thought made her feel like a bad mother, but she was finding it rather trying. She hoped the double excitement of the recital and Sam's visit would help to keep Kate's mind occupied. Perhaps, when the weekend was over, Kate would have forgotten her fears and her need to keep Juliet close. Or perhaps that was wishful thinking.

The recital went well. Kate was in high spirits and her excitement increased when Sam announced he was taking them all to Sofia's for dinner. Juliet wanted to refuse Sam's invitation because she was still annoyed with him, but she agreed to go to dinner because she didn't want to disappoint the children. She didn't want to be like Sam and put more importance on her own feelings than on those of her children. It was bad enough that one parent had higher priorities than the family. She wasn't going to go down that same path.

Juliet was still giving off a frosty vibe. There was no doubting that she was still mad with him but at least she'd agreed to join them for dinner. He had something important to tell them all and on neutral ground was a good place to do that.

Sam waited until dessert was served before he began. The children were focussed on their usual order, a massive serving of *gelati* each, four scoops of different flavours, which would be enough to keep them occupied for the next twenty minutes, or until it melted over the table, which would give Sam enough time to make his announcement.

'I have some news.'

'Good news?' Juliet asked. She looked wary.

'I hope so. I've got a temporary posting to HMAS *Cerberus*.'

'What's that?' Edward asked.

'It's the navy base down south, sort of on the way to Philip Island. It's where I'm going to be working for a while,' he explained.

'It's near us?' Ed clarified.

Sam nodded. 'It's in Victoria.'

'We can see you every day?'

'It's about an hour and a half away so I'm going to stay down there during the week, but I can see you every weekend and I'll be able to come up to Melbourne whenever you need me.'

Juliet was staring at him. She'd said nothing. Something was bugging her.

'What is it?' he asked.

'Can we talk about this later?' She glanced at the children. They'd forgotten about their *gelati* and were concentrating on the conversation. Sam recognised Juliet's body language. They were obviously heading for a discussion that needed to be out of earshot of the children.

He'd hoped it would be good news; he'd thought he was making a good decision, but he must have got it wrong. Again.

'Sure.' He picked up a spoon and pinched a taste of Ed's dessert, changing the topic completely to avoid an argument in public. 'Looks like you're gonna need help with that one, mate,' he said as he swallowed a mouthful of chocolate *gelati* and tried to ignore Juliet's icy expression. He just hoped she would calm down before they got home.

But he was out of luck. He drove them all back to the house, his old home, and the conversation continued once the children were in bed.

'What's the problem with this posting?' he asked. 'I thought you'd be happy to have me close by. I thought it would take some pressure off you.'

'It's a temporary posting, you said?' Her voice was tight and her blue eyes flashed fire. He recognised that look—she was ready for an argument.

He nodded and decided to stick to answering her questions as straightforwardly as possible. There was no point in fanning the flames of her anger by telling her things she didn't want to hear. So, until he worked out what she wanted, he thought it best to keep things simple. He thought he was less likely to get into trouble that way. 'Until July, at this stage.'

'And why are you taking it?'

'So I can spend time with the kids. So I can give you a hand.'

'For five months and then what? We're back to the same point again. You'll move on. We'll stay here.'

It wasn't a question.

'You're welcome to move with me.' His mouth was faster than his brain. He hadn't meant to say that, even though it was true. She glared at him, and he tried again. 'I thought a few months would be a good start. I thought it would be better than nothing and maybe it will lead to something more permanent.'

'But it might not.'

'It might not,' he agreed.

'And that's my point. I understand you're doing this for the right reasons, and you think you're helping, but all you're doing is delaying the inevitable. You won't be here for ever.'

He would be filling in for another officer who had
been diagnosed with cancer. It was unlikely that officer
would return to the job, in which case, if Sam was happy,
the position could become his permanently, but he didn't
want to make assumptions at this stage and he didn't
want to bring up the subject of a colleague with terminal
cancer. He'd be best sticking to a simple explanation. 'It
was the best I could do at short notice.'

His response didn't seem to appease Juliet.

'If you can do this now, why couldn't you do it eighteen months ago?'

Because he hadn't thought about it. Probably best
not to say that. 'These jobs don't come up often. People
tend to hang on to them,' he replied.

'But why now?'

'The kids need me.' This was part of the answer but
not the whole truth.

'They needed you eighteen months ago too.'

'I know and I'm sorry that it's taken me this time to
realise that. I admit, if it hadn't been for your health I
probably still wouldn't see it your way. But you were
right when you wanted to keep the family together. I
didn't realise, I didn't see why it was so important. My
childhood was very different from most but I didn't
know anything else and I couldn't see why having two
parents was so important. One good full-time parent
was more than most kids had and ours had you plus me
when I was home. I figured as long as the children had
you, that would be fine. But...'

He was hesitating with his explanations now, finding
it difficult to explain his feelings and reasons. He hadn't
really thought this part through and he was heading into
territory that was a bit risky. Territory that could open
up arguments.

'But what?'

'But you gave me a hell of a fright with your drama in hospital and I thought what if—?'

'What if they don't have me?' Juliet finished his sentence. As usual she knew what he was thinking.

'Yes. But it's not as sudden as it seems. Spending those months with you prior to Christmas made me realise how much I'd missed you, missed you all, and I didn't want to go back to Sydney. I wanted to be with my family. Or at least nearby. When I got back I put some feelers out, trying to work out how I could arrange things, but your experience in hospital made me realise that perhaps I didn't have the luxury of time. I had to have something quickly.'

'And this is it? This is the job you want?'

'I don't know.' He felt it was important to be honest, even if it meant heated discussion ensued. He couldn't afford there to be any misunderstanding. 'But, even if it's not, my priorities have changed. My job doesn't come first any more. I know you think I gave up too easily last time. I know you think I should have put my family first, and I agree with you now. I made a mistake. Nearly losing you has put things into perspective. I'm trying to fix things. Taking this position is the first step. I want a chance to prove to you that things are different. That I've changed.'

'But don't you see? Nothing is different, nothing has changed,' Juliet argued. 'You made me promise to call you first if I needed help, if the children needed you, but where were you when I went into hospital in January? You still had work commitments. Nothing changed.'

He wanted to tell her that wasn't fair. She hadn't given him fair warning. 'I thought I had time.' Time to fix things. But he'd been forced to act quickly and he just hoped he could get it right.

But Juliet hadn't finished with him. 'This latest surgery was just step one of the reconstruction. Where will you be six weeks' time when I go into hospital again? You're not only telling me you'll be around to help but you're promising the children you'll be around for them too. How is that possible? You're still an officer in the navy. You're still going to be doing the navy's bidding, put their demands first. That's what you have to do as long as you are serving with the defence force. I get that but I don't think you do.'

'This job is different—this is a shore-based position.'

'Shore based! Why are you interested in it if you're stuck on land? I thought that was a deal-breaker before.'

She was right. He'd hated the job with the oil company but it wasn't solely because it had been land based. 'There were lots of things wrong with the civilian job. For a start this one is still with the defence force, so I keep my rank and all my entitlements.' He tried to explain. 'The navy is the only life I've ever known. I grew up as a defence force kid, I was surrounded by defence force personnel and their families all my life and that's how I see myself. When I took the civilian job I lost my identity. I like the structure and formality of the defence force. I define myself by the code of the navy and when I took leave I lost something of myself in the process. That was the biggest problem, but I didn't realise it at the time. Leaving the navy diminished me in my own eyes, to the point where I lost respect for myself and I had nothing to give you. I need the navy but I also need you. My life doesn't work when I only have one. I can't be the man you need without the navy and this might be the perfect solution for us. For our family.'

'How do you figure that?'

'I'm going to be running training courses within the engineering faculty for electronics, technical and marine, with a bit of ship safety and survival training work as well. I'll be on base Monday to Friday, no weekends.'

'Monday to Friday? So you *will* be around for the children?'

'There will be a few trips to sea—' He broke off when Juliet gave him 'the look'. He clarified his statement. 'There are some overnight trips out into the bay for training purposes—firefighting and technical pracs, that's all.' Selling this posting was proving much harder than he'd expected. He'd really thought it would be an easy exercise, an opportunity too good to pass up and one that would suit everybody. 'I thought this would be a win-win situation for us all.'

'So you're doing this for us?'

He nodded. 'I want my family back, Jules. You included.'

'You want us back? What does that mean exactly?'

'I love you, Jules. I always have and I always will. It's not too late for us. I know it's not. We can have a second chance. You just have to give it to me.' He knelt on one knee and took one of her hands in his, holding tight just in case she wanted to pull away. 'I want my family back, Jules. I love you and I want you to marry me.'

'Don't be ridiculous. Get up.' She snatched her hand back. She definitely wasn't seeing his vision. 'This changes nothing. It's a temporary posting, you said so yourself. I appreciate what you're doing but please don't assume that it's going to change things between us. I can't rely on you and I'm not going to pretend that I will. I know I have to get on with things on my own. I think you're making promises you can't keep and I need to do what's right for the children, and that includes putting my needs first too. I have to move on. It's over, Sam.'

He supposed he deserved that. He might be in for a long battle but it was one he was determined to win. He enjoyed a challenge and he didn't doubt Juliet would test his resolve, but he had no intention of going down without a fight this time. There was too much at stake. 'I'm going to keep proposing until you say yes,' he declared.

'Well, I hope you don't mind disappointment.'

Sam wasn't too disheartened. He knew Juliet—he knew exactly how stubborn she could be, and he'd never expected it would be easy to convince her to give him another chance. But he knew that if he could plant an idea, and give her time to get used to it, maybe she'd even eventually think it had been her suggestion. If he could show her he was serious, show her he was committed to his family and to her, then perhaps she'd start to see his point of view and perhaps he'd get what he wanted. Perhaps he'd get her back.

CHAPTER ELEVEN

June 2009

JULIET lay in bed, a year's worth of thoughts running through her head. Today was her birthday and it was almost impossible to believe what had transpired over the previous twelve months. From one birthday to the next she had gone from being a healthy, married mother of two to a divorced mother of two recovering from breast cancer. Not a great year. But, she thought, at least she'd made it this far.

Her overwhelming feeling was one of relief. Her last blood-test results had been good and she'd actually made it through the final stage of the breast reconstruction without any dramas. She'd had the tissue expanders replaced with the implants and that had marked another step in her recovery process, a step in the right direction. Physically she was complete. The breast prostheses had been relegated to the back of a drawer. They'd served a purpose but she was glad to see the last of them, and her wigs were in boxes on top of the wardrobe. They would eventually end up in the dress-up box. Her hair was a few inches long now, long enough to be styled into an authentic pixie cut, similar to the wig she'd worn, but she'd stuck to her own hair colour. She was a brunette again.

Her hair colour she was used to, her new breasts were taking a little longer to feel as though they belonged.

She was lying on her back and she looked down at her chest. She was still getting used to seeing her boobs pointing at the ceiling when she was lying down instead of disappearing under her armpits. That thought made her smile. Ben had used teardrop-shaped implants because they looked more natural than round but, still, when she was lying down they were obviously fake because they were unaffected by gravity. And they felt heavy. But it was nice not having to worry about stuffing her bra with prosthetic breasts or worrying that the prostheses had slipped out of position or looked lopsided.

Yes, a lot had changed in the past year but overall things were looking up. She'd made it this far. Was there any harm now in planning for the future? What did she want it to bring her?

She knew what today was bringing her. It was bringing Sam.

They were going to celebrate her birthday as a family. He was still trying to convince her to make it official. He was still proposing every chance he got and she was still refusing. She wondered how long he would persist. She loved him, there was no doubting that, but in her mind they were going around in circles. Loving each other wasn't enough.

The last four months had unfolded just as Sam had told her they would. He'd been living on the naval base, ninety minutes from Melbourne, but he'd kept his part of the bargain and had spent weekends in town, just as he'd promised the children, and they loved having him around. Juliet enjoyed his company too—she didn't pretend otherwise, and she was more than happy to celebrate her birthday with Sam, but she wasn't planning any further than that.

The children were incredibly excited about the day's outing and that made everything worthwhile. Ed was at the age where he needed his dad. He needed the physical rough and tumble that he got from Sam, and Juliet wasn't up to that at the moment so Sam's presence was especially important. Kate's anxieties had diminished as well with the increased amount of time she was able to spend with both her parents. Juliet had to admit there were plenty of positives for their family with Sam's transfer to Victoria but it was still temporary. The kids were happy but she was hesitant about enjoying his company too much because, in the back of her mind, there was always the thought that he'd be gone again.

But there was no denying they still had a connection, one that had nothing to do with their children and everything to do with chemistry. All it took was a glance, an unconscious touch of his hand or one of his lopsided smiles and Juliet could feel herself falling under his spell. She had managed to refuse all his proposals so far but a girl could only resist so many times and she was fighting it with everything she had.

She got out of bed. It was time to get up. Time to get on with the next year of her life.

When she opened the door to Sam an hour later she was surprised to see him standing there empty-handed. She'd assumed he'd give her yellow tulips, just as he'd done every birthday since they'd got engaged. Yellow tulips were their thing. He'd never forgotten before, which could only mean that it was a deliberate omission today.

She swallowed her disappointment. Every day she had was a bonus and she wasn't going to waste time sulking. Sam certainly had no obligation to buy her anything any more and she shouldn't expect him to. She was determined to enjoy the day.

'Happy birthday.' He greeted her with a smile, his unique, irresistible smile, and her petulance vanished in an instant. She forgot all about the tulips as she let the warmth of Sam's smile wash over her. He bent forward, kissing her cheek, and she closed her eyes and savoured the soft touch of his lips on her skin.

There wasn't time for a prolonged greeting as Kate and Edward arrived at the door in a flurry of excitement. They were heading for the Dandenong Ranges, south-east of Melbourne, where they were going for a ride on Puffing Billy, a restored steam train, and Edward had been bouncing off the walls since early morning, bubbling with anticipation. Juliet had read the entire collection of 'Thomas the Tank Engine' stories to Ed when he'd been younger and this excursion was still one of his favourite things to do. They all loved this trip through the hills, which was why she'd chosen it as her outing.

There were some intermittent showers as they wound their way in the car through the foothills but by the time they reached Belgrave the rain had eased, although low mist still hugged the treetops and obscured the sun. The air smelt clean and fresh with an underlying scent of eucalyptus, and drops of moisture fell from the grey leaves of the gums and wet their heads as they walked beneath the trees and made their way to the station.

The train was waiting at the platform, steam billowing from its chimney as it waited for its next departure. Edward dragged Sam to the front of the train, watching in fascination as the engineer stoked the fire.

'We'll buy tickets and get some seats,' Juliet called to

Sam as she and Kate headed for the ticket window. They found seats looking out over the platform and waited for the boys to join them. The carriages had bench seats and the top half of the carriage sides was open with just a couple of horizontal bars dividing the space. Green tarpaulins made makeshift walls but these were rolled up out of the way for the journey to allow the passengers to enjoy the view. The children scrambled to the sides of the carriages and clambered up to sit on the edge, legs dangling outside the carriage, bodies inside and arms clinging to the horizontal bars.

Despite the fact that her children, and hundreds of others, assumed this position every trip, Juliet was always nervous. She had one hand ready to reach for Ed if he started to topple and she jumped as the sound of the train's whistle pierced the stillness of the morning. A cloud of steam drifted past their window as the train lurched and began to pull away from the platform, and the children cheered as the train gathered speed.

'Relax! He'll be fine—he always is,' Sam said.

He was sitting opposite her and he recognised her discomfort, knew she was always worried about the perceived danger. He reached across and rubbed her knee, shooting a smile in her direction. A delicious tingle raced through her with his touch and she felt her nervousness abate. She took a deep breath and relaxed into her seat, reminding herself that she was going to have fun and commit every minute of the day to memory. The scent of eucalyptus was strong in the air, released from the leaves of the trees by the recent rainfall, and the rocking of the train was hypnotic. She closed her eyes briefly as the fresh air rushed over her face, ruffling her short hair. The noise of the train's wheels clacking on the rails made conversation almost impossible so Juliet didn't bother attempting to make small talk and instead watched as the world went past.

The train pulled into Emerald station, where they were stopping for lunch before returning to Belgrave. The sun had come out and the air was muggy with humidity. The kids stripped off their jackets and handed them to Juliet before racing off. There was a model railway exhibit here, which was Ed's second favourite thing after the train ride. Sam had given them money for the entrance fee and they wanted to make the most of the time they had before they'd be called back for a picnic lunch. Sam carried the basket he'd packed and they walked together looking for a spot to settle.

'Sun or shade?' Picnic tables were being claimed quickly but Sam had a picnic rug under his arm so they were self-sufficient.

'I'd like a bit of time in the sun—it's such a beautiful day now,' Juliet said as she pointed to her left. 'Under that tree looks like a good spot.'

She shrugged out of her coat as Sam spread the blanket on the ground. He opened the basket and started to pull out provisions.

'I can do that if you want to catch up to the kids,' Juliet offered. She unpacked hard-boiled eggs, ham and salad sandwiches and lemon tarts. Sam brought cold drinks back with him and they shared the picnic under the trees. The children returned to the model railway as soon as they'd finished their dessert, leaving Juliet and Sam lying on the picnic rug.

It brought back memories of New Year's Eve when they'd shared a blanket on the beach. When Sam had kissed her. Despite his tireless proposals, he hadn't kissed her properly since that night. He'd been a perfect gentleman and Juliet still didn't know whether she should be relieved or disappointed. In the cold light of day she knew she wasn't ready for anything more than a kiss but at night, alone in her bed, she often imagined how it would feel to be back in Sam's arms, how it would feel to have his comforting bulk wrapped around her.

She fiddled with the bracelet on her wrist—the one Sam had given her on New Year's Eve. Except for when she'd undergone surgery she hadn't taken it off. Sam reached across and put his hand over hers and the warmth from his fingers spread through her like liquid gold. With his other hand he pulled a parcel from the pocket of his jacket.

He handed her the present. 'Happy birthday, Jules.'

The present was small, the size of a jewellery box. Juliet unwrapped the gift, opening the lid to reveal another charm for her bracelet. It was a miniature spray of flowers.

The flowers had silver stems and golden petals.

'Yellow tulips.' Her voice was husky and soft, and her emotions were running high. He hadn't forgotten. Her eyes filled with tears. It was the most beautiful charm she'd ever seen. 'It's gorgeous. Where on earth did you find this?'

'I had it made. Tulips are our thing.' Sam sat up, kneeling on the picnic rug. 'There's something I want to ask you.'

Juliet smiled. 'My answer is still no.' She knew what was coming and part of her recognised she would have been disappointed if Sam hadn't proposed today, but her answer was still the same.

'But why? I know you, Jules. Better than anyone. I know that every year on your birthday you make plans for the year ahead. I want you to include me in those plans. Let's make a fresh start.' He looked directly into her eyes. His green eyes were dark, their colour intense. 'Today is the perfect day to begin again. I love you, Jules, and I want to marry you.' She shook her head but he held up a hand. 'You've finished your chemo treatment, your blood tests are clear, you've had your last surgery, you're running out of reasons to say no. Unless you don't love me?'

He was tracing little circles on her wrist now with his thumb, sending sparks of desire shooting up her arm. There was no doubt in her mind that she still loved him. Still wanted him. But she wasn't going to let her heart rule her head.

She looked back at him, forcing herself to keep her gaze steady. 'This isn't about me not loving you, it's about priorities. Our family is my priority but I still don't think we are yours. The navy is your first love.'

'No. It was, I admit that, but things have changed. I've changed. Almost losing you has made me realise how foolish I've been. A job is nothing compared to my family.'

'But time after time the navy has taken you away from me and that hasn't changed. I did think for a while that maybe I'd been unfair, making you choose between us and the navy. I thought maybe I should have continued to follow you wherever you went, but now I'm tired. I could pretend I'm fine but the truth is I'm exhausted and I don't want to move. I'm not going to say it's because of the children. I just don't think I have the energy any more.'

'I didn't choose the navy over you. I tried the alternative but I couldn't do it. That job with the oil company was killing me. I felt like a failure because I couldn't enjoy that job. I was a failure at civilian life and a failure as a father and husband. The navy was what I was good at.'

'You weren't a failure, Sam. You were a fantastic dad, you *are* a fantastic dad. I love you but I can't keep moving. I just can't do it. I'm sorry. I can't marry you.'

'You love me?'

She nodded. 'I always have but I don't think loving you is enough. I can't compete with the sea.'

'Is that your only objection?' he asked. 'What if you didn't have to compete any more? Would you take me back then?'

'There's no point in having this conversation, is there? That's purely hypothetical.'

Sam shook his head. 'What if I told you this job at HMAS *Cerberus* could become permanent?'

'Permanent? A desk job? Are you sure it's the right thing for you?' Juliet had her doubts. She'd seen the fallout of Sam's last attempt at sitting in an office and while she knew he'd been testing the waters for the last five months, that was still a very different proposition from accepting a permanent posting in her mind.

'This is everything a desk job should be. I'm not crunching numbers, doing someone else's mundane tasks. I'm doing practical stuff and it means I can be home with my family. With you. I'm begging you, Jules. Please marry me.'

He reached out and tucked a strand of hair behind her ear and her senses sprang to life. It was her birthday, a day for making decisions.

'Are you going to take this job regardless of my answer?' she asked.

Sam nodded. 'I've already accepted it. I want to be

here for you and the children in whatever form you'll have me.'

It was a day for making decisions but was it a day to follow her heart? She took a deep breath. 'I'll think about it.'

Sam's smile lit up his face. 'That's so much better than no!' He jumped up, pulling her to her feet as Puffing Billy blew its whistle. He gathered her in his arms and kissed her, and she nearly changed her mind then and there. Perhaps they could have a future. Perhaps she could do this. Sam's kisses were very persuasive. She couldn't think of any good reason not to spend the rest of her life with him. She couldn't think of anything at all.

And that was why she knew she couldn't give him an answer now. She needed some time and space to get some clarity. She had to think logically.

The children were in bed, exhausted after their big day out. Juliet had just said goodbye to Sam and made herself a cup of tea to take to bed when the phone rang. She had been planning on using the quiet time to work out what she could tell Sam and she debated about whether or not to answer the phone. A quick phone call wouldn't hurt, she decided.

'Happy birthday, Jules.' Maggie's voice came down the line. 'How was your day?'

'Good,' Juliet said with a smile.

'Did Sam propose again?' Maggie was back in Sydney but she knew that Juliet had spent the day with Sam and the kids.

'Yes.'

'He hasn't given up yet?'

'Not yet,' Juliet replied.

'What did you say this time?'

'I said I'd think about it.'

'Really!' Maggie gave an excited squeal. 'I'm not interrupting anything, am I?'

'No. He's gone back to the base. He's got an early start tomorrow, some big training exercise.'

'So tell me what's happened. Why have you changed your answer?'

'Sam is staying in Victoria. He's transferred permanently to *Cerberus*.'

'You're kidding? That's great news. So why didn't you say yes? What are you thinking about?' Maggie peppered Juliet with questions.

'I don't want to make the same mistake twice.'

'What mistake? Marrying him? Sam has done everything you wanted him to. He's obviously committed to your family. Are you? Do you love him?' The questions kept coming.

'Yes.'

'Then I think you'd be making a mistake *not* to marry him. What are you waiting for?'

'I'm scared.'

'Of what?'

'I'm scared of the physical side of things.' Juliet hadn't told Sam that because it hadn't been until he'd stopped kissing her and she'd thought of what would come next that she'd realised what had been holding her back. She knew it was silly, childish even, to worry, and it wasn't Sam's reaction that concerned her. He'd told her everything she needed to hear but she knew from past experience that the reality might be very different. To her at least. And she didn't know if she had enough confidence.

'Why? I thought that was why you decided to go ahead with the reconstructive surgery.'

'That was part of the reason but I haven't tested the waters yet. I still don't know if I'm ready for the whole naked thing.'

'There's only one way to find out. The two of you need a weekend away together.' Maggie loved to organise things and Juliet could tell she sensed a chance to take over. 'Why don't you book something? I'll come down to Melbourne to mind the kids, or you could drop them off with me in Sydney and go to Lilianfels in the Blue Mountains—it doesn't get much more romantic than that. What do you think?'

Juliet knew she'd only be allowed off the phone after she agreed to Maggie's idea. She conceded her idea probably had merit. If she couldn't relax with Sam there was no hope for her, so in the interests of an early night she accepted.

'Okay. I'll look into it, I promise.'

Juliet had dropped the children at school and she was planning on using her free morning to get her new tulip charm attached to her bracelet and then look into a romantic weekend getaway. She would surprise Sam with the trip, she'd decided. It was her turn to do something nice for him. Maggie was right. This weekend would be just what they needed.

She got into the car and nosed out into the traffic just as the nine o'clock news came on. What she heard made her forget all about a romantic getaway. She sat frozen. She'd pulled away from the kerb and the car was sticking into the traffic, blocking the road, but she was completely oblivious to the hold-up she was causing.

'Repeating our lead story—there has been an

explosion on board a navy vessel in Western Port Bay, south of Melbourne.'

Her heart started racing.

'A navy spokesman has confirmed that at six-twenty this morning there was an unscheduled explosion during a training exercise being run out of HMAS Cerberus.'

Her stomach twisted, tying itself in knots. She took a deep breath, trying to stop herself from gagging. Cars were negotiating their way around her vehicle now, tooting their horns at her as they passed, and she suddenly noticed she was causing a delay. She reversed back into her parking spot as the newsreader continued.

'No fatalities have been reported but two navy personnel were seriously injured and have been airlifted to hospital. Several others have sustained minor injuries and are being treated at the scene.'

Juliet felt physically ill. Sam had gone back to the base last night because he had a two-day training exercise starting today.

She scrambled in her bag for her mobile phone. She hit the button that was the shortcut for Sam's mobile. It went straight to message bank. He was either on the phone or it was switched off. She couldn't bear to think of the third option—that it had been damaged.

She threw the phone onto the passenger seat, checked for traffic, pulled back onto the road and began driving. She wasn't aware of making a conscious decision to head to the base but when she realised she was heading south it seemed as good an option as any and she kept going. She hit the redial button as she drove but the result was the same each time—Sam's message bank.

A round trip took three hours. She had six hours until she had to collect the children. Either she'd reach the base or she'd get through to him on his phone. Either way, she had to speak to him. And she knew what she would say, what she should have said yesterday. Why had she waited? What had she been waiting for?

If the cancer had taught her any lessons, it was that life was short. She hoped she hadn't missed her opportunity. No. She couldn't afford to think like that. Sam would be all right. He had to be. But she wouldn't hesitate again. She was going to get her husband back.

She kept the radio on but there were no further updates.

She kept her phone on but the farther south she got the more concerned she grew. Surely Sam would assume she'd heard the news. If he was all right, why hadn't he rung to tell her? He'd have to know she'd be worried. Why hadn't he called to say everything was okay?

She tried his number again. Nothing.

She was almost there now. She was approaching Hastings. Another ten kilometres to go. Another ten minutes.

An ambulance drove towards her as she exited Hastings. Its lights were flashing but the siren wasn't on. It headed into town, to the hospital, as she continued to drive south.

The gates of HMAS *Cerberus* loomed in front of her. She pulled into the car park on the public side of the gates. She hadn't stopped to think about what she would do once she reached the base. She'd never arrived unannounced before. Sam had always known she was coming.

The gates opened as she neared the sentry post and another ambulance emerged. Juliet watched it pass her by, hoping Sam wasn't inside. Hoping Sam wasn't injured. Or worse.

Traffic was all one way. Coming out. Nothing was going in the other direction.

A small crowd milled around on the outside of the gates. Juliet recognised them for who they were. Navy families, waiting for news. Juliet knew they wouldn't be able to tell her anything. She wondered if anyone could.

Two defence force personnel manned the gate. Both of them looked harassed. Juliet didn't recognise either of them but she figured the sentries were the only defence force personnel she'd be able to talk to as she doubted she'd get into the base.

She approached the sentry post on foot.

'Can I help you, ma'am?' The slightly older-looking sentry addressed her. She obviously wasn't the first person to come looking for information.

'I'm trying to reach my husband, Commander Samuel Taylor? He was supposed to be involved in the training exercise. He's not answering his phone.' Her voice sounded wobbly and she had to make an effort to speak clearly.

'The phone system is jammed, ma'am. Too many calls.' The sentry was holding a clipboard in his hand, and he looked down and wrote something on the paper. 'I'll add his name to the list and if you can wait here, we'll get back to you when we know more.'

She nodded silently, and returned to her car. She'd been hoping for something more definite but this was obviously as much information as she was going to get at this stage. Was that good or bad? Would they have a list of the people who were injured? Would they tell her?

Probably not, she thought. It wasn't in their job description; they were too far down the chain of command.

Information like that would come from an officer, a captain or higher, she supposed. She would have to wait. Just like everyone else.

She sat in the driver's seat at ninety degrees to the wheel, leaning her shoulder on the seat, her feet resting outside the car, tapping on the ground. She couldn't sit still; she wasn't good at waiting. Two ambulances had passed her. The radio had said some personnel had been airlifted out. People had been injured. How many? she wondered. Was Sam one of them?

She pulled her phone from her handbag. Her hands were shaking. Was it worth trying him once more?

An officer, a lieutenant judging by his insignia, exited the base and came to stand in the centre of the car park.

'Ladies and gentlemen, if I could have your attention. The chapel has been made available for those of you who would prefer to wait inside the base. You'll need to undergo security checks but you may be more comfortable waiting in the chapel instead of here. If you'd like to come forward now, we can start the process.'

Still no captain. Who would be coming to give them news?

Most of the people quickly gathered together at the gate, obviously keen to get inside. Juliet joined the queue. They had to show identification and metal detectors were waved over them before they were checked for traces of explosives. Only then were they allowed on base but everyone willingly subjected themselves to the checks. The idea of being on the base instead of waiting outside the gates gave everyone hope. It felt as though they were making progress.

The chapel was an attractive building. It was built of stone with stained-glass windows, light wooden floors and pews to seat a couple of hundred people. The morning sun was streaming through the eastern windows and the interior of the chapel glowed in the sunlight. Juliet sat alone at the rear of the chapel, unaware of the beauty of her surroundings.

Dust motes kicked up by the throng floated in the air, tiny specks dancing in the currents, coloured pink and gold and green by the light pouring through the stained-glass windows. Juliet noticed the dust and was reminded of a similar scene almost a year earlier when the dust motes had been pale grey. Last July, when she'd been sitting waiting to go before the judge, waiting for her divorce. Now she was waiting again. Waiting to see if the man she'd divorced, the man she loved, was all right. Waiting to see if she was going to get another chance or whether she was too late.

She sat in a pew and stared ahead vacantly. No longer seeing the dust motes. No longer seeing anybody.

How many chances did she deserve? She'd survived the first stage of breast cancer and she'd been resuscitated on an operating table. If Sam was okay, surely that made third time lucky. How many more chances could she expect? This was it. She couldn't wait for life to be perfect—it obviously didn't work like that.

'Jules?'

She turned at the sound of her name. At the sound of his voice.

'Sam!' She sprang from the pew and flung her arms around him. She felt him flinch. She pulled back, just enough to get a look at him, not so far that she had to let go. His blond hair was damp—was it from sweat or water? He had streaks of dirt on his cheek and he looked exhausted, even though it was only late morning. Juliet wasn't used to seeing him look dishevelled when he was in uniform. He was normally immaculate. 'What's wrong? Are you hurt?' She ran her eyes over him, looking for damage. His left arm was tucked close against his side and he had a bandage wrapped around the palm of his left hand. Without thinking, she reached for his arm. 'What happened?' She saw Sam wince as she moved his arm.

'I'm fine,' he said. 'Just bruised ribs and a burn on my hand. It's nothing.'

He didn't look fine.

'Really, I'm okay,' he insisted. 'What are you doing here?'

'I was worried. I heard about the explosion on the radio but I couldn't get through to you,' she explained. 'Next thing I know I was driving this way. I guessed you'd answer my call at some point but before I knew it I was here.'

'You were worried about me?'

'Of course I was. The news said people were injured. I knew you had a training exercise. I thought you'd ring me…'

He pulled her in close with his right arm, holding her tight. His arms were strong and comforting.

'My phone was in my cabin. I couldn't get back there after the explosion.'

'You were on that vessel?' She felt her heart skip a beat and her knees were weak. She wobbled slightly and Sam quickly pulled her into a pew and made her sit.

He nodded. He didn't seem perturbed by what Juliet could only assume was a near miss. Was he that used to things blowing up around him?

He probably was.

'So what did happen?' Now she was glad she'd driven down here. If she'd heard that he'd been on the ship and hadn't seen for herself that he was okay, she'd be a nervous wreck. More of a nervous wreck, she amended her thoughts.

'We're not sure yet.'

'And the others? I saw ambulances. They said on the radio that people had been airlifted out.' Now that she knew Sam was alive she could afford to think about the others involved, about all those other families waiting to hear something—anything.

'The injuries were relatively minor, thankfully. Some burns and broken bones, a concussion or two but no fatalities. They airlifted a couple of sailors out who had compound leg fractures but they should be fine. It could have been much worse. We've got the details on the injured now, and their families are being informed.'

Juliet looked around the chapel and saw that clusters of people were being spoken to by officers. Information was being imparted.

'What are you going to do now?' Sam asked her.

'I don't know,' she said. She hadn't got to that part of her plan yet. She didn't really have a plan. 'I guess I'll drive back to Melbourne.'

'I'd drive you but I have to go back to work. Things are going to be rather hectic for a few days, I reckon.' He lifted his left hand and brushed his thumb across her cheek. The gauze of the bandage scratched her skin but his thumb was soft. 'Will you be okay?'

'Yes, yes.' He leant forward to kiss her cheek and she knew he was about to stand up and leave. She put one hand on his forearm, stopping him. 'Before you go, there's just one thing I need to ask you.' Sam relaxed into the pew. 'I was going to save this for a more romantic setting but I think I've wasted enough time already.' Very carefully she took Sam's hands and held them in her lap. 'When you proposed yesterday I said I would think about it. And this is what I think.' She took a deep breath and continued. 'I know I've been stubborn and demanding, I know I've been difficult, but I was afraid. I was afraid of coming second again, of always competing for time and attention with your career. And I was afraid of intimacy. Not emotionally but physically. But I decided last night that I had to get past that but then, this morning, when I couldn't reach you on the phone, that's when I knew what fear really was. I've coped with a lot of things over the past year but I didn't know how I would cope if something had happened to you. I realised I've been worrying about things that don't matter. Thinking I had all the time in the world when I should have known better. I've wasted enough time.' Sam was watching her, his green eyes intense. She could tell he knew what she was about to say. He smiled and that was all the encouragement she needed to continue. 'I love you and, if you'll still have me, I will marry you.'

His smile grew wider, the left side of his mouth caught up to the right and his eyes shone. He pulled his hands free and hugged her again, hugged her hard. 'Of course I'll still have you. We're meant to be together.'

'Scars and all?' she asked as he released her.

'Scars and all.' He ran one hand up her side, sliding it under her shirt, stopping at the bottom of her ribs. Juliet gasped as a surge of desire shot through her. Sam was still smiling as he slid his hand around her back and pulled her close. 'However you come is fine with me, you know that. And put back together is better than not having you at all. Your scars will remind us of what is important, of where we've come from. I love you more than you can imagine and that has never changed.'

'You're sure?'

'I've never been more certain of anything in my life. I chose you fourteen years ago and I choose you again today and I will choose you again tomorrow. We have a lifetime ahead of us. I just wish it could start right now.'

So did she, but even Juliet knew that sometimes she just had to be patient. 'It's okay. I actually do understand that work comes first in this case. I can wait.' She smiled. 'Not for ever, mind you, but for a little longer. We will have the rest of our lives to make up for tonight, won't we?'

'We most certainly will, my love, we most certainly will.' His smile spread slowly this time, full of promises, teasing, enticing, and her smile matched his. Slowly, so slowly, he bent his head to hers, joining them together with a kiss, sealing his promise to her with tenderness. Juliet kissed him back, using her lips to send him a message of love, trust and hope. She could feel her spirit responding to Sam's touch, her body and soul growing warmer with every passing second as the heat spread from her lips to her heart and rushed through the core of her, swamping the adrenaline that her fear had unleashed.

Juliet shook as she realised how close she'd come to losing everything. She could feel Sam rubbing her back to keep her warm but it wasn't the temperature that was making her shiver. The adrenaline was wearing off now that the danger had passed. The fear had gone but she was still tense and jittery.

Sam broke the kiss. He was watching her, his green eyes dark and intense, and she imagined she could see through them like windows to his soul.

'I love you, Jules. You are everything to me.' His eyes

lightened in colour as he spoke and she could almost see his love for her pouring out from their emerald depths. 'When I can get away from here we are going shopping for an engagement ring. I want to make this official. I've waited long enough.'

'I don't need a new ring,' she protested.

'You don't?'

'No.' She slid her old engagement ring from her right hand and gave it to Sam. 'I don't even need a new husband.'

Sam was frowning now, looking puzzled. 'But—'

'My old husband was perfect for me,' she explained. 'I just didn't see enough of him. If I can have him back, I'll be happy.' She held her left hand out, fingers spread, waiting for Sam.

'Are you sure?' he asked.

'Positive,' she replied. 'I love you. All I ever wanted was to be with you.'

Sam held the ring between his right thumb and forefinger and slid it onto Juliet's left hand. 'You will be, I promise. I am yours, now and for ever,' he said.

Juliet looked at her hand, at where her finger was encircled by the gold band. The ring signalled their promise to each other. They had come full circle and she was back where she belonged. She had her husband back. Her family was complete. Her world was perfect.

'We made it.'

'Yes, we did,' Sam agreed as he bent his head to kiss her once more. 'Yes, we did.'

2 FREE BOOKS
AND A SURPRISE GIFT

We would like to take this opportunity to thank you for reading this Mills & Boon® book by offering you the chance to take TWO more specially selected books from the Medical™ series absolutely FREE! We're also making this offer to introduce you to the benefits of the Mills & Boon® Book Club™—

- **FREE home delivery**
- **FREE gifts and competitions**
- **FREE monthly Newsletter**
- **Exclusive Mills & Boon Book Club offers**
- **Books available before they're in the shops**

Accepting these FREE books and gift places you under no obligation to buy, you may cancel at any time, even after receiving your free books. Simply complete your details below and return the entire page to the address below. You don't even need a stamp!

YES Please send me 2 free Medical books and a surprise understand that unless you hear from me, I will receive 5 superb stories every month including two 2-in-1 books priced at £ each and a single book priced at £3.30, postage and packing fre am under no obligation to purchase any books and may cancel n subscription at any time. The free books and gift will be mine to kee in any case.

Ms/Mrs/Miss/Mr _____ Initials _____

Surname _____

Address _____

_____ Postcode _____

E-mail _____

Send this whole page to: Mills & Boon Book Club, Free Book Offer, FREEPOST NAT 10298, Richmond, TW9 1BR